Too Many Cooks

Also by Rosemary Shrager

The Last Supper
The Proof in the Pudding

Too Many Cooks

A Prudence Bulstrode Mystery

Rosemary Shrager

C

CONSTABLE

CONSTABLE

First published in Great Britain in 2024 by Constable

1 3 5 7 9 10 8 6 4 2

Copyright © Rosemary Shrager, 2024

The moral right of the author has been asserted.

A CIP catalogue record for this book
is available from the British Library.

ISBN: 978-1-47213-541-4 (hardcover)
ISBN: 978-1-47213-542-1 (trade paperback)

Typeset by Hewer Text UK Ltd, Edinburgh
Printed and bound in Great Britain by Clays Ltd, Elcograf S.p.A.

Papers used by Constable are from well-managed
forests and other responsible sources.

MIX
Paper from
responsible sources
FSC
www.fsc.org   FSC® C104740

Constable
An imprint of
Little, Brown Book Group
Carmelite House
50 Victoria Embankment
London EC4Y 0DZ

An Hachette UK Company
www.hachette.co.uk

www.littlebrown.co.uk

To Freddie, my grandson

Chapter One

Devil's Corner was not the official name for this particular bend in the clifftop road, but – now that her camper van was parked precariously upon its verge, dangerously close to the crumbled sandstone edge and the perilous drop to the sea below – Prudence Bulstrode decided that it was rather apt. 'Devil's food cake I can cope with,' she said to her grand-daughter, Suki – who was currently absorbed in her iPhone, watching instructional videos on how to change a flat tyre, 'but the Devil's Corner might be the end of us, dear. Now, help me with this jack, won't you? I'm afraid, at this age, I can't do it alone.'

The afternoon was growing old, but the journey from Prudence's sleepy home village to the uttermost end of the earth (or 'Cornwall', as it was more commonly called) was a long one – and, owing to a three-hour traffic jam around Stonehenge, where at least the stranded drivers might gaze out upon the majesty of a few old stones, it had taken longer still. Now, with the light paling and the sun beginning its descent toward the sea, Prudence wondered if they were going to have to spend the night right here. It wasn't that she hadn't done her share of wild camping and foraging in her life – *Prudence's Meals for Nothing!* had been a big hit in the latter stages of her career, and featured such startling recipes as 'Nettle and

1

Bilberry Tarte Tatin' and 'Rabbit and Seaweed Stew' – but the scrubby roadside of Devil's Corner did not immediately offer many opportunities to dig up delicacies from the natural world. There was, Prudence saw, a stand of fat hen – which did perfectly well in place of spinach – and she'd seen flowering yarrow in a hedgerow five hundred yards back. But, aside from this, there was just scrub grass and an occasional Coke can, no doubt thrown out of a passing car window. Hardly the basis of a feast, even for the most adept of cooks.

'I've got a Twix, Grandma,' said Suki, ferreting in her pocket. 'And some gum.'

Prudence was on her hands and knees, contemplating how on earth you utilised a jack on a camper van. The thing seemed to be made for a Mini. She wondered why she'd bought it. 'I'm quite good for gum, thank you, Suki,' she said, cheerily. Suki, eighteen years old, was finally looking more like a professional kitchen assistant (her hair was still dyed black, but she had finally foregone the pale make-up which made her seem like a ghost) – but she was still alarmingly naive. 'Gum won't get us out of this, but good old elbow grease might.'

'Gum *might* get us out of this, Grandma. There's a TikTok here showing you how to patch a punctured tyre with Wrigley's Extra. He's doing it on a bike, but I imagine the principle's the same.'

Prudence had stopped listening at the word 'TikTok', but when Suki repeated the advice, she just wryly shook her head and looked around. She could, at least, take in the beauty of their surroundings. This, she reasoned, was good for the soul – even if ferreting around in the dirt, with grease under your fingernails and blisters from using the wrench, wasn't. It had been some decades since she last came along this road. Behind them, the fishing port of Penzance clung to the coastline – and, in front of her, only the pale blue of the summer sea. The cliffs here might have been perilous, but there was splendour in them as well. Beneath them stretched out all the manifold hidden beaches and coves of Cornwall. Only eight miles separated them from Land's End, the furthest a soul could voyage in mainland Britain. For half a century she had carried this particular corner of the world in her soul. Breathing in the salt air was like breathing in a bit of her history. One day, when she finally settled down to write her memoirs (she had long ago decided to call it 'The Pru Stew: Stories from My Life'), her years in this corner of the country would feature heavily, and showcase recipes like stargazy pie, hevva cake – and, of course, her own inimitable take on the traditional pasty.

'Grandma, I think we—'

'Yes, I know what I'm doing,' said Prudence, whose cheer was finally giving way to exasperation. She had just smeared grease across her aquamarine glasses. They wouldn't be so glitzy ever again.

'No, Grandma, I think there's . . .'

This time, Prudence looked up, meaning to tell Suki, in no uncertain terms, that she did not want any TikTok tips or advice from the nameless multitudes of Suki's precious internet; what she wanted was for Suki to get down on her knees and engage with the problem in front of them. She was about to open her lips and say as much when she saw Suki pointing further along the coast road. Her eyes flashed in the same direction. Only partially obscured by the greasy smears on her glasses, Prudence finally saw what Suki had clocked some moments before: a second camper van was approaching along the coastal road. Dipping in and out of sight as it followed every bend, soon it was coming, in a cloud of dust, around the Devil's Corner – where it promptly stopped, disgorging two girls of about Suki's age, with Suki's taste in dark clothing, dark make-up, and even darker expressions.

In a flash, Prudence was back on her feet, wringing her hands on one of the camper van's dishcloths, then polishing her glasses on her sleeve. By the time a third girl, the driver, had stepped out of the new camper van, she considered herself at least reasonably presentable.

'It's *you*, isn't it?' the girl said, in a voice as shrill as one of Prudence's old PR representatives every time she'd got Prudence the coveted slot on *Saturday Kitchen*. 'I'd know that face anywhere!'

Prudence looked around. She suspected the reason the girls recognised her was more to do with the fact that her camper van, iconic in its vivid peach and cyan paints, bore the legend PRUDENCE BULSTRODE'S TRAVELLING KITCHEN in florid red letters. Even the numberplate, PRU BU 1, had a kind of fame of its own. Whatever the reason, Prudence was quite certain that girls of this generation had never watched any of her old television shows, nor browsed for her books in the libraries and bookshops where she still went to do readings and offer all manner of advice.

'Girls, you catch us at a most unfortunate moment

– but you might be our angels, come to earth. Now, do any of you know how to change a flat tyre?'

The faces of two of the girls flashed immediately to their own phones. A symphony of beeps and whirrs accompanied their frenzied attempts to find whatever instructional videos Suki had already unearthed.

It was the third girl, evidently the brains of the bunch, who shook her head wearily and declared, 'I've got a better idea than that, Mrs Bulstrode. We'll take you there ourselves.'

Prudence and Suki shared a look.

'Well,' the girl went on, 'it's only fair. You've come all this way to teach us cooking. We can hardly leave you standing on the side of the road like lemons, can we? Hop on up, Mrs Bulstrode. We can ask Ronnie Green, up at the school, to come back and change the tyre. Ronnie's an absolute *darl*, he's been handyman for twenty years. There isn't a thing he doesn't know about that school, or this coast. Well, what do you say?' The girl grinned. 'You'll want to lock her up, Mrs Bulstrode.' She looked up at the sky. 'There's a storm coming on. We'll have to ask Ronnie to jump to it, or your camper'll be blown clean over the cliff.'

The thought of this prompted Prudence to unload as many of her supplies as she could into the second camper van, which took some considerable time. By the time they hit the road again, sailing down the cliff road to the cove at the very bottom, darkness was curdling – but even this brought back memories for Prudence. In Prudence's day, every journey along these old country roads had been undertaken by rickety old bus. The thought of girls as young as Suki owning cars, let alone camper vans, was quite unthinkable. But, as Suki insisted on telling her just about every other sentence, time kept on turning.

She was lost in thoughts like these when, all at once, they rounded the bend – and there, nestled in the cove beneath them, sat St Marianne's School for Girls.

Prudence was not often given to waves of nostalgia, but one crashed over her now. From on high she could see the whole school: the west wing where the dormitories used to be, the hall and gymnasium, the outdoor blocks where girls did mathematics and science (as well as sewing and religion, quite often – when they had to make their own samplers – in the same lesson). There were the greenhouses, there the hockey pitch, there the kitchen garden and the very same building in which Prudence had taken her first ever domestic science lessons with dear old Mrs Jubber, and – for the first time – fallen in love with cookery.

'Well, girls,' she said, and tried to pretend that tears weren't misting her eyes, 'I have to say, I didn't think I'd ever be back here. You won't understand the gravity of this – not yet! – but it's been nearly fifty whole years.'

'Oh yes!' the driver chirruped. She had introduced herself as Sophie, and had a double-barrelled surname with far too many syllables to safely pronounce. 'We know *all* about it, Mrs Bulstrode. They've been talking about you coming ever since it was announced last Christmas. Your face has been in every newsletter. They've got a big picture of you up in the reception hall. A cardboard cut-out, no less – life-size! They're very proud of you here, Mrs Bulstrode. And, well, when they invited sixth-formers to come back for a couple of weeks' extra lessons over the summer break, a crash course from the world-famous television chef, well, we could hardly turn our noses up, could we? None of us can make more than a sandwich, Mrs Bulstrode – and Hetty here can't even do that.'

One of the other girls, evidently named Hetty, looked up from her phone and shrugged. 'I just don't like bread,' she remarked. 'So I leave it out.'

Up ahead, the school was coming into clearer focus. Prudence could make out the groundskeeper's little house, the little orchard where the girls used to pick apples and plums, the corner of the playground where she and her old friends used to gather and gossip.

Yes, she'd been quite unable to resist when the invitation landed. Two weeks, to run a crash course in cookery for girls from her *alma mater*, preparing them to go off into the world and fend for themselves. Now, *that* was the kind of commission Prudence's retirement was made for.

'Look, Suki,' said Prudence, and took her grand-daughter's hand, 'it's going to be a true trip down memory lane.'

Later, Prudence would look back and wonder at the simplicity of that statement.

Later, after the body had been found, she would wonder if all of her golden days here had been a lie.

But all of that was to come. For now, as they finally reached the boarding school and swung into the car park, Prudence was filled with all the wonderful feelings of a childhood revisited.

There was a little time yet, before murder reared its ugly head and changed everything.

Mrs Chastity Carruthers, forty-five years old (for the fourth time) and wearing the most garish of all the garish lipsticks found on the counter at Barker's Department Store in Penzance, had been impatiently hopping about the school reception hall for some time when she saw the camper van approaching through the windows. At first, her heart sank – for this certainly wasn't the camper van she'd seen in the glossy pages of *Country Living*, nor the article in Marks & Spencer magazine which had first prompted her to invite dear old Mrs Bulstrode back to the school – but then the doors opened up, and out stepped the very same lady whose cardboard cut-out was standing at her side, cardboard egg whisk in hand.

'You look even better in the flesh, Mrs Bulstrode,' she said to the cut-out. Then she rushed forward to open the school doors.

Mrs Carruthers, the doyenne – she preferred the word to 'headmistress', which made her seem so *matronly* – of St Marianne's, had been rehearsing her welcome speech for some hours, slaving over it during a long, lonely night in the staffroom, but the moment she opened the doors, the rain started coursing down from the hills, robbing her of every breath. Consequently, it wasn't until Prudence Bulstrode, her kitchen assistant, and three of the most disreputable girls attending the summer school had charged through the doors, that she found the wherewithal to speak. Even then, her carefully planned speech seemed to vanish.

'Girls,' she shrieked, 'look at the state of you!'

She was referring to the copious amounts of black make-up, which were now cutting rivulets down the faces of her students, but suddenly she stopped, clapped a hand to her mouth, and started gabbling an apology to Prudence instead.

'Oh, Mrs Bulstrode, please don't think I meant you. You, Mrs Bulstrode, look just *divine*.' She shot a look like daggers at the girls. 'It's this rain. It's made a mess of everything, but we'll have you dried out in a second. We can light the fire in the staffroom, should you wish – though we've radiators as well, of course, and have done for many long years! – and we'll get you out of those dirty clothes and . . .'

Prudence had just about finished polishing her glasses again, when she felt Mrs Carruthers grappling with her arm. 'I'm afraid we got caught on the headland. My camper van caught one of the potholes up there and burst its tyre, so we're a little behind the times.'

'Behind the times? No, Mrs Bulstrode, *never*! You mustn't listen to what they say on these new-fangled cookery shows. You're *classical*. You're *refined*. You're stately and traditional, and that's precisely what these girls need.'

Prudence saw the look she was giving the students again – she'd been on the receiving end of one or two looks like those back in her own schooldays – and decided to throw the girls one of her own looks: this one filled with commiseration and understanding.

'I'll have Ronnie get your camper van back to base, Mrs Bulstrode. We simply *must* have the Pru-mobile here

9

for when classes begin. There's a local photographer very keen to document the whole thing – for posterity's sake, you understand – and she'll be more keen than ever to have that camper in shot. Just think of the headlines: "Local Wonder Returns to the Stage". We're proud as punch to have you, Mrs Bulstrode. Proud as punch.'

Prudence had three times tried to get a word in, but Mrs Carruthers evidently had no intent on letting her. Suddenly, she was barking orders at the girls – 'Find Ronnie Green, and find him this instant!' – and steering Prudence along the hallway. Prudence, who was rather used to excitable PR assistants whisking her along – but was yet to meet a headmistress quite as excitable – threw the girls another consolatory look as she departed. Suki, beached somewhere between them, seemed to think momentarily about following the girls, then trotted after her grandmother instead.

'Of course, Ronnie's got an awful lot on this summer,' Mrs Carruthers was saying as they ventured from the reception hall, deeper into the school's achingly familiar warren of corridors. As they went, the rush of old feelings was almost overpowering to Prudence. It wasn't that the school hadn't changed since her day – modernisation was the name of the game for schools as suddenly moneyed as this. Rather, it was that the *feel* of the place had somehow been retained. The footsteps echoed in the very same way. Somehow, the smell of beeswax and vinegar polish rolling out of the performance hall was the same, redolent of those heady summers in the 1970s when Pru and her friends had staged shows here. The way the light fell into the corridor outside the school office sparkled just as it had in 1974. The noise of the rain drumming on the plate glass windows . . .

'Oh yes, *lots*,' Mrs Carruthers went on, quite oblivious to the way Prudence was daydreaming. 'I'm afraid it's fallen to dear Ronnie to organise the contractors. You'll soon see, Mrs Bulstrode, that time marches on here at St Marianne's. Thanks to a very generous local investment, we've raised the funds to erect a state-of-the-art gymnastics facility – so I'm afraid it's goodbye to the hockey pitches, and hello to the St Marianne's Olympic Arena!'

Prudence wasn't quite sure why St Marianne's girls needed a state-of-the-art gymnastics facility at all – what gymnast needed more than a few bars and a pommel horse? – but she wasn't sad to hear that the hockey pitch was to be no more. She'd been three times passed over as hockey captain in her time here, and (yes, she knew it was *pathetic*) it had rankled ever since.

At once, Mrs Carruthers stopped dead and turned on her heel. Prudence, whose daydreaming stopped just as suddenly, realised they were standing outside the site of the school staffroom. Several times, she'd been compelled to stand here, awaiting the emergence of whichever teacher was about to admonish her and her friends for some minor infraction. She glanced sideways at Suki. Yes, she thought, it was better not to share memories like this with Suki; Prudence's grand-daughter had only just found the road marked 'straight and narrow' herself.

'I *completely* forgot to tell you. You and I, Mrs Bulstrode, have a very special connection.'

'Oh yes?' asked Prudence, whose fans often said something along a similar line.

'Indeed we do. Mrs Bulstrode, I'm proud to announce that I was born on the very same day you were awarded *this* . . .'

And Mrs Carruthers stepped aside, to reveal a single certificate – now browned around the edges, yellowed with age – mounted behind the Perspex glass of a wall-hanging display.

Prudence had to creep a little closer to see exactly what it said.

PRUDENCE BULSTRODE
Form 13a
HAS BEEN AWARDED THE
ST MARIANNE'S PRIZE FOR HOME ECONOMICS
12 June 1976

Presented by:
MISS AGATHA JUBBER
Domestic Sciences

'Oh,' said Prudence, and felt another rush of fond memories. 'But . . . but this hasn't been up on the wall all these years, *surely*?'

'Oh no, Mrs Bulstrode, it's been in the school archive – looked after by our erstwhile librarian. I chanced across it some time ago, and I've been hoarding it ever since. You see, Mrs Bulstrode, I rather feel as if we both began in the very same moment. Our stories are as one. Here you were, trotting up to stage to meet this Miss . . .' Mrs Carruthers had to squint at the certificate to make sure she had the name right, ' . . . Jubber, taking what I like to think is your very first step towards being the nation's sweetheart, the shining light of the cookery world. And there was I, my head just crowning, my little face appearing between my mother's—'

'I see,' said Prudence, tactfully, before Mrs Carruthers was able to continue that particular description. 'Well, I have to say, it *is* rather remarkable.' What was truly remarkable was that Suki was not already corpsing with laughter. 'And I remember that day very well. Miss Jubber – well, that really *is* where it started for me. I have Miss Jubber, and this school, to thank for all of it. Without Miss Jubber, I don't think I'd have fallen in love with food at all. Somehow, she just made it so *alive*. When we were in that classroom ...' It was hard to put it into words, that magical feeling of finding your vocation, of falling headlong into it and realising, suddenly, that your entire life was being mapped out. 'I shall enjoy cooking in the domestic science block again.'

'It isn't quite like you used to know it,' said Mrs Carruthers, wagging her finger. 'We're a little more *state of the art* than we were. All the ovens are voice activated now, of course. And the smart fridges can tell you exactly when your eggs are on the turn.'

Prudence thought: *So could I, by simply dropping them in a bowl of cool water.* But she managed not to breathe a word.

'Well, shall we get going then?' Prudence ventured. 'Dinner with the staff tonight, isn't it? I made sure we transferred as many of our packs from my camper van as we could. We didn't quite gather everything up, but there's more than enough to get started.' By instinct, Prudence rolled her sleeves up and wrung her hands

13

together, as if in keen anticipation. 'Any requests, Mrs Carruthers? I'm quite able to make a menu up on the spot. In fact, I rather think of it as my party piece. And I was thinking . . . Well, the school kitchens here used to serve the most dreadful beef and dumplings. For dessert: treacle sponge. I had it in mind, Mrs Carruthers, that I might jazz up the old menu. Show you all what beef and dumplings can *really* be like . . .'

Mrs Carruthers' face had suddenly contorted. 'Oh, but Mrs Bulstrode, don't you think of it! *You* cook for *us*? Well, I should be delighted, of course, to have any meal cooked by a lady of your pedigree – but you're our star, you're our guest of honour, you've come back to this school to give back to our students what we once gave to you. There'll be plenty of cookery going on this week, but tonight *you're* to be cooked for.'

Prudence screwed up her eyes. 'Mrs Carruthers, I wasn't aware that you wanted to rustle something up – but really, it's no problem to me if . . .'

'*Me?*' Mrs Carruthers squawked, then threw her head back in such laughter that Mrs Finch, Prudence's old drama teacher, would have summarily ejected her from the classroom for overacting. 'Mrs Bulstrode, unless you want jammy toast, I shan't be cooking for you tonight. No, we have something much better in store. We're to take you out on the town. We have a wonderful evening planned to welcome you back – a trip to the most hip, happening place from here to Tintagel Castle.' She inclined her head, as if to share in some confidence. 'The Bluff, Mrs Bulstrode. It's the pride of Penzance. Two Michelin stars, and just waiting on a third. You must have heard of it? The chef there, didn't you do a show with him once?'

Prudence didn't have to dredge her memory banks particularly deeply to summon up this oddity. The Bluff had sat on a lonely corner of coastland west of Penzance for half a generation, but only recently had it achieved the stardom over which Mrs Carruthers was salivating. That was down to the efforts of a young chef named Benji (though Prudence was quite certain his mother hadn't christened him with that particular spelling) Huntington-Lagan, one of the rising stars who'd got his start in cookery by posting endless videos of himself online, videos in which he sought to tutor others in skills he'd scarcely seemed to master himself. He and Prudence had been partnered together for a celebrity challenge one year, in honour of the BBC's Comic Relief charity appeal. It was the kind of thing Prudence's old agent used to sign her up for without hesitation – because, of course, it was 'just *puuuurrrrr-fect* for the public *prrrrr-ofile*, darling' – and that was how Prudence Bulstrode had ended up as one of the eight competitors in *Chefs Go Ape*, tasked with cooking a three-course dinner for a troop of mountain gorillas in the Bwindi Impenetrable National Park in deepest, darkest Uganda.

Through gritted teeth, and with a perfectly painted on smile, Prudence said, 'It sounds *fantastic*. I can't wait to see how Benji's getting on. He's certainly ... grown his brand,' that terrible saying he used to parrot every other sentence, 'since we worked together.'

'Yes, and let's hope he isn't serving us up grubs fit for a gorilla,' grinned Mrs Carruthers. Then, her face suddenly darkening, she turned to Suki and said, 'You can sort out Mrs Bulstrode's supplies while we're gone, dear. Make sure everything's ship-shape for her return.'

Suki had her face buried in her iPhone, no doubt looking up the indignity that was *Chefs Go Ape*, so there was a second's silence before she looked up, bemused. By then, Prudence had already weighed in: 'Suki's very much a part of the team, Mrs Carruthers. Where I go, Suki goes. This girl's learning so fast that, someday soon, she won't need me at all . . .'

'But still *learning*,' said Mrs Carruthers, her heels clicking as she marched on. 'Mrs Bulstrode, this is a night for the adults. Some adult companionship and conversation. And . . . well, our table's already booked.'

'It's all right, Grandma,' said Suki, quietly. 'I'm not sure I'm in the mood for . . .' And she squinted at the menu on her phone as if trying to decipher hieroglyphics. 'Deconstructed Cornish Lobster Wellington, Sequestered in a Saffron and Parmesan Velouté. Or . . .' This next was even more difficult to get her mouth around. 'Peruvian Ceviche Amidst Clusters of Sea-kale and Salsify Gel.' Suki looked up, puzzled. 'Grandma, why does it say "Aggravated Shrimp"?'

Prudence lowered her voice. 'Because chefs like Benji can't just serve scampi and chips, my dear.'

'I don't mind giving this one a miss, Grandma. I can take the packs up to our rooms, and I did promise I'd call Mum when we got here.'

Prudence nodded. Of course, what Suki didn't know was that Prudence had observed her messaging a boy named 'Doogie' (what was wrong with the good old names? Where were the Matthews and Thomases any more?) every time they stopped on the long road west. No doubt, what Suki actually intended to do was dash off a quick text to her mother, then spend the rest of the evening sending little hearts and pictures back and forth with this boy she'd met. Well, you were only young once – a fact that Prudence was being starkly reminded of, now that she walked through her old school halls – and perhaps the evening would flash by more swiftly if she didn't have to keep an eye on her grand-daughter as well.

Then, tomorrow morning, they could get on with the proper business for which they'd been hired: Prudence Bulstrode, passing on all the knowledge she'd acquired in a long, storied career to the next generation of young cooks.

There was almost something poetic about it.

'Save me some tea and toast, Suki,' Prudence whispered as she and Mrs Carruthers hurried away. 'I have a feeling I'll need something to settle my stomach after our visit to the Bluff . . .'

Coastal rain is the most dramatic kind of rain. It churns up the ocean, merges sea and sky, turns the world to a shifting, rippling curtain of grey.

So it was as Mrs Carruthers's private driver chauffeured both the headmistress and Prudence along the winding, clifftop road – until, some distance further west, they reached the little fishing port of Castallack Cove.

The village itself had grown since Prudence used to come this way: she and the girls from St Marianne's, out on their bicycles on a lazy Sunday afternoon – off, perhaps, to meet one of the boys from St Cuthbert's on the other side of the cove. Prudence herself hadn't had much time for those boys (well, not *many* of them), but among her friends there had been girls with an insatiable appetite – not necessarily for the boys, but certainly for the thrill that came with breaking a sacred school rule. A few more houses had been built, and the village post office had been joined by a little café and delicatessen – but, compared to the sprawl of London, progress here was practically mute.

That was why the Bluff, sitting on the headland above the town, up a long, sweeping track with only the restaurant as its destination, stood out so starkly.

It had been a local watering hole in Prudence's day. A pub that served perfect pasties and fish and chips – and, on a Sunday, whole roast pollock and plaice. Back then, the Bluff had taken a 'progressive' view with underage drinkers, and Prudence was quite sure she'd had her first illicit tipple up here, a cider lemonade which would have made her feel quite giddy if it hadn't been for the crispy whitebait at the bar.

Now, however, everything had changed. As the car reached the top of the headland, Prudence saw that only the shell of the old Bluff remained. Instead of the old fisherman's retreat, there now stood a gleaming palace of white stone and plate glass. Pale mauve light spilled out of the front windows, with a constellation of miniature stars gleaming around the welcoming door. Taken in its craggy, windswept surroundings – and especially with the rain still lancing down – it looked to Prudence like the bastard offspring of a novel by Daphne du Maurier and a particularly indulgent episode of *Grand Designs*.

At her side, Mrs Carruthers seemed to be thrilling. 'It isn't often you get to eat at a Michelin-starred restaurant, Mrs Bulstrode. No, this will be a true treat for us both.'

It was a short dash through the rain's rippling curtain to the restaurant doors. Then Prudence was standing in the Bluff, being met by a maître-d' who looked as if she might have been cast in any one of those horrendous reality shows Suki insisted on watching – and being led to the heart of the restaurant, where a table was already bustling with diners calling Pru's name.

'Mrs Bulstrode,' Mrs Carruthers began, settling into her seat at the head of the table. 'Might I introduce our party? First and perhaps foremost, St Marianne's loyal governor, Mr Bernard Hogg.'

A porcine man with the bristles of a nineteenth-century ship's captain stood up, snapped his braces tight, and grasped Prudence's hand. 'You may call me Bernie,' he snorted, evidently delighted to make her acquaintance. 'Bernie Hogg, of Hogg's Tackle. We're the third biggest fishing goods firm between here and Plymouth – we don't hold a candle to Franks & Scotts, of course, but we get along just fine. My daughter was a student at St Marianne's. A finer school, you won't find. I'm proud as punch,' and he punched Prudence playfully on the shoulder, 'to have stuck around as governor.'

'And prouder still to have you here, Prudence,' added Mrs Carruthers.

'Well, precisely!' Bernie declared.

On Bernie's right-hand side was a face Prudence

recognised in an instant. 'Poppy?' she ventured. 'Are my eyes deceiving me, Poppy, or is that . . .'

'It's *me*, Pru!' announced the woman as she flurried from her seat, throwing her arms around Pru and dangling there in a quite ungainly manner. 'My goodness, how long has it been? Thirty years? *Forty?*' The woman named Poppy gave a crumpled kind of look. 'Gosh, it's hard to believe we got so *old*, Pru. But . . .'

'Poppy,' Pru ventured, still staggered at her presence, 'what on earth are you doing here?'

'Well, it's right where I belong, of course.' Poppy gave a lopsided smile. Her blue eyes sparkled. At more than sixty years old, and despite the silvery hair that now flowed around her shoulders, she had retained something of the cherubic about her appearance. But Poppy Balloon always did have something youthful and magnetic about her, even back when she and Prudence used to prowl the halls of St Marianne's together. 'I'm *teaching*, Pru! Don't you see my Facebook posts?'

Prudence just smiled.

'I'm head of Home Economics! I'm . . . I'm the new Miss Jubber!' Her eyes sparkled. 'I bet you never thought you'd hear those words, did you? And, granted, I wasn't the *best* student in Miss Jubber's class. But I did pick up a few tricks here and there – and then, well, about ten years ago, there was an opening at the school. The advert found me, quite by mistake. I was thinking about early retirement – but I decided it was fate, put in an application – and, well, here I am! It's *my* kitchen you'll be teaching those girls in, Pru.' She lowered her voice. 'I have to say, I'm actually a little anxious. You'll be seeing what skills I've taught them over the years, and most likely you'll find them wanting. But domestic science isn't like it was in our day, Pru. They might be lacking a few of the . . . *basics*.'

Prudence hadn't stopped smiling throughout. 'Poppy Balloon,' she said, 'as I live and breathe . . .' There were still a couple of girls from school that Pru had kept in touch with over the years, but the sight of Poppy brought back a million memories. 'There's so much to catch up on.'

'Not for me, Pru. I've been watching you on TV for *years*. Yes, all us old St Marianne's girls have followed what you've been up to with interest.'

'That includes me,' said the final voice around the table.

Prudence looked round to see yet another familiar face. This one was more heavy with lines than any other at the table, the lady herself shrunken with age, but the way she held herself – with her eyes cast fractionally down, and her hands folded in her lap – immediately told Pru who this was. 'Miss Downer?' she ventured.

'Yes,' the old lady said, her voice whispery and full of cracks, 'you girls *did* call me that, over the years. It's Miss *Down*, Prudence.'

Prudence's heart sank, even while – in the corner of her eye – she saw Poppy stifling a laugh. Yes, Miss Down had started at St Marianne's as a youthful library assistant in the same year that Prudence, Poppy and the other girls had begun their studies there. She'd been a glum young woman then, the perfect person to haunt the library stacks, and with a name like 'Verity Down' it was only natural that the girls should start calling her 'Veritable Downer'. Pru had quite forgotten that it was a nickname at all. She was about to gabble an apology when Poppy burst in, 'Miss Down's the longest-standing member of staff there's ever been at St Marianne's. You fell in love with the library there, didn't you, Miss Down? You just couldn't leave.'

'Well, a place like St Marianne's rather gets under the skin,' said Miss Down, primly. 'There isn't a place in the world I'd rather be.'

'Well, there we have it,' Mrs Carruthers interjected, rising again to her feet, even as Prudence sat down. 'We merry few are the beating heart of St Marianne's, Prudence – and now here you are, to tantalise us across the next two weeks. But there's something I wanted to say first.' She gazed around the bustling restaurant floor. It was, thought Prudence, like something out of the space age, plonked down on a Cornish headland. 'A school has stood on the site of St Marianne's since the seventeenth century, and I am honoured to be the woman tasked with carrying its torch for this generation. It is a proud school, with a noble tradition . . .'

Here, Poppy bowed her head and whispered to Pru, 'She fancies she has a touch of nobility herself. Get her talking about it, Pru – she'll soon chew your ear off. Reckons she's descended from Gwendolen, one of the old Cornish queens. And from that,' she lowered her voice further, 'all the way back to Brutus of Troy!'

' . . . and Prudence, here, is one of our exemplary stars. It is my fervent hope that the next two weeks will not only bring our girls some vital education in the business of cookery and kitchen management, but a little inspiration as well. For who else, of all St Marianne's daughters, could ever be as inspiring as Pr—'

Mrs Carruthers didn't get the chance to finish that sentence (a good thing too, because Prudence felt a little sickly at all the praise being poured on to her), because at that moment a waiter bedecked in white and gold brocade appeared at the table – and, with the most obsequious of smiles, declared, 'Chef has been notified that we have another star of the foodie firmament in the building tonight, and he has consequently arranged for some special starters to come to the table. I've been asked tell you how honoured he is, Mrs Bulstrode, to be cooking for a fellow gastronome tonight.'

Everyone else at the table started cooing, and making wide-eyed expressions in Pru's direction, so it was only right that Prudence said, 'Thank you – and you must pass my love to Benji as well.'

'Mrs Bulstrode, he shall be *delighted*.'

Prudence wondered if that was quite true – that business with the mountain gorillas had been rather exasperating for them both – but didn't have to hide her confusion for too long. Next moment, other waiters were waltzing into place, bringing with them platters of strange charcuterie, roses crafted out of Sardinian lard, ramekins filled with mussels and steaming in sake.

'And for your delectation, the Bluff's *pièce de résistance* . . . '

The final waiter had come armed with a rack of tiny phials, each capturing a constantly writhing green steam beneath their stoppers. It looked, to Prudence, like

23

something out of the dungeons in those Harry Potter movies she sometimes watched with Suki's brother, her grandson George – but apparently everybody else at the table thought this the very height of sophistication. As each phial was placed in front of its diner, the waiter proclaimed, 'Draw into the lungs, as one would the bouquet of a fine wine,' and proceeded to illustrate this very taxing procedure by unstopping the cork of his own phial, snorting up the steamy insides, and making the kind of satisfied sound that a cat makes upon curling up to sleep.

'It's like we're stepping into a pine forest,' Mrs Carruthers began.

'Heady stuff!' Bernie Hogg declared.

Old Miss Down seemed to be luxuriating in hers, while Poppy had snorted it right up.

As for Prudence, she was game for anything – and imbibed the steamy concoction exactly as she'd been told. It was pleasant enough, she supposed, though nothing like those Persian *shisha* pipes she'd tried when she was filming *Pru's Spice Up Your Life* on her trip around the Middle East. 'Doesn't anyone remember a good old prawn cocktail?' she dared to venture. 'It's dreadfully old-fashioned now, of course, but there's a part of me still hankers for prawns and Marie Rose sauce. And . . . I rather think we've all forgotten the simple pleasures of a good old melon-baller.'

'Not so!' came a silky, baritone voice.

Upon looking over her shoulder, Prudence was met with none other than the dark, bestubbled face of Benji Huntington-Lagan himself.

Benji was a tall, beanpole of a man, with waves of black hair and eyebrows to match. His strong jaw and aquiline nose were as much part of his star appeal as his cookery, for Prudence had once seen a calendar devoted to sexy shots of him hunkered over his stove – and knew, in that moment, that the worlds of cookery and tawdry reality television had truly intertwined. There he stood, in pristine chef whites (you couldn't trust a chef whose clothes were pristine; it was practically a matter of honour), one hand on his hip and, in the other, a delicate glass bowl.

'May I present for you, Mrs Bulstrode . . .'

He set the concoction down – and Prudence was staggered to see three fat prawns balanced there, drizzled in a delicate pink sauce.

'My deconstructed prawn cocktail,' Benji declared, 'and melon balls . . .'

Next he placed, beside the glass, a single porcelain spoon – upon which was piled a pyramid of tiny globules that might easily have been mistaken for caviar, were they not luminous yellows and greens. 'A hundred little melon balls, made with my signature gel – and each designed to burst with flavour upon your palatte.' When Benji beamed, Prudence was quite certain that his teeth were luminous as well; they were certainly not the same teeth he'd had the last time she saw him. 'This ought to tickle those tastebuds better than those crock-pot recipes you cooked up in Uganda, Pru. *Bon appétit!*'

It was then that the dinner truly began.

Back at St Marianne's School for Girls, Suki was quietly convinced that her grandmother would find the

25

domestic science classrooms something of a sacrilege. Every countertop had a KitchenAid standing in pride of place. Every refrigerator sparkled with lights, recording not just temperature but humidity, shelf space, and estimates of the longevity of every foodstuff stored within. iPads were mounted on every wall, and every cooking station had what appeared to be a voice-activated timer unit so that the students barely had to use their hands at all.

There were, at least, wooden spoons in the canisters at each station – and, though there wasn't a hand whisk in sight, the appearance of a good, well-used wooden spoon (ingrained with the residue of decades of dishes) might be enough to make Pru feel all right.

Now that their packs were safely decanted into the refrigerators and larders, Suki supposed it would be all right to head upstairs to their rooms. Back home in Chelwood Ghyll, Doogie would still be up – no doubt studying for his exams, because Doogie never shied away from his studies like Suki did – and might be in need of a distraction.

The hallways of St Marianne's echoed strangely as Suki plodded up the great staircase, up to the girls' quarters at the very top. Prudence had put in a special request that she be housed in the very same rooms where she had lived as a girl, and Suki take the room next door – but, when Suki got there, she couldn't really see what all the fuss was about. It would be hard to get nostalgic about a room as small and basic as this: just a bed, a bedside cabinet, a chest of drawers and little writing desk in the window.

Still, there was a box of chocolates on the pillow, and this was surely a better evening meal than whatever hoity-toity guff her grandmother was currently devouring up at the Bluff.

Before she settled down to call Doogie – would a video call be out of the question? – Suki went to the window and gazed out over the grounds. Her grandmother spoke with such fondness of this school, but there seemed to Suki something inordinately sad about children packaged off to board all term long. Once upon a time, her grandmother had gazed out of this window and seen the very same sights as Suki was seeing now – just the outbuildings, hunkering under the rain, the wilderness of the construction site that had churned up the old hockey pitch, and the last of the workmen accepting defeat and tramping off home for the night. *Boarding schools*. There would come a time, Suki suspected, when the very idea was tantamount to child cruelty.

She was still standing there, trying to summon up something witty and charming to ease into the coming conversation with Doogie, when there came a knock at the door. Nor was there any time to answer it, for soon the door was opening up – and two of the girls who'd rescued them on the roadside, Hetty and Sophie, were standing there with a bottle in hand.

'Ronnie Green's still not back,' said the girl named Hetty, with a dark shake of the head. 'So your camper's still beached on the hillside, I'm afraid. He must be up there now, trying to get it sorted.'

'Either that or he's driven it straight off a cliff,' Sophie chimed in.

Startled, Suki looked back at the scene through the window – but all she saw was the construction site, the swamp the rain was making of the works, the last lights of the workmen as they left the grounds.

'Still, while the cat's away,' grinned Sophie, and soon both she and Hetty had gambolled into the room, flopped on to Suki's bed, and extended the bottle towards her with devilish grins. 'It's only sherry. I haven't got much taste for the stuff myself, but devils can't be choosers.'

'Beggars,' said Suki.

'I beg your pardon?'

'It's beggars who can't be choosers.'

'Yeah, them too,' said Hetty. 'We pinched it from the staffroom just now – well, while your grandmother and mine are off living the high life up at the Bluff.'

There was something in this that Suki didn't quite understand. '*Your* grandmother?' she queried.

'Old Ms Balloon belongs to Hetty,' laughed Sophie, opening up the bottle and taking a long, half-troubled sniff of its contents. 'She reckons she went to school with your old bird.'

'And she hasn't stopped talking about it, ever since it was announced.' Hetty groaned. 'Prudence this, and Prudence that. Let me tell you about the time when Pru and I went picnicking up at Castallack Cove . . . Let me tell you about this boy old Prudence was sweet on . . .' Hetty's eye roll was so dramatic her eyes nearly vanished into her head. 'It's enough to put you to sleep. But I bet you know what that's like, if you *work* for your grand-mother! That's got to be just as bad as being taught by one. Here . . .' Hetty offered Suki the bottle. 'Why should it be the old folk who have all the fun? All that posh grub up at the Bluff, and they'll be back here half-sozzled later – and there's us, with just a few DVDs in the common room and soup in the microwave. It stands to reason: we deserve some *fun.*'

Suki recognised that tone of voice. It was the same tone that the little voice inside her often adopted, the one that told her to live for the day, to care not what tomorrow might bring, that she was only young once, that her parents were boring, stuffy old fools – and life was for living, and living right now. She'd given into that voice on many occasions in the past, but never when she was out on a job with her grandmother. This job had started out as her grandmother's way of scaring her straight, teaching her some life skills, making sure she didn't get into too much trouble. It had put a second voice in her head, a much more sombre and sober one, telling her in no uncertain terms: DO NOT LET YOUR GRANDMA DOWN.

But then again, what the girls said *had* been right: her grandmother was out on the town right now, living it up with a fancy meal and, no doubt, a glass of something strong of her own.

'Just one, then,' said Suki, and scrabbled around in her bag to find some paper cups. 'One to get the week going. Just to start things off on the right foot, you understand . . .'

'*That,*' Mrs Carruthers declared, 'was *delicious.*'

At the side of the table, Benji Huntington-Lagan looked as proud as a peacock. He seemed to preen like a peacock as well, strutting up and down the table and accepting compliments from each of the diners like a king soaking up the offerings of peasants at court. The main course, which Prudence was just finishing off, had been a seared salmon with pickled vegetables and watercress salad – and would have been perfectly lovely, if only Benji hadn't insisted on serving the salmon in six different ways: in crisps and powders, cakes and batter, frozen raw and burned to a crisp. There was talent in what he'd done, that much was true, but Prudence was quite certain the whole thing would have tasted better cooked *en papillote* with a nice knob of butter and a dash of fresh lemon.

Even so, 'It was magnificent,' Prudence said as Benji's eyes lit on hers.

'Coming from you, Mrs Bulstrode, that makes this evening more special than any. And now, here comes dessert!'

There were few things more awkward in the culinary world than a chef loitering over you as you ate the dishes he'd just prepared. To Prudence, it had the feeling of an exam about it – and, at once, she was back in the examinations hall at St Marianne's, the old mathematics tutor, Mr Scott, walking up and down the rows of students, peering at each as he came. The difference was: at least, in mathematics, you weren't expected to sing your teacher's praises every time you resolved a simple equation.

Waiters fanned around the table, setting down delicate china plates upon which whole tails of lobster seemed to sit.

'Lobster!' Bernie Hogg trumpeted. 'Lobster, for dessert? I've heard of some fancy things, but nothing like this!'

Prudence watched as Bernie Hogg reached for his lobster, only to find his hand sink through its delicate pink shell and get lost in the crème pâtissière, raspberry preserve and fluffy pink sponge within. 'By jingo, it's not lobster at all! It's—'

'Ladies and gentlemen,' Benji pronounced, 'consider the way the meringue shell dissolves at your touch. Think, perhaps, about the way we eat with our eyes, our ears, our fingers – every last one of our senses.' He looked at Prudence again, fluffed up with pride. 'This is not just dessert, of course. It is a commentary on the fragility of our senses. I bid you: enjoy!'

Prudence found herself compelled to join in the applause that followed Benji as he returned to the kitchens – and, as she took her first bite, she had to admit that he'd done a decent job with the sponge, the meringue work was precise and impressive, and even the raspberry sauce had a wonderful piquancy to it, offsetting the sweetness in the rest of the dish. It just all seemed so . . . unnecessary, somehow. The whole thing had the taste of her very own raspberry roulade – and she could have made twenty roulades in the time it had evidently taken Benji to craft this.

'A message from chef, ma'am,' intoned one of the waiters, bending down to Prudence's ear. 'He should very much like to see you again while you're in Cornwall – perhaps, even, to take you on a tour of the Bluff's kitchens. If not tonight, then one day soon. We have a kitchen fit for the twenty-first century, Mrs Bulstrode. It really is a wonder of engineering.'

Prudence paused while she let a fragment of pink

31

meringue shell dissolve on her tongue. 'I should like that very much,' she lied – wondering how long she could bite her tongue for as Benji showed her all his gadgetry, pontificating on gels and smokes and how cookery was really just chemistry. Well, there'd been no chemistry, no phials and dry ice and other paraphernalia back in the Bwindi Impenetrable Park. In lots of ways, Prudence decided, those mountain gorillas had been the truest diners of all. All they cared about was taste . . .

On the other side of the kitchen doors, Benji Huntington-Lagan ripped off his chef's hat and dragged his cuff across his brow.

At the pot wash, his sous-chef Sonny looked up and stared.

'By God, that *woman*!' Benji growled. 'She thinks if you cook with anything more than a wooden spoon, you're breaking an ancient taboo. If you season with much more than salt, it's an affront to a woman like that. It's no wonder she's not on the telly any more. You've got to move with the times. You've got to embrace the new. Otherwise we'd all be eating pottage and dump-lings. I tell you what, Sonny, if mankind only ever had the imagination of people like Prudence Bulstrode, we'd never have started cooking in the first place. We'd still be eating our meat raw. It would have been too adventurous to even *try* putting meat on a spit. There'd be men out there, just discovered fire, and along Pru would come and say, "Ooh, don't put a nice loin of wild pig over that – it's too *scientific*!"'

Sonny, a slight, rangy boy with a mop of dirty-coloured

hair, and as much grease on his face as in one of the pans just used to sear scallops, snorted at that. Sonny was many things (a talented pot-washer, excellent at taking orders, a half-decent pastry chef and reliable prepper), but the thing he was very best at was bolstering his Uncle Benji's ego. Sonny knew exactly when to laugh, because he'd learned it by rote.

'Yes, chef, and fish too!' he cackled.

Benji stared at him, severely, but Sonny just chortled on: 'We'd be eating all this fish raw as well, if it was up to old Pru Bu out there.'

'Well, Sonny, eating fish raw is ... Well, it's on our menu, Sonny, so ...' There was no point going on – Sonny was lost in some merriment of his own – so Benji decided to change tack. 'I've invited the old bird to look at our kitchens. That'll show her how far she's been left behind. That'll show her how times are moving on.'

And with that delicious thought on his lips, he turned back to the kitchen serving hatch, caught sight of Prudence through the opening, and proceeded to give her a dainty little wave.

Prudence was waving back, wondering how on earth she might extricate herself from that particular appointment, when dessert came to its satisfying end – and, with Poppy clinging to her arm as if they were still teenage girls out on a jolly, they ventured back to the night.

The rain had not yet abated, but at least the cars were waiting: one private hire to take Bernie Hogg back to his seaside manor ('I'm afraid it's tea and bed for me, Mrs Bulstrode; my wife passed on some years ago, but I should *love* to entertain you one evening, if you're of a mind'), a taxicab to take Poppy and Verity back to their homes in Penzance, and the final car waiting to ferry Prudence and Mrs Carruthers back to the school. By the way she was reeling around, giddy with the night, Prudence was only glad Mrs Carruthers had declined to drive them herself.

'We simply *must* catch up properly, Prudence,' said Poppy, as she slipped into the taxicab. 'A proper, girly catch-up – just like in the old days! And . . . and you must come with me to see poor old Miss Jubber! She's up at the Cherry Garth, the retirement home just up the coast. Not one hundred per cent *compos mentis* these days, I'm afraid, but I've been visiting her every month ever since I came back. She can talk the hind legs off a donkey if you catch her in the right mood. That mind of hers might have its cracks now, but it's a treasure trove of stories, all about the old days!'

'And *we* must have a proper catch-up too!' added Bernie Hogg out of his car window as his driver whisked him away.

'I think you may have found yourself an admirer, Mrs Bulstrode,' said Mrs Carruthers as they took again to the mountain road, winding slowly down the steep path into Castallack Cove, the sea waves crashing somewhere beneath them. 'I do hope you enjoyed your evening, Prudence. I wanted to show you that we're deadly serious about giving our girls the best education we can. It's such a responsibility. I take it very seriously indeed. And, in two weeks' time, when it comes to our end-of-course banquet – we're going to invite all the parents, you understand – we ought to see some *real* development in them. I can't wait to see it!'

'I don't think we'll be preparing anything quite as flash as at the Bluff, Mrs Carruthers. Girls need to know the basics if they're to have a solid foundation. That's what Miss Jubber taught me. You can't go the distance if you don't know where you're from. Using all Benji Huntington-Lagan's fancy contraptions is all well and good – but if you don't know how to cook a chicken, you're going to get salmonella.'

'Yes, well, something a *bit* flash might be just the thing. Something just a *bit* impressive? I don't want to be serving the parents boiled eggs in two weeks' time. They'll want to know they've got their money's worth.' Mrs Carruthers beamed. 'So will I.'

Oh, thought Prudence, so *that* was how it was going to be: the delights of returning to St Marianne's for the summer would be offset by a thoroughly modern headteacher, one who was absolutely in thrall to her spreadsheets, one who was absolutely determined to get exactly what she'd paid for.

Prudence didn't dwell on this for very long. She simply said, 'I'll have those girls in good order, Mrs Carruthers, you can count on it.'

Then she turned to the window and watched the night whooshing past.

And it was only because she was fixed on this particular window, attempting to ignore Mrs Carruthers nodding her head as she tried to fight sleep, that Prudence didn't see the construction works on the old hockey pitch up close; it was only because she was gazing in the opposite direction that she didn't spot, through the rain lashing down, the place where the downpour had washed a mound of earth clean away – revealing a skeletal hand, still wearing a tarnished gold wristwatch, reaching up out of its unmarked grave, as if desperate to take the hand of another, as if desperate to be hauled back into the light, as if desperate to be *found*.

Chapter Two

Suki woke to a pounding head, a sticky body, and a sour taste at the back of her throat.

It didn't matter at all that, sometime in the night, the rains had abated, and beautiful, buttery, summer sunshine now poured in through the windows. It didn't matter at all that the birds were singing on the gutters just above her bedroom, nor that her phone had registered half-a-dozen messages from Doogie during the night. On any other morning, these things might have made her feel fit to face the day – but, right now, all that she could think about was the taste of that sherry, the whooping of the girls, and the fact that there was simply no way on earth that she would be able to hide this from her grandmother. Prudence knew *everything*. She'd known about it when Suki used tangerine instead of mandarin in the upside-down pudding on their last job; she'd known about it when Suki basted a pork loin in vegan margarine instead of butter; she'd even known about it when Suki hadn't tied her hair back properly when making the desserts for the Chelwood Ghyll parish council (although, to be fair, anyone would have noticed a thick black hair curling out of their egg custard).

Prudence sniffed out *everything* – and it wouldn't take more than one second to sniff out the sourness on Suki's breath.

Time was already against her. Her iPhone showed it was creeping past 9.30 a.m., and that meant that the girls would soon be congregating for their first lesson in the domestic science classroom. Suki ought to have been there, helping her grandmother with the morning prep, and instead she was lurching across the room, dropping her head at the sink in the corner and swilling her mouth out straight from the tap.

There was only one thing for this: a little concoction her old friend Numbers had given her – for Numbers, despite being a teetotaller, seemed to have the recipe for everything. Soon, she was filling a paper cup with his patented mixture of toothpaste, a healthy glug of mouth-wash, and just a few drops of the supermarket own-brand perfume her mother had bought her last Christmas, then stirring it up with the shaft of her toothbrush.

A cocktail like this was heady enough to banish even the worst of morning-after smells. Suki threw her head back and began to gargle it around the back of her throat.

Then, when the acidic tang of the mouthwash – with just its dash of perfume, like Tabasco added to tomato juice to give it a kick – was too much, she bowed suddenly forward and spat it back out.

When she opened her eyes and looked in the mirror, she was furious to see how red and puffy her eyes had become. There wasn't a recipe to get rid of that, and her grandmother absolutely *hated* it when she wore sunglasses inside.

But that wasn't the only thing that caught her attention – for, reflected in the mirror, she could see not only the construction works stretching out across the hockey pitch outside, but the flashing blue lights of police vehicles, innumerable constables milling around a cordon that had magically appeared overnight, and a van suddenly disgorging forensic officers cloaked in white overalls.

After that, Suki suddenly felt sober after all.

Downstairs, Prudence was searching the domestic science classroom in vain for a clock – but, of course, this being the twenty-first century, she couldn't find one. There'd been a big old clock, a golden face set in walnut surrounds, here when she was a girl. Miss Jubber had timed everything by it, and counselled the girls to do the same: 'Cookery, like a good joke, is all about timing,' she'd once said, and it was advice that had stuck with Prudence across the years.

What a joy it was to be back here. Even if the place was unrecognisable now, there was something about standing in the same spot as Miss Jubber that pleased Prudence immensely. Somehow, it felt like holy ground. Prudence's own work station had been in the corner, right beside the countertop where Poppy used to work. She gravitated there now, still in search of a blasted clock.

It had been 8.30 when she came down to begin the day's prep – today, the girls were going to be thinking about 'eggs', and all the manifold uses they could be put to; tomorrow would be about simple sauces, both savoury and sweet – and she felt certain, by the changing of the light, that an hour had passed. The problem was: there was still no sign of Suki, and if the girl didn't appear soon, the students would have arrived before her. Suki hadn't always been reliable, but of late she'd been growing into her role. It caused Prudence some not insignificant vexation to think she'd overslept – or, worse, that she was dallying around, chatting on that iPhone of hers. It caused her even more vexation when she realised that same iPhone would have been able to tell her the time.

Wearily, she called out, 'What time is it?', as if expecting one of the smart fridges or state-of-the-art ovens to reply. When there was only silence, she marched to the classroom doors and pushed them open.

If she had to go and find Suki herself, that was what she would do.

Yet, Prudence didn't get more than two footsteps out of the door – for Mrs Chastity Carruthers was almost immediately upon her, swooping in from some unseen vantage with a wild smile plastered across her face. 'Mrs Bulstrode!' she announced. 'You wouldn't be rushing off anywhere, would you? Your lesson's about to begin, is it not?'

'I just need to dash off for two—'

'Oh, but Mrs Bulstrode, the girls are coming!' Was it Prudence's imagination, or was she *really* whirling her arms like a windmill, trying to stop Prudence from venturing any further from the classroom doors? It seemed, for a moment, as if she was fifteen years old again, being warned against playing truant by a dictatorial housemistress. 'They'll be here in a jiffy. Anything you want, *anything at all*, you tell me – and I'll have it done. I'll send for Miss Down – she's just tidying in the library all summer; she'll be happy to help.'

'It's my grand-daughter. My kitchen assistant. She's—'

'Let you down, has she? Well, I'll go for her *personally*,' Mrs Carruthers declared. 'So back to the classroom, Pru! Your show's about to begin!'

Suki was halfway down the school stairs, stopping at every landing to peer out and catch some fresh angle on what was going on at the edge of the old hockey fields, when Mrs Carruthers spotted her. 'There you are, young lady,' she said, with the same scolding tone that Suki knew from her own schooldays. 'Your grandmother's worried sick. She's been waiting for you. Just *waiting*. And you – you're dallying about on landings where you shouldn't be, while my students are . . . '

Suki could hardly be bothered to listen. What was happening out there, in the grounds of the school, was *much* more interesting. She peered through the nearest window, just in time to see a grey car pull up at the cordon, and a striking young woman of perhaps thirty-five years old, with auburn hair and dark glasses, step out to meet the constables. Each of them acknowledged her with something Suki could only describe as 'deference'; then, like court guardsmen, they stepped aside to let her pass.

'What's *happening* out there?'

Mrs Carruthers had taken her arm, and now seemed to be heaving her bodily down the stairs. 'It's what's happening *down here* that you ought to be concerned with. Mrs Bulstrode needs your help, your singular devoted attention, to get this course off to a good start. Don't forget who's paying your wages, young lady. You let me worry about what's happening out there, and we'll get this day off to a good start.'

Suki could resist the pull no longer; trying not to tumble over her own feet, she took off down the stairs. 'But – but what *is* it?'

'It's . . . a little situation,' Chastity announced. 'A little discovery of some historical significance. Some . . . *archaeological* significance. Yes, there's been a bit of a find in the groundworks and . . . well, we've got a few boxes to tick, a few I's to dot and T's to cross, before we can get on with the building. It's nothing you need to trouble yourself with. It's certainly nothing you need to mention to dear old Mrs Bulstrode. Do you hear me?'

By now, Mrs Carruthers had hauled her to the bottom of the stairs, and was guiding her around the reception hall until they were almost at the domestic science doors. 'Now look lively,' she announced, proceeding to help Suki straighten her (frankly dishevelled) clothes. 'We've got a local journalist coming down to document today's lesson for a feature in the *Tregurnow Times*. St Marianne's deserves a little time in the spotlight, wouldn't you say?'

'Well, yes, but—'

'Then give it to us!' Mrs Carruthers opened the class-room door. 'I'll have the girls guided through promptly. I've got them in a little holding area back here.'

Guided? thought Suki. *Holding area?*

But she didn't get the chance to ask, because in that moment Mrs Carruthers propelled her through the open door, where she crashed directly into her grandmother.

'Suki!' Prudence cried out. 'What the devil's going on?'

Prudence didn't have time to take in the look of Suki; she didn't even have time to comment on the faint aroma of fresh-mint and eau-de-parfum that was emanating from her. Suki was already clattering across the classroom to look out of its every window, craning her neck at odd angles as if trying to see the school grounds beyond. 'Grandma, there's something going on. There's . . .' Suki looked back. 'Mrs Carruthers says it's an archaeological find. But . . . Grandma, they don't bring police officers to archaeological finds, do they?'

Thanks to a particularly memorable trip to Yorkshire last Christmas, Prudence knew more than a little about archaeological finds – and, while it was true that the law often had to get involved, the appearance of police officers at a site of interest didn't seem usual at all. With this in mind, Prudence sashayed across the classroom floor to join Suki at the windows – but, from here, the view of the hockey pitch was obscured: only a thin passage of land between two of the sports buildings, with a white forensics van parked at its uttermost end, hiding the hockey pitch altogether.

Now that she was up close, Prudence scented the minty perfume. 'Oh Suki,' she began – but, once again, Suki was saved, for the classroom doors flew open. Mrs Carruthers marched through – and behind her tramped all sixteen of the summer-school girls.

Prudence was not mistaken: Hetty and Sophie, two of the girls who'd heroically brought them down from the

43

headland before yesterday's storm, gave sheepish – and entirely green-around-the-gills – looks to Suki as they filed into the classroom, taking up their workstations. Inwardly, Prudence groaned – but, outwardly, all she could do was give Suki her familiar quelling eye. She ought to have known that, let loose among girls not far from her own age, temptation might strike.

'Well, girls,' Mrs Carruthers began, clapping her hands together. 'Here we are, and it makes me inordinately proud to introduce you all to the most shining member of St Marianne's alumni, Prudence Bulstrode herself.'

The girls turned as one – and, obviously drilled in the best way to greet a celebrity of Prudence's stature, began a respectful applause.

'Mrs Bulstrode has kindly donated her time this summer to help you girls with some important life lessons. In two weeks' time, we'll be welcoming your families to our dining hall, and there they'll be being served a banquet that you yourselves will have developed, all under the watchful eye of our darling Pru. Girls, I'm positively *salivating* at the idea of it!'

She didn't seem to be salivating, thought Prudence. She seemed to be shiftily looking left and right, checking every window, her mind evidently on whatever was happening beyond these four walls.

'Of course, two weeks is not a long time to prepare – and, while I'm sure that Mrs Bulstrode's influence on you all will be *magnificent*, it falls to each of you girls to make the best out of these two weeks. I already know, of course, that you will be affording your guest lecturer your utmost respect. And I impress upon you now that, as in every field of life, you will get out of this what you put in. So I implore you: for today, and the next days, ignore *everything* that is happening outside this classroom. Focus your energies *entirely* on what is going on in front of you, right here in these kitchens. Cookery, as Mrs Bulstrode is about to tell you, is a grand endeavour – and it requires one's *full and undivided* attention.'

Now that this was off her chest, Mrs Carruthers seemed to soften.

'Now, as many of you know, this very classroom was the one where Mrs Bulstrode was taught how to cook. There's history here, girls, and it's yours to grab hold of with both hands. Because that's what Mrs Bulstrode exemplifies to me. It isn't just her talent with an egg whisk – though I'll dare say she can whip up a mean Italian meringue. It's her can-do attitude! It's the way she's lived her life, seizing opportunity, living for the moment. *Carpe diem*, girls! *CARPE ... DIEM!* Mrs Bulstrode once stood where you are right now, listened to the instruction of her own domestic science teacher – and, some years later, found herself splashed across the cover of the *Radio Times*. It all started here, girls. If Prudence Bulstrode can make a life for herself, then start dreaming of what you can do too!'

Mrs Carruthers seemed to think this was the perfect celebratory note on which to hand over to Pru, and swiftly exited the classroom. As for Prudence, she wasn't quite sure whether the spiel she'd just listened to was congratulatory or not. There seemed a faint whiff of the back-handed to it – 'if Prudence can do it, girls, just think of what *you* can do!' – but there was evidently something else

45

on Mrs Carruthers's mind. As Pru returned to the head of the classroom, she could have sworn she heard the clatter of the headmistress's feet, bursting into a sprint the moment she passed through the classroom doors.

'Well,' Prudence began, reaching the very spot where Mis Jubber used to introduce each lesson and feeling a sudden shudder of pride, 'I'm grateful for the introduction, I'm sure. But let's dispense with all of the silly formalities, shall we? First off: in this kitchen, I'm not Mrs Bulstrode. You may call me Pru. I want this kitchen to be a . . .'

From the back of the classroom, Suki's voice piped up, 'A safe space, Grandma.'

Safe space. Prudence had heard those words used so much over the last year – everybody needed their 'safe spaces', as if the world was filled with pits and booby-traps waiting to ensnare you. But, despite all that, she supposed Suki was right. 'Well, this classroom *was* my safe space,' she went on. 'Nearly fifty years ago, I stood where you girls stand now, and knew next to nothing about cookery. I'd grown up in a family where food was highly prized – my father was a greengrocer, back in the days when that meant so much more than simply filling up the fresh produce aisle at the local supermarket – but I didn't have a passion for cookery. I hadn't yet fallen in love.'

This last provoked various titters around the classroom, but Prudence barrelled on regardless:

'But I had a good teacher. No, a *great* teacher. And it wasn't just cookery she taught me. It wasn't just the practicality of it all. It was this: that, when you care about something, when you find the little things in front of

46

you inspiring, it doesn't feel like work – or even school-work – at all. Miss Jubber's most important lesson to me was: find wonder in whatever you do. And—'

'Mrs Bulstrode?'

The voice had come from Sophie, sitting in the back of the classroom and still looking as green-around-the-gills as Suki. So, thought Prudence, that definitely solved *one* mystery of the morning. And yet . . . Her eyes flashed back to the corner where Suki was standing. To her irritation, the iPhone was out and Suki was hurriedly hammering in some message.

'Yes, dear?'

'Well, here's what I'm thinking,' Sophie said. 'You're famous, right. You've cooked for the King! But we've had a domestic science teacher for years.' Her lips curled in a smile. 'Haven't we, Hetty?'

Hetty – who also still looked green – hung her head.

'And Ms Balloon – well, *she* loves food too. *She* cooked in this classroom with your old Miss Jibber-Jabber as well.'

Prudence wrinkled her eyes, but had to bite her tongue. To Prudence, making fun of Miss Jubber in this room was tantamount to blaspheming in church. But young girls these days thought they knew it all – even more so than Pru and her gang had, back in their day. You had to forgive the hubris of youth, because you'd been there once yourself.

'So how's *this* going to be different?' Sophie concluded.

It was, Prudence decided, a good question – and she was still ruminating on it when she caught sight of Suki's horrified face, still peering into her iPhone screen . . .

* * *

47

The message had buzzed up the moment her grand-mother began to speak to the class: her old friend Numbers's whiskery face, covered in orange fur, and one of the messages he always rendered entirely in capital letters:

IT *IS* ST MARIANNE'S YOU'RE AT, ISN'T IT, DARLING? CHECK THIS! IT'S ALL OVER THE SOCIALS!

So Suki followed the little flashing link he sent, and then the next one, and the one after that. By the time she was finished reading and dared to look up, her grandmother was glaring at her intensely, silently commanding her to step up to the front and join the demonstration.

And Suki would have done exactly that, but the moment she took the first step, another phone started trilling somewhere in the room, and then another, and then another one after that – and suddenly, though it made Prudence quite aghast, iPhones were being drawn all over the classroom, like swords from their sheaths.

At the front of the classroom, Prudence was endeavour-ing to launch into the first lesson of the day. 'Our morn-ing is to be spent embracing *simplicity*,' she declared. 'Simplicity: the first of Miss Jubber's rules for kitchen life, and a rule I've been happy to embrace – whether potter-ing around my own kitchen garden, or cooking at Wembley Stadium for two teams of hungry footballers. Simplicity is the key to good . . .'

At once, the room was alive with the irritating beep

and trill of mobile phones – and, because young people were seemingly programmed to attend to their mobile phones more devotedly than penitents praying to God, sixteen pairs of hands darted into bags and pockets, drawing out the forbidden objects and getting lost in their glimmering screens.

Suki, too, seemed to be rapt. Prudence called out her name, but got only a single finger raised – 'Just a second, Grandma!' – in return.

'Girls,' Prudence began, 'there'll be time for—'

'Mrs Bulstrode,' Sophie suddenly piped up, her phone still trembling in her hand, 'have you been outside today?'

Prudence furrowed her eyes. Of course, she ought to have known that something was wrong long ago, if not by the eagerness at which Mrs Carruthers had been corralling her in the classroom, then by that white van sitting by the hockey pitch, Suki's talk of police constables on the premises, and all that hot air about an archaeological find. Dropping her tea towel pointedly on the counter, she marched towards the window where Suki was still standing. Soon, the other girls were crowding at her shoulder. By now, Prudence had decided there was no holding them back.

'There's nothing to see, girls,' she said – for the white van was still obscuring their only narrow view of the hockey pitch.

But, of course, that wasn't true. At once, Prudence realised why the iPhones had been trilling with such ferocity, like a synchronised dawn chorus. The world was a small place, nowadays. Whatever was happening outside, somebody outside these classroom walls was already

49

pontificating about it on that dreaded internet of Suki's. The news was being beamed all over the world.

'There's nothing on the BBC,' said Suki, fingers tapping wildly. 'Nothing anywhere official, but it's all over Twitter. Look, Grandma, it already has its own hashtag...'

The gasps of the other girls told Prudence that she really didn't want to know what this 'hashtag' business was all about.

'#murderatstmariannes!' somebody crowed.

'Grandma, look...'

Suki flipped her phone around. This time, Prudence had no choice but to look. At first, it just seemed a strange chain of random bleatings – people couldn't have a spare thought, nowadays, without deciding to publish it – but she adjusted her glitzy aquamarine spectacles and tried to read on.

POLICE SWARMING ON ST MARIANNE'S. ARE THEY FINALLY ABOUT TO LOCK UP THE LUNCH LADY? THAT SEMOLINA THEY USED TO SERVE WAS #DISGUSTING #GROSS #TOILETQUICK

ANYONE ELSE NOTICED THE CONVOY HEADING THROUGH CASTALLACK COVE?

I ALWAYS KNEW #CARRUTHERS WAS A BAD BITCH! HA HA HA, COMEUPPANCE AT LAST

ANYONE KNOW WHY FORENSICS ARE AT ST MARIANNE'S?

And this next message seemed to be in direct reply to the last:

THEY PROBABLY FOUND HORSEMEAT IN THE BOURGINON AGAIN

Prudence looked around. So, it seemed there would be precious little teaching to be done this morning. Precious little anything, except to speculate on what might be happening outside.

She turned on her heel, left the girls to their gossip, and headed straight for the door.

This time, she got further than she had before. Indeed, she was already through the reception hall, off into the grounds and able – for the first time – to hear the hubbub going on beside the hockey fields, when Mrs Carruthers appeared from around the outbuildings. This time, Ronnie Green was at her side.

All of a sudden, Ronnie looked pale as a ghost.

'Mrs Bulstrode,' Ronnie began. He was a gentleman of Prudence's own vintage, his face riven with wrinkles as deep as ravines, and a cigarette dangling from his lips. 'I'm glad I've caught you, ma'am. I'm afraid I haven't kept my promise. That camper of yours – well, I got up there, but I had a devil of a time trying to change that tyre in the storm last night. I'd have been back up already this morning, if it wasn't for—'

At this juncture, Mrs Carruthers had no choice but to cut him off. 'Can I help you, Pru? How's that lesson of yours going? My girls shaping up, are they?'

'Actually, Mrs Carruthers – they're quite distracted . . . '

51

'Those girls,' Mrs Carruthers replied, shaking her head stoutly. 'They were told to pay you the utmost respect, Mrs Bulstrode. If I wasn't quite as harassed as I am at this present moment, I'd come in there and box some ears. As it is, I'm—'

'I think you mistake me, Mrs Carruthers. They're distracted by what's happening out here. Is there something I should know, Mrs Carruthers? Only, it seems to me – from my limited vantage, of course – that you have something of a *situation* going on. My Suki said something about an . . . archaeological discovery?'

Ronnie Green spluttered at this; the cigarette flew directly out of his mouth, turning tip over tail to land in the gravel path at his feet. 'I'll say it's archaeological. Almost medieval, by the looks of it. And here, on my own school! Underneath my own green field.'

'Ronnie,' Mrs Carruthers snapped, 'the way you speak about these grounds, you'd think you were a disinherited prince, forced to mow lawns at his own kingdom. No, Mrs Bulstrode, it's nothing you or our girls need to concern yourselves with. A perfectly ordinary hullaba-loo, and we'll have it tidied away in almost no time whatsoever. And, in the meantime, aren't those girls supposed to be thinking about *eggs*?'

There were meaningful looks, and then there were looks that could eviscerate a soul. Mrs Carruthers was evidently a dab hand at delivering the latter, for even though Prudence was many years her senior, the look gave her pause enough that Mrs Carruthers could leap forward, thread an arm through Pru's, and begin steering her away.

This time, more convivially, she said, 'I'll explain in good time, Mrs Bulstrode. I promise I will. But, in the meantime, if you could please keep the girls where they're not poking around, occupy them with your knowledge of albumen and yolks, I'd be *more* than grateful.'

Back in the classroom, the girls flurried up from their huddle of phones and cantered towards Prudence. 'We've got a picture!' Hetty thrilled. 'We've only gone and got a picture!'

'They rolled the van forward, Mrs Bulstrode,' one of the other girls chipped in, 'and now we can see.'

Several of the girls were flourishing phones in Prudence's face, but she batted them away like so many houseflies, and returned to the window instead. 'Better to see it in person, girls,' she said – but, of course, when she got to the window, there was still precious little to be seen. It was true that the van had moved forward, revealing the digging works on the hockey pitch – but the scene was still so far away that, even through her spectacles, Prudence could see nothing but a sergeant standing at a cordon, and a heap of earthworks on the other side.

'That's why they were showing you their pictures, Grandma,' said Suki, keeping her voice to a whisper. 'See?'

When Prudence looked at the image captured by Suki's iPhone, all she saw was the same distant sight she'd seen through the window. Then, Suki performed some side-show magic with her fingers, and at once the picture magnified. She flicked her fingers again, and the picture magnified once more.

Now, Prudence saw.

On the other side of the earthworks, just underneath the cordon – where the hockey field had been scythed apart by the industrial diggers, where the rains of last night had turned the field to deep rivers of silt – a single hand extended from the earth: a hand denuded of all flesh, a hand of begrimed white bone, a hand still wearing a golden wristwatch, its face frozen forever in time.

Prudence took a breath.

The girls in the room watched as her expression twisted, as if trying to make sense of some incalculable riddle, dredging her memory for something even she could not say. The silence that had gripped Prudence quickly spread around the room, until finally – by some strange miracle – every girl among them had set her iPhone down, their interest captured instead by this celebrity cook and the way the gears seemed to be turning in her mind.

'Suki,' Prudence said at last, 'I wonder if you might fetch Mrs Carruthers.'

Suki looked as puzzled as every other girl. 'Grandma?'

'Now, Suki,' said Prudence, with the sudden severity she had reserved for only the most idle and self-congratulatory of producers back in her television days. 'It's rather important.'

Suki was used to taking instruction from her grandmother, but never quite like this. In a moment, she was off – and, when she returned, some minutes later, it was to discover that not a thing had changed in the classroom, that her grandmother still sat there in ruminative silence, that the girls still stood reverentially around her,

54

as bewildered by what was going on inside Prudence's mind as they'd been at the hullabaloo on the hockey pitch outside.

'Suki,' Prudence said, 'you appear to be alone.'

'I'm sorry, Grandma. Mrs Carruthers started sniping, almost the moment I set foot outside. She doesn't want us to know, Grandma. She's trying to keep the whole thing a secret, but . . .' Suki held up her iPhone. So too did Sophie, Hetty and the gathering of other girls. 'She doesn't understand the modern world, Grandma.'

At least the corners of Prudence's lips curled into a smile at that. 'One doesn't need to understand the modern world to have a little logic and reason, Suki,' she said – and suddenly it was as if all the deep thought and concern of the past moments had melted away. She was immediately back on her feet, perambulating around the front of the classroom, as if preparing to restart her lesson. 'Well, Mrs Carruthers wants us to learn about cookery, so I suppose that's what we'll do – regardless of what's happening out there. It's just such a damnable shame, because if only she'd let me speak to her, I might be able to help. For a start, I could tell them *exactly* who they're digging up out there.'

The reverential silence transformed into a startled one. The girls, who had begun gravitating back to their work-stations, suddenly set up a hullabaloo of their own. 'What do you mean, Mrs Bulstrode?' said one. 'Are you having us on, Mrs Bulstrode?' said somebody else. 'You can't be serious. All it is, is a hand . . .'

This last came from Hetty. Prudence shot her a know-ing look. 'Is that what you saw out there? Only a hand?'

55

Hetty waved her phone. 'It's right here. You can't *really* know who this is. You're pulling our legs . . .'

'There *is* one problem with it all,' said Prudence, still pacing up and down. Suddenly, an egg whisk was in her hand. She beat it across the other palm. 'You see, it's certainly not archaeology happening out there. I think we're all agreed upon that. We are, none of us, the fools Mrs Carruthers seems to take us for. But the truth is . . . well, I'm not quite sure *what* it is – because, if I'm right, it can't be as simple as murder.'

At least one of the girls looked away this time. At the sound of the word 'murder', her intrigue had given way to something much more unsettling. 'Oh, Mrs Bulstrode, *please*,' she said, evidently hoping they might return to the business of eggs on toast – but the other girls took her meaning incorrectly and soon joined in with, 'Yes, Mrs Bulstrode, *please* – please tell us what you're talking about. Tell us what you know! Tell us *how*!'

'This is much more interesting than raspberry roulade!' called out Sophie.

Prudence's eyes went agog. 'Sophie, my dear, *never* disrespect a raspberry roulade.' She gazed around the classroom. Even Suki was staring at her, rapt. She even looked rather sober – and if that was the positive to come out of this situation, Prudence would take it. Dead bodies did tend to have a sobering effect. 'This is a cookery class, girls,' she said, 'not a crime-solving academy . . .'

And yet . . . Prudence could feel a little frisson moving through her. She looked again at the window, and the distant, imperceptible vision of that skeletal hand. It had been nearly half a century since Prudence last roamed the

56

grounds of St Marianne's, but that skeleton had lain there all this time. 'Bring me that photograph, girls,' she said.

'I can do better than that,' said Hetty, eagerly.

Prudence was constantly astounded at how adept young people were with technology. It took mere seconds for Hetty to have performed some technical wizardry, fiddling with both her phone and a little projector unit on the front desk, before the white board lit up – and there, superimposed upon it, was an enormous rendering of the same photograph they'd been poring over moments before. You couldn't do that with a blackboard and chalk, Prudence thought, as everyone gazed upon the earthworks and that wraithlike hand.

'What are we looking at girls?'

By the tone she'd adopted, she supposed that this really had become a crime-solving academy now. Eggs would have to wait.

'It's a hand,' Sophie called out. 'Just a hand.'

'*Just* a hand?' said Prudence. 'Girls, I would have told you this at some point this morning in any case, so I may as well say it now. *Detail* matters. You young people are so used to flicking on to the next thing that you never quite stop and *see*. Just a hand? No, this isn't *just* a hand.' And she reached out, casting a shadow across the image as she pointed. 'There are only four fingers on this hand.'

The girls gasped.

'But Mrs Bulstrode, one could easily have gone missing in all that earth. There've been diggers all over that field.'

Prudence nodded. 'It's not a bad assumption, Sophie – and on any other day, we'd have to take it into consideration. But no, I'm afraid you're wrong. You see, between these four fingers and that gold wristwatch, I can confidently say that this skeleton belongs to a man named Adam Scott. I ought to know, because I knew him personally. In fact, so did your grandmother, Hetty. Mr Scott taught at this very school. He was our maths tutor. Our slightly dishevelled, slightly eccentric, but very lovely maths tutor. That middle finger he's missing – he lost it in an incident of some considerable local note. And that gold wristwatch? Well, we all thought it was a bit flash for the Adam Scott we knew, because Mr Scott was certainly not a flashy kind of man, but it was a gift from his family, and he treasured it for that.' Prudence peered at her students over the rim of her spectacles, considering each in turn. 'But if you want to know the strangest thing about all this, the thing that doesn't make one ounce of sense . . .'

'We do, Mrs Bulstrode!' cried Hetty, though at least three of the other girls had now shrunken inside themselves, happier with the idea of learning how to make a good hollandaise than hearing Prudence Bulstrode's insights into murder.

'The strangest thing of all is that, even though that body out there is certainly Adam Scott, it also certainly is *not*. Because the Adam Scott who taught me mathematics, the Adam Scott who had four fingers and wore *that* exact gold wristwatch, took himself out to sea one morning in the long hot summer of 1976, wrote a note to his loved ones to tell them he was sorry, and drowned himself in the ocean. It was a sad day in this school. It was a sad day up and down the coast, because Adam

58

Scott was the eldest son of one of the big fishing families out of Penzance – and everyone loved him. The funeral they held for him was chronicled in all the local newspapers. The mayor of Penzance organised a memorial. It seemed the whole coast turned out for him.' Prudence reached out for the projector and, after a couple of false starts, found the button to terminate the whole thing. 'So quite how he's ended up in a slag heap in the hockey pitch, I've no idea.'

Then she dusted off her hands, reached for the cookbook on the counter and hoisted it up.

'Eggs,' she declared, 'the most humble – and yet the most versatile – of the staples in our kitchen. Boil them, fry them, scramble them, poach them. Girls, by the end of the day, you'll know exactly how to . . .' Prudence paused. The girls were all staring at her, trapped somewhere between horror and disbelief. She lifted her glasses, rubbed the bridge of her nose and said, 'Well, like I say, it's a shame Mrs Carruthers didn't want my help. I'm sure I could be of some estimable service.'

Chapter Three

Across the bottom of the screen the words BREAKING NEWS: BODY OF DEAD MATHS TEACHER FOUND FORTY-EIGHT YEARS AFTER HE VANISHED rolled in bright red letters.

The newsreader, a taciturn man with a sunken, doughy kind of appearance, adopted his most sombre air and began: 'The remains of a man last seen forty-eight years ago, and presumed to have committed suicide, were discovered today at St Marianne's School for Girls on the coast of Cornwall, outside Penzance. The discovery of Adam Scott's body, and the confusion it has provoked regarding his assumed suicide in 1976, have sent shock-waves through local communities. Mr Scott was first reported missing in the evening of 1 August 1976, but it wasn't until the following morning that a local fisher-man came across a boat anchored out at sea, some two miles off the coast at Castallack Cove – and discovered a suicide note, believed until today to have been written by Mr Scott himself and apologising to his wife Elizabeth for the pain he was about to put her through. Scott, a mathematics teacher at the same school where his remains have been found, had been struggling for some time in his marriage – and had last been seen taking one of his family's flotilla of fishing rigs out to sea for a calm morning fishing. Now it seems that the accepted truth of

Scott's disappearance has been proven incorrect – and that this presumed suicide may actually have been a cunning murder in disguise. Local police remain on site at St Marianne's, while Detective Bryher Rose, of the Devon & Cornwall Police Department, has been put in charge of this very unusual – and very cold – case. Anyone with information pertaining to Mr Scott's disappearance – or anyone who lived locally in the area in 1976 and may have information to contribute to the investigation – is being asked to contact the Penzance police department on . . . '

With a flick of the wrist, and the press of a button, the television went black.

In the back office of the Bluff restaurant, while the last of the kitchen hands scrubbed down the surfaces in the kitchen outside, Benji Huntington-Lagan looked sharply around – only to discover that his nephew Sonny had come in by the kitchen door, carrying a plate of pilchards and toast for his after-shift supper. By instinct, he had taken up the remote control and started spooling through the many hundreds of channels on the television above. Only once he'd found his favourite show did he set the remote down, drop into a chair, and start filling his face.

'Turn that back,' Benji snapped, impatiently. 'That's the biggest news on this stretch of coast since . . . since Adam Scott disappeared!'

Sonny looked up glumly, his lips trailing pilchard. 'But this is a new episode, Uncle Benji. I've not seen this one. Look, they've rebooted it, Uncle. *The Two Ronnies* – but two completely new Ronnies! Go on, give it a try – it'll give you a chuckle.'

'This is no chuckling matter. Turn it *back*, Sonny.'

Sonny was much slower in spooling back through the channels than he had been scrabbling forwards. Then he sat, dejected with his pilchards, while Benji watched.

'You should listen to this too, Sonny. Our family used to do business with the Penzance Scotts. My father, *your* grandfather, fished these waters. He never took allegiance, but some seasons he'd go off working for the Penzance Scotts – and some for Franks Fisheries, from up in St Ives.' The screen was suddenly lit up with a picture of Adam Scott on his wedding day: a young man, rendered in the faded sepia hues of an early 1970s photograph, smiling in his inimitable crumpled way alongside a wife who (Benji thought) was several degrees better looking than him. She was certainly a few years older, for while Adam still had the gangliness of youth about him, his wife looked regal and statuesque. The rolling tape underneath the photograph said that this was ADAM SCOTT AND ELIZABETH FRANKS ON THEIR WEDDING DAY, APRIL 1972.

'Yes, that's right,' Benji mused, 'Adam Scott married Elizabeth Franks. Before my time, of course, but the way my father used to talk about it, you'd think it was a royal wedding. They certainly treated it like a royal wedding in these parts.' And Benji adopted his best theatrical air. 'Two rival houses, both alike in dignity, in fair Penzance where we set our tale . . .'

Sonny had evidently not studied his Shakespeare at school, so just stared open-mouthed at his uncle, no doubt hungering for this to all be over so that he could return to the *Two New Ronnies* again.

62

'Maybe Grandpa knows something about it all,' said Sonny.

'Getting it out of Dad's addled mind would be the problem,' said Benji, lost in deep thought now. 'But you're rather missing the point.' And he jabbed at the remote control, freezing the image on screen once again. Up there, the detective in charge of the investigation – a Detective Rose, according to the caption underneath her, a woman with flowing auburn hair who looked altogether too young to be in charge of a murder investigation – was making a plea to the public to come forward with whatever information they could, no matter how insignificant it might seem. 'There's going to be a lot of attention on this corner of the world now, Sonny – a *lot* of attention. And attention is good for a business like ours. Attention gets bums on seats.'

'You reckon we can get some more customers, Uncle?'

'It's not customers I'm after, boy. We fill the restaurant floor most nights. No, it's *reputation*. It's . . . to be noticed, outside of Penzance. This might be our ticket. This might get the eyes of the country upon us.' Benji returned to the office desk and picked up the telephone receiver sitting there. 'Let's make sure this Detective Rose is photographed taking dinner here. That ought to do our standing some good. Who knows, maybe this infamous case might be solved over salmon en croute, right here at the Bluff . . .'

In the same moment that Benji Huntington-Lagan was making a flurry of phone calls to local journalists, the same *BBC News* broadcast came to its end in the sixth-form common room at St Marianne's School for Girls.

There hadn't been a television here in Prudence's day – back then, a girl had to make up her own entertainment – but Prudence was glad of it now. Some of the girls from class had gravitated back to their rooms, but others were lounging here, as rapt by the news as Prudence was herself. They kept flitting between the big screen and the little screens in their hands, each hoping to be the first to announce some exciting development. The problem was that, whatever developments there were, had all happened half a century ago. The photographs that kept cycling around all seemed of a bygone age.

'My father wants to come and collect me,' said Sophie, tossing her phone on to one of the plush, velveteen sofas (they'd been much more rustic in Prudence's days; modern girls needed their creature comforts). 'He says I'm not to be left one more minute at a school where a maths teacher can be murdered just like *that*.' She clicked her fingers.

'It *was* fifty years ago,' said one of the other girls.

'But what if the murderer's still local?' said another. 'It stands to reason, he might be back to cover his traces. One of us might come a-cropper!'

'Murderers *do* go back to the scenes of their crimes,' said Hetty, 'don't they, Mrs Bulstrode?'

Prudence, who had been walking up and down the common-room window, gazing out across the hockey pitch – where the forensics teams had completed their work and the remains of Adam Scott had apparently already been carted away – looked up and said, 'Whoever killed Adam Scott will be an old, old man by now. It's very possible he's already dead.'

'Or *she*, Grandma,' Suki interjected.

'Pardon?'

'Well, you said *he*, but it's rather sexist, isn't it? To think Adam was killed by a man? Now, I know it's a 1970s murder – and things were a bit more sexist back then – but . . .' She shrugged. 'I'm just saying.'

'And you're quite right, Suki,' said Prudence, thoughtfully. 'I've fallen into my own trap. One mustn't make assumptions. And yet . . .' She thought again. 'I remember Mr Scott's suicide so well. I always liked Mr Scott. Now, I didn't like mathematics very much – but I suppose I found him *charming*. Unconventional. Do you know, Suki, he wasn't unlike your grandfather in that.' She glanced at the other girls. 'My late husband Nicholas used to compose crosswords for the broadsheets. He published a few compendiums of puzzles and riddles in his time. It was just the way his mind worked – he had a unique way of looking at things. So did Adam Scott. Everyone liked him for it.'

'Not *everyone*,' said Suki. Then, when Prudence screwed up her eyes in perplexity, Suki added, 'Well, somebody did *kill* him – and they must have planned it to perfection, Grandma, to stage his suicide like that.'

'Now it's you making assumptions, dear,' said Prudence, returning her gaze to the windows. 'Whoever said you have to dislike someone in order to kill them? I should think that most murders are committed out of love – or something very much like it.'

'So they all loved Mr Scott, did they?' asked Sophie.

Adam's wedding portrait had just reappeared on the *BBC News*. She scrambled for the remote control and froze it. 'He doesn't look too much of a hottie. I mean . . . not much of a *dish*. That's what you'd have said in your day, isn't it? He isn't too *dishy*.'

'Dishes are what we're meant to be preparing this week,' Prudence said, smiling, 'but that's not the only thing you have wrong. Girls, it sometimes seems to me as if your generation doesn't really understand what makes one person attractive to another. You're lost in those little pictures on your gadgets, and you've quite over- looked the fact that a man isn't attractive because of his appearance; it's his character that draws you to him. You'll have to trust me on this, and don't spend too long learning that lesson for yourselves – you'll waste the best years of your life on absolute *rotters*.' At last, Prudence left the window and found herself drawn to the televi- sion screen. 'No, Adam Scott didn't give a fig about his appearance – but, girls, that just means he was a man of his time, not one of your pampered generation. He had intelligence and charm by the bucketload. And he was a man who ploughed his own furrow – I think I found that rather compelling as well. You see, Mr Scott ought to have been off running the fishing firm his fathers had founded. But Adam Scott wasn't a man who liked the ocean very much. What he liked was . . .'

'Mathematics?' groaned one of the girls.

'Did he show any signs he was going to kill himself?' asked Sophie.

'Well, evidently not!' exclaimed Hetty. 'Because he *didn't*, did he? Somebody offed him!'

At this, Prudence intervened: 'As I remember, there were often whispers about Adam being a little depressed. But you mustn't read too much into that, girls. I'm afraid I knew a few folk who took their own lives, back in my London days. You wouldn't have thought there was anything untoward about them, not until the day you got the news. You see, suicide's a—'

The girls were growing enraptured again – it seemed that Prudence Bulstrode was at least as engaging when she spoke about murder as when she spoke about shakshuka – but at this point there came a knock at the common-room door, and in strode old Ms Balloon. Immediately, Hetty sank into the cushions of her sofa, instinctively embarrassed by her own grandmother's appearance.

'Pru, can I have a word?'

Prudence looked over the girls. 'It'll be sauces tomorrow, girls. Hollandaise, bechamel, velouté, good old-fashioned gravy and stocks. Suki's put some recipes from *Saucy!*' – it was Pru's second book, and one of her most famous, ' – on the . . .'

'The online portal, Grandma.'

Prudence just shrugged. 'So you can do some evening reading, should you wish.'

Outside the common room, Poppy was looking ashen and tired. 'It's been quite a day, Pru. Too much for my heart, if you want to know the truth. I've been on blood pressure meds for a few years, but this has got me racing. And . . . we're *so* sorry. It's all rather taken the sheen off, hasn't it? The journalists were meant to come down and take your picture, Pru, you and your camper, but instead it's . . . Mr Scott! I can't believe it.'

Pru decided that now was not the time to ask about the camper van, but no doubt it remained on the hillside above the cove, exactly where Pru had left it.

'Mrs Carruthers is beside herself, Pru. She's worried she's upset you – all those shenanigans this morning when she was trying to figure out what was going on. She sent me to ask: would you mind, perhaps, popping down to the staffroom to see her?'

Prudence nodded. 'Let's go, Poppy – and you can tell me a little about your time here on the way.'

There wasn't enough time for an actual catch-up – in light of today's extenuating circumstances, that would have to wait – but Prudence was pleased to hear that Poppy had had a fulfilling time across the last forty-odd years. 'I've two children, Sam and Helen, and that gave me seven – seven, Pru! – grandchildren. And I'm not sure Sam's wife Hayley's quite finished yet. I never meant to stay in Cornwall, of course, but then I met Bobby – and he has the coast in his veins, so I taught for a while at a college in Falmouth, then we were in Plymouth when the kids left home . . . and a return trip to St Marianne's, this close to retirement? Well, that was too good an opportunity to pass up.'

'And you're still known as Poppy Balloon?' Pru asked.

'Yes, I didn't want to take Bobby's surname as Poppy Flower sounded a bit silly.' Pru raised an eyebrow but kept silent as Poppy Balloon continued: 'Bobby puts his feet up these days. Mostly, he likes to watch the racing on the telly and do a spot of fly-fishing on a Sunday. I leave him to it. He's a decent cook, Pru – you'd like him.'

Prudence remembered well the kind of young

gentleman Poppy had always been drawn to, and doubted very much whether she would get along with Bobby – but, 'I'm happy for you, Poppy,' she said. 'I'd love to meet him.'

'We should never have fallen out of touch. *Never.* A wedding cake cooked by Prudence Bulstrode would have been *just* the thing.'

An old tension touched her, the moment Poppy brought her to the staffroom door.

'It feels funny, doesn't it?' said Poppy. 'Like you're about to get told off. Say, do you remember when old Mrs Arkwright called us both in here after that incident with the toilet block? I'd heard people say "my knees are knocking", but I never knew it could actually happen! She's still with us, you know. Mrs Arkwright. She's over at the Cherry Garth, just like Miss Jubber – not that they have much to do with one another. I rather think they can't stand the sight of one another, in fact. Well, here we go . . .'

Poppy was gabbling on so fiercely that Prudence was rather alarmed when she flung open the staffroom door and harried her within.

If the common room had been 'gentrified' in the years since Prudence boarded here, the staffroom had been turned into a palace. In Prudence's mind's eye, this place used to be cosy but rustic, filled with dusty old armchairs, magazines, and books. Now, it looked like the first-class departure lounge for an exclusive airline. Mrs Carruthers was reclining in a leather armchair, fanning herself while her eyes were glued to a television screen half the size of a cinema, mounted on the farthest

69

wall. An air-conditioning unit hummed, while Ronnie Green stirred sugar into his tea and Verity Down sat primly at a table in the corner, playing a game of solitaire.

'Mrs Carruthers, Pru's here.'

Mrs Carruthers didn't have the energy to leap up and greet her guest. She called out, 'Television – pause!', then pressed a button and waited for the armchair itself to elevate her, until at last she was standing. Such was the fate of humanity, thought Prudence – humankind's endless ingenuity, put to work helping middle-aged ladies to stand up, instead of solving the manifold crises of the world.

'Pru,' Mrs Carruthers said. 'May I call you *Pru*? I feel that I must. And I also feel that I must apologise after my dreadful behaviour this morning. I wanted it all to go away, you see. I truly thought that it might. An archaeological discovery – well, it's all a matter of definitions, isn't it? So much is nowadays. And who's to say how far back a body needs to be to be *archaeological*?' The effort of these mental contortions seemed to be affecting Mrs Carruthers unduly. Ronnie Green – who was studiously not catching Prudence's eye, having singularly failed to rescue her camper van once again – hurried to fetch her a glass of water. 'I hope you can forgive us. This was meant to be a joyful day, but all seems lost. I'm only sorry that it tarnishes your stay. I did so want to show you how far we've come as a school.'

Prudence was about to tell her that she had no such obligation when she directed her gaze back to the television screen. It seemed that a press conference had just been convened. There, above a caption which read

MYSTERY OF THE FOUR-FINGERED MAN, stood the auburn-haired detective who Prudence had caught a fleeting sight of on the edges of the hockey pitch earlier that day. In the frozen image, she was in the process of settling at a table alongside a woman Prudence could only take for Adam's wife Elizabeth. Fifty years on, she still had the same noble look as she'd had in the wedding portrait. She'd aged well – helped, no doubt, by the family's wealth – and might easily have been mistaken for twenty years younger than she truly was. The caption, when the image started moving again, referred to her as ELIZABETH DUGGAN, though her name had once been 'Scott', and sometime before that 'Franks' as well.

'As you can imagine,' she was saying to the gathered photographers, 'this day has shaken me almost as fiercely as that day, forty-eight years ago, when the police knocked at my door to tell me my husband was gone, and to deliver me the letter he'd left for me. I'm as shocked and appalled as anyone to learn that, for all these years, my late husband has been lying in a field, not at the bottom of the ocean. I'm sure you'll understand that it's all rather paralysing. It has been many, many years since I grieved for Adam – but something of that grief never really leaves you, and it's been a surprise how vividly it's flowered in me again. I only hope that somebody out there knows *something*. I only hope that, decades on from this terrible crime, today's discovery ignites some flame of recognition – or that, perhaps, it plays upon somebody's conscience. Somebody out there simply must know what happened to Adam. I beg you to please come forward.'

One of the reporters cast an unheard question at her, and Elizabeth quickly added, 'I don't know. It all seems like some Hollywood movie to me and my family. I'm grateful for the unending support of my husband Mac in all of this – he's been in a rock in an unusual and unsettling situation – and the love being shown to me by my children and grandchildren is unmeasurable. I've lived under a cloud for forty-eight years, but today it seemed that cloud got so much darker.'

'Television – pause!'

The screen froze once more – and it seemed a blessed relief to Mrs Carruthers. 'It makes one feel so weak. It's inconceivable, Mrs Bulstrode. The very worst a headmistress ordinarily deals with is a spot of smoking and drinking on the premises.' Beyond Mrs Carruthers, Poppy's eyes opened wide, and she gave Prudence an enormous, dramatic wink, as if to acknowledge some shenanigans decades in the past. 'But this? This is a . . . well, it's a terrible thing for the family, of course, but it's a public relations *disaster* for St Marianne's. My girls have been playing hockey on an unmarked grave! My new gymnasium's going to have to be delayed – and even a single week's slippage is going to deprive us of it once the new term begins. There'll be ghost stories and rumours about it for years. You know the thing, Mrs Bulstrode. Girls have overactive imaginations. They'll be seeing ghostly men bench-pressing weights at night – that kind of thing. A spectral presence on a Peloton bike, moaning and moaning and moaning.' She paused, seeming to take stock and gather her composure. 'I don't want this to affect your stay with us, Pru. I want you to know we'll do everything we can to make sure your time with us isn't interrupted. And yet . . .' She gestured to the television screen, and in particular the flame-haired detective alongside Elizabeth Duggan, formerly Scott, née Franks. 'Detective Rose has been in touch, Pru. She's asking for statements from anyone who was here at the time of Mr Scott's disappearance. Poppy here's got to deliver one, and so's our Verity. They're contacting all the old alumni. It's possible, just possible, that she may want to interview you. Indeed, she's to be back on site tomorrow, and . . . and . . .'

The moment had seemingly got too much for Mrs Carruthers. In an instant, Ronnie Green had redelivered her to the chair, and in the next instant the chair itself was lowering her down, cradling her like a babe.

'I'm sorry, Mrs Bulstrode. I . . . I haven't eaten today. Stress does funny things to a woman.' Then she turned her face upwards, her face alight with a sudden idea. 'Pru, dear, you wouldn't . . . you wouldn't mind rustling me up something, would you? A little something, just to take the edge away? It's been *such* a taxing day.'

It was almost, Prudence thought, as if that had been the purpose of her visit.

'I'll bring you something shortly,' she said, retreating to the staffroom door. She was fairly certain that the last time she'd been summoned to this staffroom she'd been sent away on some errand as well. Then she looked back at the television screen. The caption MYSTERY OF THE FOUR-FINGERED MAN had been replaced with DID THE SCION OF A FISHING DYNASTY REALLY DIE AT SEA? and Detective Bryher Rose was speaking, in even terms, about how a long-dead investigation was urgently being resurrected. 'It's a very strange feeling when all our recollections about the past, the things we've always held on to as true, are suddenly upended,' she was saying.

As Prudence hurried back along the self-same corridors she'd trodden as a young girl, she knew exactly what Detective Rose meant.

Outside the common room, Suki was gazing into her iPhone with all the intensity of a wicked stepmother staring into her magic mirror.

Gazing back out at her was the freckled face, banked in vivid red hair, of her oldest friend Numbers. Two years Suki's senior, Numbers had proudly called himself her 'partner in crime' since the long, hot summer when he had successfully guided her through her GCSEs with a hearty dose of revision, his excellent knowledge of educational loopholes, and the bottle of rum Suki had stolen from her father's drinks cabinet. Since then, and much to Prudence's chagrin, Numbers had often been on hand to offer advice whenever it was needed. Suki's grandmother, of course, felt that young men who lived in their mother's basement flat and seemed to make avoiding regular employment their *raison d'être*, were in no position to offer life advice – but that was just another of the ways Suki's grandmother had fallen behind the times. Numbers was the most successful careerist that Suki knew; it was just that he'd chosen online poker, and the occasional black market job mining data for a nefarious tech company, as his career.

'You and old Mother Hubbard do find yourselves in the most deliciously *interesting* situations, Suki darling. Go on, tell me what you've found.'

'Nothing more than's on the news, but . . .' Suki looked over her shoulder. Inside the common room, the girls were still glued to the television set. 'There's something altogether *fishy* about this.'

'And not just because of this Adam Scott's heritage, I presume?'

'Numbers,' Suki said, sternly, 'I'm being serious. Look, we've a job to do here – that old headmistress isn't about to let us go sniffing about Adam Scott's grave, when she's doing all she can to pretend it hasn't even happened – but I was thinking that maybe *you* could have a look round. There are fifty years separating us and him. It's not as if all the old newspaper reports of his "suicide" are up there, waiting to be found. But I thought – well, you know your way around an archive or two. Maybe, while I'm running around after my grandmother, you might . . .'

'Suki, do you *really* think I'm lounging around in my pyjamas, waiting for you to call with some little odd-job?'

Suki peered even more intensely at the screen. 'Numbers, I think you're wearing your pyjamas *right now*.'

'I'm having an early evening, darling. I'm in a rather stressful situation of my own. I was approached by a certain gentleman working for a foreign currency exchange – he's requested my services to move a little money around for him. It seems it's the sort of thing that can only be done from inside the United Kingdom – and, alas, he's in Malaysia. Well, I've had my credentials up on certain, shall we say, *less legitimate* corners of the internet for some time now. This sort of work can be terribly well paid. If it keeps the wolf from the door, Suki, I'm all for it, but—'

There were footsteps in the hallway behind her. Suki knew that sure-footed, deliberate tread anywhere: it was her grandmother, returning from her staffroom summons.

'Numbers, stop it. Can you help or not?'

This time, the voice that came back was not as imperious and teasing as usual. Numbers rolled his eyes, dropped his voice an octave and said, 'I suppose I have a spare half hour here and there. Suki, you may await my call.' Then he hung up.

Just in time, because here came Prudence, her face set in deep, thoughtful lines as she rounded the corner. 'Suki, dear, we have a job to do.'

Almost as soon as she said it, Prudence had pivoted on her heel and vanished the way she had come. Suki, sensing some urgency in her stride, floundered after her.

'What is it, Grandma? You're thinking of something – I can tell. You've had an idea.'

Prudence didn't so much as look over her shoulder as she called back, 'I'm thinking of a scrambled-egg supper, Suki. Some crispy bacon bits and tomato salsa. Chop chop, we can talk about it while we cook.'

In the domestic science classroom, the lights burst into life.

'Get out some mixing bowls, Suki, and warm up the stove. There's four of them in that staffroom wanting some supper – and I'll be damned if we're serving them up rubbish, whether I'm the "most shining member of St Marianne's alumni" or just the hired help.'

Soon, Prudence was clattering around with mixing bowls, cracking eggs, directing Suki in the chopping of chives and baby shallots, and drizzling a little olive oil around a pan. 'A quick vinaigrette next, Suki – but bring those pomegranates out of the hamper. I'll show them the difference a little burst of freshness can make . . . '

'Grandma, are we *really* making Mrs Carruthers her supper? You're – you're a famous cook!'

'But still a cook, Suki.' Prudence grinned. 'I'm humouring her. I've told you before – it pays to keep the client happy. And, besides, I wanted to be back in this kitchen tonight. Something about the atmosphere of the place appeals to me. It stirs up the memories. If I look past all these gadgets and contraptions, if I get into the *feel* of it,' and here she started whisking the eggs, adding in liberal salt and pepper as she went, 'I almost get the sensation that I'm here again. *Adam Scott . . .*'

'What about him, Grandma?'

Suki had set about preparing the tomatoes, dicing them into tiny cubes in the way Prudence had taught her, then sprinkling liberal amounts of rock salt over the top. Next came the parsley, shredded so fine as to almost be powder.

'Well, everybody liked him. I don't know a soul who didn't. The teaching profession attracts certain sorts of people. Genuine altruists are few and far between. There are more bullies than those – you know the sort, Suki, you'll have come across a few yourself. But the rarest breed of teacher – or so it's always seemed to me – is the

77

one with a real passion for his subject. Make no mistake: Adam Scott was a mathematics teacher because he *loved* mathematics. To him, it was like a riddle. Mathematics was a puzzle box, and he wanted to show it to us all, to infect us with that enthusiasm.'

'He sounds like Numbers,' Suki grinned.

Prudence's eyes darkened. 'Adam Scott wanted to share his love of a good puzzle with the world, Suki, not sit in his mother's basement clickety-clicking on his little computer.' The eggs went in the pan, and Prudence started stirring them gently, never taking her eyes off them as the scrambling began. In went two great knobs of butter: butter and salt, the gateways to *taste*. 'What I'm trying to say is: Adam Scott was just indisputably his own man, and it drew people to him. I daresay he didn't mind the attention, but he wasn't like some men, soaking it up and luxuriating in it. He was . . . gentler than that. A true one-off. Why anyone should want to kill him, I can't say.'

'You almost sound like *you* were in love with him, Grandma!'

'No, no,' Prudence said, smiling wistfully, 'not *love*. But if there was a hint of that about it – well, it was only a teenage passion, and I wasn't the only one . . .'

Prudence could still remember that golden summer of 1974, the first sight she'd caught of Adam Scott. Halfway through their tenure at St Marianne's, Prudence and her close friends thought they ruled the school now: no longer innocent first years, preyed upon by the seniors in their houses, they knew every shortcut around the school premises, dared to sneak off along the coast whenever the whim took them, and fancied they had the faults and foibles of each one of their teachers sewn up. If Prudence was the most prudent among them, that was only because Poppy, Collette and Vivienne had each inherited what the headmistress Mrs Arkwright called 'the wild gene'. 'A gene that comes to life in these headstrong teenage days,' she said darkly, when she had cause to admonish them – Mrs Arkwright coming from a generation that hadn't had 'teenagers' and consequently believed that children should be as responsible as adults from the age of eleven-and-a-half. 'You girls have overactive wild genes. Unless you learn to keep it in check, it will mar you for the rest of your days. No good man wants a wild woman, girls. You must remember this.'

There were precious few male teachers at St Marianne's, and perhaps this was what piqued the interests of the girls when it was announced that the former maths master, Mr Bottom, was to retire over the summer holidays – to be replaced by a much younger, and much more intriguing, model. Mr Bottom was a teacher of the old school – which is to say that he was one of the last teachers Prudence knew who had fought, not against the Nazis, but in the even earlier Great War. Part of him still seemed to believe he was in the trenches at Verdun – and, the more ancient he got, the more partial he was to setting arithmetic problems concerning the number of men lost to dysentery in a particularly virulent outbreak of disease, the ratio of rats to soldiers in a British barracks, and the most efficient way of sending a message between two distant points. Naturally, very little of this inspired a love of mathematics in the girls he was teaching – so the promise of Adam Scott, twenty-five years old and from a local fishing dynasty, had titillated the girls all summer.

It was titillating them still on that September morning when he first arrived. On reflection, Prudence would later decide that they had built him up to be more than he could possibly be – a knight in shining armour, come to vanquish the despicable Mr Bottom – and their first impression was never going to live up to expectations. 'Nevertheless,' Prudence told Suki, 'PVC were waiting at the end of the lane for his car to arrive. We'd determined to be the first ones to see him.'

'PVC?' Suki ventured. 'Grandma – *PVC*?'

Prudence smirked. 'It was what we called ourselves. Poppy, Vivienne, Collette: PVC. Well, it wasn't perfect – Poppy and I used to bicker like dogs over which one of us really stood for "P" – but we fancied ourselves rather stylish. We each had a PVC jacket – all the rage back then – and thought we were queens of the year. Nobody could touch us.'

'It sounds a bit,' Suki made a ridiculous face, 'to me.'

'So, one day, will all that black make-up and loud music *you* listen to, Suki. That's just the way of the world. Anyway, there we were, PVC, waiting at the end of the drive. And there was Mr Scott, rattling on to site – not in a dashing sport's car like we'd imagined, but in that little Mini we'd come to think of as . . . well, as an extension of his personality, really. A bit battered around the edges, a bit unkempt, but . . . fascinating, all the same. The moment that car arrived, we were on to it. We cantered after it, up the drive – and I daresay we were the first, other than Mrs Arkwright who'd interviewed him, to catch sight of Mr Scott. No, he wasn't the Adonis we'd been hoping for . . .' Suki made that face again, the one that said she didn't *ever* want to hear her grandmother use the word 'Adonis' again. 'Collette and Vivienne weren't so interested at all. They quickly wandered off. They'd wanted their dashing hunk, you see, not this slightly stooped, vaguely dishevelled, very *average*-looking man, who got out of the car. A bit ramshackle – that's how you'd describe Adam Scott. He had his suit jacket slung over his shoulder, a kind of gingery fuzz of a moustache, and his shirtsleeves were rolled up. In fact, I think Poppy would have taken off after the others and left me to it if those sleeves hadn't been rolled up.'

'Why's that, Grandma?'

Prudence remembered it well. Adam Scott had stepped out of the Mini, looked up at St Marianne's basking in the warm September sunshine, and stood with one hand on his hip. 'Do you see that, Pru?' Poppy had said – and it wasn't until Poppy had pointed further that Prudence knew what she was looking at. There, on Adam Scott's forearm, was a tattoo in deep, inky blue: an anchor, and beneath it the words PENZANCE SCOTTS.

'Of course, a tattoo in a young man was intriguing back then. It's ten-a-penny these days. Young men get their favourite cartoon characters on their arms, completely forgetting that, one day – if they're lucky – they'll be old.' Prudence continued to scramble the eggs, reaching out now for more of the chives Suki had been chopping. 'Back then, tattoos were for soldiers and sailors. We'd seen plenty of those. But this was a little different, somehow. Adam Scott wasn't the sort of man who had a tattoo. But here he was, sporting it proudly. And so he might: it was the family crest, the mark of the Scotts. Because we quickly discovered that Adam was a notable on this part of the coast. The eldest son of Glynn Scott, who owned the Penzance Scotts fleet. One of the biggest fishing families on the south Cornwall coast – and Adam was his heir. One day, if he played his cards right, he'd inherit eighty fishing boats and their crews, warehouses, sorting facilities, a flotilla of wagons. An empire, in this part of the world.'

Suki had almost finished her salsa. She stopped with a teaspoon of it poised at her lips – about to test it for taste, in the way Prudence had always shown her. 'But Grandma, why on earth was Adam Scott starting a career as a maths tutor, if he had all *that* waiting for him?'

The eggs were done. Prudence turned down the heat, stirring them for the final time. The chives were still green upon the creamy soft clouds in the pan. Yes, it was simple – but the finishing touches would be divine. That, Prudence reflected, was where the best cookery lay – in taking something familiar, and giving it a twist. In a roundabout way that was what Benji Huntington-Lagan did as well – but sometimes you tried so hard you lost the point of a dish.

'We never truly got to the bottom of that,' said Prudence. 'There was a story there, but not one Mr Scott ever told – not between simple accounting and algebra, in any case. Every now and again, we'd see Mr Scott out in Penzance with his wife – or perhaps she'd come to the school to meet him – and it sometimes seemed, or we *thought* it seemed, that she didn't really want him to be a schoolteacher. That he'd disappointed her somehow

– she, so very grand, and Adam just talking about mathematical puzzles all day long. But, as I say, Adam did what Adam did, and he was completely unapologetic about it. There's a magnetism in that.'

'His wife, Elizabeth, from the press conference just now?'

'You see, she was an heiress too. The daughter to Lionel Franks, of Franks Fisheries. They were the biggest fleet on the *north* coast of Cornwall. Now, of course, as a woman, she couldn't really inherit the firm, but—'

'Excuse me, Grandma?' Suki had thrown down her spoon, flabbergasted.

'Yes, dear?'

'*As a woman?*'

'We're talking fifty years ago, Suki. The past is a different country. Sometimes I think that your generation don't really know what mine was fighting for. You have your own little crusades, but you don't *really* know what prejudice feels like. You mustn't forget, the world has changed very much. If I'd been born ten years before, it's doubtful I'd have even learned any mathematics. Your generation do harp on about feminism, Suki, but it's mine who . . .'

Prudence had much more to say on this matter – she'd met so many young people in her television days, all of whom told her they were 'activists' for some cause or another, but all it often amounted to was one of those dreadful hashtags, and perhaps a nice Sunday picnic with a banner or two; OCCUPY ST JAMES! said the T-shirt one of her old PR assistants had worn to the shoot of *Pru's Posh Puds*, striking a blow against corruption in Westminster by eating Scotch eggs and M&S sandwiches on the grasses of Green Park – but, at once, she fell silent. Setting the pan of scrambled eggs down, she bustled across the classroom, returning to the corner where Suki and the girls had spent so much of today peering out of the window.

'What is it, Grandma?'

'Turn those lights off, dear.'

There was no light switch in the classroom, but at least Suki was *au fait* with modern technology where her grandmother was not. After clapping sharply three times in quick succession, the lights in the classroom dimmed – and there stood Prudence, in the dark, still staring out of the window.

Outside, in the deepening summer darkness, the light of a torch bobbed up and down.

Suki rushed to Prudence's side. 'Who is it, Grandma?'

Prudence stared. Some moments later, now that her eyes were accustomed to the dark, she could see the silhouette of the figure wielding the light: a slight, rangy-looking man, loping through the outbuildings between here and the hockey pitch.

'That's not one of those policemen, is it, Grandma?'

It most certainly was not. What constables had been left on site were in the little lean-to erected by the cordon, pacing up and down the edge of the hockey pitch, warding off sleep with radio chatter and the flasks at their sides.

By instinct, Prudence reached for one of the wooden spoons from the workstation nearest to her. A wooden spoon: the oldest, most venerable of all the implements in a good cook's kitchen. Somehow, Prudence always felt better with one in her hand. 'Wait here, Suki. I shan't be a moment.'

Through the glass, the figure picked his way methodically forward. In front of him, his torch-beam roamed, picking out first the edges of the outbuildings, then the windows of the domestic science block itself.

'You're not going out there alone, Grandma,' Suki insisted, and followed Prudence out of the door.

Out here, the night was balmy and still. A wave of heat and the scent of cut grass washed over Prudence as she emerged from the school reception, then quietly picked her way, wooden spoon in hand, around the circumference of the building.

Between the outbuildings she came, gesturing wildly for Suki to remain behind. Up ahead, between the two buildings, the figure seemed to be creeping forward, bound for the hockey-pitch edge. The torchlight bobbed, close to the ground. Each pace, he stopped. Each pace, he lingered a moment before inching further on.

'Grandma, that wooden spoon won't do anything if—'

The figure turned around.

It was too far away to see his face, but the appearance of Prudence and Suki had rooted him to the spot. Suddenly, his boots seemed heavy; he was trying to lift his feet, but succeeding only in shuffling backward.

The torchlight lifted. It dazzled Prudence's eyes. Cringing away from it, she called out, 'Can we help you?'

'I – I was . . .'

That voice belonged to no man. This was a voice that was hardly broken, a teenager perhaps, light and crackling.

'Are you looking for someone?' Prudence went on.

'Yes!' the figure exclaimed. 'I'm . . . I'm looking for the police. They're here, aren't they? Somewhere on site? I've . . . I've got a delivery.'

'Delivery?' Suki drew close to Prudence's side, trying to see through the dazzling light.

'It's dinner time,' the figure stammered. 'That is to say – I've brought out an order. Pizzas, from PenzanceEats. I just – well, I just wasn't sure which way to go. The hockey pitch, it's right up here, no?'

In spite of the light that seemed to be driving her backwards, Prudence strode forth. 'I'll show you, young man.'

'No,' he stammered, stumbling backwards. 'It's quite all right. I know which way to go now. I won't put you to any bother. I'm late enough as it is. I . . . I miss out on tips if the delivery's cold.'

Before Prudence could say another word, the figure dipped his torch beam, turned on his heel and ran. Soon, he had vanished between the buildings. Soon after that, there came the sound of an engine firing, the rattling purr of a low-grade motorbike or scooter as it came to life. For a moment, the engine roared; then it guttered into silence, fading as it took off into the surrounding hills.

In the balmy darkness, Prudence and Suki stood abreast of each other, listening to the distant susurration of the sea coming in from the cove.

'Grandma,' Suki said, 'those eggs will be getting cold.'

But Prudence only stood there, idly shifting her weight from foot to foot, still staring off in the direction the young man had fled.

'You told me never to microwave eggs, Grandma.'

Still Prudence was silent – until, just as Suki was about to take her arm, she suddenly said, 'Do you know, Suki, it's the funniest thing. I *know* things have got terribly modern – and I *know*, better than any, that progress is fast in the twenty-first century. New technologies take over just about every season. It's hard to keep up.' Now she looked at Suki, and her eyes seemed to twinkle as brightly as the stars plastered across the heavens above. 'But I'm fairly certain that, however far technology's come, it's still necessary for a food delivery driver to at least be carrying a bag . . .'

Chapter Four

Dreams dogged Prudence through the night.

Prudence had never been a woman given to night-mares. Days spent thinking about choux pastry and crème pâtissière, or perhaps showing a group from the Women's Institute the correct way to fold air into a light summer sponge, did not ordinarily breed night terrors. Yet there was something about being back here, at St Marianne's, that had ignited parts of the memory that had lain dormant for decades – and now those memories coursed through her, making her toss and turn all night long.

The first day she'd arrived at school, trailing from her father's hand, and said goodbye to her parents among all the other milling families on the step . . .

The day her mother had been late in arriving to pick her up for the Christmas holidays, and for several hours a thirteen-year-old Prudence had been left to entertain the impossible: a Christmas with only the school care-taker to look after her . . .

The very last day of term, the end of Prudence's third year, when the fire alarms had been triggered and the school's new sprinklers set off, drenching them all in the middle of exams . . .

Nightmares had been made of fiercer stuff, and perhaps

these were dreams that unnerved rather than frightened – but, whatever they were, periodically they sent Prudence flying up out of sleep, until at last she gave in and sat in her old dormitory window, looking down across the school and trying to think upon happier times.

Of course, it was Mr Scott to whom her thoughts kept returning – Mr Scott, and occasionally that phantom delivery driver, no doubt a ghoul come sniffing about the site of a murder. Somewhere past 4 a.m., just before the first pale band of sunlight appeared somewhere over the Celtic Sea, her meandering thoughts had brought her to a sports day, the summer that followed Mr Scott's arrival. It was a matter of school tradition that the teachers competed against each other at the end of the day-long gala – not even Mr Bottom had been excused his turn, so despite Mr Scott's initial protestations there was no chance that Mrs Arkwright was going to bend tradition to suit him. Adam Scott, the girls had discovered by then, was not an athletic man – perhaps that was what had separated him from his family of doughty fishermen – but nor was he afraid of making a fool of himself, and soon succeeded in doing exactly that, tripping over his own feet as he strove to hand the baton over in the teachers' relay race and bloodying his left cheek in the process.

It was the English mistress, Prudence seemed to think, who'd tended to Mr Scott that day. Dot Ellen was voluptuous, vivacious – and, so the girls thought, rather *vulpine* in the way she rushed to Mr Scott's side. There was a school nurse employed for exactly this kind of thing, but somehow she'd been relegated to handing out segments of orange and beakers of water at the end of each race

– vitamin C and 'hydration' being paramount to the welfare of St Marianne's girls. As PVC had watched Miss Ellen cleaning up Mr Scott that day, Poppy had put her fingers between her lips and dared to wolf-whistle – for there was practically something *indecent* about how close Miss Ellen got to him, and how her fingers caressed his every graze with soft, moist cotton wool. Nor were Pru and her friends the only ones who found this scene startling: Miss Jubber appeared quite put off by the whole scenario, turning away and crossing her arms firmly across her breast. It was said that Miss Jubber had once been stood up at the altar, and consequently held no truck with love affairs – so perhaps the sight of Miss Ellen getting so personal with Mr Scott was even more unseemly to her than it was to everybody else.

'I don't know what they see in him,' Collette had said, with an air of dismissiveness the other girls evidently did not feel. 'There's real men in town. I'll have a real man one day. She's just starved of attention. That's what it is. Anything in trousers would do for Miss Ellen.'

In the dormitory window, as the day's first light spilled on the school, Pru wondered what had become of Miss Ellen now. Had she married, in the end? Was she happy? Had she grown old and already passed on? Even if it hadn't been for the discovery in the hockey pitch, coming back to St Marianne's was somehow like taking a holiday to the past.

She was thinking of this as the day truly began and, having first roused Suki and asked her to follow sharp-ish, wended her way down to the domestic science block. Today it was sauces – every good cook had to have a reliable repertoire of stocks, sauces and gravies – but Prudence had to admit that her mind wasn't on hollandaise as she prepared each workstation and tried to think through her opening speech. No, it was that phantom delivery driver to whom her thoughts kept returning – so much so that, fifteen minutes before the girls poured into the classroom, she bustled on out to the edge of the hockey pitch, approached the constables who were just about to go off shift, and asked them, 'Long night, was it, boys?'

The two constables looked haggard and drawn, and grateful for the next shift who had just arrived on site. The first of them, as lean and gangly as the phantom PenzanceEats driver had been the night before, said, 'Thank God it's summer, Mrs Bulstrode, that's all I can say.'

'But I'll bet that pizza helped,' Prudence went on.

By the quizzical look on the constables' faces, Prudence immediately knew she'd been right.

'Oh, no pizza for us, Mrs Bulstrode. My mam packed me some jam sarnies, but it's not much for a long night like that. I'm off for a fry-up and a sleep. Then it's back here at six p.m. And . . . pizza?' he suddenly said. 'That's an idea. That's not a bad idea at all. Pizza and Coke, that'll do the trick. I don't suppose . . . No, it's too much to ask. It's *too* much. Only, since you're here, Mrs Bulstrode, and since you've got that lovely kitchen in there, you wouldn't mind putting us a plate together, would you? Homemade's always better than delivery. You can't beat a homemade dough.'

By the time Prudence had returned to the classroom – marvelling at the fact that, twice in twelve hours, she'd agreed to cater for people working at St Marianne's – the girls had started arriving. In her absence, Suki had prepared all the workstations, ready for the morning's first bechamel – but, if the girls showed any interested in sauces at all, it was only out of duty and deference to Prudence. She'd hardly begun her opening spiel, rhapsodising on the power and potency of a good stock, when one of the girls slumped on to her desk in mock theatrics, declared, 'It's all well and good, Mrs Bulstrode, but it isn't quite as *gripping* as a proper whodunit, is it?'

'Yes, Mrs Bulstrode,' Sophie piped up. 'I'm afraid the game's up. We've been doing some digging and . . .'

Prudence plucked up her wooden spoon again. It always gave her strength. 'I hope you're not about to put *me* in the dock, Sophie?'

'No, Mrs Bulstrode, not *that* kind of digging. And actually, *digging*'s not the right word, is it, given that digging's how we get a body in our school in the first place.' Sophie hoisted herself up, took a breath (if only to overcome her sudden bout of verbal diarrhoea) and went on, 'It's Hetty who found it, but it's not just cookery you're famous for, is it, Mrs Bulstrode? Go on, Hetty – you tell her.'

Hetty looked up miserably, as if she really didn't want to go on. 'I've been searching you, Mrs Bulstrode.'

'*Searching* me?'

'You know – online. You don't have to search too far before you find all that business at Farleigh Manor – that other cook, with her face planted down in the rhubarb patch. And that strangeness up at Scrafton Busk – that poor old tramp type, bludgeoned over the head and buried in a snowman. You helped the police out with those investigations, didn't you? If the reports are anywhere near right, I reckon you just about *solved* those cases.'

Prudence looked sidelong at Suki – who was keeping her smirk to herself, her head still buried in the copy of *Saucy!* open on the counter.

'Well, girls, I have to say, those trips were quite different.'

'But don't you *want* to help, Mrs Bulstrode? Have you even been out there to see where he was buried?'

'Come on, Mrs Bulstrode!' one of the other girls piped up. 'You were *here* when it happened. You must know *something*. What was Mr Scott like? Maybe he had an enemy, right here in the school? Your mind must have been ticking over, Mrs Bulstrode. You must have *some* ideas. I reckon, Mrs Bulstrode, if you just thought about it a *little* – half as much as you've been thinking about this course – you could close this investigation, and we'd still have time to fix the end-of-course banquet. What do you say?'

It was on the tip of her tongue to reply, *I say: sauces are the base of every good meal, whether that's the stock that starts a soup or the roux which underpins every good gravy,* but the zealous looks on the girls' faces somehow made her lose track of her words. 'You girls have *got* to promise me you'll pay proper attention to the rest of the day's lesson,' she started. 'If Mrs Carruthers were to think I was training you in the solving of an old crime, instead of . . . '

'Oh, Mrs Bulstrode, we can blag our way through a half-decent dinner! But it's murder we need to know about,' said Sophie.

This time, Prudence did catch Suki's eye. Suki had been there at Farleigh Manor as well. She'd been there in Scrafton Busk when the body was unearthed. It seemed to Prudence, suddenly, that murder had a terrible gravity about it: once you were in its circumference, you couldn't help but be dragged near.

'Well, the school was very different in those days, of course. We'd have taken a look at all this,' and she waved her hand airily around the classroom, 'and thought it was something out of the space age. The idea of a state-of-the-art gymnastics block? Well, we didn't need much more than the hockey pitch – and even half of that was given over to the old air-raid shelters left over from the . . .' Prudence paused. Here was that gravity again: her eyes were drawn back to the windows. 'Actually girls, perhaps a little trip is in order. Just a little potter to the edge of those excavations?' The girls' faces lit up; most of them were up and out of their seats in seconds. 'And then it's back to sauces and stocks,' Prudence announced, hurrying to keep in front of them as they headed for the doors. 'And no bones about it!'

Suki was about to join the stampede following her grandmother when the wild vibrations in her back pocket told her that someone was calling. Lingering in the background – and grateful that Prudence had bustled ahead, and that therefore she could avoid her withering eye – she scrambled the phone to her ear, clicked 'green' to accept the call and said, 'Numbers?'

'Darling,' Numbers purred back, 'have you got two

94

ticks? Or has Old Mother Hubbard got you sorting her curds and whey?'

Suki rolled her eyes. 'You're getting lamer and lamer. You don't even know your nursery rhymes.'

'I mash them together. I sample one and splice it with the rest. It's called culture, darling.'

Suki spun around. Through the windows, she could see Prudence and the girls all filing through the outbuildings, bound towards the excavations. 'This is dreadful timing, Numbers. My grandmother's out on a recce.'

'Well, I *can* call back, darling. I *can* go back to my day job – out of which I've just taken some not inconsiderable time, and all to do *you* a favour. Say the word, Suki, and I'll do it. I'll hang up and—'

'Oh, get on with it, Numbers! You've found something, haven't you?'

'Well, dear, I thought you'd NEVER ask. You see, I did have a spare hour yesterday evening, so I set about trawling through the old digitisations at the British Newspaper Archives. A tremendous project – but incomplete, of course. Some poor graduates are toiling like medieval monks to digitise every copy of every newspaper ever printed – so, just in case you fancied finding out what a housewife from Grimsby wrote to the editor in 1948, you'll be able to find it. Positively Sisyphean, of course – it's a job they'll never get finished – but apparently they've got far enough for OUR purposes. I'm sending you a jpeg now – see what you think.'

Suki waited patiently for her phone to buzz, staring out of the window all the while. Only when she heard the beep did she look down at the file Numbers had just zapped through. When she opened it up, the words *Penzance Gazette* leapt out at her. The date, written in tiny script beneath that, was April 1975 – and the headline, rendered in striking bold capital letters read:

A-SALT AND BATTER-Y!

'Numbers, I haven't got time. What is it?'

'Some reading material, darling. Time to get reading – I'm not your secretary.'

'*Numbers!*'

Down the line, all the way from Chelwood Ghyll, came the sound of Numbers's braying laugh.

'Did you know, darling, that Adam Scott only had four fingers on his left hand?'

'It was all over the news. THE MYSTERY OF THE FOUR-FINGERED MAN. Grandma knew it too – she spotted it straight away, on the morning they found the body. Numbers, that's how she identified him – that and the gold watch, hanging from his wrist.'

'Well, do you know *how* he lost that finger, Suki? Do you know *when* and *why*? Do you know that a perfectly pleasant local businessman spent fifteen months in the slammer for the loss of that digit? Did you know that Mr Barry Topps, once the Fish and Chip King of Cornwall, pleaded guilty to detaching that finger from Adam's hand?'

Suki had heard many grisly things in her time pottering around kitchens with her grandmother. Prudence was not a squeamish woman and had often described to her, in intimate detail, the various kitchen accidents she'd seen over the years – always with the express purpose of teaching Suki some lesson, of course, but never without some element of glee in the telling. Yet this image of an amputated finger made her wince, somehow. 'He *cut* it off?' she managed to say.

'Oh no,' returned Numbers, with his own faint air of glee. 'Nothing quite as sophisticated as that. Well, it's all there in the headline, darling.'

Suki read it again: '"A-Salt and Batter-y". Numbers, I don't understand.'

Numbers beamed. 'Barry Topps himself put it on record. Adam Scott went in for one of Topps's famous fish-and-chip pasties – he'd built his empire on those, Suki – but Topps had other ideas. It wasn't a piece of haddock he battered that day. It was Adam Scott's hand. According to those court reports, the old devil reached out, took hold of Adam's hand, heaved it over the counter, into his bucket of batter, and then straight into the deep fat fryer. Adam's hand suffered unimaginable burns, and the infection set in so badly in one finger that the doctors had to lop it off.' Numbers barked a shrill laugh. 'I mean they amputated it, dear Suki. So *fitting*! It's almost medieval. And all from this King of Fish and Chips . . .'

'But . . . but *why*?' Suki stuttered.

'Well, *that* isn't in the record, darling. Topps pled guilty, so the whys and wherefores don't seem to have mattered much. Off to prison he went, and there he stayed – for precisely a year and a day. But here's the stickler. Along comes the summer of 1976, and Barry Topps – who's spent twelve hard months cooking fish and chips for the inmates of HMP Exeter – is finally released back into the world. And who should vanish off the face of the planet, presumed to be a suicide, three weeks later?'

'Adam Scott,' breathed Suki.

'Precisely!' Numbers announced. 'And if that isn't worth a little ferreting around, I don't know what is.'

Beyond the outbuildings, around the earthworks where the foundation stones for the new 'state-of-the-art' gymnasium were yet to be laid, Prudence gathered her girls. The two day constables, who'd only recently relieved the ones who'd stood guard all night, watched curiously from their little lean-to – but did not seem unduly bothered when Prudence paced up and down the cordon, gazing out over the place where the body had been unearthed.

'What do you see?' she asked the girls.

Though the girls might have been thrilling at the thought of Mrs Bulstrode involving them in an investigation (it sure beat a velouté, whatever the hell that was), none of them seemed to have a satisfactory answer.

'Just a load of old dirt,' Hetty said.

'Just the old hockey pitches,' added Sophie.

'Yes,' said Prudence, 'I suppose that is what girls of your generation would see. But if you were of *my* vintage, you'd see something quite different: you'd see the place where the air-raid shelters used to stand.'

'Air-raid shelters?' grinned Sophie. 'Mrs Bulstrode, don't tell us you're *that* old!'

'Not quite, my dear. But when I was a girl, this field was still bordered by three clusters of shelters – not tinny old Anderson shelters, like you might have seen in your history books, but proper brick shelters, dug half into the earth, with corrugated iron for roofs. We were banned from going near them, of course – there hadn't been much upkeep of them, so one or two had already caved in, and there were others where the masonry was only held together by the brambles and vines left to grow here. But, well, have *you* ever done precisely as you're told?'

The girls shared furtive looks, evidently uncertain how much of their bad behaviour to let spill.

'Those old shelters often got used. The teachers turned a blind eye to it, I'm sure – but, if you wanted a smoke, or even a drink, these shelters were the perfect spot. I oughtn't to say it, but some of the more risqué among us might even bring the odd boy from St Cuthbert's here for some,' Prudence chose her words carefully, *'private entertainment.'*

Titters and groans morphed into one another all around. 'There isn't even a boys' school any more,' a girl named Adeline snorted. 'And no air-raid shelters to bring them. Mrs Bulstrode, it's a *desert*. An actual *desert.*'

'Well, I'm sure that's a terrible shame, dear.' Prudence paused. 'But at least we now know how the body was hidden, at any rate.' Then she turned on her heel. 'Come on, girls. The secrets of a good hollandaise won't learn themselves. I want to be tasting your beurre blanc by lunchtime.'

'Mrs Bulstrode!' Sophie cried out. 'You can't do that!'

'I'm with Sophie,' Hetty exclaimed. 'You can't throw us a crumb like that and then . . . and then not give us the cake! It's like taunting a toddler. You let them lick the spoon, but won't give them a muffin!'

Something in the idiocy of this image appealed to Prudence very much, so she turned around and said, 'Let's use our logic, girls. It seems to me that burying a body here, in an open hockey pitch, would be foolhardy in the extreme. I can *see* this hockey pitch from my dormitory window. So, I'd wager, can most of you. Imagine it's some balmy summer night, 1976: the night Adam Scott disappeared. Our killer can't possibly have been out here, digging him a grave. No, there are too many risks in that. Too many opportunities to be seen.' Prudence paused. 'But now imagine there are still air-raid shelters here. Imagine Adam Scott lies dead inside one of them. Well, in that case, you could bury the body unseen. Completely hidden from sight! Then, some years later, when the brick walls got torn down and the ground levelled off, it was like poor Mr Scott was being buried for a second time – this time under a much deeper landslide . . .'

The girls all murmured their appreciation at this. Prudence would have been lying if she had said those murmurs didn't bring her some satisfaction.

Then Hetty piped up, 'But isn't the real question how the body of a man who was actually *seen* getting on to a boat and sailing out to sea, who then threw himself overboard, ended up buried in an air-raid shelter?'

The girls murmured their appreciation at this too – and this only dampened Prudence's satisfaction in their first wave of voices. If they could find this riddle perplexing, perhaps their approval wasn't worth quite so much after all.

'Well, quite clearly it *didn't*,' Prudence ventured. 'That is to say, the body very clearly ended up buried here. But

I think we have to conclude that this business of the suicide note and the boat is all part of a very clever deception – one which fooled Adam's family, the police, and in fact the whole world, forty-eight years ago. No, the real question, the one the police ought to be asking, is: who propagated that deception? Who had the means to stage something quite as elaborate as all this?'

There, thought Prudence, that ought to satisfy them for the morning. She only hoped it wouldn't distract them from the hollandaise.

She was just about to lead them back to the domestic science block when a voice called out from further down the cordon: 'Maybe, Mrs Bulstrode, that's *exactly* what the police are doing.'

Prudence looked around, to be met by a face banked in striking waves of auburn hair. There, some ten metres along the edge of the hockey pitch, stood the same willowy detective she had last seen sitting alongside Elizabeth Duggan at a press conference on the television screen. The only thing that distracted from Detective Bryher Rose's beauty – the bounce of her hair, the startling green of her eyes, the lithe way she stepped forward, her suit of navy blue clinging tightly to her body as she came – was the vision of Ronnie Green standing at her shoulder. The school caretaker seemed to lurk fractionally behind her, with the air of a troll under a bridge.

'I'm sorry, Mrs Bulstrode,' he said as he followed Detective Rose to where the girls were gathering, 'I'll be up on that hillside by lunchtime. It's been a hell of a business, all this, but I'll make time to get your camper down. I swear it, ma'am, on my mother's grave.'

Prudence was not sure there was any need for quite such a sombre promise, but said nothing, for Detective Rose had already extended her hand. Prudence shook it swiftly, then whispered her greeting. 'You might have to forgive me, Detective. The girls have been very intrigued. All this business with the air-raid shelters, the burying of the body – well, it just occurred to me that it's one way of thinking. There may yet be others. I'm just a cook.'

It was the perfect line on which to shuffle away, but Detective Rose had other ideas. 'Not just any old cook, Mrs Bulstrode. That's rather why I'm here. My colleagues at the station said you were on site – and of course we'd like to take a statement about your time here, your memories of Mr Scott, any inkling you might have had that something was wrong, back in the day. Of course, fifty years is a long time. Memories get corrupted. Memories change. We think we're infallible in that regard, but we rarely are. But ... I *know* you, Mrs Bulstrode. Not just because I saw every episode of *Moreish Cornish Dishes* either – though that was a favourite in these parts. I very much admired your work on the murder at Farleigh Manor. I was most intrigued by your deductions in the matter of the body in the snowman, up at Scrafton Busk. And it occurred to me that a riddle like the one I've been presented with must be igniting your synapses too. That a clear, methodical mind like yours might have some insight I'm missing.' Detective Rose smiled. If she had seen the way the girls were goggling at her, eyes open wide, she seemed not to acknowledge it. She'd stoked yet more of their wonder, that was for sure; the curiosity the girls had already shown for this unexpected detour in Prudence's career was being ignited even further with every word she spoke. 'I wondered if you might join me for lunch, Mrs Bulstrode. I've already extended the invitation to your colleague, Ms Balloon. I believe she boarded here in Adam Scott's time as well. A little light repast, a glass of something fizzy, and some convivial chatter. What do you think?'

Prudence saw the way the girls were geeing her on with their eyes and said, 'I have obligations here, Detective. A banquet to prepare these girls for. Our clock is ticking.'

'I can have you back by mid-afternoon, Mrs Bulstrode. Give me but two hours of your time, while these girls are recharging their batteries. I should like to hear about St Marianne's in 1976 very much – and I should like to hear it from the horse's mouth.'

Prudence heard footsteps behind her. Over her shoulder, she saw Suki cantering out of the main school building, her iPhone clutched tightly in her hand.

'Isn't the station more ordinary?' she asked, at last.

At least Detective Rose seemed to agree with this. 'Well,' she said, rolling her eyes, 'the PR bods at the station have had an approach from a local restaurateur – and, somewhere far above my paygrade, it's been decided that a little community engagement might be beneficial to this case. The public pay for us, they say, so the public must *see* what we're up to. I'm afraid it's the modern world, Mrs Bulstrode. It isn't enough to catch a killer. Nowadays, we must be *seen* to catch a killer.'

Inwardly, Prudence seethed. Everything was a

performance for the younger generation. In her day, you had to be on television to deliver a performance; nowadays, all you needed was two legs.

'What do you say, Mrs Bulstrode? I can have a car ready to pick you up at twelve.'

Prudence cast a look at Ronnie Green, who only shrugged, 'The camper won't be ready, Mrs Bulstrode,' then proceeded to blather on about how sorry he was, how he'd have it down as soon as was humanly possible, how he wouldn't break a promise, not one as important as this, not to somebody as important as Mrs Bulstrode.

Suki had clattered to Prudence's side. 'Grandma,' she whispered, 'wait until you hear this . . .'

But Prudence's gaze was fixed upon Detective Rose.

'Two hours, Detective. I'm afraid these girls have got a lot to learn – and we've barely even begun.'

The Bluff.

Of course, it would have to be the Bluff.

The car had arrived at twelve on the dot, by which time the domestic science classroom was bubbling and smoking like a medieval apothecary, as Hetty, Sophie and all the other girls concocted hollandaise of varying thickness, Béarnaise with more lumps than a casserole, curdled beurre blanc (which, admittedly, might have been the sort of 'exciting new cookery' Benji Huntington-Lagan devised), and in one case a roux with more adhesive properties than Gorilla glue itself. Poor Suki had been left behind to bring some semblance of order to the classroom before the afternoon's endeavours (sweet sauces, custards and crèmes) began.

Prudence wondered if it wouldn't have been better to stay behind, scouring burned béarnaise from a pan, than step back into the Bluff again – but she stepped through the revolving door all the same, moving (as if through a portal) from a Cornish seaside cove to some sterile vision of a space-age diner.

The Bluff was always busy at lunchtime, but Prudence was quite certain it didn't ordinarily have a crew of local journalists loitering between the tables, one cameraman and his lighting assistant, and a provincial journo with a pencil tucked behind her ear. Their eyes were on Prudence immediately as she crossed the restaurant floor. Prudence didn't mind that – at this stage in her career, waving to the press and sharing a few nondescript words of welcome were as ordinary as walking – but, even so, she had the distinct impression that she was walking into a stage-managed event as she headed for the table in the window. Here, Detective Rose was already sitting with Poppy (who was waving effervescently), each of them with one of those pine-needle phials in front of them, like a very chaste apéritif.

'Ladies,' Prudence said, and was about to take the last remaining seat when a waiter waltzed in from nowhere, drew it out for her and beckoned her to sit.

The lights of the cameras flashed, capturing Prudence in the glamorous act of sitting down on a chair.

'We'll have to ignore them, I'm afraid,' said Detective Rose, calmly. 'A few flashing lights must be nothing to you, Mrs Bulstrode, and we've much we need to discuss . . .'

*   *   *

In the Bluff kitchens, Benji Huntington-Lagan had to tear himself away from the serving hatch and redirect his attentions to dressing the plates at his side. The sea-kale gel and salsify crisps he was delicately perching around the chorizo-seared scallops might have made the plates look like perfection, but his hand had started trembling comically. 'But what's *she* doing here, Sonny?' he seethed, whirling rock salt across the plates like a meteor storm. 'We set this up for the benefit of the Bluff, not for the benefit of Prudence *bloody* Bulstrode. Those cameras are on *her*, aren't they? What the devil's she been invited for?'

'I heard them jawing,' said Sonny, tending to his big pot of bisque. 'She was at school when that maths teacher was offed. I reckon they think she knows something. And . . .'

Benji shook his head wearily. 'She'll end up the star of the show. Feted cook, helping police with their enquir-ies. It'll be just like it was in bloody Uganda.'

'She helped the police in Uganda, Uncle?'

Benji gave him a withering look. 'No, but somehow she became the star of *that* show as well.'

'She's helped with a couple of murders before, Uncle. Maybe they think she's got a knack for this kind of thing.'

A salsify crisp shattered in Benji's hand. 'Time to stop talking, Sonny.'

'I'm just saying, Uncle—'

'Well, don't.'

The plates were ready, the scallops served up. Benji took them to the service counter, summoned his waiters, and watched as they whirled their way across the restaurant floor, depositing the plates on the table in front of Detective Rose and her two guests.

'I don't want her in any of the pictures, Sonny. Make sure they know it.' Snatching a paper and pencil from the counter, he scribbled a note, pressed it into Sonny's flailing hand, and sent him out on to the restaurant floor: an instruction to the official newspaper photographer to focus his attention on the detective, the scallops, the dramatic view out of the window, anywhere but Prudence *bloody* Bulstrode. 'This is our moment, Sonny. Being at the centre of something like this leaves an indelible mark in the memory. We've worked too hard to let an opportunity like this slip through our fingers. This is the Bluff's time to shine.'

Prudence had to admit that the plates were dressed beautifully. Her scallop was cooked to perfection as well, with just the right amount of colour – and the chorizo crumb added a hint of heat that brought all the other flavours on the plate to life. It was only a shame that it was so difficult to enjoy it amid the flashing of cameras, and the way the photographer kept reaching in to rearrange the table to better suit his picture.

'I'm just glad you could come,' said Detective Rose, once the pleasantries (and the first wave of photographs) were out of the way. 'As you can imagine, this case is creating more than a little unease back at the office. It's exactly the kind of attention the department doesn't need – not least because murders almost half-a-century old don't have the best chances of being solved. The world changes a lot in fifty years. Half the people who knew Adam Scott are already gone, and the other half only really have scant memories. It's not unlike those dedicated few who still think they might unmask Jack the Ripper – but end up relying on their imaginations to fill in the blanks. The passage of time is a devil. So anyone on hand who was there at the time, who might have any light to shed on what happened to Mr Scott, is most, most welcome.'

Prudence said, 'I should think there's a case file, buried somewhere in your archive?'

'A very slim one, Mrs Bulstrode. By good fortune, the detective in charge of the investigation back then is still with us. Brian Hall. He retired some decades ago, of course – but, if you can believe it, he's still rather active at the age of ninety-two. I went to see him yesterday evening. He has the most wonderful flower garden, up in St Ives. But of this case, he could recall very, very little – it stuck in his memory, of course, because the Penzance Scotts were such a notable family at the time. But the case of Adam's suicide was so open-and-shut that it didn't put a significant drain on Detective Hall's time. There was some paperwork to file, a few corroborating statements to take – and that was that.'

'Corroborating statements?' Prudence asked.

'Well, that's one of the vexing things about this whole case. There are two statements in the file from locals at the marina down in Penzance, who swore blind that they'd seen Adam Scott getting on that fishing boat the morning before it was reported missing. The boat's still in the fleet. The *Sally-Anne*, they call her. Patched up a number of times in the intervening years, and of course there's no forensic value in the boat, but she's still with us.' Detective Rose turned obliquely, gave a thoughtful, brooding look, for the cameras, and then returned her attention to Prudence and Poppy. 'Ladies, it seems to me that what I'm really missing is a true portrait of what Adam Scott was like, what pressures he was under during that summer of 1976, what his relationships were like at St Marianne's. Now, I understand you were but students – and consequently might not have been privy to some of the school's goings-on – but, at this point, any *texture* you can give me might be useful. I need to *feel* as if I'm back at St Marianne's. I need to *know* what Adam Scott was really like.'

It was Poppy who spoke up: 'I just think he was a lovely man. Just a *lovely* man. He was very popular at school, wasn't he, Prudence?'

Prudence opened her mouth to agree, but didn't get the chance to breathe a word, for soon Poppy had gone on: 'Almost too popular, I'd say. We *loved* him. There weren't many men to admire at St Marianne's, but Adam Scott fitted the bill. And do you know what? I can't even say *why*. There was nothing particularly special about Mr Scott. He just had a kind of easy-going charm about him. His office door was always open. He became a bit of a guru to us girls, I think.' Here, Poppy blushed slightly – and only by catching a glance from Prudence could she bring herself to go on. 'There was a time, and I don't mind telling you I'm embarrassed about it even now, when I needed some advice. You'd have thought there was someone more suitable to go to – and I did think about going to Miss Ellen, the English mistress, because *she* knew all about boys! – but for some reason I just went to Mr Scott. I'd been seeing one of the local boys, you see – one of the fishing boys from over in Littlerock. Well, we used to hang about with them when we could, didn't we Pru?'

Prudence gave a purse-lipped smile, but said nothing. It was true that she had, on occasion, shared a walk – and even a cigarette or two – with one of the fishing boys from Littlerock, but, as memory served, it was Poppy who was always most enthusiastic about this kind of thing.

'Oh, don't hide it all away, Pru! No prude Prudence, that's what we used to call you.' Poppy elbowed her, as if to gee her along, but still Prudence only silently smiled. 'Well, there was this boy. Michael McMinn, I think he was called. And the long and short of it was that I thought I was pregnant. I wasn't, of course, but that's what I thought – and it was Mr Scott I went to, not anybody else. That's the kind of confidence he inspired in us girls.'

Detective Rose had brought a notebook out and was hurriedly scribbling away. Prudence saw that the local journalist was scribbling too; she only hoped that the decades-old story of Poppy's promiscuity and indiscretion didn't make it into the pages of the *Tregurnow Times*.

'And what did Mr Scott do?'

'Well, he was mortified!' laughed Poppy. 'Mortified, as I should have known he'd be! He sent me to Miss Ellen himself, in the end. That's Dot Ellen – now, *there* was a woman who'd had a few dalliances of her own, and one or two accidental pregnancies along the way, I shouldn't wonder. She collected men like postage stamps. As a matter of fact,' Poppy turned to Prudence with a quizzical look, 'didn't we think she'd got her claws stuck into Mr Scott too? Whenever Mrs Scott turned up at school, she always looked so pained about it – it was like Mr and Mrs Scott didn't really fit. And there was Dot Ellen, known to like a fling or two, and sometimes you'd see them hanging out around school. Mr Scott liked his pipe, and Miss Ellen enjoyed a cigarette. You'd see them on classroom duty, just chatting to each other when they ought to have been looking over us girls.'

Detective Rose looked up. 'Do you know where we can find this Miss Ellen?'

'I'm afraid she's gone, Detective. Live fast, die young – that was Dot Ellen! If I'm right, she didn't quite make it to sixty. Mrs Carruthers would know better than me. She was still teaching at school, but she got unwell, and it was all done and dusted in such a short time. An ugly business all round, if I'm right.'

'Well, this is *all* a very ugly business,' the detective went on, 'because – and I can tell you this, ladies, because it will be in tomorrow's newspaper regardless – the forensics report on Adam Scott's remains suggests that he died by blunt trauma. To wit: somebody clubbed him over the back of his head.'

Poppy gasped, brought her hand to her mouth in horror – and there it stayed as the waiters waltzed in, took the scallop plates away, and deposited in their place a trio of lobster tails with seared asparagus, pickled sea vegetables and drizzles of rich lemony butter.

'I was right, then,' said Prudence. 'Mr Scott was killed in the air-raid shelter, and buried where he fell.'

'It's our working assumption, but it leaves gaping holes

111

in the narrative. I already said that we have witnesses that place Adam Scott out at sea. There's no record of the *Sally-Anne* returning to shore after Adam took it out that morning – so, at one and the same time, we have Adam Scott taking the *Sally-Anne* out to sea, and then being killed on the grounds of St Marianne's.'

'Are the witnesses reliable?' asked Prudence.

Detective Rose consulted her notes. 'Ray Cockfosters worked at the pier down in Littlerock. He knew Adam Scott reasonably well because of his connections with the family firm. And then ... Ricky Grigg,' she read. 'Ricky swore blind he'd bumped into Adam that same morning, eating a fried breakfast in the pier café. Now, memory is a hazy thing, but these statements were taken within a day of Adam vanishing. If it was a deception on the marina that morning, it was a very good one. And that's before we come to the sticky matter of this ...'

Detective Rose had reached into her file and produced a plastic sleeve, in which sat a yellowing, frayed piece of paper.

'I'm going to show this to you, ladies, on the proviso that its contents go no further. It's been lying in our evidence lock-up for nearly fifty years – and, of course, it was taken at face value back in the day because there was no reason to suspect otherwise. But it underwent expert analysis by one of the graphologists up at Scotland Yard yesterday afternoon, and they've confirmed to a degree of 97 per cent certainty that the handwriting here is genuine.'

'Genuine?' asked Poppy.

'Genuinely Adam Scott's. Ladies, this is the letter that Mr Scott left on the *Sally-Anne* that day he disappeared.

It's been compared to examples from the Scott archives, to his wedding certificate, to an old love letter his widow Elizabeth has kindly provided. We have to assume it's bona fide.'

Detective Rose cleared a space between the lobster tails, turned the paper around, and presented it to Prudence.

This is what it read:

My dear Elizabeth

It brings me the greatest sadness to write this letter, and please know that I dearly did not want to let you down. But some men are made for this world and some men are not, and it has taken me too long to truly realise that I am of the latter.

And so today I end the rot. I solve this Final Problem and shall not see you again. I know I have wasted your years, but also know that you are yet young enough to begin again, to find the true love of your life and to have the children you so desire. You are a wonderful woman, Elizabeth, and you will not live in an Empty House for very long. Do not feel too much grief or pity. You have always known I was not made for the world I was born to. It is time to accept it at last. So the sea shall have me.

Take care, live long, be happy,
Adam

Prudence lingered over the letter, even as Poppy drew away, wiping the sudden tear from her eye. Forty-eight years separated the reading and the writing of this letter, and yet the emotion still seemed to leach out of the page.

'It's all a bit . . . cryptic,' Poppy said at last, even as Prudence still pored over the letter. 'Like those crosswords he used to do. You'd come into class, and he'd have his head buried in some puzzle.'

'Well, we have some sense of what he's referring to,' said Detective Rose. 'Adam's sense of not being made for the world he was born to – well, according to Elizabeth, this was a direct reference to the expectations placed upon him by their families. You already know how the Penzance Scotts' and Franks' fisheries united?'

Prudence still stared at the page, even as she said, 'Adam and Elizabeth became a kind of arranged marriage, didn't they? Their fathers organised it, so that the businesses could merge. One day, Adam and Elizabeth would have a son – the heir of both lines, and the one true king . . .'

Poppy said, 'Oh, Pru, you always did have a way with words! Like . . . like Mr Scott, actually!' And she returned her attention to the letter again.

'It's curious, isn't it?' breathed Prudence.

'What is, Mrs Bulstrode?' asked Detective Rose.

'Mr Scott was a literate, articulate man, but these words . . . *Final Problem*,' she whispered. '*Empty House*.'

'What of them?'

'Capital letters,' said Pru, and looked up suddenly. 'A child scatters capital letters in the middle of everything she writes, because she doesn't know any better. But Mr Scott . . .'

'Cryptic!' Poppy exhaled. 'Just like those puzzles your Nicholas used to write, Pru!'

Prudence returned the letter to Detective Rose's hands, then watched as it was slipped back inside the file. A strange, faraway feeling had washed over her – the feeling that she was trying to see something just beyond the bounds of her vision, just out of reach. She came from the reverie only when a waiter hove into view, asked the table if everything was satisfactory with the lobster tails, and sallied on.

By that time, Detective Rose had begun to speak once more. 'Of course, I didn't just ask you here to get your take on life at St Marianne's, circa 1976. Ladies, my principal problem in investigating this case is that, though I can gather voices like yours, it's rather impossible for you – students as you were – to help me peel back the layers of what was happening at the school that summer. What I really need are the voices of Mr Scott's colleagues – and, of course, many of them have passed beyond us. But there are still some who remain . . .'

'Miss Jubber,' Poppy piped up, 'and Mrs Arkwright, over at the Cherry Garth.'

'Precisely,' went on Detective Rose. 'Now, we've been out to see them, of course – but to no satisfactory ends. I'm afraid age plays havoc with our minds as we grow old – and both Miss Jubber and Mrs Arkwright are suffering with varying degrees of vascular dementia. It's a very sad situation – but we were discussing best next steps at the office, and it is the suggestion of one of my colleagues that we might have more luck getting an insight from Miss Jubber and Mrs Arkwright if, rather than some unknown detective coming to interrogate them, it was the familiar face of an old student. An old student who was there at the time of Mr Scott's disappearance. An old student who went on to become quite a familiar face in this country . . . and who provoked no small amount of pride in her old favourite teacher.' Detective Rose smiled. 'Mrs Bulstrode, what do you think?'

Prudence felt Poppy grip her arm, as if in encouragement. 'I did say we should go and see Miss Jubber, Pru. This might be just the chance we need!'

Half of Pru's mind was still fixated on that old, yellowing letter now slipped back into Detective Rose's file – but the other half had rather come alive at the thought of seeing old Miss Jubber again. It was just a shame that the talk would not centre on butterscotch sauces, hotpots and stuffings, strawberry pavlova and raspberry roulade.

'It might be of great help with this investigation,' Detective Rose ventured, sensing some hesitance on Prudence's part.

And, at last, Prudence nodded. 'Anything I can do, Detective,' she said, and reached across the table to shake Detective Rose's extended hand.

Hovering by the kitchen serving hatch, Benji Huntington-Lagan froze. Out there, cameras were flashing, the photographer – seizing his moment – leaning in close for the perfect shot: Detective Bryher Rose clasping Prudence Bulstrode's hand across a landscape of lobster shell and seared asparagus tips.

Benji let go of the dishcloth in his hands, flinging it on to the counter with a wearisome sigh.

'Throwing in the towel, Uncle?' chortled Sonny, who was just preparing the plates for dessert: the Bluff's patented thousand-layer apple tart, served with shards of frozen Chantilly.

'They've asked her to help,' Benji said. 'Sending her on some mission. Do you know, Sonny, I'm dog tired of it all. You work hard all your life; you *innovate* and *imagine*. And do you get any thanks for it?'

'Not a jot,' said Sonny – who at least knew the right thing to say.

Benji returned to the plates Sonny was dressing, then began choreographing his perfect dessert. 'I'm the one with local knowledge,' he said, crouching to consider the plates at eye level. 'Our family's been entwined with the Scotts and Franks for a generation – but did they come to *me* for help? No, they're happy to eat my food, but wouldn't dream of asking for a single thought from my mind. And there's Prudence Bulstrode, doyenne of the raspberry roulade, treated like the greatest thinker of her age . . .'

Sonny crumpled his face up and said, 'We'll still be in the papers, Uncle. Your lobster tail was in every one of those pictures.'

'"Bulstrode at the Bluff with the Boys in Blue", that's what they'll say.' For the first time, Benji looked wan, defeated, a shadow of his ordinary, strutting self. 'Service!' he called, and watched as waiters materialised at the hatch, ready to whisk the apple tarts out to Prudence and her posse.

'It's a shame *you* can't solve the murder, Uncle,' said Sonny, as he proceeded to tidy up.

Benji Huntington-Lagan stood stock still. Out on the restaurant floor, the desserts had landed – and seemed to be being cooed over, at least by that teacher at Prudence's side – but all of that seemed suddenly distant to Benji. He turned around and looked his imbecilic nephew up and down. 'What did you say?'

'Well, if you solved the murder, Uncle, they'd have to put *your* picture in the papers. They'd be writing stories all about *you*, Uncle, and not about old Mrs Bulstrode out there. I reckon you'd be back on the telly if you did a thing like that. There'd be a podcast all about you. How a famous seafood gastronome filleted a very fishy murder, that kind of thing.' Sonny looked up from his counter with a sudden grin. 'I could be like your Dr Watson, Uncle. Helping you sniff things out, that kind of thing. You have to admit, it'd cause a bit of a stir. The eyes of the world, Uncle – isn't that what you said you want?'

Chapter Five

By the following afternoon, though the girls could not claim to have mastered any of the finer arts of the pastry section, the domestic science classroom was at least awash with impressive concoctions of cakes, cream and elaborate constructions of chocolate ganache. Prudence had awoken that morning and, on a whim, abandoned her plan for the first half of the day – core knife skills: deboning fish, butchering a chicken, finely chopping vegetables and herbs – and decided that *skill* was not what these girls were interested in. As with most things in the modern world, *style* came before substance, and perhaps the way truly to inspire them was to subscribe to one of Miss Jubber's old rules: 'We eat with all five of our senses,' she'd once told Prudence, 'but the most important sense of all is the magical sixth sense that few of us acknowledge: our sense of . . . FUN!'

She'd been thinking of Miss Jubber all night. She was thinking of her all day as well. She was thinking of her still as, at afternoon's end, she judged the girls' creations and found them, if not always technically impressive, then at least embodying a sense of fun and adventure that far surpassed anything else they had accomplished that week. If the end-of-course banquet was going to be a hotch-potch affair, at least it would all end on an indulgent sugary high.

After the last of the confections had been judged, and found to be 'dizzying in flavour Sophie – just dizzying!' (which was Prudence's kind way of saying it was nauseatingly sweet), the girls started drifting back to the common room and dormitories – but Prudence was intrigued to see Hetty and Sophie lingering behind. Soon, she had observed them gravitating towards Suki, cajoling her with invitations to 'hang out' and 'shoot the breeze', two idioms Prudence was surprised to find alive and well among Suki's generation, whose chatter was more often than not unintelligible to her. At first, Suki seemed to be resisting the calls but, as she scrubbed at a particularly sugary baking sheet one of the girls had left behind, Prudence sensed her grand-daughter's resistance melting. Certainly this spelt trouble – for Prudence hadn't quite forgotten the *interesting* scent of Suki on the morning after they'd first arrived – so she made a point of hurriedly sashaying over and intervening. Suki would find a trip to the Cherry Garth Retirement Home stultifying, of course, but not as boring as Prudence would find it tomorrow morning if Suki showed up to class having gargled some priceless cocktail of mouthwash and perfume again.

She was about to ask Suki to accompany her when Suki suddenly declared, 'Chips!' and the girls looked at her curiously. 'Chips,' she repeated. 'We should go and get some. There's a place in Littlerock, isn't there? The old Topps place?'

'Oh, *that* place,' said Hetty, rolling her eyes. 'It's like somebody saw a picture of Las Vegas and decided to try and build it on the Cornish coast. All gaudy neon lights and gambling machines.'

'But the fish and chips are good,' interjected Sophie.

'And I suppose they *did* invent the fish-and-chip pastie, with mushy-pea dipping sauce,' Hetty mumbled.

Prudence was almost on top of the girls now. As she drew near, Suki looked up and gave her a knowing look. Prudence inclined her head, as if to acknowledge some secret. And, of course, there was really no secret in that news story Numbers had dug up – for decades the barbaric assault of the fish-and-chip merchant upon a local school teacher had been a matter of public record. No harm could come from poking at the edges of the story a little, overturning a few stones and seeing what came out, so Prudence was inclined to let it happen.

And if it stopped Suki from stinking like a spillage in a vineyard tomorrow morning, so much the better.

'Well, that solves a little problem of my own,' said Prudence warmly, as she approached.

'Oh yes, Mrs Bulstrode?'

'Ronnie Green *still* hasn't brought my camper down from the hill,' she said, 'and I'm bound to go a little way up the coast myself.' Her eyes twinkled. 'Girls, I'm sure you wouldn't mind giving your old teacher a little lift again, would you?'

In the end, Sophie offered to take Prudence all the way to St Austin, where the Cherry Garth Retirement Home sat in a serene spot overlooking the seaside, just beyond the boundary of town – but some deep-seated sense of nostalgia was rising in Prudence, and the thought of travelling the coast road by bus again called out to her, somehow. That was why, a short drive later, Sophie was pulling her camper van to the kerb by the bus stop on the outskirts of Littlerock, then watching as Prudence lifted herself down into the gathering dusk. 'We'll pick you up on your way back through, Mrs Bulstrode,' Sophie called down from the driver's seat. 'Just give us a call when you're finished.'

Prudence locked eyes with Suki, and in that short, silent look, they shared a wealth of meaning.

'My grandmother doesn't have a phone,' Suki snorted, half embarrassed. As for Prudence, she rather enjoyed the mortified looks of the other girls; they would have looked less surprised to discover that Prudence was walking on wooden legs.

'I'll get by perfectly well, girls. I won't fall off the edge of any maps.'

'But ... but it looks like it might rain again, Mrs Bulstrode!'

Prudence looked back at the girls quizzically; she hadn't been aware that, on top of all the other miracles a mobile telephone could perform, it might also keep her dry in a storm. 'I shall see you girls back at school,' she declared, 'bright and early – for doughs and pastas.'

Prudence didn't have to wait long. The girls and their camper van had wended off into Littlerock only two minutes earlier when the coastline bus arrived and welcomed her aboard. The driver seemed to recognise her, though without being able to put a name to her face. He waved her aboard with some element of perplexity, Prudence settled in a seat up top, and then they were off.

It was the perfect spot from which to watch the coast sliding by, the buttery sunshine of midsummer paling as evening approached, the sea beyond the windows turning a warm shade of pink. She'd quite forgotten how beautiful it could be in this part of the world, how mellow you felt when you watched a serene seascape like this. It might have been nice to sit on the upper deck of that bus all evening, just letting it carry her wherever it might go.

But then the call came for St Austin, and soon Prudence was pottering down a country lane on the edges of town, following a single-lane track through carefully sculpted rhododendron bushes, until she reached a wide, sweeping driveway and the miniature redbrick palace that was the Cherry Garth Retirement Home.

It was difficult to step inside. Prudence's mother had spent her last years in a place not unlike this, and the scent as she stepped through the doors – of freshly cut flowers, antiseptic, and something close to sun lotion – was familiar enough to fill her with a sudden breath of sadness. She had to remind herself that she was here to see the one woman who, her mother aside, had most influenced the story of her life. There was a strange nervousness that came with the prospect of seeing Agatha Jubber again, the student's eagerness to please a former teacher, tinged at the same time with the feeling that they ought to have outgrown such desperation by now. But Prudence's heart had started beating just a touch faster, her thoughts were stampeding just a little too strongly – and, by the time she approached the reception desk and rang the bell, she was having to quietly tell herself to *calm down*.

'Mrs Bulstrode,' said the bosomy blonde lady who emerged from an office behind the desk. Evidently, Prudence had been expected. The name on the woman's badge read DAISY LANE, and she had quickly produced a copy of Prudence's magnum opus, *A History of English Desserts*, expecting it to be signed. 'I have to say, I was so taken aback when the police department said you might be visiting us that I swapped shifts, just so that I could be here. You've been a big presence in my family, Mrs Bulstrode. The face of our Saturday-night TV! I hope you don't mind?'

Daisy had offered Prudence the book, along with a flashy fountain pen to sign it. 'Not at all,' Pru replied, and started signing the title page. 'I'm always delighted to know the books are still being used.'

'This old book would be getting much more use if it was up to me, Mrs Bulstrode. I've been trying to get management here to experiment a bit. You know, get the old girls trying something a bit more adventurous than stewed apples and cinnamon.' She took the book back, looking enormously pleased with the signature Prudence had provided. 'One day, some months back now, I convinced the kitchens to try your pineapple compote and brown butter biscuits.'

'And how did it go?'

Daisy froze. 'Well, I'm afraid – well, it's just that – well, the old dears *do* get set in their ways. We had to stew extra apples that day and rush them out, with brown sugar and black treacle. Some of the girls still talk about it like it was the End of Days! And them with dementia too!' Daisy shuffled the book out of sight, caught her

124

composure, and dared to look Prudence straight in the eye. 'It was Miss Jubber you're here for?'

'And Mrs Arkwright,' Prudence said smiling, deciding that to completely ignore the drama over her brown butter biscuits was the best policy she could possibly take.'

'Oh, Mrs Arkwright's got a visitor already,' Daisy said, eyes flashing to the computer on the desk, 'but Miss Jubber's just up in her room. She's been out playing rummy with Mrs Gadfly and Mrs Inglis, so she might be a little weary. I'll hazard she's actually nodded off in her chair again! But I'm sure she'll be wide awake once you come, Mrs Bulstrode. Would you like to come this way?'

The smell was more powerful the deeper Prudence went into Cherry Garth Retirement Home. Some of the residents were still sitting up in one of the common rooms, shrunken creatures sitting in sofas that seemed to devour them, watching an old Technicolor movie on an enormous television screen. 'We had a tea dance this afternoon,' Daisy went on, taking Prudence across the common room (with its smell like bonbons and carbolic), along another corridor – where doors were left ajar, revealing the sleeping residents within – and through a smaller sitting room, where two elderly men were playing on a video games console. 'It helps with the reactions. Keeps the mind young. It may sound funny, but time moves on – it isn't just dominoes and cards any more, though there's plenty of that as well. We've got the Ludo championship next Monday, and the following weekend it's the Over 80s Draughts League. Cherry Garth's up against Greenhill Crescent in the quarter-finals. Come on Cherry Garth!' Daisy had cheered just a little too enthusiastically, and moments later looked suitably embarrassed. Thank goodness then that, having followed a corridor round the back of the sweeping common room, they appeared to have reached their destination. 'It's just down here, Mrs Bulstrode.'

Prudence followed Daisy past another open door. Inside, a portly, elderly man was sitting at the bedside of a long, withered woman, a small television set buzzing by their side. It wasn't until Prudence saw the name on the door – MRS GERTIE ARKWRIGHT – that her memories lined up. How strange it was to see her old headmistress so diminished, to truly, starkly see the passage of time. It made you feel vulnerable, somehow – because, of course, you suddenly knew you were walking the very same road, still some miles behind but catching up with every breath.

Mrs Arkwright's voice flurried up, then faded away: 'I don't like this one. No, not one bit. I've seen it a hundred times. It wasn't funny the first time, and it's not funny now.' That voice, which had once made Prudence and her friends shudder, now seemed so frail and faraway: the monster of her schooldays, thoroughly unfanged. There was some sadness in this too. Prudence was glad to be hurrying on her way.

Some doors further along, Daisy had stopped at the end of the hall. 'She's just through here, Mrs Bulstrode,' she said, and knocked gently on the closed door. 'Miss Jubber?' she called out. 'Agatha? I'm just coming in, dear. I've got a very special visitor for you.'

The door opened up – and there, wrapped in a shawl,

a pile of knitting in her lap, sat a shrunken version of the woman who had kickstarted Prudence's career, the woman who had inculcated her love of food, who had kindled her passion, buoyed up her talent, showed her that anything was possible if you just indulged a bit of your passion.

Miss Jubber looked up as Prudence stepped through the doors.

There was a moment in which Prudence might have been any old stranger, looming there in the doors. Then some unnerving sense of recognition came over Miss Jubber. It took a long time to place Prudence's face, because some part of her was unable to believe that the woman she'd watched so often on her television screen was standing in front of her. It was only some moments later, when her mind at last filled in the blanks of her confusion, that she dared to say, 'Pru?' Then she lifted her spectacles from the bridge of her nose, polished them on her sleeve, and peered again. 'Little Pru Cartwright? Can it *be*?'

'It's been a long time since anyone called me Cartwright,' Prudence said softly, and took another step into the room. 'But it's me, Miss Jubber. I've been in the area a few days. I hope you don't mind me looking you up.'

'Oh Pru!' Miss Jubber exclaimed – and it seemed, somehow, that she'd shed several decades in an instant, that her mind and body had suddenly woken up. Already, she was setting her knitting down on the bedside; already, she was heaving herself from the chair and, using the frame at her side, hobbling across the small chamber to meet Prudence. 'Look at you, my dear!' she said, with the fresh tremble of emotion in her voice. 'Pru Cartwright! Well, I never. Prudence *Bulstrode*, right here.' She clasped Pru's hand. 'Oh Lord, it's really you. I haven't forgotten, you know. They'll tell you that I have, but I haven't forgotten my favourite pupil.'

In the corner of her eye, Prudence saw Daisy taking a step backwards. 'Well, I can see you've no need of me here,' she said. 'Miss Jubber, you'll be the envy of the common room tomorrow.' Then she dropped her voice a little, whispered a few words meant for Prudence alone. 'Try not to get the old girl *too* excited, Mrs Bulstrode. She'll be worn out tomorrow as it is. Miss Jubber's often asleep by eight. She likes listening to a few old records, that sort of thing. Some Goons on the tape deck over there. Give me the nod when you're ready to leave, Mrs Bulstrode, and we'll take care of the rest.'

After Daisy had gone, Miss Jubber – still clasping Prudence's hand – said, 'She thinks my hearing's worse than it is. That's the worst thing about being old, Pru. Your body starts packing up, and sometimes your mind too, but everyone thinks you go from fit-as-a-fiddle to decrepit in an instant. Well, there's a lot more to me than they know!' She paused. 'Well, come on! Sit down, dear. Let's have a little catch up. It just fills my heart to think you might come and visit your old teacher . . .'

Miss Jubber had put up a valiant defence of her faculties, but the truth was this brief moment of excitement had already left her quite exhausted. Pru helped her back into her seat, then took up her own position on the foot of the bed. 'I could pour the tea, Miss Jubber?' she said, noticing the Teasmade on the dresser.

'I'd like that. And . . . I think I should like it if you called me Agatha, after all this time.'

Prudence said, 'I'm not sure that would ever feel right, Miss . . . *Agatha.*'

The two women both creased their brows.

'No, it doesn't sound right!' they said in unison – and, after that, it was decided that 'Miss Jubber' she would remain.

There was much catching up to do, and all of a sudden Prudence didn't know where to start. 'I can hardly remember the last time we were in touch, Miss Jubber. I know I wrote to you a few times, after I started out. I know I sent you tickets for the demo I was doing, at the Expo in Plymouth that year.'

'Oh yes!' Miss Jubber enthused. 'I came as well. I watched you make that raspberry roulade and thought . . . that's *my* recipe, that is!'

'A variation on a theme,' grinned Prudence. 'I hoped you wouldn't mind.'

'Mind?' grinned Miss Jubber, showing her mouth full of missing teeth. 'Pru, I dined out on that story for *years.* Every time the ladies from the WI got together, I made sure each and every one of them knew: that's *my* recipe Prudence Bulstrode's mixing up on the BBC.' Miss Jubber paused. 'I haven't seen as much of you on the old goggle-box of late, Pru. Those television types locked you out, have they?'

'Oh, I rather locked myself out,' grinned Prudence. 'I had a good few years – half a lifetime, in fact – of cookery shows. I went all over the world, Miss Jubber, making programmes, finding new flavours, digging up new recipes and sharing them far and wide. But, after a time, I started to think . . .'

Miss Jubber pitched forward with a gummy smile, 'There were no new worlds to conquer.'

'I wouldn't have stated it quite as grandly as all that,' Prudence returned, with a smile of her own, 'but you cut to the heart of it. It was time for a change. And the change I wanted was: somewhere quiet, with my husband and my grandchildren, and my little kitchen garden. Well, of course, that plan got upended as well. I'm afraid I was widowed soon after we retired to the country. Nicholas was buried in the little church up the road, and I was at rather a loose end.' Prudence shrugged. 'In a roundabout way, Miss Jubber, that's why I've ended up back in Cornwall this summer. St Marianne's invited me back to teach a few lessons. Well, I didn't need to think twice about it. I'm in the old domestic science block, Miss Jubber. Oh, it's changed so much since we were there! But I'm standing where you used to stand, and I'm teaching girls about stocks and sauces and . . .' Prudence shrugged again. 'I don't suppose an ounce of what I'm saying is going into their heads, but it got me thinking, again, how much you did for me back then. It's filled me with . . . not just nostalgia. A kind of love, I suppose. So I had to come and see you, Miss Jubber. When I found out you were still with us, I wanted to come and say: thank you.'

Prudence hadn't meant for her voice to be brimming with such emotion – in truth, she hadn't really meant to be so heartfelt at all – but now that she saw her old teacher, all of the feelings were coursing out of her. There had been so much she'd wanted to say to Nicholas that she'd never got the chance to say, but here was a gift: Miss Jubber, perhaps the only surviving guiding light in her world, and she could say everything she'd ever wanted to.

'Prudence, dear, you've nothing to thank me for.' Miss Jubber took her hand. 'It's a terrible thing to lose someone you love, Pru. Not even a gilded life protects you from that heartache. I should know.'

Prudence looked down. The wrinkled, papery hand that had taken her own was wearing a simple golden wedding band – and it occurred to her, suddenly, that she'd been using the wrong title all evening long. 'Miss Jubber, did you get married?'

'Oh, don't be silly, Pru. You know me. That lark was never for me, not after the first time. No, this is my mother's old wedding ring. I took to wearing it some time ago. I don't know, but it helps me feel close to her somehow. You've got to feel close to the people you loved. That's how you keep them alive.' She stopped. Then, with something approaching devilry, she said, 'I heard the new headteacher's a bit of a fruit.'

'A fruit, Miss Jubber?'

'A lightweight, in the intellectual department . . .'

Prudence had taken a mouthful of the tea she'd prepared, but now she half-choked it down. 'That's not for me to say!'

'Oh, come on, you can tell *me*,' whispered Miss Jubber. 'Old Arky's here, you know. Mrs Arkwright, from back in the day. She can't string a sentence together now, of course, but I reckon she's got as much malice in her as ever. I stay out of her way, whenever I can . . .'

Prudence hadn't appreciated there might have been any animosity between her old teachers. In a roundabout way, that brought her thoughts back to Mr Scott, the body in the hockey pitch, the true purpose of her visit. She was about to dare and broach the topic when, suddenly, Miss Jubber's eyes lit up. 'All this talk of that classroom, it's got me thinking. I should quite like to do a spot of cookery with you again, Pru. It's been an age since these old hands got dirty.' She lifted her aged hands and wriggled her fingers. 'I don't get to chop or knead, or even whisk an egg around a pan any more. A piece of toast's about the limit of what they'll let me do. But . . . you'd be a dear, wouldn't you? Help me up and along that hallway? They have the kitchens down at the end. We could rustle something up together, couldn't we, Pru? Mrs Bulstrode . . .' she said the words with a particular emphasis, as if trying them on for size, 'I should be delighted to cook with you. There'd be a nice poetry to it. It would bring things full circle, wouldn't you say?'

A warm feeling had rushed through Prudence. 'It certainly could,' she said – and was on her feet in a moment, ready to help Miss Jubber up.

It took a little while to wend their way down the corridor. As they passed, the portly man was still sitting with Mrs Arkwright, and Miss Jubber snorted merrily as they crept past. 'She doesn't get many guests, doesn't old Arky. But you can't begrudge her it when one comes. It's awfully lonely when you've got nobody.'

That only pulled on Pru's heartstrings more, and for the first time she felt a surge of guilt that she hadn't kept up a correspondence with Miss Jubber. All of those strained feelings melted away the moment they crept into the kitchens, however. This place was not nearly as stately or grandiose as the domestic science block at St Marianne's, and consequently it suited a couple of old cooks like Prudence and Agatha perfectly. The wooden spoons were ingrained with a decade of dishes, the most fanciful thing about the fridges were the lights that flashed on when the doors opened up, and instead of automatic KitchenAids there were but mixing bowls and whisks.

'What do you fancy, Pru?'

Miss Jubber even seemed to move more fluidly, now that she was back in a kitchen. Once or twice, Prudence looked over her shoulder, half-expecting Daisy Lane or some other member of staff to appear in the door and remonstrate with them fiercely – but, when nobody appeared, Pru simply said, 'A little bowl of pasta, perhaps? A simple sauce, like you showed us how to make that spring term?'

Miss Jubber beamed. 'Tagliatelle was such an indulgence in 1974. Only the most refined diners ate anything as delectable as tagliatelle.' She stooped to one of the cupboards and brought out a pan, a strainer, two serving dishes. Next, she started directing Prudence to search through the cupboards for tinned tomatoes, jars of peppers in oil, a bundle of fresh shallots. 'Of course, fashions change,' said Miss Jubber. 'Once upon a time, you ate a chicken Kiev as a status symbol! Now you just pop into the newsagent and look in his freezer.' She paused. 'It makes you feel old. I used to like the old days. I don't suppose you'll be teaching your girls about tripe, will you? Nobody uses the whole animal any more. The world loves waste.'

Prudence tried to picture tutoring the girls in the correct way to brown a calf's liver, or explaining to them exactly what a sweetbread was. Already, she could sense the outrage, Suki's face contorted in a horrified mask.

'You've heard, I suppose, about what's happening up at St Marianne's? You've heard about Mr Scott?'

Miss Jubber paused, the kettle she'd found poised just under the tap. 'It's so sad to talk about offal and Adam in the same sentence,' she said, wanly. Then she turned on the tap and watched as the kettle filled. Too late, Prudence realised she was only stalling for time, trying to feel stronger. Her voice cracked as she said, 'It's just so frightful, that he was there all this time. All of us, going about our daily business, teaching our lessons, and Adam was so *near*. I must have looked out on that hockey pitch hundreds of times. I didn't know I was looking at a grave.' The kettle was filled. She set it to boil. 'The police popped round. Did you know that? They wanted to chat about Adam, but it's just so long ago. I can hardly remember. I can't hear his voice, you know? I know he was a lovely man, an *unexpected* man – him, who should have been out reaping his family's riches, and all he wanted to do was teach arithmetic at our school! – but everything's so fuzzy.'

'Miss Jubber,' said Prudence with sympathy, 'it's been nearly fifty years.'

Miss Jubber started ferreting through another cupboard, pulling out salt, stock cubes, mixed herbs. 'Not a lot's happened in my life, Pru. Now, don't get me wrong, I've enjoyed the time I've had – but it's been rather quiet, and that's suited me fine. St Marianne's was the happiest time of my life, and now . . .' She shrugged. 'It's not nice when things aren't what they seem, is it? It feels dirty somehow. Just a bit uglier than I'd thought. I told the police – they ought to go poking in that family of his. I always thought that the Scott family was why he was in teaching. He didn't fit with them – he *certainly* didn't fit with that beast of a wife he had – and you just knew he got along with *us* more than he got along with them. I always thought that's why Adam came into teaching: a bit of him just longed for the comfort of being somewhere lovely and safe, and he found that in us. But on the *outside* world . . . those fishing families and all their *drama*! You'd think they were medieval courts, the way they carried on. And then, when Adam and Elizabeth couldn't have a baby . . .'

'They were trying?' Prudence asked.

'Well, I didn't pry, of course, but of course that was the point of the marriage. A son, to unite the houses. Like I say, positively medieval! But a baby didn't come, and Adam spent almost all of his time at school – and you got to thinking, well, it was all a sham really. You take your little happinesses wherever you can when your life doesn't feel right. He loved his students – your friend Poppy, I remember, really relied on Mr Scott! He made good friends with everyone in the staffroom too. I'm fairly certain he even got along well with old Arky out there, and, in my eyes, that made him a saint.'

The kettle had boiled. Miss Jubber directed Pru towards it and said, 'A healthy sprinkle of salt and a glug of oil as well – that will get us going. Then we can think about a sauce. Nothing fancy – a watered down ratatouille, I suppose. More tomatoes, less chunky veg. Well, come on Pru, let's see your knife skills. They must have come on, after all these years . . .'

A test from Miss Jubber? The thought delighted Pru. 'There are more skilled chefs, Miss Jubber, but I fancy I can—'

A noise silenced Pru.

The opening of the kitchen door.

A single, abrupt cough from the figure who had just appeared.

With all the synchronised timing of a vaudeville double act, Prudence and Miss Jubber turned over their shoulders. There stood Daisy Lane, a mortified look on her face, her head shaking from left to right in teacherly disappointment.

'Mrs Bulstrode,' she declared, 'I thought *much* more highly of you. And Miss Jubber – you *know* the kitchens are out of bounds to residents. One of you has led the other astray, and I can scarcely tell which!'

The pink neon lights read TOPPS FISH MEGA PALACE in garish letters two metres high.

From the newspaper reports, Suki had imagined this place to be a small fish-and-chip shop on a busy seafront boulevard, the kind of little takeaway joint they had in

136

Chelwood Ghyll – just somebody's converted front room, or a repurposed shopfront, just about big enough for a few deep fat fryers, a menu board and a queue snaking out of the door.

It wasn't until Sophie pulled the camper van up on to the kerb that Suki realised the girls hadn't been joking. Topps Fish Mega Palace was the screaming, garish anomaly on the otherwise refined seafront. As broad as all five of its neighbouring buildings, it was nothing less than a palace: three storeys of slot machines, flashing lights and restaurant floor. 'They have a disco in the back,' Hetty said as the girls left the camper van behind and approached the extravagant exterior. Music that Suki had never heard before (did any song *really* contain the refrain 'Hi ho – silver lining!'?) was blasting out on speakers as powerful as any in a London nightclub. A bouncer on the door gave the place the air of some exclusive (if somewhat tacky) nightspot – but, as they approached, they realised his real purpose was to hand out flyers offering a free curry sauce with every meal.

The smell of fish, peas and batter was thick and cloying in the air – but not unpleasant, Suki reflected, as they came through the doors, certainly not as unpleasant as the sticky floors and the subterranean look of the busboy currently mopping round the slot machines, where someone had got a little too energised with his squirty tomato ketchup. All around them, great obelisks in the shape of pickled eggs, battered sausage and one particularly luminous six-foot gherkin stood on dramatic plinths. A muscular copy of Michaelangelo's *David* stood brandishing a bright-pink saveloy dripping in curry sauce.

137

Suki wasn't sure what she had stepped into: a fish-and-chip restaurant, or an alternate planet.

'She's got that look, Hetty,' said Sophie as they led her through.

'What look?' Suki asked.

'*That* look. Like you've smoked something dodgy,' grinned Hetty, 'or chowed down on some magic mushrooms.'

'Of course, it never seems *perfectly* normal in here,' Sophie went on. 'You kind of get used to the bright lights, but ... it's kind of the appeal, isn't it? Like having fish and chips on a distant planet.'

Suki wondered how anyone could eat a simple saveloy and chips in a place of such deafening music and bright, flashing lights – certainly, this place ought to come with a warning to epileptics – but her eyes did not deceive her: on the other side of the dance floor, where glittering disco balls revolved and a lone dancer was pulling some rather improbable moves on her roller skates, the restaurant floor was teeming. Local families out for the evening, day-trippers filling their bellies before heading home, even one or two prim-looking businessmen seemed to have stopped in for their dinner. A waiter, in a silvery suit that shimmered in perfect imitation of a fish's scales, marched past, his outstretched arms laden down with cod and haddock, battered burgers, beanies and potato patties.

The queue at the counter was long, but advanced quickly – for the man tending the fryers seemed born to the task, constantly tending the great vats of beef dripping while issuing commands at his minions further down the counter. Suki hadn't been intending to eat here, but as she waited the smells of fat, fish and vinegary batter filled her up so intensely that there was nothing else she could do. More and more bewitched as the queue advanced, she decided on the 'Topps Fish-and-Chip Supper #6, inc. Battered Tartare Scraps' from the board above.

They had almost reached the head of the queue when Hetty let out a sudden groan. Looking up, Suki saw her burying her head. From a table at the other side of the disco floor, a young man was furiously waving at them while polishing off his 'Hake & Hash Brown Combo #3', and glugging back the rest of his curry sauce as if it was a fine after-dinner wine.

'Sonny,' Sophie laughed, poking Hetty in the ribs. 'You know, he's down here an awful lot for someone who works in fine dining.'

'Fine dining?' asked Suki. In the corner of her eye, she saw that the young man named Sonny was waving even more furiously still.

'He's sous-chef up at the Bluff,' Sophie went on, 'but, more to the point, Cupid's arrow hit him square between the eyes the first time he saw Hetty here.'

'Oh, give over!' Hetty protested. 'He gives me the *ick*.'

The ick: that undefinable notion that, if a boy got close to you, you might throw up. Yes, Suki'd had that feeling more than once before as well. Even her grandmother understood that feeling – it was one of those things that transcended the generations.

'He keeps asking Hetty out.'

'But I'm not like my grandmother was. I don't like rolling with the local boys.'

139

'You watch him – he'll be over here by the time we're finished, to ask you on a stroll. He thinks he's in with a chance, and all because his uncle runs that restaurant. He reckons he's gonna be a *star*.'

Hetty was still asking Sophie to 'shut the hell up!' when, suddenly, they had reached the end of the queue. Across the deep fat fryers, a hulking man with the faint air of a pirate about him – certainly in the great gold hoop he wore in his ear, and the gnarled, seaman's look about his face – bent forward and asked, 'What'll it be?' The name badge he was wearing read OGGY TOPPS in pink letters every bit as garish as the neon lights outside.

Suki's mouth had suddenly gone dry. She knew she ought to be asking about the man named Barry Topps and the incident for which he'd become notorious, that ludicrous headline – A-SALT AND BATTER-Y! – but she hadn't anticipated being met by someone with the same name. By the look of him, she took him for the ex-convict's son, or perhaps his nephew, for he was certainly at least fifty years old. He looked as if he'd spent every one of those years gorging on the family delicacies as well. Even now, his moustache seemed to be rimed in mushy pea.

'Spoilt for choice, aren't you, girl?' he cackled, cheerfully. 'This your first time at Topps, is it? Expecting to order a cod and chips and be done with it, were you? Well, *not here*. Folks said it couldn't be done – fish and chips was a classic and couldn't be bettered. Well, look around you, girl. We're the one place in England that'll batter mushy peas for you – little bombs of green, sludgy perfection, with a crispy crust. That recipe's patented, by the way. Don't go believing all those sods who'll

140

serve up a pea fritter like they thought of it themselves. *We're* the first to put curry sauce *inside* a battered sausage. Scampi chips with whitebait batter. Double-battered chips with a curry sauce spicing.' He bowed his head even lower, as if in conspiracy. 'But you want to know what I'd recommend a girl like you?' This man seemed to think he could divine a customer's fish-and-chip preferences simply by the cut of their gib. 'For you, girlie, I'll slather a burger in peas, pop another on top and batter it. How's that sound?'

'That's not the only thing you batter in here, is it?'

Suki had blurted the words out, semi-accusingly, before she'd given them much thought – but Oggy Topps seemed not to hear the accusation in them. Rather than thinking of a newspaper headline from half a century ago, suddenly he was reeling off a list of their other extravagant creations. 'Pineapple rings, of course, but we're the first to deep fry banana. Try that, girl – it's positively exotic. Serve it with some vanilla ice cream – which, by the way, I can batter up too, so that the inside's still frozen solid. Have a sweet tooth, do you? Fancy something of that?'

'I was meaning . . . Adam Scott,' said Suki, finding her courage at last.

Oggy Topps's piratical face darkened a shade further. 'Oh, you're one of *those*, are you?'

Suki just stared. Behind her, Hetty was still busily trying to keep out of the line of sight of her admirer across the restaurant.

'Every now and again, one of you lot comes out of the woodwork,' said Oggy Topps, angrily turning some fish in the deep fat vat. 'Activist scum, the lot of you. One little mistake, fifty years ago – and paid for a hundred times over, by the way – is all you obsess over. Leave alone the fact that my father single-handedly reinvented fish and chips. Leave aside the breadth and depth of all his creations. That man's a bloody *pioneer*, but you don't come around asking about that, do you? No, your lot stumble across that cunning old fox, and it's all you want to talk about.' Oggy drew two fish angrily from the fryer and proceeded to slather two more in his signature batter. 'We damn near lost all this because of Adam Scott. We had to fight to keep this place alive, all because of him.'

Suki had been blindsided by the man's sudden anger, but now she found some outrage of her own. 'I think Barry Topps might have had *something* to do with it. He *is* the one who battered and deep-fried Adam's hand, isn't he? It even cost him his finger!'

'Yes, well, if Adam Scott had been able to satisfy himself with just one woman, none of that would have happened. That fox got what was coming to him – there mightn't be a court in the land who'd agree, but there's plenty of folks who would.'

Suki could feel the press of bodies behind her now, the queue growing impatient as they slavered over the save-loy on the rack. 'One woman?' she asked, intrigued now.

'Well, that's my father's story to tell. My father was spotless before Adam Scott came along. He didn't do no wrong to anyone. Rising star of the coast. King of Fish and Chips. My mam had died when I was only a bairn, and he'd been raising me alone – and then along comes . . .'

142

Oggy Topps had let his fury carry him away again. 'As I say, that's not my story to tell. That's my dad's.'

Suki blurted out: 'Can we talk to him?'

'Talk to him?' Oggy exclaimed, reeling back. 'By Neptune, he's an old man now. I don't see why he should talk to you at all.'

'You do know what's happening over at St Marianne's? You do *know* Mr Scott's body was found?'

'What's that to do with us? We haven't thought about Scott for fifty years, except when gawkers like you come poking around. My dad's not the man he once was. He's near ninety years old, for God's sake. He's not long for this world. Just look at him. Look at him yourself.'

Oggy gestured across the disco floor, to the edge of the restaurant itself. At the table alongside Sonny – who still seemed to be flashing eyes in Hetty's direction – an old man sat in the confines of his wheelchair, some medical apparatus seemingly propped at his side. He was a strange shape, rangy on top but sporting a portly belly, and his white hair and whiskers clearly hadn't been tended in an age. Upon seeing him, Suki felt a sudden rush of sadness: so this was the ultimate fate of Cornwall's King of Fish and Chips.

'All he can eat nowadays is mushy peas and milk,' said Oggy. 'Now, there's not a finer diet to keep a man alive in his old age. All that Mediterranean diet is for the birds – there's more sustenance in peas and milk. There's tribesmen in Africa who thrive on it.'

'I think that's blood,' Sophie interjected.

'What?'

'Blood and milk. The Maasai. We did it in geography.'

'Nonsense, girl. There's nobody going around drinking blood when they could just as easily have mushy peas.'

'Can't we just go and have a chat?' Suki asked.

She was almost tempted to take off in that direction, but the look of fire on Oggy's face stopped her dead. 'You want to talk to him, you'll have to make it worth his while. And what have you possibly got that a man like my father could need? What could you possibly provide? Look at what he's built.' Oggy opened his arms, flicking scraps in every direction, as if to take in the entirety of Topps Fish Mega Palace. 'A man like this, the culinary star of his age? What could you possibly have to offer?'

Suki looked from Hetty to Sophie, and then from Sophie to Hetty again.

'I have my . . . grandmother?' she shrugged.

A few quizzical moments later – once Oggy Topps had been supplied with the details of who exactly Suki's grandmother was – the girls watched as Oggy tramped across the restaurant, picking his way between Michaelangelo's *David* (with saveloy) and the giant pickled egg, until he had reached his father's side. The two were lost in conversation for some moments, the elderly Barry Topps casting the girls a few harried looks along the way, before Oggy tramped back across the restaurant, a ruminative look on his face.

'That bloody Sonny's listened to everything,' said Hetty. 'Look, he's coming this way now.'

It was true: Sonny, too, had leapt up from his table, the moment Oggy Topps left. Yet, just as he got near to the girls, he turned on his heel and scurried off towards

144

the restaurant doors and the seafront beyond. Apparently his bravery had faltered at the last moment; he hadn't summoned enough courage to speak to Hetty after all.

Oggy returned to the counter, swept the girls aside and start doling out fish and sausage to the punters who'd been so patiently waiting.

'Well?' said Suki.

'Well,' said Oggy, 'here's the thing. Dad doesn't want to talk. He's done reliving that part of his life. There's all this to be celebrated, without getting lost in that quagmire again. *But ...*' And Oggy gave them a devilish look, as if about to relay to them some fiendish riddle. 'Barry Topps is happy to make a deal. He's seen your grandmother on the telly and reckons she's got something about her – but it isn't gonna be enough for her to just come in here and have a chat about the business with him. No, no, no, he's going to need to see something special if he's to talk about that most delicate time of his life.' Oggy paused. 'So here it is: girls, if you want him to spill his story, your grandmother's going to have to come here and *cook* for him. She's going to have to make him a fish and chips like he's never seen before – something so special it'll change his view of it, something so simple and different it could define fish and chips for years to come. A recipe, cooked here on the premises and gifted to us – the next great advancement for my father's empire. Yes, he'd like to see that very much. That might round out his retirement very nicely indeed.'

Suki ventured, 'I'm sure my grandmother can—'

'Barry Topps has been doing fish and chips since the fifties, girl. This is no easy task. Your grandmother might have been on telly, but she'll have to have her wits about her if she's to impress *my* father. But there you have it. That's your deal. You can take it girls, or you can leave it. It's up to you.'

Suki hadn't felt like this before. Somehow, it seemed as if her grandmother's talents were being called into question – and, through them, her very purpose in life itself.

Nobody thought of Prudence Bulstrode like that.

She leaned against the counter, muscling the woman at the head of the queue out of the way, and said, 'Mr Topps, your father won't know what's hit him.' Then she smiled, with some fresh devilry of her own. 'And I'll take a curry-basted sausage, battered with spice, and a tub of minted mushy peas to dip it in.'

Prudence had never felt like a naughty schoolgirl in front of Miss Jubber. There'd been plenty of times she'd been scolded at school – but never by Miss Jubber. Perhaps that was why, even fifty years later, she flushed bright red as Daisy Lane marched them out of the kitchens and back along the hallway, muttering appalled invective as they came. 'I've never known disrespect like it, and from someone as lauded as you, Mrs Bulstrode! These old dears need calming down, not riling up this close to bedtime. It's all right for you – you're not the one who'll have to deal with the night terrors and tummy problems.'

'Oh, *phooey*!' Miss Jubber spat – and now it was Prudence's turn to be amazed, for she'd never heard such a rebellious tone in Miss Jubber before. 'I needed a proper meal after all that mush you serve!'

'Our *mush* is filled with the vitamins and essential fats and oils to keep you in good working order,' Daisy announced, still frog-marching them on (at an interminable pace, for no amount of haranguing could transform Miss Jubber's joints). 'You ought to be grateful to our chefs. They've kept your heart in good working order for some years, Agatha.'

'Oh, but I want some *proper* cooking!'

They had almost reached the open doorway, beyond which old Mrs Arkwright sat with her guest – and here Miss Jubber stopped and suddenly declared, 'Proper cooking, yes, that's it!' She beamed at Prudence. 'What if I was to come to this end-of-course banquet of yours, Pru? Well, one last look at the old school might be good for the soul. I should die happily to see it again. And maybe . . .' She flashed a look at Daisy, 'I could get some proper food along the way.'

Then, cackling, she resumed hobbling forward, bound for her quarters.

Before Prudence had followed, a sudden mournful noise came from the door of Mrs Arkwright's room. There were no words in that noise – at least, none that Prudence could follow – but there seemed no doubt it was the voice of a woman in deep distress. Daisy set her face in a scowl and said, 'You've set her off again, Miss Jubber!' Miss Jubber herself was already halfway along the corridor – she seemed to have gained some sprightliness from somewhere, perhaps from the adventurousness of the evening – but now Daisy muttered darkly at Prudence,

'Mrs Arkwright isn't a well woman. She doesn't need these disturbances, not at this time of night. Mrs Bulstrode, perhaps it's better if you brought this visit to an end.'

Prudence had just begun uttering her apologies when the door to Mrs Arkwright's room opened up and, out of it, appeared the face of her portly visitor. Now that he was up close, Prudence took him for the nonagenarian that he was. Kind, dark eyes sat in a face that had become jowly over the years, and his silver hair had a little wildness about the edges, as if this was a man who had, for some years, had to survive without the usual tender care of his wife. He was wearing a smart charcoal grey suit and braces, and at his wrist a watch hung loosely on its strap. 'I'm sorry, Mrs Lane,' the man said, in a thick Cornish brogue. 'I'm not sure what's got into her. She was perfectly calm up until just now.'

Prudence looked through the open door. The room beyond was a perfect mirror image of Miss Jubber's own – except that Mrs Arkwright's shelves were lined up with photographs of family members now either living in different corners of the world or themselves passed on. In the bed, propped up by pillows, the shrunken form of Prudence's old headmistress sat in a shroud of duvets and shawls, her long white hair spread around her like a halo.

There was something ghostlike about Mrs Arkwright. At once, every bad memory Prudence had of her melted away, and all she wanted to do was to go through that door, take her hand, and speak to her of the old times.

She chanced a look at Daisy Lane, as if she might let

that happen – but Mrs Arkwright's lowing was only increasing in intensity. Daisy was sadly saying, 'I think you may need some sedation tonight, Gertie,' and in the room Mrs Arkwright lifted a long, bony arm and pointed it straight out of the door.

The next words that came out of her mouth caught Prudence and Daisy quite by surprise, though the gentleman in braces seemed to have heard them already.

'SHERLOCK HOLMES!' Mrs Arkwright moaned. 'SHEEERRRRLOOOOCK! HOOOOOOOOOOLMES!'

The gentleman looked over his shoulder. 'Gertie, I keep telling you. I'm very flattered by the comparison, of course, but I'm just Brian. Brian Hall.' He shrugged, and smiled oddly at Prudence. 'I'm not even a detective any more, but the old dear's got it lodged in her memory. It's funny what they dredge up, isn't it?'

'SHERLOCK!' Mrs Arkwright bellowed. There seemed to be terror, as well as fury, in that voice. Prudence sensed an unearthly desperation as she bawled out the word. 'SHERLOCK HOLMES!'

Daisy Lane's face had purpled. 'Out of here, you two. I'm meant to be off shift in fifteen minutes, but it looks like I'll be here all night!'

Then she bustled past Prudence and the stranger, approached Mrs Arkwright's bedside, and started plumping her pillows, fussing with her sheets, whispering to her all the while that she really did *need* to calm down.

'It gets all mangled in their minds, the poor old woman.' The man named Brian Hall stopped himself. 'Old!' he laughed. 'She's three years my junior. It's just rotten luck. The hand of fate.' He pottered off along the corridor. 'I've left my toffees in there as well,' he said wearily, as he left, 'and I'll be able to get no more until morning.'

There was just enough time to dart back to Miss Jubber's room, make a proper farewell – 'I had a hankering for that pasta as well, Pru!' – and a promise to come back soon, certainly for the night of the banquet at St Marianne's, before Prudence left. As luck would have it – and because she was herself more sprightly than the nonagenarian Brian Hall – Prudence caught him again in the empty reception hall, just before he stepped out into the night.

'Detective Hall?' she ventured.

The older man turned round. 'You're as bad as Gertie Arkwright up there. I told her, and I'm telling you, it's been thirty years since I was a detective. She fancies me Sherlock Holmes himself! Isn't it funny how we still think of others in the jobs they used to do, though? I've been a retired detective longer than I was a detective at all, and I still get called it. Nobody calls me "Gardener Hall", though that's what I do with most of my time. Nobody calls me "Allotment Keeper Hall", or "Fisherman Hall", or "Pottering Round the Supermarket Hall".' He grinned, cheerily, then bowed through the doors, back to the balmy summer's night. 'I know who you are, of course,' he said, when Prudence followed. 'I suppose they've got you trying to coax something out of the old dears' minds, have they? Yes, that's what I'd have done too. You've got to think laterally when you're a detective. Matter of fact, it's why I came here tonight as well. Not that I'm on *official business*, of course . . .'

Prudence said, 'I didn't recognise your name at first,

sir. Detective Brian Hall.' It was Detective Bryher Rose who'd first mentioned that name, over lunch at the Bluff. 'You're the detective who worked the Adam Scott disappearance, back in the day.'

'Oh, but there was hardly anything to work at all, Mrs Bulstrode. As far as we could say, it was open and shut. Young men commit suicide. It's a sad fact of life – and nobody seems to have grappled with it in all the decades since. I scarcely remembered the case when Detective Rose came calling. Now, it was nice to talk about police-work with someone after all this time, but I'm afraid I didn't have much to offer.' He pottered a little further down the Cherry Garth drive, Prudence following closely in his wake. 'But it kept coming back to me. Just playing on my mind, every time it cropped up on the radio, or that spread of you and Detective Rose having a lunchtime jolly in the Bluff.' He shook his head wryly. 'In my day, we'd have just had a cup of tea at the station. Nowadays, it's all for the camera.'

'I can assure you,' said Prudence, 'that wasn't my choice. A cup of tea, and a piece of shortbread, would have suited me fine.'

'It just felt like unfinished business, you see? A damn silly feeling, but it felt like someone had got the better of me, that some bastard really pulled the wool over my eyes in 1976 – and been pulling it ever since. So I thought: well, I'll just poke around a bit, lift a few stones, see what turns up. But what turns up is an old headmistress thinking I'm Sherlock Holmes, and not a lot else. The old dears in there can't remember what they had for breakfast, let alone what happened one summer fifty years ago.' At last, they had reached the main coast road. Detective Hall banked left, and picked his way slowly to a little parking area off the verge just up ahead. 'The mind's a funny thing, Mrs Bulstrode. Full of cracks and ravines.'

'I prefer to think of it like a deflated cake,' said Prudence, sadly. 'It's got all the right ingredients, it's just got no rise to it.'

Detective Hall nodded; apparently he approved of this image very much. 'My wife ended up in the Cherry Garth. Three years she was there before she passed. That's twenty years ago now. Twenty years, Mrs Bulstrode! Two decades I've plodded on, without my Miriam.'

By now, they had reached the parking place, and the rustic old Morris Minor waiting patiently there for its master to return. As he fumbled for his keys, Prudence touched him tenderly on the shoulder. 'Did Mrs Arkwright say nothing at all?'

'She talked about that English mistress a bit. Dot Ellen, if I recall. A wild one, that woman. She was known a bit in these parts. A regular in the Lonely Hearts columns. That's another thing that's fallen by the wayside, of course. Now you just order up a new partner on one of those little gadgets.'

Prudence smiled. Here was a man with less interest in the vagaries of modern technology than she had.

'Is it, perhaps, possible that Dot Ellen and Adam . . . ?'

'An affair?' Detective Hall ventured. 'I seem to recall something about her and Adam enjoying a tea together, after hours. But Adam Scott was like that with a lot of folks, or so I was told.' He paused. 'You know, I'm starting to get forgetful too. Maybe there's something *I'm* misremembering about it all. That's the thing, Mrs Bulstrode – how do you solve a murder when your own mind's starting to fray around the edges, when everything's become a jumble?'

'I've been turning it over,' said Prudence, 'but every time I think of it, it makes less and less sense.'

'Welcome to policework. Skulduggery abounds . . .'

'If you wanted to kill Adam Scott and make it look like a suicide, and somehow you managed to lure him on to that boat, then why not just kill him at sea? Why not put a knife in him and throw him overboard right there and then? Why go to the trouble of setting up the hoax at sea, only to kill him back at school?'

'The instinct says he was already dead,' said Detective Hall. 'Somebody offed him at school, and in a panic had to set up his suicide to cover it. So they go down to the marina and take out a boat and leave his suicide note there, for everyone to see.'

'The problem is Adam was *seen* getting on to the boat. You had witnesses who swore to it.'

Detective Hall mused on this for but a moment as he unlocked the car. 'Witnesses, Mrs Bulstrode, can be *bought*.' He slid into the driver's seat. 'Are you looking for a lift, Mrs Bulstrode?'

Prudence had decided this would be an inestimably good idea, for it was getting late and the thought of waiting for the bus again did not seem as nostalgic and inviting now that she'd spent the evening talking about murder – but, just as she prepared to accept Detective Hall's invitation, she lifted her eyes to the undergrowth at the edge of the track.

From the bushes, two sad eyes watched her.

Two sad eyes she recognised almost at once.

'Mrs Bulstrode?' Detective Hall ventured.

Suddenly, Prudence felt very far away. Of all the puzzling things she'd seen and wondered about this evening, this was the strangest by far.

Stranger still, the figure was waving furiously toward her, beckoning her to come near.

'I think I'll take a stroll, Detective Hall,' she said, 'but it's been . . . wonderful to speak with you.'

'Wonderful might not be the word,' said the aged ex-detective as the Morris Minor choked into life, 'but it's been enlightening. Here, I still have an old card somewhere.' He reached up out of the window and pressed it into Prudence's open palm, but her eyes barely dropped down to meet his, for her gaze remained fixed on the undergrowth above. 'Well, cheerio, Mrs Bulstrode. You might have made a wise choice not to get in this car with me! My daughter's been telling me to sacrifice my licence for years, but I reckon I've got a few good years in me yet.'

Soon, the Morris Minor had rattled back on to the road. Soon after that, it was rattling off into the darkness. Then, just as the rattling had faded into silence, Prudence dared to say, 'I am right. It is *you*, isn't it?'

The luminous eyes opened wider, the boy in the shadows fervently nodding his head.

'And you're not a PenzanceEats driver at all, are you?'

'I'm afraid not,' came a sad and fearful voice, the very same she'd heard that second night at St Marianne's when the delivery driver had come snooping around.

154

Then the figure half-stepped out of the bushes, revealing himself as the same rangy, shaven-headed teenager she'd seen through the classroom window. 'But I do need to talk to you, Mrs Bulstrode – and I need to talk to you right *now.*'

Chapter Six

In the little fishing village of Littlerock, not two hundred yards along the seafront from the gaudy neon lights of Topps Fish Mega Palace, a country bus pulled away from the bus stop, leaving behind only a middle-aged man with two carrier bags of shopping and a particularly disgruntled-looking sausage dog.

In the camper van parked on the kerb, Suki shook her head in mounting concern and said, 'When's the next one come along?'

The three girls dived, as one, for their iPhones and started dementedly scrolling through the options, eager to be the first to divine the answer from that great modern-day oracle of all human wisdom and knowledge: the internet.

'There's only one more before the service ends,' said Hetty, evidently the competition's winner.

'One hour to go,' said Sophie.

Suki's phone had started flashing with messages from Doogie – she felt terrible, but she'd only been responding to one in three since the news of Adam Scott; no doubt Doogie thought she was letting him down – but she crammed it quickly in her pocket. 'Something's happened,' she said.

'Just call her,' Sophie said. 'Find out where she is.'

'I *told* you. My grandmother doesn't . . .'

'Yes, Sophie,' Hetty pompously intervened. 'Mrs Bulstrode doesn't want or need a phone.'

'Well, you can't navigate the modern world by Mrs Beeton alone,' said Sophie – and, in the same moment, turned the key in the ignition, bringing the camper van's engine to life.

'What are you doing?' Hetty exclaimed.

'If Mrs Bulstrode won't answer her phone, we'll just go and get her.'

'I *told* you,' Suki insisted, 'my grandmother doesn't *have* a phone.'

Even after being told so many times, this information did not seem to penetrate Sophie's mind. 'We can't just leave her out there. We'll just head on up to the Cherry Garth and stake her out. Maybe she's already found something out. Maybe she's still there with these old teachers, hearing all about Adam Scott. Maybe—'

Hetty's jaw had suddenly dropped open. For a second she was frozen; then she slumped down in her seat, scrabbling to sink as deep into its cushiony surface as possible.

Soon, Suki knew why. Sonny had just emerged from Topps Fish Mega Palace, a meaningful look on his face.

'Let's just get out of here,' Hetty said, waving her hands frantically. 'Just go, Sophie. I can't bear letting the silly boy down again. And I *absolutely* can't bear having a nice, polite chat with him while he constantly tries to take my hand. Just go. *Go, go, go!*'

*   *   *

157

The boy was still standing in the bracken at the edge of the road, half-hidden by the undergrowth, his eyes darting in every direction. That was either nervousness or anticipation, thought Prudence. A sudden chill took hold of her, and she cast her own eyes in every direction as well. Something told her that the fake delivery driver wasn't the only one watching her, but no other figures were materialising out of the summer night. She focused her attention back on the boy, listening out for the sounds of other footsteps as they might approach.

'Are you following me?' she ventured. For the first time, she felt Detective Hall's card pressed into her hand. She dared to glance at it. BRIAN HALL, HANDYMAN AROUND TOWN, it read, with a telephone number underneath. A second career, she thought – just like Prudence herself. She rather wished he was here right now; whether he was a handyman or a detective, she didn't quite care.

'Mrs Bulstrode, come on!'

The boy threw himself bodily out of the bracken and grappled for her arm. Too late, Prudence stepped back, slipping in the uneven earth at her feet. That gave the boy every opportunity he needed: his hand closed over her wrist, he wrenched her back – and, if it was only the boy that kept her from falling, that did little to bring Prudence any cheer. The boy was slight, but his grip was firm. She tried to wrench her hand free, but he was holding her fast. The only thing she could do to resist being heaved into the undergrowth was to dig down deep, to plant her feet firmly in the earth. At least, now, she had found some purchase.

It occurred to her that she wasn't screaming. Another woman might be, but Prudence had sunk deep into silence instead. She had to concentrate to find her voice. 'What do you think you're doing?' she cried out. 'Let go of me. Let go of me this instant!'

'You're coming with me, Mrs Bulstrode,' the boy insisted. This time, when he wrenched backward, Prudence near toppled after. 'You *have* to.'

At last, Prudence sensed some hesitation in the boy. It was enough for her to slip free of his grasp, enough that she could stumble back, out of the range of his immediate reach. 'Have to?' she exclaimed. 'Young man, I don't *have* to do anything.'

The boy was rocking on his heels, as if he might spring for her again – but then he hesitated once more, and everything changed. 'You're helping police with their enquiries,' he said. 'I *know* you are.' Next second, he reached into the waistband of his baggy jeans and drew out a rolled-up newspaper, like a knight unsheathing his sword. This he unfurled, revealing the front page of the *Tregurnow Times* – and a picture of Prudence Bulstrode, sitting at a restaurant table with Poppy and Detective Rose, fat tails of lobsters half-eaten in-between. 'This is *you*, isn't it?'

Prudence ventured, 'Why, yes, but—'

'Then you'll have to follow me.'

'Young man, I'm not following you anywhere until you tell me exactly what this is about.'

'It isn't that simple,' said the boy, with mounting irritation, mounting unease, mounting dread. 'I can't be seen talking to you. It's more than my life's worth. So

159

you'll just have to come with me. Look, my hog's just on the next road. I hid it in the bushes. You ever ridden pillion, Mrs Bulstrode?'

Hog? thought Prudence. *Pillion?*

Her furrowed eyes must have betrayed her confusion, because the boy snapped back, 'My ride, Mrs Bulstrode! My sled! My . . . my motorbike! It's right round the corner. Come on, we've got to go.'

Suki did not need to know this – but there had actually been a day when Prudence was quite partial to a ride on a motorcycle. Nicholas had owned one, back in their halcyon days, and there had been a memorable summer hostelling around the south of France, Prudence often riding in the sidecar and navigating the roads ahead. Nicholas, of course, hadn't been quite as rebellious and uncouth as to call his motorcycle a 'hog' – he'd called it his 'darling' instead – and Prudence had often been wryly amused at a man's ability to dote upon an inanimate object. Personally, she'd never named any of her favourite whisks, mixing bowls or kitchen knives – but 'each to their own', as her mother used to say.

But there was no way she was riding pillion with this young man, and certainly not with that wild, frenetic look in his eyes.

'You came poking around the hockey pitch,' Prudence began, pointedly ignoring the boy's pleas. 'News had got out about Adam Scott's body, so you sneaked on to St Marianne's and started snooping around. But . . . what did you expect to find? You must have known there were police constables standing guard.'

'Mrs Bulstrode, you're wasting time. It isn't far, not on

my sled. I'll have you back before bedtime, you can count on it.'

'I'm not going anywhere, young man, not until you tell me exactly who you are.' She stopped, for a sudden thought had occurred. 'Are you in trouble? You can't be mixed up in whatever happened to Mr Scott, but—'

Lights flared.

One second, there was darkness – only Prudence staring into the half-frightened, half-furious eyes of her assailant. The next, the roadside was bathed in a bright white glow. The boy let out a shriek, cringing from it like something vampiric, then staggered back into the undergrowth as if the light itself had propelled him. Prudence, too, cringed away, lifting her arm to provide some shade from the worst of the brightness.

There were noises too. A door opened, then slammed shut. Somebody called out Prudence's name. 'Mrs Bulstrode?' came one voice. 'Mrs Bulstrode?' came another.

'Grandma?'

That was Suki's voice – and now came Suki's footsteps, clattering nearer and nearer.

Prudence turned.

Now that her eyes had grown somewhat accustomed to the light, Prudence could see the girls' camper van looming in shadow on the other side of the road, its headlights bathing them in their fearsome glow. Moments later, one of the shadowy figures had resolved into Suki herself. Prudence's grand-daughter took hold of her wrist, every bit as fiercely as the boy had some moments ago.

'Was he attacking you, Grandma?' Suki gasped. 'Was he trying to . . . abduct you?'

Prudence had not always thought her grand-daughter had the most common sense in the world, but until that moment she had never taken her as hysterical. 'Certainly not,' she replied, 'he was just . . .' She turned back to the boy, but the only sign of him that remained was the back of his shaven head as it bowed into the undergrowth, the frantic flailing of his feet, and his panicked voice carried on the wind: 'Justice for Adam Scoooooooooooooooott!'

For a time, there was silence. Prudence supposed it was the girls' dawning realisation that they hadn't interrupted an abduction – but instead scuppered some possible avenue of investigation – that dampened their enthusiasm. Still brooding on the matter, Prudence dusted herself down, then bowed down to the dirt at her feet and retrieved Detective Hall's card from where it had fallen. 'This one's for you, Suki dear,' she said, and handed it over. 'Pop the number in that little doohickey of yours. We might have cause to call it yet.'

Then Prudence, still ruminating inwardly on the sudden appearance of the youth, pottered back toward the camper van, where Sophie and Hetty were waiting with frantic, wide open eyes. 'Mrs Bulstrode, you were . . . you were fighting a . . . a *skinhead*!'

'Oh nonsense, girls.' Prudence swung up into the camper van, then found herself a seat amidst all the mess these girls left around. 'We had proper skinheads, back in my day. You wouldn't dare look one in the eye. That boy was no more a skinhead than you or I. He'd simply taken a razor to his scalp – very inexpertly as well, judging by the look of him.' She paused. 'But he did *know* something. He did come snooping around St Marianne's. He's tied into this somehow.'

'Justice for Adam Scott, Mrs Bulstrode?' asked Sophie, as she slipped back behind the wheel.

'There's plenty who want truth and justice in this world,' said Prudence, 'but why *him*?'

'Never mind that, Grandma,' said Suki, as she too arrived at the camper van and slipped within. 'We've got bigger fish to fry.'

Prudence gave her a quizzical, questing look.

'Quite literally,' Hetty chimed in.

'The biggest fish of them all,' said Sophie, as she brought the engine back to life.

'I'm sorry, Grandma,' Suki declared, 'but you're going to have to revolutionise fish and chips.'

The girls had wanted to play drinking games again, Prudence had wanted her help setting up the classroom for tomorrow's lesson – knife skills and butchery – but, that night, Suki had other ideas. After hammering out a quick message to Doogie (it was no good; she'd been ignoring him for too long – that was another boy lost to trekking around the country on her grandmother's tail), Suki retired to her room, looked out upon the upturned hockey pitch, and summoned Numbers to the phone.

'Darling, I thought I'd played my part with all this "A-Salt and Batter-y" business,' Numbers's whiskery face yawned, after he'd finally picked up the phone. 'I'm on sabbatical, darling. I've had it up to *here* with this Malaysia lot, so I've retired from the game. A few days R & R ought to sort me out.'

By 'R & R', Numbers evidently meant lounging around in his pyjamas with endless mocktails and milk-shakes. Suki had only rarely visited Numbers's family home, and the sight of it through these video calls – his basement room littered with dirty crockery, glasses and cans of Pepsi Max – didn't encourage her to go more frequently.

'I need you to go hunting for me. Numbers, I'm blitz-ing you some links.'

For a little while, Suki just hammered at her iPhone, before then drawing it back to her ear. 'Well?' she asked.

'Justice for Adam Scott,' Numbers read out loud. 'Pray, tell.'

So Suki told him about Barry and Oggy Topps. She told him about the challenge laid down. She told him about her grandmother's visit to the Cherry Garth, and the skinhead boy who'd accosted her on the roadside. 'And after he said that, Numbers, I did a little digging. There's a hashtag trending on all the socials. #JusticeforAdamScott. As far as I can tell, it's just a load of randoms sticking their noses into the investigation, trying to rile up a bit of attention for themselves. Benji Huntington-Lagan's in on the action – look, he's hashtagging like crazy after every post the Bluff makes. But there's this little group who are persistently posting. Look – @spiderwoman66, @UptheWolves, @ PBandJPenzance . . .'

'Smart work, Suki, but what precisely are you asking me here?' Numbers's face loomed large in the screen, grinning from ear to ear. 'Because you don't call me for a chinwag any more, sweetness. You don't call me for a catch-up. You don't bring me flowers . . . '

'Numbers, this is serious!'

Numbers faltered. 'You only call me when you *want* something.'

There was a time when Suki found Numbers's mock petulance almost *charming* – but that time was not today. 'I want to know who that boy is,' she said, stoutly. 'I want to know why he's so desperate to talk to my grandmother, and exactly how he's bound up in all this. And Numbers, I need to know *fast* . . .'

The following morning, Prudence woke to a miracle.

When she drew back the curtains of her dormitory room, it wasn't just the palatial grounds of St Marianne's School for Girls that she looked down upon.

It was her camper van as well.

There were still two hours before the girls congregated for the morning's lesson, so as soon as Prudence was washed, dressed and ready to face the day, she bustled down to the ground floor and out, through the reception hall, into the school grounds. The camper van had been left alongside the hockey pitch, half a furlong from where the police cordon still rippled in the wind. She picked her way towards it. Even at a distance, she could tell it was a little worse for wear. The peach and cyan paintwork, which she took pains to keep so pristine, looked discoloured by the storm of the night before – but, as she got closer, she could tell that one of the window panes was splintered as well, that half a forest's worth of foliage had become entangled in the contraption from which the awning unfolded, and that (most egregiously of all), half-a-dozen plastic-wrapped parking notices seemed to have been stuck underneath the one windscreen wiper that wasn't currently bent out of shape.

Yes, Prudence had thought it rather comical how much Nicholas used to dote over that motorcycle of his – his 'hog', as that young man would have called it – but she thought she understood, now, how a heart could break over an inanimate object.

'Oh, what have they done to you?' she whispered, as she finally drew near.

Up close, it was even worse than she'd thought, for it wasn't only the outside of the camper van that had been despoiled. The sliding door at the back was still an inch open, and when she heaved it aside, the inside looked as if some vagabond – or perhaps some feral schoolchildren – had been using it as a dosshouse. Empty beer cans were crushed in a corner, among the remains of supermarket tinned pies, which had evidently been burned to a crisp in Prudence's own cooker. Shreds of newspaper gave the place the impression of an animal's nest, while the dirty impressions of hands and boots on the surfaces were so distinct that a neophyte detective ought to have been able to identify a culprit straight away.

'You were meant for finer things than this,' said Prudence, stroking the discoloured paintwork tenderly.

'She certainly was, Mrs Bulstrode,' came a voice from behind.

Prudence turned. There stood the caretaker Ronnie Green, looking about as derelict as PRU BU 1.

'I didn't want you to see her like this,' he said, with the air of a pathologist welcoming some bereaved family member to a morgue. 'I wanted to tidy her up for you, before you got down.' At least, in this, he was telling the truth: the bucket at his side was overflowing with soap-suds, and from his hands hung all manner of disinfect-ants and sprays. 'I'm afraid the foxes got into whatever stores you had in them drawers, Mrs Bulstrode. All those tubs of frosting you had in there, that kilo of brown sugar, even those tins of chickpeas and whatnot. They've eaten every last one of your pies.'

'The pies weren't mine, Ronnie,' said Prudence sadly. 'I don't go in for Fray Bentos.'

'I'm partial to one myself. Taste of childhood, is a tinned pie. But . . . there's ne'er-do-wells up and down this coast, Mrs Bulstrode. One or two vagrant types too. You get them lurking round school sometimes. I reckon one of them decided they'd live in your camper for a while.' He paused. 'But I'll have her fixed up for you in no time. I'm only sorry I couldn't get to her sooner. The thought of her, alone up on that hill . . .'

'But the parking tickets, Ronnie? *Why?*'

'Local constables must have thought it was a party bus. They take a dim view of that kind of thing. You wouldn't believe what happens in some of these lay-bys.'

Prudence wasn't quite as prudish as people seemed to

167

think. Whatever happened in the local lay-bys was nothing compared to what happened at the Groucho Club after the end of a long day on set. She said, 'I'm just glad she's down from that hillside, Ronnie,' and turned to return to the school . . .

. . . only to discover Mrs Carruthers waiting for her, with her arms opened wide and a smile plastered across her expertly made-up face.

Mrs Carruthers must have been up at dawn to have perfected that appearance. Not a hair was out of place – not a hair even blew in the stiff breeze now coursing across the hockey pitch – as she approached Prudence and began, 'I understand you had a rather late night, Prudence, and with some of my girls in tow, mmm?'

Prudence had already started walking back toward the school reception, and Mrs Carruthers kept pace with her as she walked. Funny, but she hadn't been aware that she herself was subject to the St Marianne's student curfew. This job, such as it was, was beginning to feel more and more like Prudence was back at school herself.

'Just a few errands, Mrs Carruthers. I took the chance to stop in at the Cherry Garth and see Miss Jubber. Do you know, it rather warmed my heart. It made me *remember*. And, more than that, it made me think that – well, getting old isn't ever for the faint-hearted, but it doesn't have to mean the end of all *fun*. As a matter of fact, Miss Jubber might join us for the end-of-course feast . . . '

'Well, that's why I thought we might have a little word this morning, Prudence. Now, I'm an understanding, generous woman, kind of heart and even kinder of spirit . . .' Prudence had never heard anyone outside television talk about themselves in such glowing terms, but decided to let her go on; sometimes it was easier that way. 'But I'm fully aware, thanks to that little picture in the *Tregurnow Times*, that you've been asked to take on some, shall we say *extra curricular*, activities while you're staying with us. Now, we all want Mr Scott's foul, loathsome brute of a killer to be found. It is in my personal interest that this investigation is wrapped up neatly before term begins again. Heaven forbid we lose students because of all this! And yet it leaves me with something of a predicament.'

'Oh yes, Mrs Carruthers?'

By now, they had reached the front doors of St Marianne's, where Poppy had just arrived for her day's work, readying lessons for next year's intake. As she stepped from her car, Prudence caught her eye. That look they shared had echoes of half a century ago: one girl being scolded by a teacher, even as the other dreamed up ways to extricate her friend. Prudence was pleased to see Poppy quickly marching over. Some distraction was going to be very necessary indeed.

'The governors of this school entrust me with the budgets, Pru. I'm sure you understand. Mine is a position of much responsibility, and chief among those is managing our assets wisely. I have staked my reputation on running a tight ship, and have sworn to be accountable for any lapses in this. So when I see the – esteemed, of course, talented and inspirational! – cook I have hired to tutor our students, off indulging *other* interests . . .'

Mrs Carruthers let the sentence hang there, and gave Prudence a supercilious smile.

169

'You want your money's worth,' Prudence said.

'Understandable, is it not? I simply can't have these girls serving up slop next week, and their parents wondering what on earth we've been teaching them. I'd be dragged before the governors and *thrashed*.'

This was quite the image, but Prudence had to admit, to herself at least, that it was one she rather enjoyed. 'Mrs Carruthers,' she said, adopting a supercilious smile of her own, 'you'll get your money's worth.'

It was at this point that Poppy's face appeared alongside Mrs Carruthers's own. 'Everything all right, girls?' she said, with enough cheeriness to light up the Blackpool Illuminations. Over Mrs Carruthers's shoulder, she winked at Pru. 'I hear you've been cooking up a storm in that kitchen, Pru. Anything I can help with?'

It was like the double-act of old: one girl expertly blazing the trail along which the other could flee from their teachers. 'It's funny you should ask,' Prudence began, 'because there *is* one thing. I took the trip up to Cherry Garth last night, and had a chat with Miss Jubber. She's going to join us for the end-of-course feast.'

'Oh, how splendid!' Poppy thrilled, summoning yet more cheer with which to drown out the headmistress.

'But I didn't get the chance to sit with Mrs Arkwright. Maybe you could take a trip up there, like Detective Rose asked? See if she has anything to offer?' After the weariness and hysteria of the night before, Prudence was quite sure it would be a wasted trip – but it had to be done.

'That's OK with you, isn't it, Chastity?' Poppy beamed

– and, faced with this much bubbliness so early in the morning, there was nothing Mrs Carruthers could do but nod sharply and scurry off.

'Leave it with me, Pru,' Poppy said, with a wink. 'We'll get to the bottom of this thing, I'm sure of it. The dynamic duo, just like back in the day. The two P's in PVC!'

Between the sight of the camper van and Mrs Carruthers, the day had not got off to the most positive start – so Prudence was happy to hustle back to the domestic science classroom to clear her mind and think about nothing but cookery for a time. To her surprise, Suki was already up, hurrying around the classroom laying out ingredients at each station, excavating mixing bowls, a platoon of miniature deep fat fryers, flour, salt and all manners of spice.

'It's knife skills this morning, Suki,' Prudence announced. 'Clear all that away. We need to get prepped.'

'Oh, Grandma,' Suki said, shaking her head with almost enough condescension to make Prudence think the spirit of Mrs Carruthers had possessed her, 'you're missing a golden opportunity. Here we are, with sixteen pairs of hands, sixteen minds and imagination, sixteen young souls eager to do whatever you tell them.' She stopped. 'Well, we have a challenge, don't we? Barry Topps wants a fish-and-chips invention so original it will keep his empire strong for a generation. We've got to give it to him.' She flicked a switch, and across the classroom sixteen deep fat fryers started humming into life. 'Might as well make use of these girls while we can, huh?'

*   *   *

'Mrs Bulstrode, might I present: fishy chip surprise!' Sophie and Hetty had been working together on this one, and the twinkle in their eyes showed the whole class how very proud they were of their creation. 'You cut into the fish and realise it's just a single big chip. And look . . .'

Here, Hetty took over the telling. 'You take a bite of this chip, and realise . . .'

'Fish!' Sophie declared.

The girls had evidently been expecting a rapturous applause – and, indeed, this was what they got from their classmates, who all thought they had scaled the dizziest heights of artistry and originality. Prudence only wished she might have felt the same wonder.

'Girls,' she said, 'I think you might have invented fish fingers.'

It had been an *interesting* morning. Yes, *interesting* – that was the word. In the midst of all the waffle-cut chips, crispy pea batter, Scotch fish-and-chips (peas wrapped in minced fish and deep-fried in breadcrumbs) and battered bisques (this had been a particularly messy half hour), there had at least been one or two triumphs. The globules of battered tomato ketchup and tartare sauce that one of the girls was working on had started out a disastrous slop, but been refined close to perfection by the time lunchtime came. On reflection, Prudence decided that it was not a completely wasted endeavour; given a month in an experimental kitchen, and infinite resources of potatoes, cod, dried peas and batter, these girls might actually have created something.

It was just a shame that they didn't have a month to hand.

And a further shame that the classroom couldn't take a month's worth of mistreatment at these girls' hands. Prudence heart rather quailed at the sight of it now: a kitchen that needed cleaning was very often the sign of a kitchen well-loved, but this was more like a warzone.

'Girls,' she announced, 'I'm stepping out for half an hour. By the time I return, I expect this place spic and span.' She looked around at the glazed faces, the horrified expressions. 'Make it happen, Suki,' she whispered, 'or Mrs Carruthers is sure to have a fit.'

'But Grandma, where are you going?'

Prudence smiled. 'There's one more member of staff here who must remember Adam Scott, Suki. I'm going to catch her if I can.'

Like the domestic science classroom, the St Marianne's library had been revolutionised in the decades since Prudence used to sit among its stacks, diligently rushing through all her homework so that she could get on to more important things, like gallivanting with PVC. Indeed, the only one of its fittings that looked remotely the same to Prudence was the willowy, slight figure of Miss Verity Down, who looked up curiously from her desk as Prudence came through the doors.

Miss Down was different, of course – fifty years had provided her with lines and long, silvery hair – but the way she inclined her head in greeting was much the same, and the way she ignored the library's visitors and returned to the affairs of her desk was precisely as it had been fifty years ago. What was different, this time, was that Prudence didn't scuttle off to find a quiet corner in the stacks. For a start, there seemed to be precious few actual books here – only the shelving set into the deepest walls. Where the rolling stacks used to be, the endless spiral of bookshelves making up a labyrinth, there were only desks with computer workstations, iPads on long cords and headphones jacked into the back of each chair. But Prudence had no need to lose herself in the library today. The moment she stepped into its glistening white surrounds, she bustled towards the front desk, where Miss Down was hard at work.

'I rather thought you might come along soon, Pru,' Miss Down said, smiling. On one side of her desk was a mountain of periodicals, and in particular a teetering pile of the *St Marianne's Student and Alumni Newsletter*, which the students here published each term. On the other side of the desk was a contraption Prudence took to be a scanner, for Miss Down seemed to be spending her summer feeding each periodical into the machine and storing it, for posterity, in the school's computer network. Now that Prudence had approached, she set down the most recent issue she was working on and lifted the iPad on her table. This she turned around so that Prudence could see its display: the front page of the *Tregurnow Times*, with Prudence herself feasting on lobster tail over at the Bluff.

'I think I preferred it when newspapers were actual news *papers*, Miss Down.'

'I'm minded to agree with you, Pru, but if I don't move with the times, Mrs Carruthers will have me out of the door – and no doubt I'd soon be ferried off to the Cherry Garth, like so many of our old crowd. I understand you've been there too, Pru?'

'News travels fast.'

'Staffroom gossip,' Miss Down said, smiling again. 'And did Agatha and Gertie have anything to say on poor old Mr Scott?'

Prudence gave a non-committal shrug. 'You remember Mr Scott too, of course.'

'I even dreamed of him,' said Miss Down sadly. 'And do you know the thought that's dogged me all morning? The thing that won't leave me alone?' She paused. 'When Adam Scott died, he was scarcely a man. Twenty-six, twenty-seven years old – and the world's rolled on fifty summers, leaving him behind. He was my contemporary once. Now, when I picture him, he's more like those girls you've got in your classroom over there – one of the young crowd, a *youth*. Such a silly thing to observe, but it's made me inestimably sad.'

'Do you have any recollections of him, Miss Down? Anything at all?'

'Nothing I haven't already told that detective. Adam Scott was a good man. A fine man. A well-loved man. Why anybody should want to kill him, right here, right under our noses, I just can't say.'

'They're saying that his marriage was in trouble, that he wasn't happy?'

'You're looking at a woman who twice turned down proposals of her own, Prudence. In my experience, marriages are rarely what they look like from the outside. Was Adam Scott more unhappy than most? I should say that he found his fulfilment in other ways. If there was unhappiness in him, it came from the expectations of his family, not from Elizabeth. Teaching was his escape.' She paused. 'But you already know that, Pru. There isn't an observation I can make that you haven't already made yourself. So tell me, what's the famous Mrs Bulstrode *really* doing in my library?'

Prudence smiled. It was nice to feel transparent, on occasion. There were enough secrets in the world without carrying them around yourself. 'I was hoping there were photographs from the old days,' she said. 'Adam Scott, the staff, the students – something, *anything*, to get the mind going.'

'Well, you came to the right place,' said Miss Down, and promptly stood up. 'Take a seat, Pru.' Prudence went to take Miss Down's seat at the desk, but the old librarian gave her a look of mounting horror. 'At one of the *workstations*, young lady,' she said, shaking her head. 'You youngsters will never learn.'

It was nice to be called a youngster again, however comically Miss Down had meant it. It was less nice to realise that Miss Down expected her to take one of those dreaded iPads in hand and perform all kinds of quackery with it. 'All of the school history is archived on our intranet,' Miss Down explained as soon as Prudence sat down. 'That's a localised network, Pru – I'm sure your grand-daughter would be able to tell you. Just a few clicks and a swish here and there, and look, you're in.'

Miss Down had reached over Prudence's shoulder to flick at the screen, but now she handed control of the instrument over to Prudence herself. She'd seen Suki

176

navigate her way through one of these on innumerable occasions, but to Prudence it was like learning a different language. It was only when she decided that this was how Suki must have felt upon first being handed an electric whisk that she told herself to buck up and do precisely what Miss Down had said. Some moments, and a good number of false starts, later, she had found her way to a page called THE ST MARIANNE'S CHRONICLE and Miss Down was showing her how to spool back through the ages, dialling back time with a flick of the wrist. Soon, class photographs from the 1990s were whirling past. Then, the 1980s was exploding in glorious colour. Fashions transformed. The school uniform grew, then shrunk in size. The strange, New Romantic haircuts of the 1980s became the long, flowing trusses of 1970s hippiedom.

And then they were right there, back in the April of 1976. In the iPad frame, the whole school was lined up, gathered in rows on the very hockey pitch where Adam Scott's body was soon to be buried.

'This one's just three months before he vanished,' Miss Down said, sadly. 'Look, I can show you how to zoom in. There's Mrs Arkwright, and there's Miss Jubber, and *there's* Mr Scott.'

The picture became a little blurrier when Miss Down focused the image, but Prudence's old teachers were still recognisable. There was Mrs Arkwright, looking much more imperial and domineering than she had in her retirement home bed; there was Miss Jubber, her hands folded in front of her – her fingers devoid of her mother's wedding ring, the sign perhaps of a happier time; and there, on the edge of the crowd, was Mr Scott, squinting into the camera in his inimitable way. To look at him here, you would certainly not have suspected him of some deep-seated unhappiness. He was holding a book of what Prudence assumed to be mathematical problems in his hands, the only teacher in the school portrait who had brought his own prop to the staging.

'And *that's* Miss Ellen, of course,' said Miss Down, with a wry shake of her head. 'Now *there* was a one.'

'What do you mean?'

Miss Down looked down knowingly. 'Prudence Bulstrode, you know *precisely* what I mean. You're old enough now that we don't have to beat around the bush. Teachers are human beings with lives of their own, Prudence. You don't like to think about it when you're a student, but these are people with passions and dramas too.'

'Well, some of them,' said Prudence wistfully, gazing at Miss Jubber, trying to make the image focus further on her face. It had been a joy to see her, but Prudence had to admit that it had left a kernel of sadness in her as well.

'Don't mistake yourself, Prudence. Agatha Jubber had been stood up at the altar, remember. It made her swear off men for good! But as for Dot Ellen . . .'

'Mrs Arkwright spoke about her last night. I wondered if, perhaps, Adam and Dot . . . '

Miss Down spluttered wildly. It was really most ungracious. 'Well, Dot's private life was always very colourful, of course, but the thing you really must remember about Miss Ellen was that she was completely *terrible* at keeping secrets. If Adam and Dot had been fraternising, it wouldn't have stayed a secret for very long.' Miss Down paused. 'I always liked Dot. There were some who didn't – I believe that's one of the only things Agatha Jubber and Gertie Arkwright agreed upon in all their years working together – but she did have a charm to her. I'm a rather private woman, Prudence. I don't broadcast my personal life for all and sundry. But Dot was a woman out of time – she'd have thrived much more in this current generation, I'm sure, than she did her own. Nowadays, it's practically mandatory to publicise your personal life at every opportunity. Dot would have *loved* it. I suppose you'd say she'd missed out on the Summer of Love – she was just a few years too old for that malarkey – but she kept on trying, summer after summer after summer, you can give her credit for that.'

'But Mr Scott?'

'If they'd have been indulging in an extra-marital affair, Prudence, it wouldn't have stayed secret for long. My goodness, in later years, Dot practically *mined* her personal life in that novel she wrote.' Her eyes flashed nervously around. 'Did you happen to read it, Prudence?'

Prudence stammered, 'I . . . I had no idea it even existed.'

Miss Down had an unexpectedly mischievous glint in her eye now. 'Our copy's in the Restricted Section. We didn't have one in your day, of course, but since everything went digital, we decided to keep a few of the less suitable texts back. Lord knows why we had it in the school library at all – more, I suspect, as a fop to Dot than anything else. It certainly has no real educational value.' Prudence watched as Miss Down, her eyes still twinkling mischievously, disappeared through a door behind her desk – then, after a peculiarly short length of rummaging (perhaps Miss Down looked at this book more often than she let on?), re-emerged with the tome in her hands.

It was only a tattered little paperback book, its colour a gaudy yellow, its spine broken beyond repair – a dog-eared, well-read, much loved story by the looks of it. The author's name was written in striking scarlet: Dorothy Ellen. Above that, the title *A Girl's Life* was embossed in faux gold leaf.

It wasn't until Prudence had marvelled at the author and title that she saw the cover image in between. Two images were entwined around each other: the first, a man's stubbled face, his collar stained in red lipstick, his blue eyes dazzling. In shadow around that, the silhouette of a woman, voluptuous in the way only a scantily clad picture from the 1970s could be, leaning over and blowing a kiss out of the page, directly at the reader.

All of a sudden, Prudence felt quite uncomfortable.

'Not quite a Mills & Boon, but something rather similar,' Miss Down explained. 'Just look what they say about it on that back cover.'

Prudence almost didn't dare. It wasn't the idea of a saucy novel that unnerved her – Prudence, as she was quite keen to emphasise, had been no prude in her lifetime – but the thought of something penned by her old English mistress was only a few shades away from thinking about her parents having . . .

She turned the book over.

'If you like Jilly Cooper, you'll LOVE THIS!' There was no name attached to the endorsement, so it was just publisher's hot air – but Prudence immediately knew the inference they were trying to make. 'I met Jilly Cooper once. She came on *Pru's Big Night Out*. She had an idea to write a novel about a celebrity chef, but,' Prudence smiled wryly, 'I told her it would never work.'

'Dot didn't quite have Jilly's panache,' said Miss Down. 'I'm a dedicated bookworm, Pru. I've read *Riders*. I've read *Rivals*. *A Girl's Life* has its moments but ...' She stopped dead. 'I think Dot published a few more after that, but it never quite took off for her. More's the pity: she thought it was her ticket out of teaching! Listen, take it with you if you think it might help.' She lowered her voice to a whisper. 'But best not to let it stray into our students' hands, if you can help it. Girls their age don't need their ardours inflaming, if you take my meaning.'

Prudence felt a little dirty even taking the novel, but the iPad in front of her was flashing 1 p.m., and it was almost time for classes to resume.

'Did Mr Scott *ever* have an argument?' she asked, as she got to her feet. 'We make saints of the dead, don't we? When someone's perished like this, it's tempting to sanctify them. But it seems to me that that isn't *real*. Real people are good and bad, saints and sinners, lovely and *lousy* all at once. But nobody ever has a bad word to say about Adam Scott.'

Miss Down shrugged. 'Fifty years heals all sorts of ills. But you're right, Pru. Somewhere along the way, you got wise. But if Adam Scott wasn't truly a saint, he was certainly more saintly than others. Oh, and Prudence?'

Prudence had almost reached the library door – she would be glad to get back to fish and chips instead of this pristine, clinical environment the library had somehow become – but now she looked back.

'One more thing,' Miss Down went on. 'I've been saving this for you since the day you first arrived. I'm afraid Mrs Carruthers snaffled the certificate itself – you might have seen it, up on display outside the office – but I thought this might tickle you.'

Like *A Girl's Life*, this particular item was yet to be digitised. Miss Down opened up a drawer in her desk and drew it out, then tottered across the library to hand it personally to Pru.

There, in the fading hues of an early 1970s photograph, stood a teenage Prudence – a little rounder than she would be in later life, *sans* spectacles, with long chestnut hair falling in the buoyant waves that used to come so naturally to her. Beside her stood Miss Agatha Jubber, and between them they were holding on to the same prized copy of *Miss Beeton's Book of Household Management* that still stood, a little more dog-eared now – and imbued with all the spills, stains and annotations of a lifetime – on her shelf back home. Miss Jubber's hands cupped the book, her mother's wedding ring sparkling in the flash of the camera light, while Prudence's hovered around it, seemingly about to accept it as a prize.

'The day you won the Prize for Home Economics.' Miss Down smiled.

A rush of warmth coursed through Prudence. 'I was so proud that day.' She looked up. 'I still am.'

'I thought so,' said Miss Down, kindly. 'And that's why you must keep the photograph, Prudence. One for the memoir, if you ever get round to writing it. Now Prudence, *that's* a book I should like to read very, very much.'

Back in the domestic science classroom, streaks of batter still covered every surface (somehow, there were mushy peas smearing the skylight above), and the girls were already beginning to return from their lunchtime forays. Between bursts of frantic cleaning, Suki had spent the lunch hour noting down the recipe for those explosions of battered tartare sauce – she felt certain this was something of which Barry Topps would approve – but, consequently, the kitchen remained a state. As the first of the girls reappeared, she set them to scrubbing the surfaces – and would have joined them herself, but in her pocket her iPhone was ringing.

'DARLING!' came the very specific ringtone she'd set. 'DARLING!' She'd been meaning to change that sound file for ages; the syrupy way Numbers said the word had once seemed charming, but after a while it had the capacity to get on your nerves.

'You've got two minutes,' she said as she picked up. 'Grandma's on her way back.'

'And hello to you too,' Numbers said, with a dramatic roll of the eyes. 'I'll keep this brief, shall I?'

'If you could, Numbers . . .' With one hand, she gripped the iPhone; with another, she started scouring curry sauce from a hob. 'What have you found out?'

'Carn Euny,' Numbers declared.

It sounded like a foreign language. It sounded like

something had got caught in the back of his throat. It sounded very much as if Numbers was being deliberately obtuse. In an instant, Suki stopped her cleaning, glared into the video chat, and said, 'Numbers, I swear to God, if you don't cough up, I'll—'

'Keep your knickers on, darling, I'm being deadly serious. Carn Euny. It's a site of historical significance, just a stone's throw from that little Hogwarts place you're scrubbing at. Really, Suki, I thought you were a professional chef, not a kitchen skivvy.'

This time, Suki decided that the best policy was to ignore him. Instead, she returned to her scrubbing.

'The Romans built it, if you care to know, but now the skinheads use it.'

Suki said, 'The skinheads?'

'They're the ones behind this Justice for Adam Scott hashtag. Now, there's plenty others posting as well, but scratch beneath the surface a bit and you'll find a dedicated few. I suppose you'd call them conspiracy theorists, that is, unless they happen to be *right*. Mostly anonymous accounts, some sock puppets, online activists – you know the type, always sitting in their mother's basement, typing out their vitriol on their keyboards and sending it out to the world.'

'Mother's basements, Numbers?' Suki laughed. 'Pot. Kettle. *Black*.'

'Touché, dear, but I'm a local notable, not just your average basement dweller. I'm *going places*.' He paused. 'I'm sending some pictures to your phone. Is one of these your boy?'

Three images popped up in quick succession on Suki's

iPhone. The first was of a thickset man in motorcycle leathers, half his face dominated by a spider's web tattoo – but the second was, undoubtedly, the boy Suki had seen on the school grounds that night, the very same who'd been wrestling with her grandmother in the undergrowth of St Austin.

'That's him,' she gasped. 'Numbers, you've done it – that's him!'

'His online handle is @PBandJPenzance. PB and J? Something to do with peanut butter and jelly, one would think, but you never can tell. He seems a minor member of this crowd. But, Suki darling, they look rather unsavoury to me. Follow the trail a little deeper, and you see they're bikers: all leather and piercings and all manner of tattoos. Carn Euny's the place they get together, if the messages I've seen are right. Every Friday night. Lord knows what they get up to out there. Frightful stuff, by the look of them . . .'

Suki had flicked to the third picture, and now she recoiled. 'Numbers, who *is* this?' The woman's face was deep set with a scowl, but that wasn't the most surprising thing about her. Nor was the way she'd dyed her hair pink, then shaven it to a stubble. No, the most striking thing about this particular woman was the great tattoo that snaked around her neck and shoulders: a fire-breathing lizard, with its forked tongue aflame and its wings spread wide.

'Ah yes, the gang's leader by my reckoning. Looks delightful, doesn't she?'

Suki shivered. 'That boy was trying to drag my grandma off somewhere. What if he was taking her to *this* lot?'

'It doesn't bear thinking about.' Then Numbers paused. 'You're going to have to promise me to be careful, darling. I enjoy taunting and teasing you too much to want you dead. I'd be cut to the bone, Suki. I'd be bereft if this bunch of skinheads sacrificed you and Grandmama to their gods. Be careful, won't you, darling?'

Suki had never heard Numbers as unnerved before. She stared, glassily, into his face and found herself nodding, silently.

'Maybe it's time for the proper police, darling? Old Mother Hubbard oughtn't get mixed up with the girl with the dragon tattoo, should she?'

Prudence was almost at the classroom, the girls flooding through the doors in front of her, when she looked up from *A Girl's Life* and saw Poppy bustling across the reception hall, bound for the school office. In the milling girls, the two old friends froze. Poppy's eyes, it seemed, had taken in the book in Pru's hand. 'That old bonkbuster, Pru!?' she gasped.

Even the word 'bonkbuster' made Prudence cringe, somehow. She'd been flicking through the pages as she walked, lighting upon passages wherein a teacher named Deb strutted her stuff along the seafront at night, catcalled and wolf-whistled by all the passing tradesmen, and rarely daring to read more than a sentence at a time. 'Did you know about this?' she whispered as Poppy crowded near, eager to take a peek.

'I may have had a copy, once upon a time. My Bobby rather went off me for a couple of years, after we had kids. I had to keep the light alive somehow, Pru!'

Prudence cringed again. Perhaps now was the moment to change the subject. 'Did you get to see old Arky?'

Poppy nodded. 'I can't say she got to see me though, Pru. She's in an awful way. Just befuddled. Sometimes there, sometimes not.' She paused. 'It makes you feel scared, doesn't it? Scared for what's coming next. We're the next generation up, Pru. We're the Cherry Garth's next intake.'

Prudence clasped her by the shoulder. 'We have a few years left in us yet, Poppy. PVC until we die, remember?'

That old saying gave Poppy a thrill. 'PVC always,' she declared before she hurried off.

The girls were already at their workstations when Prudence pushed through the classroom doors. Suki seemed to be fumbling her iPhone back into her pocket – Suki was *always* fumbling that iPhone back into her pocket – but at least the kitchen looked *half* cleaned. It was as much as Pru had hoped for.

'Well, girls,' she said, clapping her hands, 'we had an interesting morning, but perhaps it was a little wide ranged. I think, this afternoon, we should focus on accompaniments. Forget the fish, forget the chips. Let's think about ways of jazzing up a mushy pea. Let's think about curry sauce and baked beans, pickled eggs and gherkins. Let's think about ketchup.'

'Ooh, Mrs Bulstrode!' Sophie exclaimed, thrusting her hand in the air. 'What if we made a stuffed crust? Like with pizzas? We took a piece of fish, slathered it in ketchup, *then* peas, and *then* batter? Do you think it might work?'

'One hour to design, girls,' Prudence declared. 'No

cooking until two p.m. Let's see where our imaginations take us.'

As soon as the girls had begun, Prudence hurried to where Suki was standing, once more staring into her iPhone screen, and foisted *A Girl's Life* upon her. 'A little light reading, Suki. Do you think you can manage?'

Suki took in the front cover, instantly balked, and said, 'Dorothy Ellen. *Dot Ellen. The* Dot Ellen, Grandma?'

'The very same,' said Prudence. 'It might be nothing, but I've an inkling . . .' Prudence froze. Her eyes, which until now had been lingering on the book, had landed on Suki's iPhone screen. There hung a face she recognised well: the boy in the bracken, the boy with his 'hog'. 'Suki, how the devil did you get that?'

'It's worse than that, Grandma,' said Suki, and scrolled onward, past the image of the thickset man with spider's tattoos, until the pink-haired woman with the serpent around her shoulders lit up. 'They'll be congregating at a place called Carn Euny this Friday night, Grandma. That boy who tried to kidnap you and all of his gang. Skinheads, Grandma. Bikers.' She paused. 'But they know something about Adam Scott. They're all over the socials, saying it's a stitch up, that Adam's killer isn't really a secret at all, that the police knew who it was fifty years ago – and they've known ever since.'

Prudence took hold of the iPhone – since the library, she was a dab hand with technology – and held it up. No, she thought, this woman did not look savoury. Her face was set in a deep grimace, her eyes shone with bitterness, and those dramatic piercings on her face could mean only one thing: she was impervious to pain.

'I suppose, then, that we're going to have to pay a visit to this Carn Euny,' she said – and, for the first time, Suki heard a tremor of real trepidation in her voice.

'OK, Grandma,' Suki said, and looked around at the girls, 'but you might need back-up.'

Chapter Seven

Across the next days, fish and chips *changed*.

There are always revolutions in food. Researchers travel the world far and wide, looking for the next great culinary delight to bring to the British masses. Things that were hitherto thought unpalatable to a family raised on meat and potatoes work their way into the psyche of a nation. So it was that pizza became a British institution. So it was that korma and jalfrezi became staples of menus from Land's End to John o' Groats. So it was that prawn cocktail and chicken Kiev both had their moments in the sun.

But fish and chips?

Fish and chips was *eternal* . . .

'There's an old adage,' Prudence said to the class on the second day she tasted Hetty's mushy-peas-with-a-hint-of-vanilla. 'If it ain't broke, don't fix it.'

The girls were trying their hardest, concocting new combinations, approaching old ingredients in radical, daring ways – but it was hard to believe that fish and chips had not already been perfected, that the reason it had stayed that way for two hundred years was because simplicity was best. By the third day, the battered balls of tartare sauce and ketchup were still the only things that

Prudence considered satisfactory at all. Sophie's minced-fish fritter was little more than an oblong fishcake. Suki's own attempt – a fish burger of cholla bread filled with cod, gherkins and tartare sauce, then dunked in batter and deep fried – was a decent effort, but hardly revelatory.

So, late at night, after the girls had gone back to their dorms, Prudence stayed alone in the domestic science kitchen, making tuiles of curry sauce, adding spices to her endless jugs of batter, devising slippery mille-feuille with the thinnest layers of haddock and hake, then firmed up in the fridge before battering and deep frying. If old Miss Jubber had been here to see it, she would have thought it quite preposterous – and so too did Prudence herself, for when she caught her reflection in the window one evening, she looked rather like a mad scientist in one of those old Hammer Horror movies: mushy peas steaming like potions in the pan, curry sauce bubbling and overflowing, Prudence hunched over her creation, scattering salt and pouring vinegar with a quite demented look on her face.

But at least the girls were learning something – every day brought a different lesson, and very soon their fish cookery would be superb – and at least there was always something to feed the visitors when they came. That was why Detective Rose, on visiting to speak with Prudence and Poppy about their twin visits to Cherry Garth, dined on fishcake and waffle chips. That was why Mrs Carruthers took miniature fish dumplings and deep-fried mashed potato balls for supper one evening.

That was why the end-of-course banquet quickly adopted a salty, vinegary nautical theme, with the girls spending the entirety of the fourth day experimenting with condiments old and new.

And why Ronnie Green – who, by now, had promised to chaperone Prudence to Carn Euny himself – had eaten his body's weight in scraps by the time Friday night came around.

'I think I've got it,' said Prudence to Suki, who sat in the corner of the classroom, her face twisting into a horrified rictus with every new chapter of *A Girl's Life* that she read. 'Come and see.'

Suki set down the bonkbuster – she wasn't sure how much more sexy pillow talk she could take – and trotted across the classroom to see Prudence's creation.

There, on a plate decorated by deep-fried lemon wedges and creamy mashed potato balls, stood Prudence's proud creation: perfectly fried haddock, with a spicy ketchup crust that, once cut into, would ooze hot tomato sauce like a perfect chocolate fondant. *They stuff pizza crusts*, Prudence had thought when she heard Sophie's ideas, *so why not this?* Put it on a plate, put it in a bread roll, serve it whichever way you wanted: here was a self-saucing fish and chips.

'It looks divine,' said Suki. 'Barry Topps has *got* to approve of that.'

'So we're ready,' said Prudence, with mounting conviction. 'You and the girls will pack the hamper, and I'll meet you at Topps Fish Mega Palace at nine. By then, I'll know what this Justice for Adam Scott lot are really about.'

'Grandma,' Suki ventured, mindful of how many times she'd said this before, 'I wish you'd think again. I wish you'd let me and the girls come.'

'Nonsense, Suki,' said Prudence. 'Your mother would ban you from working for me ever again if she thought I'd put you in danger.'

'But Grandma . . .'

Prudence clasped her by the shoulder. 'I've dealt with this type before, Suki. They're not nearly as frightening as those piercings and tattoos make out. It's all a show, rather like this . . . black hair of yours.' Prudence lifted Suki's dyed fringe by the fingers, as if inspecting vegetables at a market stall. 'I'll be *fine*,' she promised. 'I've got my bodyguard, remember.'

A knock came at the door. There stood Ronnie Green, sniffing the air as if what he really fancied was a plate of Mrs Bulstrode's new fish-and-chip creation.

'We've both got jobs to do, Suki. Let's jump to it.'

'Grandma, before you go . . .' Suki hurried back to the corner, plucked up the copy of *A Girl's Life*, and hurried back in an instant. 'This chapter, Grandma. You *have* to listen to this.'

Quick as a flash, Prudence lifted her hand. '*Later*, Suki,' she said, not sure if she could stomach another sex-laden scene, especially rendered in Suki's voice. 'Let's tackle one thing at a time. First, Carn Euny. Then, Barry Topps. And then – and only *then*,' Prudence turned quite green, 'we'll start thinking about Dot Ellen and what may or may not have been happening in the staffroom after hours . . .'

*　　*　　*

193

It would have been less foreboding if it hadn't been dark, reflected Prudence, but Carn Euny would have looked mysterious even in the full light of day.

Less than twenty minutes' drive from Penzance, past the vast, rolling waters of the reservoir outside Lower Drift, through the picture-perfect parish of Sancreed – and along the lattice of old farm roads and tracks – came PRU BU 1, its peach and cyan paintwork a strange aberration in this world of greens, greys and brown. At least Ronnie Green seemed to know where he was going. Picking at the fish-and-chip supper he'd brought from the classroom, he directed Prudence down one track, then down another, stopping to guzzle on the can of pale ale he'd had about his person. 'We used to play down these tracks when we was lads,' he said, pointing out witching trees and birdwatching hides. 'You ever come this way, Mrs Bulstrode, when you was up at this school?'

'Archaeology wasn't really my interest,' said Pru as she pulled the camper to the side of the road.

The skies above the rolling fields were clear tonight, and consequently the spiral of stars plastered across the heavens above spilled pure, crystalline light. It was by the light of those stars that Prudence first saw the stone monoliths, the ruins of old settlements that made up Carn Euny, a memory of an ancient time still imprinted upon the land. As she stepped out of the camper, she could smell woodsmoke on the breeze – and picked out, somewhere in the ruins, the orange light of a dwindling campfire.

'So, then,' she said, as Ronnie Green too clambered to

the ground, wiping his greasy fingers on the front of his jeans, 'Numbers was right. They do congregate here.'

'You're damn sure about this, Mrs Bulstrode?' asked Ronnie. By now, he'd gone to the back of the camper and produced a shovel he'd hidden there. As soon as Prudence saw it, she rolled her eyes. 'It's not much, Mrs Bulstrode, but you want protection against this sort. I should know. I was in a gang once.'

'Oh yes?'

'Now, we didn't go about on motorbikes duffing folks up, but we got up to all sorts. You wouldn't want to mess with us. We threw eggs on this old fella one day. Just dropped them off the bridge by the Pirate Inn – smack, on to his head. We scuttled a boat on the reservoir. You didn't want to cross us.'

Prudence picked her way across the barren road, then up into the scrub on the other side. 'Let's hope it's just a few rotten eggs, Ronnie,' she said, 'but I should like it if you'd put away that shovel.'

'Can't do that, Mrs Bulstrode. I've sworn an oath to protect you.'

'Yes, well, you don't have to play Lancelot right now. If they see you with that shovel, they're liable to think we're here to cause trouble – and, in my experience, that will only *start* the trouble. So let's just see what they're about, shall we? If our young man's here, we might even get a welcome.'

A sudden voice spoke out of the shadows:

'Oh, you'll get a welcome all right . . .'

Prudence startled, searching out the voice in the darkness. At her side, Ronnie Green whirled around, brandishing the shovel like it was at once both sword and shield.

A moment later, a silhouette materialised out of the gloom up ahead. Moments after that, that same silhouette put two fingers to its lips, let out a shrill whistle – and, in instants, engines were revving somewhere in the darkness, the headlamps of two scrambler motorcycles flaring as they banked around the closest outcrop of rock and cut tight arcs around the place where Prudence and Ronnie stood, blocking their way back to the roadside.

The shadowy figure stepped further forward, at last entering the halo of light from the motorcycle headlamps. Prudence had seen that face in Suki's iPhone screen, the portrait dug up by Numbers from wherever he went excavating online – but, of course, it was the tattoo that wrapped around her neck and naked shoulders that identified her the most. In the headlamps' light, the wings of the serpent looked even more fearsome than they had on the iPhone screen. Prudence could just about see its reptilian snout poking around the young woman's shoulders, its nostrils spewing flame so that it looked as if the pink fuzz of her shaven head was all that had been left after her flowing locks were incinerated.

'Hands where I can see them,' the young woman barked. Strange, but her voice was altogether more genteel than her appearance allowed.

'My hands are already where you can see them,' said Prudence, who had immediately extended her right hand in greeting. 'Young lady, my name is Prudence B—'

In the corner of her eye, Prudence saw a frenzy of

movement. When she turned, it was to discover that Ronnie Green had lifted the shovel he was wielding aloft, brandishing it at the motorcycle riders like a sword. 'Get back!' he was growling, in a trembling voice that Prudence was quite sure would not even have put the frighteners on the girls at St Marianne's. 'I'm warning you! You think I haven't had my fair share of brawls? I'm Ronnie *Green*.' He looked over his shoulder. 'Come on, Mrs Bulstrode. We're getting out of here. We're getting out of here right now.'

Prudence peered curiously between the manic Ronnie and the tattooed woman at her side. 'Ronnie, put the shovel down. You're making a scene.'

'I'm getting us out of a sticky situation, Mrs Bulstrode. It's more than my job's worth if you're sacrificed to these heathens. Mrs Carruthers will have me out the door quick as a flash, and . . . and I *need* that job, Mrs Bulstrode. Things aren't good at home. If I lose that job, I'll lose my missus for good and then . . .'

Prudence touched his arm. 'Ronnie, we're just here to talk to these good people.' Some bodyguard he'd turned out to be; even now, Prudence could hear the motorcycle riders conspiring to disarm him, then wrestle him to the floor.

'You don't know they're good people, Mrs Bulstrode. But I've got my instincts. Good people stay at home with a pint and a pie. They don't get together at stone circles after dark. It's practically pagan. That's what it is. They used to round up pagans in my day . . .'

Prudence had a sudden vision of medieval villagers falling upon the local witch, but Ronnie's 'day' had been more recent than Prudence's, and she was quite sure there weren't any Cornish witch trials back in 1976. 'People are different, Ronnie,' she said. 'I've met all sorts in my time. You wouldn't believe some of the unusual types you get in TV. You'd think lots of them were pagan too. Good heavens, sometimes I think anyone below the age of thirty-five has grown up in a parallel world. But sometimes, just sometimes, you have to look a little deeper. Trust people who aren't like you . . .'

The words seemed to have penetrated Ronnie's mind, for – with hands still shaking – he released the shovel, letting it clatter in the scrub and stones at his feet. His frenzied eyes caught Prudence's own. 'I hope you're right, Mrs Bulstrode.'

'Ronnie,' she softly said, 'I know I am.'

Then she turned back to the girl with the dragon tattoo.

In the intervening moments, the woman had closed the gap between Prudence and herself. There she stood, but inches away – in one hand, a wicked looking Bowie knife whose blade sparkled in the starlight; in the other, a black length of cloth, a bandana ripped from her belt.

'Oh,' said Prudence, who was suddenly quite lost for words.

'Blindfold them,' the tattooed woman announced, 'and lead them through the fogou!'

It was hard to cling on to the idea that these were good people with a blindfold strapped so tightly around her eyes. Harder still to believe that they meant her no harm

198

with Ronnie Green sobbing quietly behind her, the ground uneven at her feet, and the whirlwind of disorienting voices that surrounded Prudence as she was driven on, somebody's hand jabbing into the small of her back every time she stalled. 'I met one of your colleagues,' Prudence tried to say (colleague being a much more positive description than 'gang'), but nobody seemed to listen. 'It's *him* who wanted to meet me.'

But the tattooed woman only barked, 'You'll get your turn to speak,' and heaved her onward, down a rocky incline, along a more even walkway that, by the way the sound distorted, Prudence took to be underground – and up again, to a place where the wind blew more freely and the smell of woodsmoke was stronger in the air.

There were fires near. Prudence was certain of that. The smell was not unpleasant, but something couldn't stop her from harking back to that image of paganism and witch trials. She tried to speak out and tell Ronnie Green not to panic, that this was all some dreadful misunderstanding, but could not give voice to the words.

'Wait!' came a voice, from somewhere out in the fiery dark. 'Wait, that's Mrs—'

There came a flurry of other voices.

'You mean to say you *invited* her here?'

'I . . . I don't . . . No!' came the voice again, and now Prudence knew who this was: the boy from outside Cherry Garth; the boy who'd claimed to come from PenzanceEats. This stilled her heart a little, for at least she knew she was in the right place. Now, if she could only get this blindfold off and find breath to say the right words, she might be able to calm Ronnie Green, explain why she was here, and take charge of this sorry situation. She reached up, but somebody forced her arms back down. 'It was . . . wasn't an invitation,' the boy went on. Something in his voice was as panicked as Prudence felt. 'I went to see her. You *know* why. She's working up at that school. And then her picture in the press. She . . . she can help . . .'

'She's working for the filth,' came a man's deep, resounding voice.

'She's one of *them*,' came another.

'She's just a cook,' blathered the boy. 'Please. Please, Pearl, just take that blindfold off. She knows where we are anyway. You can't hurt her. You just can't. She's . . . she's off the telly!'

Prudence wasn't sure what irked her the most: the idea that she was "just" a cook, or the idea that she was only going to be excused their violence because she'd made a few television programmes over the years. What did that mean for poor Ronnie Green? Was he to be manhandled more ferociously because he was 'just' a caretaker?

'Now, listen here!' she called out, into the blackness. Then, quite without knowing she was going to do it, she reached up suddenly and tore off the bandana that had been tied around her eyes. 'I'm not here to cause any trouble. I came because *that* young man . . .' she looked for him, but her eyes were a blur and all she could see was a rush of black and orange firelight, ' . . . seems to know something about the murder at my school. In fact, you all do – all of you here! And don't go blaming that boy for telling me where you were. My grand-daughter worked that out all for herself. You young people can't go about chattering online where everyone can see it and then claim privacy . . .'

The blurring receded from her vision. The nightscape of Carn Euny resolved in front of her eyes. She was standing in a circle of some fifteen figures, half of them lounging around their motorbikes and scooters, the other half laconically propped up on the ancient stones that made up the heritage site. Just behind her, where Ronnie Green was still trembling between the motorcyclists who'd shepherded them here, the earth dropped away, leading into a rock-lined tunnel just beneath the surface. It was this, Prudence would later discover, that was the 'fogou', some remnant of the prehistoric settlement that had once sat on this site. The dark tunnel entrance was disgorging a couple more silhouetted figures now, one of them with his arms laden down with takeaway cartons, pizza boxes, and bags that seemed to be filled with ciders and beer.

She turned back around. Two small bonfires had been built between the ruins, and in front of the first one stood the boy who'd accosted her outside the retirement home. The woman with the dragon tattoo was at his side, holding him fiercely by the collar.

'For goodness sake, put him down,' Prudence said, suddenly full of vim. If these youths really thought they could intimidate her, she was going to make them try much harder. 'And Ronnie, take that blindfold off this instant.'

'I'm . . . I'm not sure I w-want to, Mrs Bulstrode . . .'

In the end, Prudence did it for him. As soon as she'd whipped it off his face – the bikers standing back in bewilderment, amazed that this old woman seemed suddenly oblivious to her perilous situation – he closed his eyes again.

'Oh, Ronnie.'

'If it's all the same to you, Mrs Bulstrode, I'll let you handle this one. I'm afraid I'm not much cop without my shovel.'

'Well,' Prudence said, 'this is a pretty sight.' She gazed around the circle. 'Firstly, I'm quite sure you're not meant to be starting fires at a site of historical significance. There must be better places to congregate. And secondly . . .' her eyes lit, suddenly, on some empty tinned pie tins littered around one of the fires, 'I suppose it's *you* who were using my camper van as a party wagon, is it? Drinking beer and carousing when it was stuck up on that hillside?'

The woman with the dragon tattoo cast the boy aside and said, 'You don't get to come here, intruding on *our* private meeting, and accuse us of crimes, Bulstrode. Not that it's any of your business, but we don't drink. We're not like you olds. We don't need to drink to feel *real*. We've got purpose outside of drink and drugs. You old people are all the same – you take one look at us and think we're worthless. Well, we ain't. And—'

Prudence dared to potter forward. 'You heard me telling my friend, here, that looks can be deceiving. But what am I supposed to think, mmm, when you blindfold us like prisoners?'

The woman fell silent for a moment. 'You better spit it out. Why you're here, what you want from us, before you really make me angry.'

'Well, let's start like civilised people, shall we? You already know my name. Why don't you tell me yours?'

Prudence could tell that the younger woman felt baited now. She had opened her mouth to snarl a reply, but before she said a word, the boy picked himself up and called out, 'She's called Pearl. And I'm . . . I'm Peter.'

The girl named Pearl glared at the boy.

'We're on the same side, Pearl,' said Peter, glumly. 'Mrs Bulstrode wants to figure out what happened, just the same as us. I thought she could help us. She was there. She *knew* my grandfather.'

There had been much to discombobulate her in the last fifteen minutes, but this was the most discombobulating of all. Prudence had to pause for some moments, listening to the flurry of conversation from the bikers on the outside of the circle, before she understood. 'Peter,' she ventured, 'Peter . . . Scott?'

'Not quite,' said Peter. 'My name's Sparrow. Peter Sparrow. But you've got the right idea, Mrs Bulstrode. Adam Scott was my grandfather. At least, that's what I've always been told. You're not allowed to *wonder* in my family. They wanted it all neat and tidy.' He stopped. 'I'm sorry, Mrs Bulstrode. *We're* sorry, aren't we, Pearl?'

'You'll be sorry after this night is through, Peter. If you were going to bring in a stranger, you ought to have talked about it first.'

'I've already explained that,' said Prudence, sharply. Then she turned to Peter once more. 'You came sniffing about the school, after Adam's body was found. Then, after that picture in the *Tregurnow Times*, you wanted to search me out, to see if I could help.'

'It's what we're all doing,' said Peter. Around the circle,

the bikers started to hoist the placards that had been lying at their feet into the air. 'I always thought my grandfather committed suicide. It's in the family, you know. They don't talk about it often, but it can't be ignored.'

'Peter, you'll have to slow down a little . . . slow down a little and help me understand. Adam Scott never had any children, *did* he?'

'Not that he knew of,' said Peter. 'But my grandmother was pregnant when my grandfather got on to that boat and left her that note. She gave birth to my mother just eight months later.' He paused. 'Maybe, if he'd known, he wouldn't have done it. That's what they said in my family. That Adam Scott desperately wanted a baby – and, if he'd known, he wouldn't have gone out to sea. But then I started seeing all that social media chatter about the body found at St Marianne's. And then it was in the newspapers: Adam Scott's body found – not at sea, but in the hockey pitch. And . . . I just had to go and check it out for myself. Because it means my family have been living a lie since long before I was born.'

'Here,' said Pearl to the figures who'd just emerged from the fogou, 'bring that grub over here before it gets cold.'

As the figures bearing the takeaway delivery marched past Prudence, Peter continued, 'I don't know, Mrs Bulstrode, but something stinks on all this. And me and my friends here, we want to find out what.'

Something else stank, thought Prudence, for some of the skinheads had started opening the takeaway delivery – revealing nothing but carton after carton of chips and

204

potato patties from Topps Fish Mega Palace. Not for the first time, Prudence cast her mind to her date for later that evening: the challenge thrown down by Barry Topps. Perhaps, by the time midnight came around, she might be in a position to draw together the strands of this mystery.

'Hold on there,' she declared, and marched over to the mountain of potato products just delivered. 'No. That just won't do.'

'Won't do, Mrs Bulstrode?' leered Pearl.

Prudence looked up. 'Ronnie, I need you to nip back to the camper, and pull out the blue plastic storage box from the refrigerator.'

'M-me, Mrs Bulstrode?' He looked quite petrified of venturing back into the fogou.

'I'm sure some of these chaps will help you if it's too much, Ronnie.'

The caretaker started shaking his head feverishly, then tumbled back into the darkness.

'Somebody better go with him,' Prudence said, 'just in case he decides to do a runner. Now, listen. I've plenty of food back in the camper. All my travelling equipment too. I won't have you youngsters eating cheese and chips all night, when I can make you up a pot of perfectly good chilli, right here on one of those fires.'

Pearl took the opportunity to leer again. 'We're not philistines here, Mrs Bulstrode, but we *are* vegans. There's not one of us here who'll want chilli from your pan.'

Prudence paused, just to take stock. Skinheads, she thought. Teetotal, vegan skinheads, gathering at a site of historical interest to organise a campaign against a seeming miscarriage of justice. Perhaps there was some hope for the next generation, after all.

'I'm perfectly capable of making a vegan chilli to blow your socks off, Pearl. So, if you'd indulge me, I can have you all fed within the hour – and Peter, I'll hear all you've got to tell me while we eat.'

In the end, Ronnie Green had courage enough not to jump in the camper van and leave Prudence stranded among the skinheads. He even had enough courage to indulge in a small bowl of Prudence's three-bean chilli himself – though he did add that he would rather have a pint and a pie, 'just, you know, to settle my stomach' – while the gang gathered and talked.

'Adam and Elizabeth are just like a legend in my family,' Peter began, as chilli was heaped on top of chips and general murmurs of appreciation spread among the skinhead gang. 'Them getting married was a big deal in these parts. I've seen the old wedding album. All the letters and cards. You'd think it was a prince and princess getting married – and the thing is, Mrs Bulstrode, it *was* a bit like that. An arranged marriage, though nobody ever said it. But my great-grandparents had been manoeu-vring to get Adam and Elizabeth married since they were tiny. Then – bang, it happened!'

'All about business, of course,' intervened Pearl. 'Business, not love.'

Prudence had heard this part of the story before. 'To unite the two fishing families. To build a proper empire, Franks & Scotts, to rule the seas around Cornwall.'

'The way I see it, it was doomed from the start,' said Peter. 'If you're getting married, you really ought to like each other. But I don't think they really did, Mrs Bulstrode. They did it out of obligation. They got a nice big house to live in together, and enough money to go round – and my grandmother's family even tolerated it when Adam decided he'd go off and be a teacher instead of going out on the boats. They thought he was a coward, of course. That he wasn't good enough for my grand-mother. But, as long as they got a child out of it, that didn't seem to matter. It was the child that counted. Because that child would be the direct heir of both families, and that would be it – job done.'

'Problem was,' said Pearl, 'Elizabeth didn't get pregnant. Not at first. They tried and tried, and it just wasn't happening. There were whispers in the family. Adam was secretly gay, they said – and, of course, you'd have to keep it a secret back then. Barbarians – it had only just been legalised! Or Adam couldn't, you know, *perform*. Or . . .'

Prudence said, 'Adam was getting his interest somewhere else, perhaps?'

'Oh, you ask enough folks, and you'll hear it all,' said Pearl. 'We should know. We've been making it our business to find things out ever since Adam was discovered. Because Elizabeth *did* get pregnant in the end. In fact, she announced it only a few days after Adam committed suicide. Now, doesn't that sound fishy to you?'

Prudence looked around at the gang. The chilli seemed to have gone down a treat. The bottles of sparkling mineral water, which had come with the takeaways – and which Prudence had, in her haste, assumed to be ciders and beer – were being popped open.

'It certainly sounds strange,' she conceded, still rather lost in thought.

'Just a few days, Mrs Bulstrode,' said Peter. 'The *Tregurnow Times* ran a piece about the funeral. Well, like I say, it was *big* in these parts. They had my grandmother in their sights, milking her for the emotion of it. And she tells them about the tragedy of it – that she's carrying a baby, *Adam's* baby. And then . . .'

'Six months later, she's married to another man,' said Pearl. 'A man by the name of Mac Duggan. A distant cousin of Adam Scott, out on the edges of the family business, just running a couple of boats out of Porthleven.'

'She's still married to him now. That was the man my mother called Dad. Only now . . .'

At last, Prudence understood. 'You wonder if Mac Duggan really *is* your grandfather. You wonder if your grandmother was having an affair with this Mac, that she carried his baby – but, what, had to pass it off as Adam's so that the union of the Franks and Scotts wasn't undermined? Had to pretend she was pregnant by Adam, so that your family still inherited both firms?'

'Oh, it's more than that, Mrs Bulstrode,' Peter trembled.

'Tell her, Pete,' said Pearl – and, for the first time, Prudence detected some tenderness in her tone.

Peter looked up, his eyes reflecting the dancing orange firelight. 'I'm afraid, Mrs Bulstrode . . . I'm afraid that what really happened is that my grandmother was having an affair with Mac. That her marriage wasn't working and she fell in love with Mac. That she ended up pregnant by him and she had to . . .'

Prudence whispered, 'To kill Adam Scott.'

Peter nodded. 'It makes sense, doesn't it, Mrs Bulstrode? That they staged his suicide – Mac knew all about boats! – and then passed off their own child as Adam's so that nothing fell apart.' Peter started trembling. 'I'm afraid, Mrs Bulstrode. That's why I came to you. I can't . . . I can't go to the police myself. If I do, my family will never forgive me. My grandmother's a powerful woman, Mrs Bulstrode. She and Mac ruled over the company for forty years before handing on the reins to my mother and father. They'd do anything to keep their secret. If they killed one man to make sure the company thrived, why not . . . why not kill another?'

'But you're the heir of that company, Peter,' Prudence breathed. 'You're their flesh and blood.'

'I'm not the heir,' said Peter, ruefully. 'That honour goes to my brother. I'm to be paid off and left to my own devices. My hog over there? That was for my seventeenth birthday, while they paid for my brother to study business in New York. Yes, they'll indulge me, my family, if it keeps me out of their hair. That's why,' he puffed out his chest, 'I've got my own people here.' He reached for Pearl's hand, and Prudence could sense the solidarity of the skinheads around him. 'We've been doing what we can. Our social media campaign. These placards, for a protest outside the police station in Penzance. There's some of us reckon the filth knew all about it, that it was all hushed up, all that time ago. But then there was you, and I started thinking . . .'

'What do you want from me, Peter?'

'Well, not just another bowl of chilli, though I'll happily take six more,' said Peter, as one of the other skinheads topped up his bowl. 'Mrs Bulstrode, my grand-mother's a fan of yours. She has all your books. So when I saw you at the school, and I saw you in that newspaper, I started thinking, maybe there's a way *you* could get it out of her? It wouldn't have to be much, just enough that you might take it to that detective and get *her* to look into it. But it's my grandmother's birthday in just a few days. And I was thinking, what better birthday gift could there be than a dinner cooked by none other than Prudence Bulstrode? What if you were there, in the house with her, just chatting away, talking about fish and chips and seafood, and all those things you'd have in common, and somehow she let the mask slip? What if *you* heard enough so that detective could do the rest?' Peter stilled. Somewhere along the way, the emotion had got the better of him. 'I don't want my grandmother to be a murderess, Mrs Bulstrode, but if she is, I want the world to know it. I don't want to live the rest of my life know-ing I stayed silent. I want . . . I want to be a good man, like Adam Scott. I don't want to be a part of any cover up, and if it spells the end of the Franks & Scotts line – then so be it.'

On the seafront, the lights were flashing in bright pink, mauve and green, the enormous letters that spelled out TOPPS FISH MEGA PALACE illuminating even the sea as it crashed into shore.

Sophie drew the camper van to a halt outside the garish

establishment. Friday night in Littlerock, and seemingly the fights had already broken out. Two brawlers ceased throwing punches at each other somewhere along the seafront, and were now propping each other up as they staggered along the promenade. Revellers kept pouring out of the doors of the Topps's place itself, and every time they emerged so too did the music rush out into the night. Somebody seemed to be hawking up their fish supper round the back, while scavenging seagulls circled overhead.

'Go on, Suki, she's not here yet,' said Hetty, peering out of the windows. 'Read us another.'

Suki had been serenading them with sections from *A Girl's Life* since they'd set off. 'Oh, this bit's a delight,' said Suki, bending back the spine. 'This is from the early years, before Deb's finished college. She's fallen in love with her best friend's father! He's only just widowed – and, you know, down in the dumps. *Down* in lots of other ways too.' Suki stifled her laughter.

When Sophie looked at her, miscomprehending, Hetty butted in, 'It means he can't keep it up.'

Sophie groaned.

'He's just a bit depressed,' said Suki. 'He hasn't had the touch of a woman in so long. And . . .'

'I can help you with that, Mr Forsyth,' said Deb, smiling demurely at Georgia's father as she sashayed silkily across the kitchen. 'My mam taught me how to cook. You have to tenderise the flesh first. Beat it around, with a mallet . . . or your fist.'

Soon Deb had taken over at the kitchen counter altogether. Steak was her favourite thing to cook.

'I don't trust a man who doesn't like red meat. You won't understand me, Mr Forsyth – nobody ever does! – but I've got an instinct. I've got an intuition.'

'Oh yes?' asked Mr Forsyth, running a finger behind his collar. 'And what's your instinct telling you now?'

Deb stood coquettishly at the counter, one finger playing with her full, red bottom lip.

'It's telling me there are other things that need tenderising instead of this meat . . .'

Deb had never ripped off a man's clothes before. Taken them off, yes. Helped him unbutton his shirt and roll down his trousers, innumerable times. But to *rip* a man's clothes off? That took passion. Soon, Mr Forsyth's work shirt, the same one his daughter had pressed and ironed eight hours ago, was in shreds on the kitchen floor, and Deb was wrapped around his hairy, naked body, just inside the pantry doors . . .

'Mr Forsyth,' she moaned.

'Call me Jeb,' he sighed. 'Call me your handsome stallion Jeb . . .'

Knuckles hammered on the camper-van window.

Suki started up from the book. There, looming in the window, was the face of her grandmother.

Suki's hands scrambled to hide *A Girl's Life*, as if she'd just been caught *in flagrante* with a decidedly dirty magazine. Then, flushing crimson red, she wound down the window. 'G-Grandma,' she stammered. 'You're back.'

'And running just a little late,' said Prudence, 'so let's hop to it.' She paused. 'Suki, you're looking quite green around the gizzards. Is everything OK?' Then her eyes drifted down. 'It's that silly book, isn't it?'

'We really need to talk about it, Grandma. I know it's silly and I know it's salacious – but you *have* to read chapters twenty and twenty-one.'

'You may precis them for me later, Suki. Right now, we've got fish and chips to cook. Girls, help us out with this hamper. Let's get in there before this night gets any wilder.'

More revellers were staggering down the seafront as the girls unearthed the hamper from the camper van's stores, then hurried after Prudence into the neon glow of the restaurant frontage. Ronnie Green had emerged from Pru's own camper and was already waiting for them at the doors; apparently vegan chilli hadn't quite satisfied his appetite, and he was eager for a cardboard tray full of scampi and scraps.

The music coming out of Topps Fish Mega Palace bordered on deafening. Prudence had never heard Gilbert O'Sullivan's 'Alone Again, Naturally' played at such inde-cent volume. She could hardly hear when Suki said, 'What about Carn Euny, Grandma? You got out of there alive, at least.'

'I told you, Suki: skinheads can be rather lovely little souls after all, even if there *was* an element of . . . kidnap about the whole thing. I'll tell you as soon as we're finished here. Just be ready with that notebook. I want you to catch every last word Barry Topps says.'

Through the doors of the palace they came, past the

213

gaudy obelisks and across a dance floor peopled with pleasure seekers whose stomachs were far too full of Spam fritter to be truly in the mood for dancing. Prudence fancied that the statue of Michaelangelo's *David* with its bright-pink saveloy was watching her as she took her place at the counter.

The man named Oggy Topps recognised her at once. 'We been wondering when you might come, Mrs Bulstrode,' he grimaced, still turning fish in his fryer.

'I told you we'd come,' Suki declared, with a pointed smile. 'Prudence Bulstrode never lets you down.'

'And I've got something rather special to show Barry,' said Prudence, tapping the top of the hamper Sophie and Hetty were holding. As for Ronnie Green, he had already put in an order for his scampi, adding on a nicely battered pineapple ring. A torrent of vinegar later, he was happily munching away. 'So where should we get set up? I'll only need a corner. Just a little surface to work on. If I get started now, Barry can be eating in twenty minutes time.'

'Well, that's the thing, Mrs Bulstrode,' said Oggy, leering over the counter at her. 'I'm afraid you're too late.'

'Too late?' Suki recoiled.

'Do you mean to say Mr Topps has already eaten?' asked Prudence, more levelly.

'Well, my old man wouldn't let that stop him. No, Mrs Bulstrode, what I mean to say is, he's already told it all. Already spilled his story. I'm not going to ask him to do it again. We've just been through all this rigmarole. You're a couple of hours too late.'

Prudence felt a strange emptiness yawning open inside

214

her. She'd had disappointments before. There were always presenting slots you missed out on, jobs you lost to other cooks, television shows you pitched for that never got picked up. But this was different. Almost an entire week had been spent submerged in batter and curry sauce. There were few things that stung a busy woman more than *wasted time*. 'The police?' she whispered.

'Take a look for yourself. Seems there's a few folks set on digging up the dirt on old Adam Scott.'

As one, Prudence and Suki turned around. There across the dance floor, through the writhing bodies (one of whom seemed to be ejecting his half-digested Spam fritters at the feet of his lover), they saw Barry Topps sitting in his throne-like chair at the edge of the restaurant floor. Two figures sat beside him, one perched on his right hand side, the other facing him across the table with a little Dictaphone in hand. On the table between them, plates had been scoured clean, leaving barely a trace of mushy pea: the sure sign of a meal much loved.

'Benji Huntington-Lagan,' Prudence breathed.

It was difficult to march across the dance floor, for bodies were twirling and hopping in every direction – but somehow she made it without stepping into anything too suspicious. It was only as she approached Barry's table that she slowed. She watched as, with a simpering smile, Benji flicked off the Dictaphone and clasped Barry Topps by the hand. 'You don't know how useful you've been, Mr Topps. Consider my recipe yours, for now and ever more.' Then, by clicking his fingers, he prompted Sonny to stand as well.

It was only as he moved to leave the restaurant floor

that he saw Prudence, standing beneath the disco ball's glittering light.

'Mrs Bulstrode. Fancy seeing you here. I didn't know you liked a dance on a Friday night. I'm afraid I can't join you. I've important work to be getting on with.'

'Benji, what are you doing here?'

For a moment, Benji seemed set on ignoring her. He swept Sonny along, and together they brushed past Prudence, marching straight into the heart of the dance floor and then out the other side. As Prudence followed, she was half-delighted to discover that, somewhere along the way, Benji had trampled in what was left of somebody's dinner. A thin trail of spammy batter dangled from his shoe.

'My sous-chef Sonny returned to the Bluff the other night with strange news, Mrs Bulstrode. It seemed that a challenge had been thrown down: that the fine, upstanding Mr Topps over there – and he *is* an upstanding gentleman, Prudence, no matter the shadows cast over his life – might recount the sorry events of fifty years ago, if somebody were to present him with a recipe to revolutionise his menu. Well, it seemed very clear that this was a job only *I* could do. And, well, suffice to say that crispy seaweed slaw will now be making its appearance on the menu of Topps Fish Mega Palace, along with my Pickled Pollock Platter.' He had already pocketed the Dictaphone. Now, he ripped the notebook out of Sonny's patiently waiting hands. 'I'm sorry, Prudence. I know how much you wanted to be at the heart of this particular story. Centre of attention, like you always are. But I'm rather tired of being upstaged by an old-fashioned Mrs Beeton.

You couldn't even let my restaurant be the star of the show. No, you had to make sure you were front and centre, and stealing all the glory. As it was in Uganda, so it was at the Bluff.' He paused. 'But not this time, Mrs Bulstrode. I've tried to show you – cookery is modern now. And so is policework. And, once I take my findings to Detective Rose, the *Tregurnow Times* won't want a thing to do with you. Do you hear?' He took a step nearer, then patted her on the shoulder with the air of a particularly presumptuous producer Prudence once knew. 'That headline's going to be mine, Mrs Bulstrode. You're not the only one whose intellect reaches further than the kitchen. *Benji Huntington-Lagan,*' he announced, as if reading an imaginary headline. '*Where Crime and Cookery Collide!*'

Prudence stood there, watching him as he strode back towards the seafront, bits of spam fritter still trailing from his shoe. Sonny soon scuttled after.

'We're not going to get that story out of Mr Topps, are we Grandma?' asked Suki, sadly.

'I'm afraid not,' said Prudence, still staring after the retreating chefs. Then, after a moment's contemplative silence, she came to life. 'So you'd better get out that book, my dear. We'd better start digging around *A Girl's Life*. This isn't about stardom, Suki. Boys like Benji Huntington-Lagan will never see that. They've grown up thinking that something only matters if it's got a hundred thousand little views and "likes" on their website. No, this isn't about glory. It never was. This is about a man who died, and a killer who never got found out.' Prudence turned. 'And there's one thing we have that Benji Huntington-Lagan doesn't.'

'What's that, Grandma?'

'The friendship of a gang of skinheads, Suki,' Prudence announced, 'and a little movement called Justice for Adam Scott.'

Chapter Eight

'SEX! LIES! HANKY PANKY IN THE STAFF-ROOM!'

Suki looked up from her copy of *A Girl's Life* and tried to detect any hint of embarrassment on her grandmother's face. A day had been lost in making egg custards – Prudence was determined to cover the ground they'd lost in a week-long ecstasy of haddock, hake and mushy peas – but now they sat together in Prudence's old dorm room, while Suki dared to spin out Dot Ellen's story. In this particular scene, Deb Elena – the book's heroine, now fully grown – had returned to the Cornish coast where she grew up (after a sensual sojourn in swinging sixties Soho) to take up a position as an English mistress at the school she once attended. But her reputation, forged in those swinging London nightspots, had followed her home.

Prudence's face did not show the hints of embarrassment Suki had been certain it would.

'Go on, Suki dear.'

Suki's own face had started purpling with embarrassment now. She flicked forward a few pages. 'This is the bit, Grandma. The rest of it . . . well, I suppose Dot Ellen was writing for a particular sort of audience. She wanted to . . .'

'Titillate, my dear?'

'Yes, Grandma,' said Suki, with her eyes buried in the book. *'Titillate.'*

'Well, go on,' said Prudence thoughtfully. 'What's this Deb Elena getting up to?' She sensed Suki's hesitation and added, 'I've seen rather a lot in my life, my dear. Whatever Dot Ellen dreamed up on those pages, I'm sure it won't shock me. Just treat it as anthropology.'

'It's more like a nature documentary, Grandma.'

'What do you mean?'

'Well, all this . . . huffing and puffing,' Suki groaned. Then, telling herself this was important, she shook herself and said, 'Listen, Grandma. Deb Elena's been around the block, right? But she wants to straighten herself out, so she takes a respectable job. No more dancing on tables or going topless in a Soho nightclub. No, she's reinvented herself as an English teacher, and she's taken a job at St Georgette's. So far, so . . . autobiographical, right?'

Prudence nodded. 'Publishing people will tell you that we all have a book in us. It's what lazy writers do – just cheaply cannibalise their own lives.'

'Hold that thought in mind, Grandma. Listen to this . . .'

And Suki began to read:

Sometimes, it just got so BORING, Deb could
hardly breathe. Sometimes, after classes had
finished, she longed for something, ANYTHING, to
lift her out of this prison she'd made. The prison
called RESPECTABILITY. Some nights, if the mood
took her, she'd take a bottle of wine up to her
room, put on an old record, and just dance – dance,

even though there was nobody to dance to. Deb liked listening to the old records. Bowie was all well and good, but what she really liked were the Animals, the Stones, the bands she used to dance to in London.

But sometimes, if dancing was not enough, she would look for other adventures. 'All I need's a little company,' she thought – and, one night, she found it. His name was Andrew Simpson, he was the new mathematics teacher – and, if he wasn't exactly Deb's usual type (he didn't exactly have the beefy forearms of Dirk, or a jungle of hair upon his chest like Gary), right now that hardly mattered. If he was a man, he was enough.

Flirting is a strange business. What on the surface seems to be a perfectly ordinary activity can take on a new level of meaning when attraction is in the air. When Deb went down to see Andrew Simpson at the school day's end, he was reading a mystery novel in his classroom. He didn't seem to want to go home. 'Fancy reading a bit to me?' Deb asked, and though it took Andrew a little time to oblige, that was all part of the dance of it. Deb liked that dance. It was a dance that didn't need music. All it needed was two willing participants, hot-footing around each other, until one of them realised what they were really dancing for . . .

Suki looked up. 'Well, it's obvious, isn't it, Grandma? Deb Elena? *Dot Ellen.* Andrew Simpson? That's got to be Adam Scott. She's writing her life, just like you said.'

Prudence mused on this. 'The less said about those Soho chapters, the better.'

'And that bit with her best friend's father!'

Prudence had filed that particular scene in the deepest, darkest part of her memory, where it might never resurface. 'You'd better read on, Suki.'

'I don't really want to, Grandma.'

And yet . . .

Andrew had been reading for some moments, his deep voice personifying each character in the story, when Deb decided she might scooch a little closer. *The Hound of the Baskervilles* was a perfectly gripping story, but that wasn't what gripped Deb. No, to Deb, Andrew's voice was like music – and music turned her *on* . . . Soon, she was drawing her chair near to Andrew's. Soon her hand, with its scarlet fingernails, was resting on his arm. Soon, after that, she had slipped it toward his collar, where she dared to touch the day-old stubble on his chin, to slip a single painted fingernail into the inside of his collar . . .

'There's more, Grandma, but . . .'

Prudence looked up, sharply. 'Oh, give it here, Suki.' Suki was only too pleased to hand over the book; what had seemed ribald and fun when reading with the girls had a distinctly different flavour when reading to her grandmother. As Prudence settled down with it, she looked up and said, 'Don't worry, dear. I'd have been a nervous wreck if I had to read something half as erotic to *my* grandmother. But then, *my* grandmother was born in

222

an era when they still considered it indecent not to cover up the chair legs, so it's rather a different thing.'

While Suki gathered her composure, Prudence returned to the novel.

No doubt Suki didn't want to read this because Deb Elena's hand hadn't just been playing with Andrew Simpson's collar. Soon, it was sliding up the inside of his leg and playing with a completely different part of his clothing altogether. Indeed, Prudence was fully expecting the play to continue without clothes, when suddenly Andrew Simpson jolted upwards, got out of his seat, lay down his copy of *The Hound of the Baskervilles* and said, 'I'm sorry, Deb. I truly am. You know I'm . . . I'm in love with another, Deb. I couldn't betray her, not like this.'

Now, at last, Prudence felt confident about reading out loud:

And Deb was soon careening directly out of the class-room, holding back her tears as she fled through the school's winding passageways, until at last she could fling herself on to her bed and stifle her sobbing with her face pressed into the pillow. Only minutes ago, she had been hungering for Andrew Simpson to be the one pressing her into that pillow. Now, she hated him. HATED him more than she could ever hate a man. In love with another? Still in love with his wife? Then why, pray tell, was he at the school after hours, EVERY SINGLE NIGHT? Well, to hell with him. He could stick with his vows, as joyless as they were. As for Deb, she was determined to conquer the very next man she met. She would show him the wildest, most wondrous night of his life. Andrew Simpson didn't know what he was missing.

Here, Prudence paused, and let the book fall shut. 'Well, that was *something*. What are you thinking, Suki?'

Suki was just glad it was over. 'I'm thinking it's tantamount to confession. Dot Ellen tried to seduce Adam Scott, right here at St Marianne's, but he turned her down.'

'Because he was still in love with his wife?' quizzed Pru. 'That hardly tallies with all we've learned.'

'It doesn't have to,' said Suki, and rushed back to the book. 'You see? Nowhere does he *say* he's in love with his wife. He just says he's in love and he can't betray her. So . . .'

Prudence nodded. 'He rejected her advances for somebody else, somebody who wasn't Elizabeth.' She paused. 'So Adam Scott really *did* have a secret, second life. You know, Detective Hall said that Mrs Arkwright talked about Dot Ellen a lot, when he went to see her. But if Dot's book is true . . .'

'Then it wasn't her.'

Prudence stood. '"A-Salt and Batter-y",' she said, softly.

'That's exactly what I was thinking, Grandma. It has to be connected, doesn't it? Adam Scott's having an affair, and then Barry Topps deep-fries his hand. So maybe . . . Did Barry Topps have a wife? Oggy's mother? Were Adam and she . . .' Suki stalled, for she didn't want to say the words – *doing it* – that had sprung to mind.

'I don't know,' said Prudence, ruefully, 'but Benji Huntington-Lagan clearly does.'

Suki had never considered her grandmother overly competitive before, but she saw something glinting in her eyes now – some element of ruthlessness, perhaps, that had always remained hidden. Perhaps you needed that streak to succeed in the world of television – but, if it was so, Prudence had done a good job at hiding it over the years.

'Well,' Prudence said, and turned to plump up her pillows, 'you can continue your bedtime reading in your own room, Suki dear. We've a big day ahead of us. Ice creams and sorbets in the morning. Meringues for the afternoon.' Then her face darkened. 'And, between those things, luncheon – though she doesn't know it yet – with the woman who was once Adam Scott's wife.'

By lunchtime the following day, Prudence was grateful to escape the kitchen. If children who gorged themselves on sugar could cause all sorts of mayhem, then teenagers who'd spent three hours taste-testing ice cream, sorbet and all manner of dessert sauces (chocolate, caramel, chocolate caramel) were even worse. Prudence had left them with the strict instruction to have some toast and butter – 'and lots of water!' – at lunchtime, but doubted very much whether she would return to an ordered classroom by the time the afternoon session came.

At least the sun was shining above Littlerock. The sea had shimmered like a daydream as she steered the camper van along the coast's winding road, and in the air the scent of cherry blossom from the town's central boulevard was sweet and strong.

Elizabeth and Mac Duggan lived on the headland just beyond the last of the townhouses, their seafront manor – commissioned by the newly united Franks & Scotts as a wedding gift, the ground broken on the day Elizabeth and Adam were wed – sitting in its acre of grounds at the end of a long driveway bordered by palms. Prudence left the camper van at the foot of the drive, then ambled the final hundred metres to the gate. If she was surprised to see a small delegation from the Carn Euny skinheads milling around here, their bikes pushed up on to the coast-road kerb, she tried not to show it. It would, perhaps, have been better if they hadn't come, for they were not exactly inconspicuous. It would certainly have been better if they might have left those placards at home. There was Pearl, proudly displaying her dragon tattoo and carrying aloft a sign that said SPEAK TRUTH TO POWER!, with a picture of a fish drawn inexpertly underneath it. Prudence decided not to waste any precious minutes working out what it might mean – and, besides, here came Peter, hurrying out of the bikers to meet her on the side of the road.

'Did they have to come?' asked Prudence. 'I thought this was meant to be a quiet affair. More espionage, less picket line.'

'Oh, they just want to show support,' Peter shrugged. 'You know, in case things go *south*.'

'South?'

'It's what they say in the movies. I suppose you'd say: in case things go *pear shaped*.'

226

This, at least, Prudence understood. 'It's just a luncheon,' she said, unloading the hamper from the camper van. 'If I can steer your grandmother back to Adam, I'll do it. But if I can't . . . sesame and tuna, fresh pea shoots and lime. I've a fresh seabass here, so I may even make a ceviche.'

By the look on his face, Peter didn't know what a ceviche was. 'Well, another vegan chilli wouldn't go amiss. That's why this lot have turned up, I reckon. A way of saying thank you. They're your honour guard now, Mrs Bulstrode. They'd follow you to the ends of the earth.'

Prudence squinted her eyes. 'For a vegan chilli?'

Peter shrugged. 'It won a few hearts.' After that, he started leading Prudence to the foot of the driveway. The grounds of the house lay behind six feet of sandstone walls, the drive protected by tall black gates – but these easily slid back when Peter tapped a passcode into the pad on the central pillar. Then he bustled Prudence through.

'I've been doing my own digging since we met,' he said. 'I know I should leave it alone. I know there'll be hell if I get found out, but . . . they were out yesterday afternoon, so I went for a recce. My grandmother keeps all her old trinkets in the armoire in the spare bedroom. The key's just on the hook, just inside the larder. So I went sifting through it, Mrs Bulstrode, and look what I found . . .'

Peter had led her into the shelter of one of the palm trees. The grounds here were lovingly tended, thought Prudence, though there was too much sand and chalk in the earth to make it much use as a kitchen garden.

Peter had produced a letter from his pocket, crumpled and yellowed with age. 'Seems my grandmother used to write to her cousin out in Orlando. Florry – I've never heard of her, but I don't suppose that's unusual. But look, just read it, Mrs Bulstrode. It's what Florry sent back.'

Prudence made doubly certain she wasn't in view of the house as she opened the envelope.

'It's this bit,' said Peter, eager to show her.

'Oh, sex is hardly all it's cracked up to be!' read the florid script.

You can hardly call time on a marriage because of s-e-x. There'd hardly be a marriage in the world if you did that! It's the other stuff that troubles me more. If Adam's intent on living a life that's nothing to do with the Company, then where does that leave you? The 'kept woman' of a man who's not interested in doing the keeping? A schoolteacher's wife? Is that enough? People make all sorts of pacts with themselves, Lizzy. But you've got to get SOMETHING out of it. If it isn't a bit of how's-your-father, then it had better be something else. To be Queen of the Company? Yes, I could see that. To be a mother? I could see that even more. But that just brings us back to the dreaded matter of the horizontal tango, and you're not doing much of that! Lizzy, are you sure Adam isn't a gentleman's gentleman, if you catch my meaning?

Prudence looked up.

'Might it make sense, Mrs Bulstrode?' Peter shrugged. 'Adam Scott was . . . gay?'

Prudence folded the letter, then slipped it back into Peter's hand. 'It would have brought a man of his standing some considerable shame to be gay back then,' she mused, carefully. 'Your generation don't have it like this, Peter – I'm glad to say – but in those days it wasn't nearly as straightforward to be different.' Suddenly, she was thinking of Barry Topps: the hand in the deep fat-frier, the secret that neither man dared give voice to in the trial that followed. An unsettling image of two men's eyes locking over the fish-and-chip counter popped into her mind. She had to shake it off as they continued up the garden path. 'Of course, Adam Scott was not what certain uncivilised people might call a *manly* man. But we've come a long way since then, Peter. I've never held any truck with the idea that, just because a man doesn't involve himself in *manly* pursuits, he might be gay. My Nicholas enjoyed his crosswords. He liked a scented candle. If you'd asked him the rules of football, he'd have laughed.' She paused. 'But Adam Scott . . .'

'He had to be killed for a reason, Mrs Bulstrode. Maybe there it is.'

They had arrived, at last, in front of the seafront manor: a broad, palatial house built from white stone, with vines running up its trellises, the greatest care and attention put into making it look pristine against the blue expanse of the sea beyond.

Prudence looked down. Peter's hand was hovering, ready to knock, but suddenly he had frozen.

'Don't be afraid, Peter,' said Prudence. 'I promise you, I won't let our secret slide. It's just luncheon. It's just your birthday gift to her.'

'That's what I'm afraid of,' whispered Peter. 'She's bound to know something's wrong.' He knocked on the door and feebly looked up. 'Normally, I just get her a book voucher.'

Prudence was not sure what she was expecting, but this was not it: when the door opened up, there appeared a sprightly young woman, with an olive complexion and wearing a maidservant's uniform that looked as if it had come straight from the set of some expensive Dickens adaptation. Her eyes glimmered as she took in Peter. 'No school today, young man?' she said, with the wryest of smiles.

'You know I don't do school, Sandra,' Peter shrugged. Then he looked at Prudence. 'I flunked all my GCSEs. They're not worth the paper they're written on.'

'Well,' said the woman named Sandra, 'they're not written on *any* paper, because you didn't do them. But little rich boys like you never think they have to work hard.' She paused. 'Can I help you, Peter?'

'Grandma's in, is she?'

Sandra nodded.

'Then you'd better lead on, Sandra. I've got her birthday present right here.'

Sandra, who Prudence now took as Elizabeth Duggan's housekeeper, seemed to roll her shoulders in a shrug as she turned and led them into the building. 'Don't worry, Mrs Bulstrode,' Peter whispered. 'It's me they're down on, not you. They think I'm a waste of space. But what did a bunch of GCSEs ever get a person?'

Prudence decided not to answer that; there were some conversational cul-de-sacs it wasn't worth wandering around. Besides, she was more interested in looking around this palatial house. Prudence had never been short of money in her life – work had been very good to her in that regard – but her instincts never extended to splashing it around. All she had ever wanted was a nice little home with, perhaps, an extensive kitchen garden, but she had met plenty of people in her line of work who liked to wear the money they earned like gaudy jewellery around their necks. So it was with Elizabeth Duggan. Fine portraiture hung from the walls; fresh cut flowers stood in every vase; the mirror in the hallway was edged in silver, and everywhere smelt of riches lavishly spent.

'One moment, please,' said Sandra, leaving them at the foot of a grand, sweeping staircase and slipping through a great oak door.

'Just wait until you see your kitchen, Mrs Bulstrode. Last time I saw you make dinner was over a fire! But this is like something out of the space age.'

She'd seen quite enough of that up at the Bluff, thought Prudence, and waited until the door opened again.

Standing in its frame was a tall, lithe woman with silvery hair. To look at Elizabeth Duggan, you would not have thought she was nearly eighty years old – but, Prudence reflected, money could buy you a lot of things, not just expensive pottery and houses overlooking the sea. What lines Elizabeth wore were faded, the crow's feet around her eyes banished by some surgical procedure to make her seem little more than middle-aged. She was wearing a delicate cashmere cardigan, and slick trousers that shimmered and rustled like chiffon. At her wrist, a collection of silver bangles jangled.

Sandra was lurking somewhere behind, like the faithful maidservant that she was – but it was Elizabeth who looked them up and down. 'Peter,' she said, 'I have to say this is somewhat unexpected. The last time you were in my house, you rather made a scene. All that talk of "taxing the rich" and "reparations to the working class". I thought I made it clear: you were not to come back into this house without an apology. And I've not received a word from you.'

Prudence tried not to scowl as she looked sidelong at Peter. It seemed, then, that Peter had not been *entirely* honest in his efforts to get her here.

'Well, Grandma,' Peter said, shuffling from foot to foot; it was curious how cowed he had suddenly become under his grandmother's withering eye, 'that's kind of why I'm here. I didn't want to let your birthday go, and I know I'm late in writing you that letter. I *have* tried – and, honestly Grandma, I'd drunk far too much apple cider that day, and I didn't know how to take it – but I just couldn't find the words. But ...' He looked at Prudence. 'Maybe I can do better than words.'

For the first time, Elizabeth seemed to take in the woman standing at her grandson's side. It took her several moments to process what she was seeing – her eyes, apparently, were a little more aged than the rest of her face. 'Mrs ... Bulstrode?' she queried.

'It's your birthday present,' Peter said, opening his arms wide, 'and your apology all in one! *Ta-da!*'

*   *   *

The kitchen was just as Peter had described it. It even looked as if it had been constructed by the same company who fitted out the Bluff.

Prudence didn't mind; at least it didn't come with a side order of the preening Benji Huntington-Lagan. She tried not to think of him as she worked through the ingredients in her hamper, preparing the light seaside luncheon she'd devised the night before – but it was difficult not to keep coming back to his self-satisfied look as he strode, proud as a peacock, out of Topps Fish Mega Palace the other evening. A little piece of Prudence (one she wouldn't *ever* admit out loud to existing) was fascinated with the idea of what he might have made to sate Barry Topps's insatiable taste for fish and chips. Perhaps Topps was the sort of man who was easily pleased – but, from everything Suki had said, he didn't seem the sort who would be won over by one of Benji's flamboyant creations. As Prudence arranged the dish on the plate in front of her, she fancied he would *much* rather eat this.

Fish and chips had been on the mind so much this week, so fish and chips it was. Instead of battered cod or haddock, Prudence had prepared a seared tuna steak, accompanied by a delicate potato latke of shredded potato, shallot and matzo meal, a pea-shoot salad (the elegant lady's replacement for mushy peas) and chilli jam. It certainly looked bright and summery. By the time Prudence waltzed out to the dining room with it, to find Elizabeth poring over her stocks and shares on a laptop computer, she was pleased with how it had turned out.

At least, now that a half hour had passed, Elizabeth seemed more accepting of the situation. It helped that

Peter had made himself scarce. After that, her instinctive politeness took over – and, some time after that she appeared to have become genuinely curious at the idea of Prudence Bulstrode in her house. Elizabeth Duggan seemed less easily impressed than some did at the appearance of a celebrity chef; Prudence could only assume she'd crossed paths with many famous people in her time – those with money often did – but now she looked up from her laptop with something approaching delight.

'Well, it *looks* delightful. It *smells* delightful.' Elizabeth picked up her silver knife and fork, their ivory handles denoting them as antiques from a bygone time. 'The question, Mrs Bulstrode, is: does it *taste* delightful?'

'I've paired it with a rosé from the Loire Valley,' said Prudence, pouring a glass. 'Would you mind, perhaps, if I joined you?'

Elizabeth had already cut into her tuna. She was inspecting it like a head chef interrogating the work of her underlings – and, upon finding it satisfactory, popped it into her mouth. 'I know I shouldn't be surprised, but it's cooked to perfection, Mrs Bulstrode.' She gestured for Prudence to sit. 'Please, have a glass. I'm sure my birthday gift isn't simply a seared tuna steak. It's an *experience*, is it not? I have to say, Mrs Bulstrode, I'm a little long in the tooth to be changing the way I do business. At Franks & Scotts, it's about weight, first and foremost: the weight of the catch each morning. But I do understand that things move on. The younger generation put so much emphasis on buying an *experience*.'

Prudence wasn't sure that she liked the idea of anyone thinking of her as an 'experience', but for now it served her purposes, so she sat opposite Elizabeth, poured a small glass of wine and took in its bouquet. 'I'm more knowledgeable on tea than I am wine, but a good rosé does make you dream of summer. I expect today is a little unusual for you, Mrs Duggan?'

'I must admit, it's rather an unusual thing for Peter to do, to arrange something like this. I'm sure you've picked up on it, Mrs Bulstrode, but Peter is a teenage boy who has . . . some issues. Yes, that's what this generation would say. It would have been different in ours! But Peter has his complications, and my family has tolerated them for some time. Indulged them, no less. No son of mine would have been gifted a motorcycle just to keep him busy. No son of mine would have an *allowance*. He'd have been sent off to work instead – out on the boats, if it came to it.'

'I had girls,' said Prudence, 'but I'm given to understand *all* teenage boys have complications of one kind or another.'

'Well, he's not cut from the same cloth as the rest of this family, that's for certain. If he was . . .' Elizabeth let her fork clatter to the plate. 'I'm sure you know this, Mrs Bulstrode, but Peter has chosen the worst possible moment for something as light-hearted and joyful as this. Perhaps he thought it would be a balm to me. I must say, I've been in need of a distraction.' She made a steeple of her fingers. 'You do know, don't you, Mrs Bulstrode?'

'Know, Elizabeth?'

'About my former husband, Adam.'

There it was. Prudence was actually rather glad it was out in the open, for there could be no denying it. 'I'm teaching a summer school over at St Marianne's. I'm so sorry, Mrs Duggan. I can't imagine the pressure you're under.'

'It has been quite considerable,' said Elizabeth primly.

'You won't remember me, but Mr Scott was actually *my* teacher for some time. I remember him fondly, Mrs Duggan. All of us St Marianne's girls do. It's a terrible thing that happened to your family.'

'More terrible than suicide, Mrs Bulstrode?'

Prudence hadn't been expecting that question. Nor had she given it much thought. What was a woman supposed to prefer: that her husband took his own life, or that somebody else did? Those sorts of questions were for the philosophers. Most weeks, Prudence preferred to think about cheesecakes. But when murder reared its ugly head, it somehow swamped all other thoughts.

'Death is always terrible, Mrs Duggan. I've had more than my share of it in my time. But no,' Prudence went on, 'I was rather thinking about the lie of it all – that Mr Scott went out to sea and . . .' She feigned not being able to finish the question, tried to judge by the look on Elizabeth's face how she was taking to this particular pivot in the conversation. 'My heart goes out to you, Mrs Duggan. It must be like having the carpet ripped from underneath your feet.'

Elizabeth took a pause in eating the tuna steak. 'Well, Mrs Bulstrode, since we're so quickly on to the subject, I'll say it straight: my life was already a lie. Everything to do with poor Adam was a lie, and there's no secret about that. Since Adam, I took a vow that I'd live my life in openness and honesty.'

Prudence furrowed her eyes. 'I'm not sure what you mean.'

'Oh, *please*, Mrs Bulstrode. If you were a student at that school, you knew all the rumours. It's fifty years ago – there's no need to play coy about it. Adam and I weren't in love. Married, yes, but lovers very rarely, and *in love*, never at all. Oh, I found it mortifying at the time. But I was twenty-two years old and I believed in fate. All young women do. I was reared on it. And then I was married and my husband . . . didn't want to be a husband to me. No,' said Elizabeth, upon seeing Prudence's pained expression, 'don't look wounded. I haven't been wounded for half a century. I think I even came to *understand* it by the end. Adam didn't want to be with me. He didn't want empire, or leadership – or even, I think, to be a Scott. He didn't belong among them, rugged men of the sea that they were. *Real* men.'

Prudence tried not to let her irritation show. *Real* men: soldiers and sailors, bruisers and brawlers, men who drank fifteen pints on a Saturday night, then went fighting at the local car park. She thought of Nicholas and how grateful she was he hadn't been like that.

Elizabeth sighed. 'For years I'd thought it was *that* feeling that made Adam take his own life. That it wasn't just me and our marriage. But now . . .'

'Now?'

'Well, now he *didn't* take his life, and a whole lifetime of thinking needs to be unpicked. None of it changes what happened. None of it makes it so that Adam hasn't been gone all this time. But you find yourself a bit at sea, Mrs Bulstrode, if you'll pardon the expression.'

'It just seems so monstrous,' she said, 'so calculated, so planned. To stage a suicide like that – it wasn't done on a whim. I suppose the police have asked you all the obvious questions.'

Elizabeth rolled her eyes. *'Can you think of anyone who would want Adam dead?'* she said, parroting back what the police had said.

'And?'

'And, Mrs Bulstrode?'

'And . . . *could* you?'

Elizabeth seemed to smart at this question. 'I thought I'd been bought a nice, distracting luncheon, Mrs Bulstrode – not another interrogation.'

'Forgive me, Mrs Duggan.' Prudence stood. 'I've a lime tart in the kitchen. Just the thing to cleanse the palate after a fish dish.'

She was pottering back towards the kitchen door when Elizabeth said, 'I'm quite aware of how it all looks, Mrs Bulstrode. *I'm* the one who had the most to gain by Adam's death. It set me free of that sham of a marriage. It allowed me to marry again, and to keep majority control of the company. I didn't lose anything in the long run – nothing except my husband, and what husband was he to me? But it's like I've already told the police: I was staying with my parents on the day Adam set out to sea; my diary shows it, and so does my father's. And Detective Rose has been very clear – it would have been near impossible for me to stage Adam's suicide. Somebody had to be posing as him that morning, and that could *never* have been me.' She flicked back her silvery hair. 'I was grey, even back then. The most distinctive hair on this part of the coast. Nobody could mistake me for my husband.'

Prudence passed through the kitchen doorway and hurried to the refrigerator where her crisp lime tart was waiting, already dusted in confectioner's sugar. She'd prodded Elizabeth too quickly, stirred her up when she had no need. It was time to slow the conversation down, and this lime tart would do just perfectly for that.

As she walked back through the door and presented the tart, she said, 'I read a little piece about Barry Topps, from that gaudy fish-and-chip place down on the seafront. They say he's the one who attacked Adam. He already had a grievance with Mr Scott . . .'

'It had entered my mind as well,' said Elizabeth, steely. 'Topps is an odious man. The sort of man who'd happily deep-fry a customer's hand. But is he brave enough to *murder*? Did he have the *intellect* to accomplish something like this? I highly doubt it.'

'And yet . . .' Prudence held up her hand, then folded up her little finger, as if to make it disappear. 'He had enough barbarism in him, didn't he? And enough about him that, even on the stand, he refused to explain . . .'

'I, for one, never needed him to explain,' said Elizabeth. 'Barry Topps is a schemer. I'll admit he's possessed of a kind of feral intellect, but that's all. I believe he told the police he had a moment of drunken madness – he'd been partaking a little too much of the beer he used to make his batter – but I'd long known how much he hated Adam. Barry Topps, you see, once fancied himself a suitor of mine. This was before Adam, of course. You might think of the Topps as the third great fishing family around Penzance – only, instead of catching it, they slather it in batter and serve it up. They had a string of little places, once upon a time, all the way from Penzance round to Sennen Cove. Then Barry came along and opened his *Mega Palace*.' Those two words could not have been laced with more revulsion if the greatest actor in the world had tried. 'He thought he was the emperor of all he surveyed. The King of Fish and Chips. And . . . I suppose you'll think me vain to say it, he wanted *my* hand in marriage.'

This, Prudence was not expecting. In a flash, she had hoisted up the bottle of wine and topped up their glasses, inviting Elizabeth to go on.

'I daresay he had some basic attraction to me, but it wasn't about that. Barry Topps was after his own kind of empire. I suppose he'd caught wind that Adam and I were circling a marriage proposal, and it got his little mind thinking. His father came to see mine. What about a different kind of merger? they mooted. Not two fishing families coming together – rather, a kind of vertical merger, fishing and fish and chips. One company to catch the fish, fillet the fish, then batter the fish. I think my father was even interested, for a little time. No doubt he strung the Topps along – that would be my father's way – but ultimately . . .'

'Barry Topps was let down. And he held a grudge against Adam ever since.'

'I'm conjecturing, of course. Topps kept his mouth shut, and so did Adam. I no more know what happened that day than those scurrilous journalists at the *Tregurnow Times*. "A-Salt and Batter-y". Yes, I imagine some greasy little oik got a nice bonus for that particular headline. It's stuck in the memory long enough to deserve it.'

'They say he was released from prison only a few days before Adam vanished.'

Elizabeth had taken her first taste of the lime tart. Her expression was suddenly trapped somewhere between ecstasy (because Prudence's lime tart was just that good), and distaste, for at last she seemed to have grown weary of Prudence's questions.

'I was a woman alone, Mrs Bulstrode. Pregnant, no less, with the child I felt certain would have transformed my marriage. Topps came sniffing around again, of course. He fancied that, even after everything that had happened, there was still a chance we could work together. I sent the man packing, and I never saw him again. A weaker woman would have fallen straight into a man's arms. I, however, did not.'

'But you did get remarried, Mrs Duggan?'

Elizabeth shifted. 'Have you, Mrs Bulstrode?'

'Me?'

'You were widowed, just like me. I read the puff pieces in the newspaper. Have you ever thought of remarrying?'

Prudence said, 'I'm at a very different stage of my life. I rather think I'm done with romance.'

'Well, there's the difference. You're done with romance – but me? I hadn't even *started*. Adam rejected me on my wedding night and kept on rejecting me ever since. It's a wonder I fell pregnant at all. But Mac was there for me, when I needed him. He became my anchor. A fitting tribute, for a seafaring family, but there it is

– Mac was my rock, my life jacket, my lifeboat. I fell in love with him then, and I've been in love ever since. Do you know a man who would willingly raise another man's child as his own? That takes something very special, Prudence. But I've heard all the rumours, all the hearsay. I suppose they all think we did away with Adam so we could set up home on our own, but it just wasn't the way. I *wanted* my marriage to work. I couldn't bear being a woman who couldn't keep her man happy. I couldn't bear being responsible for the companies and the merger. It all fell down to me and my body, you understand. If I could give Adam the baby everyone wanted, everything would have been fine.' She paused, shaking her head ruefully. 'And, do you know, I think it *would* have been fine. It was time that was against us. Only a couple of days would have changed everything. But Adam was gone and I couldn't stop being sick – and I didn't realise, until a little while had passed, that it wasn't because I was sick with worry; it was the baby I was carrying inside me, and if Adam had only lived a little longer, he would have known all about it – and we would have gone on, me and him, not in love, but as good, solid partners, raising our family. He would have been a good father.'

'You must forgive me, Mrs Duggan, it must seem very much like I'm prying. But if you and Adam were not . . .'

'Having sex?'

Prudence nodded.

'Well, there were *moments*. I rather thought Adam was taking his appetites elsewhere, but on occasion he

242

would . . . do it for England, as they say. Do it for Franks & Scotts.' She stopped. 'Lord, it all sounds so archaic. So unnecessary in the modern world. Our grandchildren aren't shackled like we were – although I sometimes wonder if Peter wouldn't be better off if someone frog-marched him down to the recruitment office and made a soldier of him.'

'It can't have been easy, to be treated like that.'

'Like a princess, to be married off.'

'Like a commodity, to be traded.'

Elizabeth carefully finished the last of her lime tart, delicately dabbed the corner of her lips with the napkin, and said, 'Well, Mrs Bulstrode, it didn't feel very good as a naive young girl. But now? Now, as a seventy-nine-year-old woman who's lived her life in luxury, who's overseen empire on this part of the coast for more than half her life? From this vantage, Mrs Bulstrode, I might say that there are worse things in the world than being used by your family.' Suddenly, Prudence heard the front door opening and closing, Sandra making some muted hello, the heavy tread of footprints in the corridor outside. 'And I got to be happy in the end,' Elizabeth went on, as the door opened up, revealing her husband Mac.

The first thing Prudence realised was how similar he seemed to Adam Scott: the same lean, wiry physique; the same rolling gait as he walked. Of course, fifty years separated the two – and Mac Duggan had evidently embraced cosmetic surgery a good deal less than his wife. His face was covered in tight black curls, his sleeves rolled up to reveal the very same anchor tattoo that Prudence remembered Adam Scott sporting. The man froze upon seeing Prudence, then looked bewildered at his wife.

'Darling, this is Prudence Bulstrode,' said Elizabeth, rising to her feet to plant two kisses in the air about her husband's cheeks. 'We used to like watching you on your adventures, Pru.'

Mac Duggan loped over, his feet making a heavy tread, and considered Pru like a particularly knotted piece of rigging, before shaking her hand. He smelt, thought Prudence, of salt and Old Spice. 'But what the devil are you doing here, Mrs Bulstrode?' he said, in a half-accusing tone. 'Of all the places to be, you're sitting right here in my diner. The mind boggles.'

Prudence smiled. Yes, she thought, it might be useful to speak with Mac as well – though it was not what Peter had planned. If there was any other person to shed light on the unusual circumstances of this union, it had to be Mac himself. 'Believe it or not, I'm Peter's birthday present for your wife. Peter's birthday present and his . . .'

Prudence had been about to say 'apology', but Elizabeth's face darkened and, curling her arm around Mac's shoulders, she fixed Prudence with a glare. '*Spy*,' she said.

Prudence blanched.

'Oh yes, Mrs Bulstrode,' said Elizabeth, 'I know what you're about.' And, turning to the sideboard against the wall behind her, she drew up a copy of last week's *Tregurnow Times*: Prudence's fateful luncheon in the Bluff, with Poppy and Detective Rose. 'Helping the police with their enquiries, I can understand. A student at the school, with first-hand knowledge of my first husband

– that much makes sense. But to start *snooping* around on behalf of my grandson, and his pack of dropouts? Mrs Bulstrode, I thought you would be better than that.'

Prudence stood. She had seen the bristling look in Elizabeth's eyes, but it was nothing compared to the sense of righteousness rising in Mac. In that moment, she knew what kind of man he was. Leave alone the fact he looked as meek and civil as Adam Scott had; underneath that surface stood a man of steel. A *real man*, Prudence thought.

'Mr and Mrs Duggan, I just came to make lunch.'

'And delightful it was,' said Elizabeth haughtily. 'I was pleased to eat it, and now I'll be pleased if you would leave. Your hamper is in the kitchen. You may fetch it now.'

Slowly, not wanting to turn her back on the married duo, Prudence inched towards the kitchen door. Then, with the hamper in hand, she backed more hastily towards the hallway.

By now, Elizabeth had let go of Mac and followed her. 'You may take this back to my grandson, Mrs Bulstrode. I neither care for his apologies, nor for the theories of his little crowd. I'm not a Luddite; I know what they're up to. Justice for Adam Scott. Well, they're barking up the wrong tree. I should like justice as well. You forget that this is *my* country, Mrs Bulstrode, and I know the detail of everything going on between Land's End and Kennack Sands. If Adam's killer is still out there, I want them found and brought to justice. But you can be sure: back then, I had much to lose in Adam dying. My world came crashing down when he vanished. The company would have split, if fate hadn't sent me the child. No, Mrs Bulstrode, as unhappy as I was, it was in my best interests to keep my sham of a marriage alive – you can bet your bottom dollar on that.'

Prudence could hardly look at the skinheads as she hurried out of the manor and through the black gates at the bottom of the drive. 'Just keep your head down,' she told Peter when he cantered up to her on the way back to the camper. 'Stay out at Carn Euny. Do whatever you must. But your grandmother knows about your move-ment. She's cannier than you take her for.'

'But is she a killer, Mrs Bulstrode?' Peter breathed, with mounting panic.

'I don't know,' admitted Prudence – but, all the way back to St Marianne's, the thought was playing in her mind: if Elizabeth Duggan doesn't have the capacity to kill, then Mac Duggan surely does . . .

The domestic science classroom was, at least, less sticky than it had been when she left. There was much less chocolate sauce underfoot – and the marshmallow she'd shown the girls how to make was not liberally coating every doorknob, drawer handle and micro-wave as it had been when she left. Suki must have marshalled the girls well, but when Prudence reap-peared in front of the class, she was nowhere to be found.

'Meringues,' Prudence announced, still trying to shake off the unnerving sensation of Mac Duggan's eyes boring into hers. If there was anything to lighten the mood, it would be meringues. 'To my mind, there is nothing more simple and divine than the best homemade meringue. One of those brittle little nests you might have bought at the supermarket is all well and good – and it will certainly do in a hurry – but by the end of the afternoon, you'll be eating Eton Mess with your own crunchy, chewy clouds of goodness, and you'll never look back.' She looked down. *Pru's Dessert Storm* was lying open on the counter, but on a whim she declared, 'Let's ignore the books, for now. The book can come later. Girls, we're going rogue . . .'

The girls looked thrilled at this, and Prudence would have launched them straight into their first lesson in correctly whipping up egg whites, if only the class-room door hadn't opened and Suki scuttled in. Prudence shook her head wryly, and gestured for her to hurry up.

'Grandma,' Suki said, 'can we have a quick word?'

It was only now that Prudence saw the grave look on Suki's face. It was only then that she saw the way she was gripping the iPhone in her hands, with knuckles strained so much they had turned bone white. No doubt it was that Numbers fellow, blitzing through some more information. Or perhaps it was *A Girl's Life*, some dark secret buried in one of the chapters. 'Suki,' she whispered, 'can it wait?'

But Suki mouthed 'no' almost before Prudence had finished, so in moments they were standing just outside the classroom doors, while the students patiently waited.

'That was Detective Rose,' she said softly. 'She's been trying to get you all morning. I told her you didn't have a phone but . . .'

Prudence rolled her eyes. 'But what did she want, Suki?'

Suki took a breath. 'Mrs Arkwright, your old head-teacher? The one you went to see up at Cherry Garth last week?'

'Yes, Suki?'

'She's dead, Grandma.'

Prudence fell silent. Every death comes as a shock, even those who have been waiting on God for far too long.

'They found her this morning, Grandma, just dead in her sleep. Peaceful, they say – but the thing is, she'd asked for you last night. They were in the common room at the home and they had the TV on, one of the foodie channels, and there you were. *Pru's Aussie Walkabout*, I think it was. You in the outback, eating witchetty grubs and making up koala burgers . . .'

'Kangaroo,' Prudence interjected. She would never eat a koala.

' . . . And it got Mrs Arkwright talking. It was the last thing she said, Grandma. "I want to see little Prudence Cartwright straight away!"' Suki fell silent. 'They wanted to let you know. There's going to be a funeral in a few days, and a wake. There won't be too many there – Mrs Arkwright didn't have many people – so they wondered if you might go.'

Prudence wasn't sure why the thought moved her so much. She let it settle over her, lingering on the idea that Mrs Arkwright was, in some way, proud of what her old student had accomplished – and then touched Suki tenderly on the shoulder. 'There's too much death,' she said, 'but perhaps Mrs Arkwright's at peace now. Old age, Suki, is not for the faint of heart.' Then she turned back to the classroom. 'Meringues,' she said, 'and strawberries and cream. Just the thing to lift the heart on a day like this . . .'

Then she marched back through, leading Suki with her.

And all afternoon, as she whisked and beat together egg whites and sugar, she couldn't stop thinking about that look on Mac Duggan's face, the tattoo on his arm, and the oddly familiar, rolling gait that put her in mind so much of Adam Scott.

Chapter Nine

'I'm sorry to do this to you, Pru. I know it's been quite a couple of weeks already – too many distractions to go round. And I'm *well* aware of how little time there is between now and our end-of-course feast. Not that you've made it any easier for us, of course, with all this showboating with the local constabulary.'

At the end of another long day, lost in a dozen different kinds of pastry, Prudence had found herself summoned to the staffroom again. At least, this time, she had come prepared. The girls had spent the afternoon making Prudence's spinach and shallot tartlets, topped with a chestnut crumb, and she had brought a little Tupperware filled with them for the staff to try. As Ronnie Green and Miss Down tucked in, however, Mrs Carruthers just paced up and down.

'I wanted this summer to go off without a hitch, but these things are sent to try us – and Mrs Arkwright was a part of the St Marianne's community for twenty-nine years, so she is something of a little legend in these halls. It's for that reason that I've agreed you should cater for the wake, Mrs Bulstrode.'

It was times like these that Prudence wished she had an agent again. An agent would have backed Mrs Carruthers into a corner and told her, 'My client was hired for a job, not to scurry around after you.' Now, however, she could only sigh and paint on a smile. The frustrating thing was that, if anyone had cared to *ask*, Prudence would have been more than happy to have helped cater the wake. She had enough fondness for her schooldays, even for the old tyrant Arkwright, to do that. It was the fact that Mrs Carruthers had offered up her services as if she was bonded labour that really rankled.

'My girls are in the thick of preparing their menus for the feast, Mrs Carruthers. I mustn't leave them for too long.'

'Incorporate it into your lessons, dear Pru. You could be rustling up vol-au-vents while the girls are focusing on their own endeavours. These little tartlets would do a treat.' Mrs Carruthers had gravitated to the Tupperware and popped one whole into her mouth. As she spoke, shortcrust pastry showered down. 'The problem is, this school's reputation is being put through the wringer. A teacher, one of our own, was murdered and buried right here on our premises. The absolute cheek of it! The parents are up in arms. I've received seventeen emails asking us to update our policies on safeguarding and premises security – as if "murder" wasn't already against the school rules. So we really must be doing something to show we're an upright, proud part of this community – that we honour our own, that we're a force for good. Ergo,' and Mrs Carruthers popped another tartlet into her mouth, 'we'll be sending a contingent to the funeral, then the wake – where *your* delicacies will be the star of the show.' She smiled. 'Keep up the good work, Pru, and

251

let's not allow some Cornish pasties with soggy bottoms to tarnish the school's reputation even further.'

At least, now that the end-of-course banquet was in sight, the girls were preoccupied with preparing their menus, rehearsing each course, working under their own steam in the kitchen while Pru filled trays with miniature pasties, tartlets and a collection of other hors d'oeuvres she'd perfected over the years. Some of these she'd have to prepare in the morning, then deliver to the pub where the wake was being held, but others she could work on in advance. Soon, she was surrounded by mountains of Tupperware containing tartlets, Parmesan tuiles, salmon summer rolls – and a hundred little fairy cakes, each delicately topped with a swirl of azure icing. It was meant to represent the sea over which Mrs Arkwright had gazed for all of her life, but Pru rather felt as if the meaning would be lost somewhere between the plate and the mouth.

She had dismissed the girls for the day, and was looking forward to an evening kneading yet more pastry, sautéing diced onion, swede and chuck steak, when she realised that Sophie, Hetty and a trio of the other girls hadn't yet retired. 'We thought we could help you, Mrs Bulstrode,' said Hetty – and, at that moment, the classroom door opened up, revealing Hetty's grandmother Poppy, already in her apron. 'Looking for an assistant, Mrs Bulstrode?'

Prudence had marshalled busier kitchens in her time, but the next hours were spent in pleasant companionship, as the tins and Tupperware filled up with enough to feed an army. What was left over could go back to the

Cherry Garth, for Miss Jubber and her fellow residents to pick at.

In fact, the only person in the kitchen who seemed distracted at all was Suki. When she looked up from her pan of bubbling chuck steak and swede, Prudence saw her staring into her iPhone with the same intensity as the rest of the girls were flaking smoked trout for the vol-au-vent cases.

'It's the *Tregurnow Times*,' said Suki, when Prudence marched over, ready to drag Suki back into the fray. 'Look – Numbers dug it out of the archive . . .'

It was hard enough to see the iPhone screen at the best of times, and with her glasses still fogged up from the chuck steak, it was harder still. As ever, it was the girls who came to the rescue. Inside moments, the article Numbers had buzzed over was being projected on to the whiteboard at the head of the classroom.

The date was September 1976, just a handful of days after Adam Scott vanished.

The headline: CORNWALL GATHERS TO MOURN ITS FINEST.

And there, underneath the big, bold letters, was a portrait of Elizabeth Duggan, then Scott, with Adam's elderly parents at her side.

An open service is to be held at Chywoone Churchyard in memory of Adam Scott, faithful husband, brother and son, with a wake hosted at the home of Adam's widow Elizabeth. Adam Scott, heir to the Penzance Scotts fishing dynasty, married his childhood sweetheart Elizabeth Franks in April 1969, and his sudden death has sent shockwaves around the community. Although his family initially asked for privacy while they come to terms with the event, the Franks & Scotts recognise that the loss of their leading light will be keenly felt up and down the coastline, and mourners are invited to both the service and the wake that follows.

Adam Scott was a proud family man, who had spent the most recent part of his career teaching mathematics at St Marianne's School for Girls, where he was a liked and well-respected tutor. 'His plan was always to come back to the family firm,' said Adam's father Glynn, 'and it is a cause of much heartache to us all that he will never sit at the head of our Board, as had always been his ambition. Adam was a dear son, a dedicated family man, and we will carry his loss with us until the end of our days.'

Elizabeth Scott said, 'It's hard to believe that the man I knew since we were children, the man I always knew I was going to marry, is gone – and that all our lives are irrevocably changed. It is even harder to accept in light of the fact that, in March, I am due to give birth to our first child – and that Adam will never get the chance to be the father he always dreamed of becoming.'

The family have asked that well-wishers refrain from laying flowers, but welcome contributions to the local lifeboat service, and the Charitable Commission for Retired Seamen, Penzance.

Mourners are politely requested to leave dogs at home when attending the service and wake.

*   *   *

The kitchen had come to a standstill while they devoured the article. A strange sadness settled across them – for here they were, preparing the hors d'oeuvres for another wake, fifty years later.

Death, it seemed, was the only constant in life.

Poppy Balloon had turned white as a ghost as she read the article. Now, she buried herself in the chuck steak again, and started gently spooning it into the pastry shells Prudence had arranged.

'It just doubles the tragedy,' she said, wiping away a salty tear. 'That a child should grow up without a parent, and all because of . . .'

All because of murder, thought Prudence. This much was true. But she couldn't help thinking, as she stared at the article, that she was missing some vital piece of the puzzle. She couldn't help thinking that the answer to all of this was staring her in the face, somehow, that it had been in front of her all along. The article, of course, was filled with bluster and rot: Adam Scott, the faithful husband; Adam Scott, indulging his love of teaching for a few years before scuttling back to the family firm. But was there another lie here too? Elizabeth's pregnancy, conveniently announced in the wake of her husband's death?

In the corner of her eye, she realised what Poppy was doing.

'That mixture's too hot, Poppy,' she called out. 'Those pasties will end up with soggy bottoms!' And she hurried over to rescue what she could of the dish. 'Miss Jubber would have had you sitting in detention for much less,' she said grinning. Then she pulled Poppy close. She didn't quite know why, but Mrs Arkwright's death seemed to be touching her more than most. Perhaps it was the inevitable realisation of how close they, too, were to the end. 'PVC forever, remember?' Prudence whispered.

'PVC forever,' answered Poppy.

By 10 a.m. the following morning – with the girls back at the kitchen, running through their dishes while Suki timed them, for the banquet was but two days away – Prudence had parked the camper van up on the roadside at St Austin, and was picking her way up the long, winding driveway to the Cherry Garth Retirement Home.

At least the sun was out. A funeral bathed in buttery light felt different, somehow, to one cloaked in the wintry dark. Even so, it was difficult to keep other funerals from your mind when you approached a fresh one; Prudence hadn't known Mrs Arkwright since her schooldays, but the idea that she'd been asking for her only hours before her death preyed on her, somehow, as she approached the home. Perhaps it was only that it brought back thoughts of Nicholas, and that saddest day back in Chelwood Ghyll. She realised, now, that she hadn't attended a funeral since Nicholas. There came a time of life when funerals were a common occurrence – just as weddings and Christenings used to be – but since Nicholas, there had been none, as if the big death of her life had somehow put an end to all of the rest.

She wished Nicholas was with her now. A puzzle like Adam Scott, the impossibility of that suicide letter – now, *that* was something Nicholas would have enjoyed unpicking.

Daisy Lane was waiting for her in the reception hall, dressed entirely in black. At least, today, she seemed more forgiving of Pru's presence than she had when she stumbled upon her rustling up a pasta sauce in the kitchens. 'It's a dreadful business, Mrs Bulstrode, but all too common in this line of work. Strange, but it's always a shock. We spend our weeks anticipating these things, putting our plans in place, keeping the waiting list moving, but then, when it comes, it always catches you out.'

Prudence thought she understood that. Death came as a surprise, whether you were just starting out in life or yourself knocking on heaven's door.

They picked their way across the Cherry Garth common room, where a platoon of old dears were variously watching daytime television or staring at their magazines, and into the residential halls beyond. Daisy Lane seemed to look purposefully the other way as they passed the kitchens (could she *really* still be bridling at Prudence's rule breaking?), but soon they were passing the doorway that had once belonged to Mrs Arkwright. Miss Jubber's room lay just ahead.

Prudence paused in the doorway. She supposed it was inevitable, but the room had already been cleared. How sad it looked, stripped bare of what few things Mrs Arkwright had. At the foot of the naked bed stood a single cardboard box, and into this had been piled all the trinkets she'd had with her at the end. On top of them all lay a single book, perhaps the one she'd been reading on the night she slipped away.

'I found her when I came on shift,' said Daisy Lane, with sadness. 'I was on rota to get Mrs Arkwright up for breakfasting. She never took much – some tea, lots of honey, sometimes a little porridge. They don't eat much as they get close to the end. The body decides it's done with all that. But she'd been a little livelier the day before. She ate a few mango pieces – called it foreign muck, of course. "What's wrong with a good old gooseberry?" she cackled. But she had a bit of life about her, you know?' Daisy Lane paused. 'That happens too. They have a little flourish in their last days. I like to think it's life's way of saying: so long, and thanks for all the memories.'

Prudence had dared to potter a little further into the room. It was the smell of disinfectant that made her the saddest: a life spritzed away by lemon-scented bleach.

She bowed down to the box, the last remnants of Mrs Arkwright's life. 'Detective Rose said she asked for me, that final night. One of my shows was on the TV in the lounge?'

She reached out to touch the book on top of the box. In gold lettering, across the front, read the words *The Collected Sherlock Holmes*.

Something stuttered inside Prudence's thoughts . . .

'Your shows are regulars out there in the lounge, and more so since you came to visit Miss Jubber,' said Daisy Lane.

Prudence looked back, brandishing the book. 'Was it one of her favourites? A comfort read, perhaps?' She'd shouted out Sherlock's name when Detective Hall came here; perhaps it had tickled her to be visited by a real detective. If she was a mystery reader, it might have made sense.

'Oh, I believe she ordered it up from the library in Littlerock. We do a trip out there once a week. A few of the oldies come – those that don't get too worn out by the travel. Mrs Arkwright couldn't make it that far, of course, but she sometimes put in requests.' Daisy took the book from Prudence's hands. 'It'll have to go back, before it gets carted off with the rest of this stuff. Well, come on, Mrs Bulstrode. We mustn't keep God waiting.'

Before they set out, of course, there was Miss Jubber to collect. When Prudence and Daisy reached her room, she too was dressed in black, already sitting in her wheel-chair, thumbing through an old album of photographs on her lap.

She looked up, with eyes already shimmery and wet. 'I know it's silly. Gertie and I never really saw eye to eye. But when someone's gone . . .'

Prudence went to her, and lay a hand on her shoulder. There it lay, among wisps of silver hair. 'Your parents?' she said, looking down at the album.

'Losing Gertie just feels like losing another bit of the old times, I suppose. It made me think of them.' Miss Jubber stared, lovingly, into a black-and-white portrait of her parents – a wedding-day portrait, saw Prudence, because there they were, decked out in their wedding-day finery, clasping hands and beaming into the camera. The big diamond wedding ring on her mother's finger sparkled madly in the flash of the camera light. Prudence lingered on it, feeling that same strange frisson she'd felt upon seeing the book in Mrs Arkwright's room. All these tokens of former lives – it was enough to make one weep. 'It just makes you think of endings, I suppose. They're buried in the same churchyard. It's been years since I visited. That's got me feeling so guilty as well. I used to go every Sunday, rain or shine. Then it was every month. Then just birthdays and their anniversary. And then . . .' Softly, she fingered the picture, running her fingertip around her mother's smiling face, then down her flowing white dress, across that diamond sparkling on her finger. 'Do you think of your parents often, Prudence?'

There was no right answer. All Prudence could say was, 'I think they stay with us, everyone we ever loved.'

Moments later, Miss Jubber closed the photograph album, laid it respectfully back on her bedside dresser, and dabbed at the corner of her eyes with her sleeve. Then she looked up. It seemed to Prudence that she had said the right thing, for Miss Jubber suddenly had a fresh conviction about her, a new readiness to face the day. 'I like to think they do,' she said, and clasped Prudence's hand.

It took some time to get Miss Jubber into the camper van, her wheelchair secured in the back while Daisy Lane took the passenger seat up front. Several taxis had been laid on for other residents of the Cherry Garth, but the last of them had already left by the time Prudence fired up the engine and steered PRU BU 1 out of the grounds. Consequently, by the time they arrived at the church, there were precious few seats left – and Prudence, Miss Jubber and Daisy had to find a corner at the rear of the congregation, obscured by one of the church's ancient, weathered pillars.

The delegation from St Marianne's was close to the front of the hall, alongside several mourners in charcoal grey. Prudence took these to be Mrs Arkwright's surviving family. Sometimes, at a funeral, there was an air of celebration; sometimes, a sense of release. Today, Prudence didn't know how to feel. As the vicar began to speak to the congregation, telling them in broad brushstrokes the story of Gertrude Arkwright's life, she gazed around and couldn't help thinking of the memorial service held here almost fifty years ago: fisherfolk and local well-wishers coming from every direction, all to pay their respects to Adam Scott, lost at sea. What a different occasion that must have been, loaded with tragedy, loaded with deceit – and all of it orchestrated by lies. At least there was no underhandedness underpinning today's event: just the long, ordinary sadness that came at the end of every life, no less tragic for that, but comforting in its normality.

There was Detective Hall, sitting in the middle of the mourners. Prudence was glad to see that he'd made the visit. Apart from Poppy, he had, perhaps, been the last visitor Mrs Arkwright ever had. No sooner had Prudence had that thought, she had a stab of guilt that she hadn't personally made the trip.

At the front of the church, the vicar had stepped aside. Now, from the front row, Miss Down was on her feet. Prudence watched as she crossed the transept and climbed the steps to the lectern at which the vicar had, moments ago, been standing.

'My name,' she began, 'is Verity Down, and I am proud to have been asked by Gertrude's family to share a few thoughts and recollections with you today. As many of you know, I am the longest-serving member of staff to remain at St Marianne's School for Girls. When I began my tenure there, our beloved Gertrude had already been in place as headmistress for some years – and it will not surprise anyone here when I tell you, my friends, that I was *terrified* of her.' Prudence listened to the muted titters rising and falling across the church; it seemed there was something in this sentiment that many people recognised about old Gertie Arkwright. At her side, Miss Jubber's face twitched in a smile, but she had started dabbing at the tears in the corner of her eyes as well. 'But what started out as fear quickly became respect, and what had become respect teetered, on occasion, dangerously close to love. St Marianne's was not quite my first job in a school, but it was the first where I observed what leadership was truly about. Mrs Arkwright had once studied Philosophy at Oxford University, and I believe it informed her thinking for the rest of her life. She was firm but fair, authoritative but kind, just but never afraid to mete out a punishment when one was needed – not only to our students, but to our staff as well. Nowadays, leadership is so often about "friendship" and being on affable, colloquial terms with those you're trying to lead. Mrs Arkwright knew differently: she knew that she was the leader, and that to lead properly she must set herself apart. It gave her great insight. I have often thought of Gertrude Arkwright in

the years since she took me on board, and when I
bring her to mind, it is this that I focus on: her calm-
ness in the face of pressure; the tact and diplomacy
with which she handled disagreements between our
students, and in our staffroom itself. A boarding
school can be a strange kind of place. It can be rife
with drama, gossip, innuendo. When those things go
unchecked, the fallout can feel seismic – but Mrs
Arkwright knew how to keep her school in perfect
balance. She was a master of tact. She looked upon us
all, not as her staff, but as people – with private lives
of our own that needed protecting. She never pried,
she never interrogated, she didn't spy or keep tabs –
but I believe she had insight enough to know precisely
what was going on in her school, whether good or
bad. I don't believe it is wrong to say that she had a
PhD in *People*. In this, I believe she was a woman
before her time.'

Miss Down left the lectern to a smattering of applause
and gentle here-heres, and soon one of Mrs Arkwright's
children – themselves as old as Prudence – was taking her
place, to deliver a eulogy freighted with emotion. But
there was something in Miss Down's last words that
preoccupied Prudence, so that she scarcely heard what
was being said next. 'I believe she had insight enough to
know precisely what was going on in her school, whether
good or bad.' Yes, Prudence, Poppy, Vivienne and Colette
had thought the same, once upon a time. 'Old Arky
knows *everything*,' they would often bemoan.

But there she lay, in the coffin at the head of the
church, and whatever she knew was now gone, gone like

all the memories she cherished, the loves and hates and passions of a lifetime.

That same coffin was soon being hoisted aloft by Mrs Arkwright's pall bearers. Two of them seemed to have come courtesy of the funeral directors, but the other two belonged to Mrs Arkwright's family: the son who had delivered his eulogy, and an elderly man whose grimace betrayed the discomfort he felt at bearing his beloved sister to the grave.

Out the congregation filed, into a churchyard dappled by sunshine. Under the trees they came, through the rolling dell of graves, that long, rambling library where all the finished stories went to rest. Somewhere here, thought Prudence, lay the stone laid in memoriam to Adam Scott. Perhaps she would come back and seek it out, wondering at the crowd who had gathered to hear the eulogies in his name, trying to picture them, to wonder if his true killer had stood there among them.

Somewhere up ahead, the coffin had been borne to the graveside. Now, the mourners drew closer, forming their huddle around the plot where the mortal remains of Gertrude Arkwright would forever lie. Daisy Lane was somewhere up there, having joined the head of the procession as the Cherry Garth's lieutenant – and that left just Prudence and Miss Jubber at the very end of the procession, lagging somewhere behind the other residents who had been taxied out from the home.

'My mother and father are here as well,' said Miss Jubber sadly. She looked exhausted, thought Prudence; the solemnity of the occasion had overwhelmed her.

'Prudence, would you think it terrible of me if I asked you to . . .' They had reached a meeting of trails between the graves, and now Miss Jubber directed her along the left-hand trail. Fifty yards along the right lay the hummock where Mrs Arkwright was to be buried. 'It's just been so long. I can feel them near.'

Prudence touched her on the shoulder, then strained with the wheelchair to change its course. 'Miss Jubber, of course,' she said, and helped the wheelchair along, down the incline, around a cherry tree surrounded by stone tablets and the statues of miniature cherubim standing sentry over the dead.

The foliage was so different to the last time she'd been here, but still Miss Jubber knew the way. Soon they were standing above the twin graves of Holly and Everett Jubber. Prudence was heartbroken to see they had died within but a few days of each other – a terrible time for Agatha, no doubt, but perhaps some consolation to a couple who had treasured each other throughout the entirety of their lives.

'Miss Jubber,' she ventured, 'are you all right?'

A facile question, she knew, but the silence was worse. Agatha Jubber took some moments to compose her reply. Then she said, 'It's hard to be the last one standing. I think, perhaps, I might feel as if my life was worth something if I'd given the family a new generation . . . it's an empty feeling to know you're last, and that nobody comes after.' She reached out to trace her mother's name upon the gravestone. 'I did want to give them grandchildren. They would have been the greatest grandparents in all of Cornwall – but I let them down in that. I think that's why I always lived with them, right up until the bitter end. To leave to raise a family of my own would have been well and good – but, when that didn't happen, I resolved to look after them until the end of their days.' She permitted herself a small smile. 'I suppose I could have moved out. I could have taken digs at the school, like Dot Ellen and all of the rest, but I didn't like leaving them, you see?'

There was a moment of silence. Prudence knew she oughtn't to ask, but still she said, 'There used to be a rumour at school, Miss Jubber. They said you'd been left at the altar, once upon a time.'

Agatha shook her head ruefully. 'Yes, but *that* was a lucky escape. Arthur Mann ended up doing hard time for embezzling money from the paper merchants his brother ran. I'd have been married to a convict. Can you imagine the shame?' This time, she really did laugh. 'My parents warned me about him!' Then the laughter faded and she returned her eyes to the grave. 'It's funny how things work out. I've had a happy life, Pru, really I have – but you do get your regrets, as you come to the end. I hope they're somewhere up there, waiting for me. I hope, when I finally see them, they'll be proud.'

'Oh, Miss Jubber,' said Prudence, moved almost to tears, 'how could they not be?' There was so much more that she wanted to say. It was the funeral that brought it out of her. Just like Miss Jubber looking back through those photographs, Prudence had spent the service brooding on the loves and deaths of her own life. There was still so much she wanted to say to Nicholas – just the banal, ordinary stuff of love and life, but it hurt that it would forever remain unsaid. There and then she decided that nothing would remain unsaid in this moment, that she would say all she wanted to say. 'Miss Jubber, thank you.'

'Thank you, Pru?'

'I wanted to say it, fully and properly, and from the bottom of my heart. My life wouldn't have been the same without domestic science. My life wouldn't have been as rich and fulfilling and filled with experience, if you hadn't shown me the right way to hold a whisk.'

Miss Jubber smiled. 'You were holding it too stiffly, I remember, treating it like a cane for whipping with.'

'You were the best teacher I could have hoped for. You made me see who I was, and what I might be.' She bowed down. 'Miss Jubber, you mightn't have had children of your own, but you had all of *us*, and you had *me*, and your influence on my life? Well, it just couldn't be counted.'

At Mrs Arkwright's graveside, the mourners were starting to cast down handfuls of earth. As Prudence finally wheeled Miss Jubber near, she heard the old teacher softly singing, 'Ashes to ashes, dust to dust, if the kids don't get you, the teachers must.'

Miss Jubber smiled again at that. 'We used to say that all of the time. I learned it in teacher training college. Gosh, it became our litany!'

But when it came her own turn to scatter the earth, Miss Jubber couldn't bring herself to do it. Prudence had to cup another handful in her palm and cast it down on her old teacher's behalf.

*   *   *

267

The Headland & Hope (Est. 1889) sat alone, halfway on the road between Littlerock and St Austin.

Daisy Lane said this had been Mrs Arkwright's favourite pub, and as they approached, Prudence had to admit that she could see its appeal. If it looked a little worse for wear, that was only because it had stood proudly on this headland for more than a century – a home for fishermen, smugglers and locals who liked to stop in for a pint glass full of cockles and a glass of the best Cornish cider. 'Oh, we came here for a staff outing once!' Miss Jubber exclaimed as the camper van drew up among all the other mourners in the car park outside. 'I had a punnet of prawns. I never knew that prawns came in punnets.' Yes, thought Prudence as they followed the rest of the mourners through the narrow doors, this was the kind of place Cornwall should be known for. It was about as far away from the space-age cleanliness of the Bluff as Land's End from John o' Groats.

The publican had dedicated the entirety of the pub to the wake, all except the back room where a few of his regular punters were idling over baskets of crispy whitebait. Pru had to admit that Mrs Carruthers had done an estimable job of dressing the place. The hampers of food that Prudence had dropped off were arrayed around the edges of the bar, and the wall was festooned with innumerable old school photographs that Miss Down had excavated from the archive. Prudence would enjoy poring over them a little later, but first there were drinks to be poured, pasties to hand around, stories to share and speeches to hear.

It was Mrs Carruthers who got things going. Soon after

the last mourners arrived, she levered her way on top of a stool at the bar, and hushed the crowd with her most headteacherly voice. 'We at St Marianne's are proud to play our part in sending our dear Gertie on her way. They say that we are, none of us, truly dead until the last person on earth whose life we touched, who holds us in memory, is gone as well. And if it is so, then we who are teachers will last the longest time – for the lives we have touched are so many, and the memory of us spreads out like ripples across this earth. So, ladies and gentlemen, enjoy the vol-au-vents, the salmon rolls, these little . . .' she squinted, oddly, ' . . . bruschetta toastie-type things. They come from my heart, to yours.'

Prudence looked down at Miss Jubber. The elder woman had reached up to squeeze her hand. 'I think they all know whose heart they come from, Pru.'

As Mrs Carruthers stepped down from the stool, the publican at the bar – a man of some significantly hirsute appearance – called out, 'First round's on us. We're ready and waiting.' Soon, the mourners were raising their glasses; soon, the plates around the bar were being depleted. Miss Jubber herself took a tartlet in her lap – 'It's like heaven, Pru, after the slop they serve at the Cherry Garth.' When Mrs Arkwright's family came to thank Prudence for coming to the service – 'She often spoke about you, you know. She was so proud that you'd come through her halls!' – Prudence started to feel as if her return to St Marianne's had in some way been pre-ordained. Pru was no big believer in Fate (Nicholas had been a man for the mystical, but never Pru), but she felt a strange belonging here, today. It helped that Poppy kept plying her with sweet apple cider. 'I'm sure *we* came up here too, Pru. The whole of PVC! But it must have been on a night when the teachers were tucked up in bed.'

It was, perhaps, an hour later when Prudence heard the tinkling of a teaspoon against a wine glass, and the inhabitants of the bar all turned to see Mrs Arkwright's son stepping up on to the stool Mrs Carruthers had some time ago vacated. A man of wrinkled appearance, he kneaded his flat cap in his hands and said, in a throaty voice, 'We've had all the eulogies, but perhaps it's time for a toast. My mother was many things. A wonderful headmistress, a devoted mother, an expert seamstress, believe it or not! Too often it felt as if she wasn't quite with us these past few years, and my family and I have had to come to terms with that. But if there's one thing my mother embodied to us all, it was . . .'

The door of the Headland & Hope flew open.

A heavy tread, a peremptory cough, a slammed door announced some new presence in the pub.

Prudence turned – and there stood Benji Huntington-Lagan, his simpering sous-chef Sonny at his side.

By the bar, Mrs Arkwright's son had stuttered into silence. The eyes of the pub no longer on him, he too turned his attention to the newcomer. 'I'm sorry, sir. This is a private function. Perhaps you might . . .'

'I'm truly sorry to interrupt,' Benji began, 'but I'm afraid this can't wait.'

'Can't wait?' somebody ventured. 'What the devil do you mean?'

'This is a wake, Mr Huntington-Lagan,' said one of the

mourners, evidently familiar with the Bluff. 'I think you've come to the wrong place.'

'I'm afraid not,' said Benji, and cut a swathe through the mourners as he reached the bar, shuffling Mrs Arkwright's son off the stool with a steely look, then stepping on top of it himself. 'I am, of course, monumentally sorry for the loss you're all suffering – and I shall make it all up to you momentarily, with an open invitation to my restaurant to continue your reminiscing about fine, upstanding Mrs . . .'

'Arkwright,' Sonny mouthed, from across the bar.

' . . . Arkwright,' Benji concluded. 'But I'm afraid it is my sad duty to inform you that one among you should not be standing where they are this moment. One among you is a cuckoo in the nest, a charlatan, a fraud – and it my sad duty to conclude the dirty business that has been despoiling this part of the coast for some forty-eight years. Sonny, the door if you will.'

At the back of the bar, Sonny opened the door again, and in stepped a figure who was suddenly familiar to Prudence. Yes, she'd seen that face before – the photographer who'd been at the Bluff on the day she took lunch with Detective Rose, the one who'd documented their meeting for the *Tregurnow Times*.

'I'm sorry, my friends, but one among you is a killer. They got away with it for half a lifetime and more – but that all ends today.'

A camera started flashing. Up on the stool, Benji Huntington-Lagan struck an heroic pose.

Prudence started forward. 'Really, Benji, this isn't the place. Come down from there.'

Benji held up a hand. 'I must be permitted the floor, Mrs Bulstrode. This isn't *Chefs Go Ape*. This time, I have to be heard. Truth and justice matter.' Benji took a deep breath, careful to launch back into his speech before Prudence could intervene any further. 'You see, ladies and gentlemen, the discovery of Adam Scott's body in the grounds of St Marianne's felt very personal to me. My father fished in the same waters over which Franks & Scotts ruled – and the idea that one of my father's old fishing folk was murdered, his killing covered up, has not left me alone for these past weeks. Since that moment, I have done all that I could to further the police investigation. Yes, yes,' and he took a deep breath again, as if the responsibility had been too much to bear, as if he was a king whose crown weighed too heavily upon his head, 'I realised very early on that I must do all I could – a man like me with local knowledge, a personal connection to the case, a man who has, all his career, learned to look at things *sideways*, to reinvent the old, to cast old favourites in new light. A man like that *had* to be able to help. And so it has proven to be.'

Prudence rolled her eyes. 'Benjamin,' she said suddenly, in her own headteacherly voice. She'd heard him waffling on like this before – God, wasn't that why the producers had cut so much of his screen time down on *Chefs Go Ape*? 'If you've something to say, Benji, get down from that stool and . . .'

'The key to this all,' Benji went on, not acknowledging Prudence, 'lies in an old newspaper headline.' With a flourish, he produced a yellowing old copy of the *Tregurnow Times* – and, upon unfurling it, revealed the

272

headline A-SALT AND BATTER-Y to the room. 'We have been taught, across the last decades, to think of Adam Scott as a saint. It is very human, is it not, to make saints of the dead.' Prudence smarted again; to speak like this at a funeral was surely unconscionable! 'Well, *somebody* knew better of Adam Scott. *Somebody* had seen straight through his mask of saintliness, and in the end was put in a prison cell for the simple fact that they knew the truth. Yes, Barry Topps – the finest purveyor of fish and chips in this fine county of Cornwall – never did reveal to the world why he battered and deep-fat-fried Adam Scott's hand. He wouldn't breathe a word of it on the stand, and he didn't breathe a word of it across the many years that follow. But, ladies and gentlemen, he's told his story at last – and what a sorry picture it paints.

'Topps Mega Fish Palace. An institution in these parts. But it was so much more than a fish-and-chip shop. So much more than a restaurant, a disco, a swinging seaside nightspot. It was, ladies and gentlemen, a centre of local gossip. Yes, Barry Topps knew *everything* about his customers. And when certain students from St Marianne's wandered into his fish-and-chip shop, one day back in 1975, he learned his juiciest bit of gossip yet: Mr Adam Scott, scion of the Franks & Scotts union, runaway mathematics teacher at the girls' school up the road, was having an extra-marital affair.'

Prudence bristled. This was hardly a revelation. Everyone knew the Scotts' marriage was in trouble. Dot Ellen had virtually chronicled a confession of the affair in that bonkbuster of hers.

'Well, some days after that, Adam himself popped into the Palace for his usual Spam-fritter sandwich. Barry took one look at his smarmy face and decided that the time was right: he simply had to confront the scoundrel. Yes, there was jealousy flowing through him – for Barry had once held a torch for Adam's wife Elizabeth – but it was the righteousness and grace in the heart of a fish-and-chip man that truly compelled him. But Adam Scott, of course, had no honour. What men who keep mistresses do? When he flat-out denied what he was doing, Barry lost his self-control. He reached across the counter, took Adam's hand . . . and plunged it into the deep fat fryer!'

There were audible gasps across the room. Mrs Arkwright's son, bewildered by this sudden turn of events, suddenly scowled – and looked set on brushing Benji bodily out of the way.

'Well, Barry knew he was done for then. Scott had to be taken to hospital in Penzance, and soon it was the police turning up at Topps Fish Mega Palace – and not for their usual order of scampi and curry sauce. Topps was arrested, charged with causing grievous bodily harm, and knew he faced a tough trial when the day came.' Benji paused, clearly enjoying the moment. Once again, the cameras started to flash. 'But Barry Topps didn't explain his actions to the police. Nor did he explain his actions in court when the moment came. The mystery of why Barry Topps kept his own counsel was used, in the gutter press of the time, to suggest it was simply the act of an uncouth vandal, a hooligan, a bully. But the truth could not be different. I can, this moment, reveal that Barry chose to keep his own counsel because, some time before the case came to court, he entered into a pact. A pact with none other than Glynn Scott, Adam's own father. Glynn Scott had spent his life organising the union of the Penzance Scotts and Franks Fisheries. His son had already near scuppered the deal, running off to teach mathematics – but Glynn knew that, if Adam's faithlessness was exposed to the world, the union would crumble, and his life's work would come undone. So Glynn did the only thing he could think of to preserve the peace: he paid Barry Topps to keep his silence, a handsome sum that would keep Topps Fish Mega Palace ticking over while Barry was in prison, that would provide for Barry's son Oggy, and set the business up for expansion once Barry was released. Yes, ladies and gentlemen, it was a corrupt payment from the Scotts that financed Michaelangelo's *David Carrying His Saveloy*. And, until but a few days ago, Barry Topps never told a soul.

'Topps was in prison, Adam's secret concealed. Now, an ultimatum was presented to the philandering cad: "Son," said Glynn Scott, "there are more important things in life than that thing in your trousers. Sex, son, will lead this family to damnation. You are to stop your philandering ways. You are to make your marriage succeed. You are, Adam, to FALL IN LINE!"'

Benji clapped his hands suddenly together. At Prudence's side, Miss Jubber shuddered and shut her eyes.

'Adam knew his father was right,' Benji went on. 'He had almost destroyed it all. For months, he agonised over the right thing to do, and for months his father made it clear: Adam's life was not his own. So, one fateful night in August 1976, he invited his lover to the secret love nest they kept in the grounds of St Marianne's – one of the old air-raid shelters, forbidden to students, on the site where the hockey fields used to be. There, he told them that their love could go no further. It had to end.

'And yet ... love is not so easily curtailed. Adam's lover was distraught. She could no more stand the thought of ending their affair than imagine the sky caving in. She begged him. She beseeched him. She threw herself at his feet. And when none of that worked, she could take it no longer. The old air-raid shelter was littered with pieces of shattered brick. She took one in her hand ...' Benji snatched the jar of pickled eggs from the bar and thrust it aloft, like Cain about to dash Abel's brains out with a stone. All around the bar, the mourners turned away, shocked, exasperated, appalled. 'And smashed it down, snuffing out Adam's life in a second.' Then Benji's eyes roamed the crowd, until at last they had picked out the one person he knew to be guilty. 'Didn't you, Poppy?' he cried out.

In the bar, there was silence. Not a voice was heard, only the shuffling of feet as dozens of pairs of eyes turned to take in the aghast features of Mrs Poppy Balloon.

Prudence looked at Poppy. Her face was etched in incredulity, but moments later that rigid mask started to change. Perplexity turned to panic before Pru's eyes. She stammered out a few words, 'What the ... what are you ... what on earth ...', before Benji went on.

His eyes were fixed on her with an implacable

intensity. 'It was you, Poppy, who was in Topps Fish Mega Palace that night. *You*, Poppy, whose gossip was overheard by Barry Topps. *You* who let on that Adam Scott was having an affair. Oh, it took Barry a little while to realise it was you yourself who was Adam's mistress – and this was too much for a man of good character to stand. Yes, more might have changed with the times, but it has always been the case that a teacher abusing their power over a student is wrong, wrong, WRONG! How could Barry let such a thing go on, now that he knew?'

'You don't know what you're s-saying!' Poppy stammered. She looked frantically around her, seeking anyone who would help.

'I think we can assume what happened next, can't we, Poppy? You met Adam in the air-raid shelter, thinking that this was going to be a fun, sexy time for you. But then – heartbreak! – Adam ended the affair for good. You pleaded with him. You begged. Perhaps you even threatened to expose him as the bastard he was, if he didn't do as you pleased. But Adam had been warned off twice now – first by Barry Topps and a deep fat fryer, and secondly by his own father. He would not be swayed, and the next thing he knew, the rock was in your hand . . .' Benji shook his head, sorrowfully. 'A charitable man would call it manslaughter, a crime of passion – but, Poppy, the law would call it murder.'

Upon saying the word 'law', Benji inclined his head to Sonny, who immediately turned and opened the pub door once again. The timing of the moment was not perfect, for the police car had only just arrived at the

277

roadside and Detective Bryher Rose – evidently summoned by a call placed just before Benji so brazenly marched into the room – was only just stepping out of the car. Not for the first time, Prudence seethed: this had all been orchestrated so that Benji got the maximum level of attention.

As Detective Bryher Rose reached the door, Benji declared, 'You can take her away, Detective,' with the same mock disgust he'd once had when a particularly truculent mountain gorilla refused to eat his bamboo-shoot salad.

Poppy scrambled backwards, but the crowd was tight around her, parting only when the detective came through. Her desperate, darting eyes returned to Benji as she said, 'You're making a mistake. That isn't how it happened. You can't honestly think *I* did all that. I was seventeen years old. Prudence, tell them, I was seventeen years old!'

Detective Rose strode through the last of the mourners, brandishing a set of handcuffs as she drew close to Poppy. 'I'm sorry, Ms Balloon,' the good detective began, 'but I'm going to have to ask you to come with me.'

In the Headland & Hope, the photographer's camera started flashing again. By tomorrow morning, those pictures would be all over the front page of the *Tregurnow Times*. Long before that, they would be proliferating across the internet. In each of them, Poppy's tortured face turned towards Prudence in horror, Benji Huntington-Lagan standing defiantly on the stool at the bar, the twisted faces of a dozen flabbergasted mourners uncertain where to look, what to do, how to feel.

'Prudence,' Poppy called out as the detective took her away. 'Prudence, it wasn't me! Tell them – it wasn't me!'

The camera flashed again.

That picture, with Poppy being dragged backward through the crowd, Benji Huntington-Lagan hanging imperiously above, would be the most iconic image of all.

By evening, it dominated the front page of the *Tregurnow Times*'s website.

And on top of it, the big, bold headline: CRIME CONNOIS-SEUR CRACKS THE CASE!

Chapter Ten

Sleep did not come to Prudence Bulstrode. Long past the midnight hour, she prowled the dormitory window at St Marianne's, gazing down upon the earthworks of the hockey field and marvelling that, once upon a time, forty-eight years in the past, Adam Scott's head had been staved in by a stone in the air-raid shelter out there – and that her friend Poppy was now locked in a police cell, charged with the murderous crime.

By the time morning came, the girls already assembled in the domestic science classroom, Prudence knew what she must do. No doubt Mrs Carruthers would tell her that only a single day, less than thirty hours, separated them from the moment when the service bell would ring and the families would gather in the dining hall to taste the fruits of their daughters' labours – and, of course, she was correct – but some things simply could not wait. Before she issued the girls their instructions for this, their final day of proper tuition, she marched into the classroom, fixed her eyes solely on Hetty – who, to her credit, had still turned up for class – and beckoned her near.

While the other girls were prepping their workstations for the day's 'dress rehearsal', Prudence led Hetty just outside the classroom doors and lay a hand on each of her shoulders.

'Listen to me, girl,' she said, firmly but not unkindly. That was the way Miss Jubber would have spoken to her, thought Prudence; that was the thing which would have given her strength. 'Your grandmother was a wild young woman. Out of all of us, she was the hellraiser. If somebody showed her a rule, she knew by instinct how to break it. She loved a drink. Believe it or not, she liked a cheeky smoke. She was talented at skipping lessons, and she was the one behind every scheme we ever concocted to get off the school grounds and go carousing in one of the towns. She was *trouble*.' But now Prudence smiled, and brushed the hair out of the startled Hetty's eyes. 'But the one thing she was not, Hetty, is a murderess.'

Only upon hearing this did Hetty find her voice. 'What's going to happen, Mrs Bulstrode?'

Sometimes, there were times in life when you had to give voice to a thing you did not quite believe. Only by saying it did you find the courage to make it true. 'You're going to go back through there,' said Prudence, 'and cook like you've never cooked before – and tomorrow, when your family comes down to take part in the feast, it won't just be your mother and father eating your halibut and mushy-pea-encrusted croquettes, it'll be your grandmother too.' Prudence paused. 'I'm bringing her home, Hetty. I don't quite know how, but I'm bringing her home.'

Suki would have to oversee the girls today. After all, she'd had enough practice this week. As Prudence steered the camper van on to the coast road, then watched the glittering seascape rushing past as she headed into the east, she made a mental note to reward her grand-daughter somehow. 'Suki,' she would say, 'you're the one who kept this show afloat. It's time for a *promotion*.' Quite what that promotion would be, Prudence did not know. Executive Kitchen Assistant had a nice ring to it, but – like many of the promotions she'd seen eager young people snapping up in the media world, back in the day – ultimately it meant nothing.

It took her some time to locate the police station in central Penzance. No doubt Suki could have guided her here more ably with that iPhone chirping in her lap, but Prudence had grown up with Ordnance Survey and AA roadmaps, and she didn't mean to change her ways just yet. In the end, it was the protestors who led her to the station door. She'd been circling the area too long, growing increasingly frustrated at the hours and minutes rushing by, when she heard the dull chanting through the window. 'Justice for Adam Scott! Down with PC Plod!' As chants go, it left a lot to be desired – but, then again, this lot were the tamest bunch of bikers Prudence had ever come across. She steered the camper van around the next corner, and there they all were, every last one of the bikers from Carn Euny, their bikes lined up like a cavalry ready to charge, their placards held aloft. For some reason, among all of the JUSTICE FOR ADAM SCOTT notices, one placard declared MEAT IS MURDER and another LET'S ALL GET ALONG.

The police station lay on the other side of the milling mob. Prudence was barely halfway through it when Pearl caught her eye. She was only a few steps further when

Peter's voice flurried up, and the young skinhead reached up to snag her by the sleeve.

'It isn't her, Mrs Bulstrode. It really isn't.' He was holding a copy of the *Tregurnow Times*. There, preening on the front cover, was Benji Huntington-Lagan, and a grainy picture of Poppy Balloon being marched into the same police station that loomed at the head of the square. CRIME CONNOISSEUR BURSTS POPPY'S BALLOON read the preposterous headline. 'And I . . . I think I can prove it.'

It was only those words that made Prudence stop dead. Instead of shaking him off and marching straight up the station steps, she eyeballed him and said, 'How?'

'I know I shouldn't have done, but look . . .' Inside the newspaper there was stuffed an envelope, frayed around the edges and yellowed with age. 'I went back in last night. Well, my grandmother's house was empty. I *knew* they were up at the Bluff. That chef they're all talking about, Benji-Holding-His-Lagan, invited them. And, well, I *know* the alarm code.' He handed the letter to Prudence. 'It's incriminating, Mrs Bulstrode. It's practically a confession! God knows why she never burned it. It was just lying there with the others, stuffed into the bottom of her armoire.'

Prudence allowed her eyes to roam quickly across the page. The signature at the bottom came from cousin Florry again. This is what she had written:

Lizzy, I'm worried about you. So worried! You've really got to keep your head. You don't really want him dead.

Prudence looked up, darkly.

'Read on, Mrs Bulstrode,' implored Peter. 'Read on, it gets worse . . .'

I know what you mean and I know why you said it. If Adam died, it would be the easy way out. Divorce isn't going to happen. Your parents just wouldn't allow it! But he's a good man – in your heart, you know this. If he's playing away from home, well, maybe that's just one of those things. Maybe it's just how it goes. And listen to me Lizzy: why shouldn't you do the same? That's what kings and queens of old did. The marriage was for politics, but they kept lovers on the side. So! There you have it! *You* should keep lovers. Hey, what about that dishy Mac?

'You see?' said Peter, grappling to take hold of the letter again, as if only he could keep it safe. 'It's *proof*, Mrs Bulstrode. Proof that my grandmother had started seeing Mac even before Adam went missing. Listen to Benji Love-Himself-Lagan and you'd think it was Adam who was cheating – but what about my grandmother? This, Mrs Bulstrode, this would *prove* she killed Adam!'

Prudence lowered her voice. 'You're playing a very dangerous game, Peter. Your grandmother knows you sent me to snoop around her. She knows you're in with this Carn Euny lot. She's a powerful woman.'

'I know what you're saying, Mrs Bulstrode. She killed once. What's to keep her from killing again? But . . . but if you keep on thinking like that, then people can get away with what they want. Powerful people. Moneyed people. People like my grandmother! No, Mrs Bulstrode, we can prove it now. All we need is a DNA test. I'm Mac's grandson, not Adam Scott's. There's been a murder hanging over my family for two generations, Mrs Bulstrode. We need to put it right.'

Peter's words were still ringing in her ears as Prudence hurried up the station steps, then waited at the counter to announce herself to the taciturn sergeant sitting there. 'You're to go straight through, Mrs Bulstrode,' he said in his thick, Cornish monotone. 'The duty solicitor's with her now, but Detective Rose is on her way. You know the understanding?'

Prudence did. She'd spoken to Detective Rose some hours after the arrest, and argued vehemently for the right to visit Poppy. 'Given the severity of this case, the duplicitousness and calculation involved, the Crown has given us a full seventy-two hours before we lay formal charges. I can permit the visit, but you should be aware the suite is being monitored. Anything Poppy says can be used in evidence.'

Prudence had never set foot in a police station before. Suki had, of course – there'd been that terrible moment when she was arrested for being drunk and disorderly outside the local amateur dramatics production of *A Streetcar Named Desire* at the Netley Pike Fringe – but it hadn't been Prudence who went to relieve her. Consequently, Prudence had little idea what to expect as she followed the sergeant into the station's innermost halls. By the time she was ushered to the end of a long, barren corridor, just in time to see the duty solicitor

285

emerging from the cell at the end, a mounting sense of dread had overcome her. She'd been pitched a series once where she'd go into one of London's most notorious prisons and teach the lags there how to bake. That had been one job she'd been only too happy to forsake.

'You've got fifteen minutes, Mrs Bulstrode. Detective Rose will be waiting.'

Prudence pushed at the door of the cell, took a deep breath, and stepped through.

There sat Poppy, ashen-faced and grey, the bags around her eyes deep and dark. The moment she saw Prudence, she started weeping. Her trembling hands extended, and Prudence would have rushed straight to her side and hugged her, if only a voice hadn't barracked them through the door: 'No touching!' Then Prudence looked up, casting her eyes around the ceiling. Beside the fluorescent strip light, two cameras watched them like beady black eyes.

'You believe me, don't you, Prudence? It's ... it's nonsense. I didn't touch Mr Scott. I was seventeen years old. Prudence, I was seventeen!'

Prudence was well aware of how old Poppy had been, but Poppy seemed to cling on to the detail like it was incontrovertible evidence of her innocence. 'They've taken a statement from Barry Topps,' said Prudence, who had read all about it in the *Tregurnow Times*. 'He's swearing on oath that he heard you in Topps Fish Mega Palace talking about Mr Scott – that you were in love with him, that you were going to make him yours, that it didn't matter what the world had to say about it, nothing would keep him from you. That you were having your way with him in the air-raid shelter – the very same one where he was killed.' Prudence took a breath. 'Poppy, you're going to have to be straight with me. I *know* you didn't do this, Poppy. I might not have known you for forty-odd years, but I knew you back then – and the Poppy Balloon I knew could no more kill a man than stamp on a spider.' She paused. 'What have you told them, Poppy?'

Poppy's eyes danced madly in their orbits.

'Well, you know me, Pru. I can't deny it – I was pretty wild back then. I just got so damnably *bored* all the time. I just wanted a little fun. All those teenage hormones were raging, and listening to T. Rex and Bowie, and that poster I had of Marc Bolan and—'

'You're getting off the point, Poppy.' In fact, she was looking positively frenzied.

'I'm just saying we were *starved* of it, weren't we, Pru? God, I was *famished*. I'm not talking about food. I'm talking about *boys*. And you know we all dallied about here and there. I was worse than you, Pru, but you can't say you didn't have a soft spot for one or two of those fishing lads from down the coast. But you couldn't get to them, could you? It was all out of bounds. I had all these *needs*, Pru, and I had to put them somewhere. And then . . . well, I didn't think much of Mr Scott to begin with. That tattoo he had *did* rather tantalise me – just like those fishing toughs out on the sea! – but he was more *your* sort, Pru. You know, studious, and wise, fond of puzzles. Fond of books! And, if I'm really honest, Pru, I think it was because *you* admired him so much that I started thinking he was . . . a bit of all right. A bit dishy, I suppose.'

Prudence's heart had hardened. For the first time, she

287

was truly uncertain whether she was about to hear an exoneration or a full-blooded confession of guilt.

'You must think me a dreadful friend, Pru, but you were so clever and bright and winning every prize – proper head-girl material, we thought back then – and I almost *never* got noticed. Not by the teachers. Not by Mr Scott. So, one night, I asked him to help me with my revision. I told him I was struggling and I needed help, and more than anything I wanted to keep it from you girls, because you'd be down on me for anything so scholarly. That's when I had the idea. Meet me in the air-raid shelter, I told him. That's the thing – that would help me keep up my street cred, you know? Only, when he got there – with his calculators and protractors, and that damn silly set square he used to carry around – I'd laid it all out. A nice rug, some candles, a picnic hamper. A bottle of wine I'd nabbed from Miss Ellen's store cupboard – God, it was like a wine cellar, that place! And I told him: I didn't *really* want revision. What I wanted was *him*.'

Prudence cast a sudden glance at the cameras above. 'Poppy, whatever happened down there, whatever it was, you've got to—'

'I didn't lure him down there and kill him, honest I didn't! They're making out like it was a thing we had – him and me, down to the air-raid shelters whenever we had the chance. But Pru, I didn't have the nous to stage something like this. I didn't have the attention span to do that comprehension exercise on *Wuthering Heights*, remember? I could hardly pull a staged suicide together! God, if Mr Scott were here now, he'd probably enjoy this puzzle, wouldn't he? It's like one of those Sherlock Holmes stories he used to like.'

There it was again, thought Prudence. *Sherlock Holmes.* Her mind flew back to Mrs Arkwright sitting bolt upright in bed, bawling out the name of the famous detective; to the library book left on top of her box of things; to an image of a man in a deerstalker hat with a meerschaum pipe . . .

'You do believe me, don't you, Pru? God, it would all be so easy if only I'd told you girls back then. PVC forever, Pru.' Then she repeated it, more feebly now. 'PVC forever?'

Pru took a breath. Something was niggling her, something deep in the back of her mind – but what it was, she couldn't say. 'The timing of the whole thing is skewed. Barry Topps deep-fried Adam's hand a full year and more before he "vanished". So a full year after he heard you gossiping about Adam in the Palace.' She shook her head ruefully, trying to figure it out. 'What did happen in the air-raid shelter, Poppy?'

Poppy just shrugged, her voice cracking as she spoke. 'He was very kind to me, Pru. That's what happened. He didn't laugh and he didn't scream. He even promised not to tell a soul – he just didn't want me to be in any trouble, for there to be any fuss, any humiliation. I'd have been a laughing stock, Pru! He just told me to think again, made me tidy everything away, and then we left, quite separately, to go back to the school. I went up to the dorm, and I never breathed a word of it again – never, until this very day.'

The terror that she'd been about to hear a confession

must have been sapping all of Prudence's energy, for suddenly she felt drained. She sat down beside Poppy, ignoring the cry of 'No touching!' that came again through the door. 'Are you sure that's everything, Poppy?' she said. 'Absolutely everything there is?'

Poppy trembled as she said, 'I couldn't sleep, Pru. Not last night, and not the night after I propositioned Mr Scott. I was just sitting there in my dorm and the humiliation was building and building in me. If I'd still had that bottle of wine, I'd have drunk it in one, but I'd left it in the shelter, so it was just me and this sick feeling in my stomach. A little bit later, I can't remember how long, I just knew I had to go and find him. To apologise, if I could. I could see his car was still out front. I knew he hadn't gone home – well, he didn't, did he? He was *always* staying late. But I couldn't find him in his office, and I just knew he wasn't in the staffroom. No, when I finally found him, he was down in the library, and . . . and . . .'

'And *what*, Poppy?'

'He was kissing her, Prudence. They were kissing between the library stacks.'

Prudence was still. At last, she said, 'You fool, Poppy. Why didn't you say this? Why didn't you say this earlier?'

'I don't know, Pru. I didn't want anyone to know the full story of that day. Don't you see? I felt like such a bloody fool. Because *I* was the one who'd turned him on, wasn't I? I'd propositioned him, down there in the air-raid shelters, and he'd gone back up to the school and he was . . . he was taking her, between the shelves! Rutting, Pru! Rutting with her, up against the bookcases! I suppose they went up to the air-raid shelter after that – because, when I went back the next day, the wine bottle was gone. So somebody had a good time that night. Mr Scott had a good time, but it wasn't with me.'

'Then who was it, Poppy? Who did you see him with, down in the library after hours?'

Poppy opened her palms. 'I just don't know. I never did. I could see them holding each other, writhing together, through the shelves – and I felt like such a fool, I just turned tail and ran. And now, Pru? Now I'm here, and Barry Topps has filled their head with stories. He got the wrong end of the stick, Pru. I can even remember it. I was down there with Jilly Bronze – you remember Jill? She enjoyed a thing or two with the local lads as well. I just had to tell someone, you see. I had to get it off my chest. And Pru, I would have told you, or Vivienne, or Colette – only, none of you ever did anything quite as stupid as this, and Jilly Bronze had done things you just wouldn't believe.' Poppy had run dry of tears now; she drew her sleeve across her nose, wiping up all the run-off still lingering on her lip. 'Barry Topps didn't attack Mr Scott because he's so morally superior, Pru. He'd been after Adam all along – just fuming it was the Franks and Scotts that united, not the Franks and Topps! But now it's fifty years later, and it doesn't matter that his brain's all Swiss-cheesed up with holes – they're taking his word as gospel, and I'm going to hang for it, Prudence, I'm going to hang!'

Prudence put an arm around her and drew her near. 'Sweet Poppy, you're not going to hang.'

The cell door burst open. There, in the doorway, stood the taciturn desk sergeant, his face set with a scowl. 'I told you: no touching, Mrs Bulstrode. You could be smuggling contraband.'

Prudence stood up and dusted herself down. 'If I was going to smuggle a file in to aid Poppy's escape, I'd have hidden it in a cake.' She marched past the sergeant, hovered in the doorway and looked back. 'Don't lose heart, Poppy. I'm told they can keep you here for seventy-two hours, but it's like I promised Hetty: by tomorrow afternoon, you'll be sitting at the banquet, just like we always planned.'

'But how, Pru?' Poppy whispered. *'How?'*

Prudence just winked, then turned on her heel and marched away from the cell.

She hadn't yet reached the police station lobby when the falsity of her promise struck her. There was, she thought, but one hope – and that lay in Peter, milling with the protestors outside, and his dreams of a DNA test. Beyond that, there was nothing, just niggling feelings, just blossoming doubts, just the vain, vague hope that she might really be like Sherlock Holmes and have the solution pop into her head in a moment. *Elementary, my dear Grandma!*, Suki would say, and then all would be resolved.

Detective Rose was waiting in the lobby. 'Mrs Bulstrode,' she began, 'I trust you did the right thing? That you encouraged Poppy to tell us everything she knows?'

'You're making a fool of yourself, Detective,' said Pru, her face still set in deep lines of concentration. 'You're staking your reputation on a hotch-potch of thoughts cooked up by that conceited, arrogant chef. Why would you listen to Benji Huntington-Lagan at all?'

Detective Rose heaved a sigh. 'Why would I listen to *any* chef?' she asked, more pointed than Prudence had ever known her. 'Mrs Bulstrode, this case is causing a lot of trouble for the chief constable. We let it slip through our fingers fifty years ago, and I don't intend to let that happen again. Franks & Scotts is an important firm in these parts. Benji Huntington-Lagan has been much help to our investigation – but it's being corroborated, even as we speak. We now have a statement from one of Poppy's friends, a Jilly Bronze, to confirm the fact that she was obsessively in love with Adam Scott. We're told she wrote poems about him. *Poems*, Pru. And Jilly's put us on to a local man, Steve Door, who's happy to attest to the fact that he and Poppy used to use that same air-raid shelter for late night . . . hanky-panky.'

Prudence shuddered at the words. Why couldn't people say just what they meant?

'It's all so . . . circumstantial,' Prudence seethed.

'The sworn statement of a respected local businessman—'

'Respected? The man battered Adam Scott's hand!'

'A confession from Poppy herself that she was in love with Mr Scott, that she was spurned, that she took him to the air-raid shelter where his body lay for half a century. I think we have the beginnings of a case here, Mrs Bulstrode. The Crown Prosecution Service certainly believes so. There are some nuances to work out, of course, but Ms Balloon will be staying with us while we work out the kinks. Then it'll be for the CPS to decide.'

'Nuances?' Prudence replied, in horror. 'You're railroading a woman towards a murder conviction, and you haven't even worked out the *nuances*. My goodness, it's like cooking without seasoning – you might make a meal, but it won't taste of anything!' Prudence marched past her, flinging open the police station doors. Out there, the skinheads still milled. 'You know what they're saying, don't you?'

Detective Rose joined her on the steps, the sun spilling like a beautiful, bright halo around them. 'They're saying it's a conspiracy – a family job, designed to extricate Elizabeth from marriage. If it was divorce, the companies would have been compelled to divorce as well – so it had to be murder. The problem, Mrs Bulstrode, is there's no evidence for any of it.'

'But there might be,' said Prudence. 'There's a boy out there. Peter. He might be all the evidence you need. A simple DNA test to prove that the Scott family line ended with Adam. That Adam didn't really get Elizabeth pregnant at all.'

'What just cause have I to order that test? You're forgetting, Mrs Bulstrode, that Elizabeth Duggan is not under my suspicion. Poppy Balloon *is*.' Then she lowered her voice. 'You have nuances of your own to work out, Mrs Bulstrode. If the Franks wanted Adam dead, why not just kill him at sea like his "suicide" note claimed? Why was his body left at St Marianne's at all, if the murderer was not Poppy Balloon?' Then she fixed Prudence with a glare. 'I like you, Mrs Bulstrode, but I believe your professional rivalry with Benji Huntington-Lagan is clouding your vision.'

Of all the things the detective had said, this was the one that inspired the more irksome feeling in Prudence.

What rivalry existed extended only one way, thought Pru. It wasn't Prudence desperate to prove herself on the world's stage. It wasn't Prudence so eager to show talent and foresight and powers of deduction that the police had been tricked into pursuing a perfectly preposterous case. 'Benji Huntington-Lagan might be a decorated chef, Detective, but his mistake has always been to value catching the eye more than satisfying the palette. He does it in his cookery, and he's doing it right now. He isn't a world famous detective – he's a rather arrogant, egotistical young man.'

She took a step into the daylight, then looked down upon the protestors still chanting their slogans.

'You may wait for my call, Detective Rose. And I promise you this: the last meal you eat on this case won't be "Gelatinous Bisque Sequestered in a Saffron and Seaweed Ceviche", nor will it be fish-and-chip pasties down at Topps Fish Mega Palace. It'll be the simple, honest cookery of the girls up at St Marianne's. The banquet is at three p.m. tomorrow, Detective.' Prudence extended her hand. 'I shall see you there.'

At St Marianne's School for Girls, Suki called out, 'That's time, girls. Let's break for lunch,' and looked up to find that – contrary to her expectations – the domestic science classroom was not nearly as much of a bombsite as she had feared.

The girls, it seemed, hadn't just learned about cookery across the last two weeks. Somewhere along the way, they'd learned the fundamentals of kitchen management as well.

It was Hetty that Suki was worried for. In her pocket, her iPhone kept buzzing with messages from Doogie – she supposed *that* was another failed romance, for so much had been going on she'd only sporadically contacted him all week – but she ignored it again and looked instead at the stricken girl. As soon as she'd announced the lunch hour, Sophie and a trio of other girls had flocked to Hetty. Suki decided to flock to her too.

The girls were all cooing over her, cooing or else clucking like mother hens. Suki couldn't cluck, but she had no need – for as soon as she drew near, Sophie took her by the wrist and hoiked her into the group. 'Do you really think your grandmother's right?' said Hetty, voice wavering. 'Do you think my grandmother's innocent? Do you think she'll be here tomorrow?'

At first, Suki stuttered in her reply. Giving false hope, making false promises, seemed cowardly somehow. And yet she had seen her grandmother as she strode out of here this morning. She knew the look of conviction that had been colouring Prudence's face.

'Let's think about it logically,' said Suki, trying to think of what her grandmother would say. 'If nothing else, Barry Topps *has* changed the complexion of the case.'

'Yes,' sobbed Hetty, 'he's changed it so that it's all about my grandmother.'

'I think it's clear, now, that *something* was going on with Mr Scott. He stayed late at school all the time. He told the English mistress Dot Ellen that he wouldn't be seduced by her because his heart belonged to somebody else – someone who couldn't possibly have been his wife.' She paused. 'He was having an affair, right here at the school. But Hetty, if it wasn't your grandmother, then who *was* it?'

'There were hundreds of students here,' Sophie protested. 'How could we possibly know?'

'No,' said Suki, 'not a student. Adam Scott doesn't strike me as the sort to become infatuated with a student.'

'Then it had to be a teacher,' said Sophie. 'Somebody who worked here. But that was fifty years ago! How are we to even tell?'

Suki stepped backward. 'Lucky, I suppose, that St Marianne's has its very own archivist.'

At least this energised the girls. As Suki led the march down to the school library – if library it could still be called, so devoid of books were its shelves – she even sensed a new spring in Hetty's step. She only hoped that, wherever she was, her grandmother was having better luck than this. It was the hope that destroyed you in the end, and Suki had just reignited the hope in Hetty's heart.

In the library, Miss Down sat at her desk, still diligently digitising the old school prospectuses and newsletters. When she saw the cavalcade of girls come crashing into her library, she flurried up out of her seat in shock.

'Miss Down,' Suki began, 'we were wondering—'

'Pictures!' Hetty cried out.

'Pictures, young lady?'

'Of the year when Mr Scott was murdered,' Suki explained. 'We want to see everybody – all the staff who worked here. Every teacher and lunch lady. Every cleaner and governor. Anyone who might have worked in the school that year. Anyone who might have *known* Mr Scott. Anyone who might have *loved* him.'

At mention of the word 'love', Verity Down's eyes darkened. Then, several heartbeats later, she fixed her attention back on her computer – and, purposefully ignoring the plaintive, searching looks of the students, started summoning the pictures from the server. 'What's this all about, girls?' she asked, stiffly.

'One of them killed him, Miss Down,' Hetty blurted out, 'and if we don't find out which, my grandmother's going to hang.'

Suki looked at her sideways. 'I'm not sure *hanging* is quite right, Hetty,' she began – but went no further, because at that moment Miss Down stood up again, stepped aside and offered her chair to the girls in front of her.

'There must have been fifty staff on site that year, and almost all of them ladies. The cooks and cleaners, the office staff, the governors – not to mention the parents who always busied themselves about the school in those days. I'm afraid, girls, that you've set yourself an insur-mountable challenge.' Verity reached over, clicked the mouse, and watched as the full school photograph, summer 1976, flashed on to the screen. 'If one of *these* ladies is Adam Scott's killer, like you seem to think, then good luck telling me which one. No, girls, I have a feel-ing the true story of that night is going to stay dead and buried – dead and buried,' she said, eyes darting around, 'just like poor Adam Scott . . .'

Prudence was still fuming as she came down the police station steps, but by the time she got to the bottom she had

298

started to feel a touch of foolishness as well. It was that line about competing with Benji that had inflamed her – because, as soon as it was said, she had realised some element of it was true, and that made her feel diminished somehow. The image of Benji basking in the glory of a crime only half-solved – and half-solved badly at that – would have been enough to convince even the most saintly of people to want to prove him wrong, but Prudence felt she ought to have been able to resist the temptation. She tried to fix her sights on Poppy instead, on setting one of her oldest friends free – and if Benji Huntington-Lagan was taught a thing or two about the ego, about cookery and crime, along the way, well, so much the better.

There was Peter, still parading up and down with the crowd, still bearing his placard aloft, still lending his voice to that unimpeachable chorus: 'Justice for Adam Scott!'

Prudence waded into the crowd and snagged him by the arm. 'Young man, come this way.'

Peter was adept at ignoring the orders of his elders – but the conviction in Prudence Bulstrode's voice meant he needed no further convincing. Moments later, placard clattering to the cobbles at his feet, he was following Prudence out of the crowd, into the shadows on the other side of the square where the bright peach and cyan PRU BU 1 was waiting.

'Peter, I need you to call my grand-daughter. Call her on that portable telephone of yours.'

Peter looked nonplussed.

'Call St Marianne's School for Girls,' she instructed. 'Have them patch you through.'

299

'Patch . . . me . . . through?'

'Oh, for heaven's sake, just hand it here,' she said.

By good fortune, Peter had already found the number for St Marianne's and hit 'dial', so when Prudence snatched the phone from his fingers, all she had to do was put it to her ear. By even greater fortune, it was Ronnie Green – not Chastity Carruthers – who answered.

'Ronnie,' Prudence declared, 'I know very well it was *you* who was using my camper van as a party wagon. Don't think I didn't notice – your love for a tinned pie, your fondness for pale ale, all those disagreements with the missus at home. No, Ronnie, there's no use denying it, and I'll make no more fuss about it, as long as you do me this one little favour.' Prudence paused, while a flurry of grovelling apologies came down the phone. 'That's quite all right, Ronnie. Now run off and find my grand-daughter, wherever she might be. I need her help this instant.'

'This instant' turned out to be several instants too long. Prudence had just about lost what reserves of patience she had left when she heard her grand-daughter's voice buzzing at her down the phone. 'Grandma? Grandma, we're down in the library, going through the old school photographs. If Adam Scott was having an affair with anyone, she has to be here . . .'

Kissing in the library, thought Prudence.

The story Poppy had told . . .

'Listen to me, Suki. I need you to call Detective Hall. Get him to call me on this number as soon as you can.'

There was a long pause before Suki said, 'Grandma, what's all this about?'

'Please, Suki.' Prudence paused. 'Oh, and Suki, I need you to get those girls in good order. I'll be back before the end of the day. I want to see those meals presented exactly as they'll be at tomorrow's feast. Do you understand?'

'Loud and clear, Grandma,' said Suki, and hung up the phone.

Prudence turned on her heel, opened up the camper-van doors and heaved herself inside. 'You'd better slide on in, Peter. I'm afraid I need use of your phone – and, if I'm right, I'll have need of you very soon as well.'

Peter looked nervously back at the protestors. 'My hog, Mrs Bulstrode, she's waiting for me back there.'

Prudence scanned the crowd, picking out Pearl – with her distinctive dragon tattoo – before she remembered that Peter meant his motorcycle.

'I'm afraid your hog will have to survive without you for a little, Peter – just until Detective Hall calls me back.' She turned the key in the ignition, listening to the familiar purr of the camper van's engine as it fired up. 'Now hop on up. We haven't far to go – but we haven't any time to lose. There are sixteen girls back at St Marianne's waiting for their teacher, an old friend shivering in a prison cell, desperate for my help, and I've a visit to pay to a particularly puffed-up chef.'

'The challenge,' Benji Huntington-Lagan was saying, his hand swaying through the air in front of him, still clasping its little phial of pine-scented steam, 'is in the *method*. Think of your favourite cookbook. Each recipe is constructed of two sections: the ingredients come first, but it's the *method* wherein lies the skill. Toss those ingredients together any other way and you won't have the dish you set out to make. Baking, frying, roasting and steaming – these are all very different skills. Don't listen to the strange sorts who tell you that it makes no difference whether you put the milk in first – or that it doesn't change things at all to add the jam before the cream. These details are what the *method* is all about. And so it is in solving a crime: an amateur may look at all of the clues in front of him, and arrange them in a way that approximates a main dish; but the more erudite among us, those with more verve and imagination, must work out the way to string these clues, these *ingredients*, together – so that the right meal is achieved. One sleuth ends up with scrambled eggs, but the purer mind makes *île flottante*. Do you see?'

Prudence had staggered to a stop almost the very moment she entered the Bluff, for the sound of Benji Huntington-Lagan pontificating at the eager journalist was almost too absurd to bear. The duo were sitting in the window, the exact same table where Prudence and Poppy had taken lunch with Detective Rose. As Prudence approached, she could hear Benji holding court on how an ingredient was very much like a clue, how the roles of chef and detective were uncommonly intertwined. What was worse, the journalist seemed to be lapping it up – as only a writer could. In Prudence's experience, writers were willing to believe just about anything, so long as it got them a good story.

She was halfway across the restaurant, preparing to burst this preposterous bubble, when the sous-chef

Sonny emerged from the kitchen door, scampered through the tables and snagged Pru by the sleeve. 'It's a very important meeting, Mrs Bulstrode,' he chirped. 'They mustn't be disturbed. Don't you know who that is? Not just any old journo from the *Tregurnow Times*. That's Dave Hodge, that is. Ghostwriter to the stars. He's working on a podcast – true crimes in Cornwall. Uncle Benji's going to be its star. True crime's the thing now, Mrs Bulstrode. It'll get the Bluff back on the telly.'

Prudence calmly shook off Sonny's arm and said, 'I'll have a Florida orange, young man, with one of those nice curly straws.'

'Florida orange?'

'It's fresh orange juice and lemonade.'

'B-but I'm not a waiter, Mrs Bulstrode!'

Sonny was taking far too long to process the fact that Prudence hadn't listened to a word he said. While he was standing there, confounded by the idea of orange juice and lemonade, Prudence left him behind and, barely breaking her stride, swept around and sat beside Benji.

'Mrs Bulstrode, we're closed for the lunchtime service,' Benji announced, slapping Prudence's hand as she reached in for one of the pistachios on the table. 'Would you mind? This is a private meeting.'

'So your sous-chef tells me,' said Prudence, cracking one of the pistachios. 'A ghostwriter keen to do a book about the case? A podcast, revealing exactly how you uncovered the truth behind this crime? That's the sort of thing, is it?' Prudence didn't wait for a reply; as soon as this ghostwriter opened his mouth to reply, she

303

continued, 'Something that will show exactly what epiphanies you came to in uncovering the truth? No, I'm afraid not, Benji – because any self-respecting producers, and I've known one or two in my time, will take one look at this codswallop story you've spouted out, and see it's got more holes in than a piece of Swiss cheese.' Prudence popped another pistachio in her mouth. 'And if you want a foodie pun in your article,' she said to the writer, 'you can have that free of charge.'

Incandescent, Benji snatched back the pot of pistachios and handed it to Sonny, who scuttled backwards again, away from Prudence's greedy grasp. 'Mrs Bulstrode, this is beyond the pale.' Then he directed his attentions upon the writer once again. 'Mrs Bulstrode and I have had something of a professional rivalry since a certain charity appeal we partook in together. I'm afraid she's out to show she's best, which is what you have to do to succeed in the television world. Personally, I prefer my dignity and integrity to a little fame—'

Prudence snorted. There was much to unpick in this statement as well, but it would have to wait for another time. The clock was ticking, Poppy was still imprisoned – and, back at the school, sixteen girls would be knee-deep in fish and chips. 'Let's begin with the biggest hole then, shall we? Benji, you've made no attempt whatsoever to satisfactorily explain the set-up of Adam Scott's suicide. You've made an accusation against Poppy Balloon – and made not even the most cursory effort to explain how a seventeen-year-old girl single-handedly staged a suicide at sea.'

'Now this is interesting,' said Dave Hodge, the

304

ghostwriter, with a new keenness. He leaned forward, gingery beard twitching, his pen dancing in shorthand across the page. 'Readers pick up on this sort of thing. Listeners don't mind making a leap of faith, but they won't stand for holes.'

'They won't stand for this business about the suicide note either,' said Prudence, cheerily. 'Verifiably written in Adam's hand – at least, according to a modern graphologist.'

Benji Huntington-Lagan had turned almost purple in irritation. 'Sonny,' he snapped, 'a double brandy, this instant.'

Sonny scuttled off to fetch the finest brandy the Bluff had to offer.

'Well, it's obvious, isn't it?' Benji blathered. 'Even to the simplest of minds. Even to a layman's layman.' His eyes kept darting. It was only when Sonny re-emerged with the decanter of brandy, and a small crystal glass, that he centred himself at all. Half the brandy spilled down his chin as he said, 'Poppy was a party girl up and down this coast. She knew all the fishing lads. We've yet to uncover him, but it's perfectly plain to see that she had an accomplice. Killing Adam Scott wasn't premeditated. No, no – Poppy panicked. And after she'd panicked, she knew she had to cover it up. So she did what she was best at: she called up one of those fishing boys she'd sometimes parlayed with, told him she'd give him what he wanted if he only helped her with this. All he'd have to do, to get a piece of Poppy Balloon, would be to pose as Adam Scott – dress himself up, take himself out to sea, leave the fake suicide note and swim back to shore.

305

Womanly wiles, you see. That's what had got Poppy into this mess, and that's what got her out.' Whether it was the brandy or some other rush of confidence that propelled Benji now, Prudence could not say. Either way, he seemed to be hitting his stride. 'The key to it all, of course, will be locating this young man, the one in thrall to Poppy Balloon. Yes, I'll have to pass this new line of enquiry on straight away. A search must be begun: a reward handed out, if needed. Somebody out there helped Poppy Balloon, and that makes them an accessory to murder.' Benji smiled, condescendingly, at Prudence. 'Your faith in your friend is estimable, Pru, but I'm afraid what at first seems a great strength is actually a weakness. We too often mistake one for another. It's this kind of thing I've been exploring in my lobster-tail cakes . . .'

Prudence was disheartened to see that the ghostwriter's pen had started dancing across his page once more. She reached out, gently touched the back of his hand – and, in that way, brought some much-needed stillness to the table.

Benji was taking his double brandy, but there was no sign of Prudence's Florida orange.

'You always did pride yourself at making recipes up on the hoof, Benji,' she said, sadly, 'but the difference is, cookery and crime aren't *actually* the same. Both processes of deduction, perhaps. Both require inventiveness and flair. But if you stir some cinnamon into a sauce and it doesn't taste right, a woman isn't going to spend the rest of her life in prison. An unfortunate half an hour in your restaurant toilet, perhaps, but she wouldn't lose her life.

And we're not dealing with a troop of hungry mountain gorillas here. We're dealing in life and death.' She looked at the ghostwriter. 'It's better you put your project on hiatus, dear, at least until the facts of this matter are sorted.' She stood up. 'Benji, the moment you can satisfactorily prove how Poppy Balloon staged a suicide, and expertly forged Adam Scott's handwriting, I'll listen to what you have to say. Until then . . .' She walked halfway across the restaurant, then looked back. 'This wasn't the work of a teenage girl, you fool. This was an intricate act, a planned act, an act which took much preparation. And Poppy Balloon? Poppy Balloon couldn't even get her homework in on time.'

She was stepping back out of the Bluff, reflecting on the fact that she'd enjoyed showing Benji up in front of his fawning ghostwriter much more than she ought to have done, when she saw Peter cantering towards her, having tumbled out of the camper. The rickety old phone was in his hand, and that hand extended towards her in something close to desperation. 'It's him,' cried Peter. 'It's Detective Hall!'

'Prudence?' came Detective Brian Hall's whisper, crackling down the line as Prudence put the phone to her ear. 'Mrs Bulstrode, I received a message I should call?'

Prudence marched back toward the camper, Peter trailing behind her, as she tried to explain. 'Detective Hall, I'm just leaving the Bluff. I'm afraid things have got rather out of hand since poor Mrs Arkwright's wake.' She paused. 'She didn't do it, Brian – I'd stake my life's reputation on the fact that Poppy Balloon didn't lay a finger on Adam Scott – but Benji Huntington-Lagan and his showboating have got everybody riled up. Detective Rose is sending her before the magistrates. Nobody's listening to reason.'

'Welcome to the world of policework, Prudence. More politics than policing, it seems.'

'Mr Hall, I need your help.' Prudence clambered into PRU BU 1, then fired up the ignition. 'I'm afraid I don't know who else to ask. I'm only hoping it isn't beyond you. One more piece of policework, Detective. It might be you could finally solve the case you closed forty-eight years ago . . .'

The hesitation on the line filled Prudence with foreboding.

'Now, Mrs Bulstrode,' Detective Hall finally said, 'I have to say, there are one too many cooks in this case already. I did think I might poke around a little, uncover a few stones – but I'm ninety-two years old, Mrs Bulstrode, and whatever Mrs Arkwright thought, I'm not really Sherlock Holmes . . .'

Sherlock Holmes. Prudence looked down. In the corner of her eye, up on the dashboard where Peter was now sitting, was the copy of the collected works that ought to have been taken back to the public library. Daisy Lane had left it there on the day of the funeral, and there it had stayed ever since – forgotten in the chaos of Poppy's arrest.

'Isn't police work better left to the professionals, Prudence? However talented the amateurs are?'

Prudence took a breath. *Too many cooks.* She dared to look back at the Bluff. Yes, she thought, but one more wouldn't hurt.

'How easy would it be, Mr Hall, for you to organise a

DNA test? To pull a few strings, even in your retirement?'

'Mrs Bulstrode, those things are ten-a-penny right now. Almost anyone can take a DNA test online, just to track down relations they didn't know they had. You can do it by mail order. I've been doing the family history. I did my own test. Two weeks later, I found I had second cousins living on a barge in Newport Pagnell.'

'I don't have two weeks, Detective. Poppy's to remain in custody another two days – then they'll present what they have to the CPS. If I can't convince them otherwise . . .'

'Mrs Bulstrode, what have you got in mind?'

She looked at Peter. 'Can you help me, or not?'

'There's an old mate of mine, from back in the force. Took a redundancy package and set up a consultancy – a little forensics laboratory, up Camborne way. Well, it's them Tories, isn't it? They started outsourcing everything in the eighties, and it hasn't really stopped. He does the usual stuff. Toxicology reports. All sorts of analysis. But he's mostly corporate now. The force still uses him, but so much of it's insurance.'

'Could they do a paternity test?'

'I don't see why not. It's not like the old days. It's practically run of the mill.'

'By the time Poppy's dragged off to the magistrate?'

This time, Detective Hall paused. 'I'll put a call in, Mrs Bulstrode. It might be asking too much. You might have to bake them a crumble, something to grease the wheels. Of course, they'll need samples to work with – and one wouldn't be enough. They'd need sample from *both* parties.'

Prudence looked askance at Peter. This, she supposed, was one of the drawbacks of being a skinhead: there was no strand of hair to pluck, no root follicle to pick out, but they would manage.

'I'll get you your samples,' she said. 'The first is going to be easy.' She thought of Elizabeth, of the hulking frame of Mac Duggan, of the way they'd glared at her as they ejected her from their home just the other day. 'Of course, the second – well, that's going to need a little bit more *imagination* . . .'

Chapter Eleven

Prudence was about to leave her dormitory room, the fresh day dawning, when a knock came at the door. When she opened it up, there stood Hetty, already flanked by Suki and Sophie, one standing at each of her shoulders for moral support.

'Mrs Bulstrode,' she said, 'I just can't do it.'

Prudence had slept for but a few short hours that night, lost in anticipating the day ahead. For countless hours, she had tossed and turned, seeing again that skeletal hand and its tarnished gold watch, the implacable look on Mac Duggan's face, the contorted terror of Poppy Balloon sitting in her police station cell. She had tried not to think of Benji Huntington-Lagan preening in front of his audience, nor that unctuous ghostwriter, gobbling up every word that he said – but the radio had buzzed that night with talk of the Crime Connoisseur, and when she'd heard a local news breakdown of the morning's headlines – BURSTING POPPY'S BALLOON! CALL MY BLUFF! – it had been impossible to push him out of her mind.

Now she welcomed Hetty and poured tea from the pot on her dresser. Prudence always woke to a peppermint, but for Hetty only strong, black and sugary would do.

'I just can't, Mrs Bulstrode. I messed it up all day yesterday. My fish was uncooked, my batter was soggy, my peas – if you can believe it – were crunchy and rough. I just can't get my head in the game, not when my grandmother's in prison.' She stopped. 'Mrs Carruthers is going to flip her lid, but I text my mother last night. They're on their way. They've taken a holiday rental in Mousehole. I'm going to stay with them there, so we can be close to my grandmother. But I can't cook today, Mrs Bulstrode. I just can't.'

Prudence stirred three thick creamers into the tea – the cream was gloopy and oilier than anything Prudence would willingly use, but for now it would do – and handed Hetty the cup. Then she sat down beside her. 'Your grandmother's innocent, Hetty. I promised you that I'm going to prove it and bring her home, and I will.' The moment she spoke the words, she wondered if she ought to have just said nothing – but, right now, all she wanted to do was console the girl. 'That's why, girls, I need you to cover for me this morning. I know, I know – I said it yesterday as well. And this morning Mrs Carruthers is going to be prowling around, making sure she's "getting her money's worth" out of me. So I need you to cover for me. Tell her the domestic science classroom is a temple. A private temple, where only cooks might be allowed. Do you hear?'

At Suki's insistence, Prudence left Hetty sobbing into her oily, sugary tea on the edge of the bed and stepped out into the hallway. 'Grandma, you can't be *sure*.'

Prudence rolled her shoulders, as if to say: *But what other choice do we have?*

'The guests will start arriving at one,' she said. 'If things go according to plan, I'll be back before they come – but, either way, Mrs Carruthers won't be a problem after that. She'll be pouring bubbly for the parents and leading them on a tour of the school. She was supposed to show them the new gymnastics facilities, but I'm sure she'll want to show them the rest of the school now, anything to mollify the rumours spreading round. But you have to man the stations until then, Suki. Make sure the girls are prepping. Make sure there's no delay in getting cooking underway. The banquet's served at three. Have the girls lunched and watered by twelve-thirty, so they can go straight into it.' Prudence looked back at the door. 'Hetty as well.'

'We can't make false promises, Grandma.'

Prudence had never been admonished by her own grand-daughter before. It took her a moment of bewildered silence before she understood what was going on. Then she simply said, 'Ronnie Green's going out to the Cherry Garth to pick up Miss Jubber. Bernie Hogg, who I met last week, is bringing himself down, picking up some of the other governors on then way. If I'm not back, take out the tartlets at one, so there's something to be nibbling on.'

'Just once,' said Suki, 'I'd like it if we were on a job that didn't turn to hell.'

At this, Prudence clasped her shoulder. 'It's just another learning experience, Suki, and you're doing just fine.'

It would not do to leave without rallying the girls first – but, as soon as Prudence had given the girls a speech worthy of Henry V at Agincourt, she hurried to the camper and brought the engine to life. 'Let's make this a day to remember,' she had said. 'Let's fill the dining hall of St Marianne's with scents so tantalising that your families won't ever want to set foot in Topps Fish Mega Palace again. They'll have no need, girls, because *here* – right *here!* – is where fish and chips reign supreme!' She had seen the thrill it had given the other girls, but Hetty's face still seemed sallow and grey. It was a wonder she'd been convinced to go to the kitchens at all.

Cornwall was glittering under the morning sun. Sometimes, the world reflected the inner turmoil you were feeling – but not today. Today, the sun was so bright and the scents in the air so summery and fresh that it was difficult to believe anyone ever meant anyone else any harm at all, leave alone the fact that a murder had been committed on a summer's day much like this. By the time Prudence reached the skinheads' camp at Carn Euny, the last of the morning clouds had dissipated, leaving only the endless blue sky reflected in the endless blue sea below.

Some of the bikers were already here. By the looks of them, they'd camped here all night again – for, somewhere beyond the ruins, low cookfires were smouldering, and Prudence noticed Pearl chowing down on a vegan bacon roll, propped up against one of the standing stones. One of the skinheads, a burly young man in imitation leathers, with LOVE and LOVE tattooed across each set of knuckles, gave Prudence a timid wave, then quickly buried his head in the paperback he was reading.

Prudence had never seen a star-struck skinhead before; she simply hadn't understood the power of that vegan chilli.

Here came Peter, yawning groggily as he picked his way towards Prudence from the cookfires, rolling his 'hog' alongside him.

Prudence's heart sank when she saw quite how dishevelled he looked. 'Peter,' she said, with the same air of disappointment she used on Suki's less sober mornings. 'You camped out, I see?'

Peter shrugged. 'I cadged a ride back here so I could pick up my hog. And my folks aren't too happy with me after I put you up to snoop around Grandma's house. I figured, with what we've got planned for today, it was better I laid low. But don't worry, Mrs Bulstrode. I'm game. I know exactly what I've got to do. I've worked out exactly what I'm going to say. It'll work like a charm.'

'It would be more charming if you'd been able to have a wash this morning, Peter.' She looked back at the camper, then began to lead him there. 'Come on, I've a bucket and sponge. There's enough water in the tank that you can sort yourself out before we get there.'

Peter looked aghast. 'Mrs Bulstrode, I've got a few baby wipes in my pack, and a bottle of deodorant . . .'

Prudence shook her head witheringly. 'You're supposed to be grovelling to your grandmother, Peter, not turning up on their doorstep looking like a vagabond.' Soon, they had reached the camper van. Prudence pulled the slide-door open, then produced a bucket and sponge from underneath the sink unit. Moments later, she had the taps running. 'Here,' she said, while they waited, 'we might as well get this out of the way. Take this.' Prudence had reached into the glove compartment and pulled out a small cardboard box. 'It's a simple mouth swab. All the instructions are inside. Detective Hall went to pick it up last night.' Prudence saw him ogling the box, his grubby fingers leaving sticky prints all over the surface. 'On second thoughts, Peter, perhaps a wash first,' said Prudence. 'Come on, you can get yourself sorted round back. And . . .' She shook her head, looked at her wristwatch, thought suddenly of Mrs Carruthers clucking round the domestic science classroom doors. 'I'll have to take you into Penzance and get you into some clean clothes as well. You might have made this easier for us, Peter.'

Prudence looked round. For a boy who'd been aghast at the prospect of it two minutes ago, Peter had quite readily stripped down to his boxer shorts.

'How on earth did you get quite so dirty *there*?' Prudence gasped.

'It's just a biker's life,' grinned Peter. 'Now, Mrs Bulstrode – pass me the soap?'

It took too long to get Peter even half-clean. It took even longer to spirit him into Penzance, bustle through Barker's Department Store, and get him dressed in something that approximated civility. After that, there were the flowers to buy – Peter favoured the local Co-op, but Prudence knew that only a bouquet from a boutique florist's had any chance of working – and after *that*, Prudence was insistent on hearing Peter's speech rehearsed over and again, until she was certain the apology he was about to deliver sounded both unrehearsed and sincere. From the back of the camper, she produced a small gift basket filled with specialist olive oils, jars of roasted peppers, aubergine and artichoke hearts in high-end marinades, and made sure he memorised each one. 'I saw all these on display in your grandmother's kitchen,' Prudence explained, parking the camper van some distance from the clifftop manor, lest they be spotted from some upstairs window. 'All out of date, of course – in homes like your grandmother's, you don't buy these sorts of oils to actually use them; it's like that copy of my *History of English Food* sitting up on the shelf – a display item, totally unread. But it will show you've been paying attention, Peter. It will show you've made an effort.'

Peter seemed to understand. 'More than Co-op flowers and a box of Milk Tray, Mrs Bulstrode.'

Prudence, who was rather partial to a box of Milk Tray at Christmas, just nodded; she was just pleased he got it. 'Just sell it to them, Peter. Don't be too showy about it, but make them see that you're sorry. You've been reflecting on your behaviour, you had no right to go stirring a hornet's nest when this is already such a horrible time for your grandmother. You've been looking at the old photographs of your grandfather – *Adam Scott*, remember! – and you suddenly understood what it must have been like, forty-eight years ago, to lose your future, to face up to motherhood alone.'

'That's when I turn to Mac,' said Peter. 'I'll reach out to shake his hand and, if he doesn't take it – which he won't, Mrs Bulstrode! – I'll tell him I understand, and that I hope one day I'll win back his trust. I hope I might even join the family firm one day – of course, they'll need to know I trust them first, so that's why I've undertaken some days charity work at the seamen's mission.' Peter paused. 'Do I really have to do that, Mrs Bulstrode?'

Prudence had put in the telephone calls herself yesterday evening, in-between fretting about the end-of-course banquet and trying not to brood too deeply upon the second lonely night Poppy was about to spend in the Penzance cells. The Charitable Commission for Retired Seamen, Penzance, had been only too happy to hear about the prospect of a new volunteer – and Prudence had deduced that it would pull at the heartstrings of Elizabeth Duggan, because it was the same charity her family had asked mourners to make contributions to instead of laying flowers at Adam's wake.

'Do it just like we said, Peter. And then . . .'

'Just as I'm leaving, Mrs Bulstrode, I'll beg leave to take a toilet break.' Peter rolled his eyes. *'Beg leave', Mrs Bulstrode? Really, Mrs Bulstrode?* 'And then I'll grab whatever I can. Mac's toothbrush. His hair brush. I'll pocket them and bring them with me – and then, that's it, we're done.'

Prudence tapped him on the shoulder encouragingly as he clambered out of the camper, arms laden down with flowers, artisanal oils and jars.

'You realise, Mrs Bulstrode, that you're sending me into a murderer's lair, don't you?'

Prudence just stared.

'Sending me to the butcher's block, that's what you're

doing, Mrs Bulstrode. This better work – because, if I end up dead and buried, it's not going to look very good on your CV. National treasure Prudence Bulstrode sent poor young fisher-boy to his certain doom . . .'

Prudence called after him, 'You can rest assured, Peter, that if you do die in there, I'll make sure to look after your *hog.*'

Then she watched him diminish as he followed the road along the coast, until finally a miniscule version of Peter tapped the code into the keypad at his grandmother's gate, and vanished.

Back in the camper van, Prudence closed her eyes. This was one of those moments she was grateful not to be enslaved to a mobile phone. She needed the stillness. She needed the solitude. She needed not to be harrying Suki down the phone, checking that everything was going well in domestic science.

Most of all, she needed Mrs Carruthers not repeatedly calling her to find out where she was.

For a time, she waited with closed eyes, hoping – because her mind was still riven with doubts – that this test would reveal some element of truth, that its result would be the key to unlocking the entire crime. She seemed to drift with that thought, pulled along by its current, until some time later she opened her eyes, hoping to find Peter cantering back along the road toward her – but saw only the stillness of the coast in front of her, the hypnotic glittering of the sea.

Peter was taking too long.

How long had he been gone already?

She checked her watch. More than half an hour had

passed. In some senses, that boded well – because at least it meant the boy hadn't been summarily ejected – but even this thought did nothing to settle Prudence's stomach. She hadn't been this nervous before she stepped in front of a TV camera for the first time, nor even when she demoed her raspberry roulade to the entirety of the World Trade Centre in Dubai.

There was no doubt about it: she needed something to lift her mind out of this worry.

That was when she saw the copy of *The Complete Sherlock Holmes* sitting in the footwell of her passenger seat, evidently where Peter had swept it when he climbed into the camper. No doubt there was a hefty fine sitting on it at the library now, but for this Prudence was thankful. A little old world literature was just the thing to pass the time – and it touched her, somehow, that these had been the last pages Mrs Arkwright flicked through, the very last stories of her life.

It was a hefty old tome; Arthur Conan Doyle had enjoyed himself, over the years, writing stories about his eminent detective. What was it Brian Hall had said? *Isn't police work better left to the professionals, Prudence? However talented the amateurs are?* Well, here, in Prudence's hands, was the perfect riposte to that – because, of course, Holmes had been an amateur detective too. The difference was: he wasn't nearly amateur as Benji Huntington-Lagan and his idiot of a sidekick Sonny.

She flicked through the pages. Here were novels everyone knew. *The Hound of the Baskervilles. A Study in Scarlet. The Sign of Four.* But here were so many stories she'd never heard of as well. 'The Five Orange Pips'. 'The Man with the Crooked Face'. 'The Adventure of the Empty House'. 'The Final Problem'.

She lingered over these last two, something stirring in the back roads of her memory.

She lingered longer still, with that sense of an idea undefined, some realisation just out of reach – a recipe idea you could scent, perhaps even taste on your tongue, but for which you hadn't yet devised either ingredients or method.

She flicked onward, deciding that the best thing to do was simply begin at the beginning, when she sensed movement in the edges of her vision – and, upon looking up, saw the tiny, stick figure of Peter hurtling up the coast road, having just come scrambling through the black iron gates.

Prudence had already started the engine by the time he reached the camper and hauled open the passenger side door. As he clambered inside, shouting 'Go, go, go!', a multitude of things spilled from his hands: an electric toothbrush, a hair comb matted in coils of black, a soiled Elastoplast seemingly rescued from a bathroom waste basket. 'Peter,' she said, hanging her head, 'don't tell me your mask slipped? Don't tell me they *saw* you take these things?'

'I thought they had. They seemed to know I was up to something. It took all my wiles, Mrs Bulstrode, to get through that door in the first place. By the time it came to asking to use the bathroom, I'm not sure I had many wiles left. They must have noticed something *iffy* about it when I asked. I'd only been in there a few minutes when Mac came, knocking at the door. I . . . I had to throw this lot out of the window, Mrs Bulstrode. What would they have thought, if they'd seen Mac's tooth-brush sticking out of my back pocket?'

Prudence took this information in with all the serenity she could reasonably muster. 'So, just so I understand this correctly, Peter, you threw these things out of the window, and recovered them as you left?'

Peter nodded. 'You'd better get going, Mrs Bulstrode. Only, don't drive past the gates. You never know if they're watching.'

The camper van rolled forward. 'I should think those items you've recovered are covered in a lot more than Mac Duggan's DNA now, Peter. I should think Detective Hall's old friend will be finding DNA from fox scat in there. Soil particles. Plant particulate. All manner of things.'

Peter looked up, startled. 'But I can't go back in, Mrs Bulstrode!' he gawked. 'They'll just *know* something's wrong if I . . .'

Prudence reached over and patted him on the knee. 'Never fear, young man. I'd no more send you back into that house than invite you to the banquet at St Marianne's.'

'That's a shame, Mrs Bulstrode. I could murder some fish and chips.'

Prudence rolled her eyes. 'I'll buy you a pasty at Topps Fish Mega Palace on our way.'

It was something of a detour to Topps Fish Mega Palace, but at least Prudence was able to pick up a basket of scampi and peas from the lunchtime menu and deliver this to Detective Hall, along with the samples Peter had provided. By the time she got to the aged detective's cottage, having first returned Peter to Carn Euny and the comfort of his 'hog', it was already approaching midday – and the banquet only three hours away.

Detective Hall took the items at the door, thanked Prudence for the scampi, and declared, 'I'll eat on the way. Bradley's ready and waiting. It might take a few hours, Mrs Bulstrode, but we'll do our best.' He looked at the samples in his hands. 'That's if there's DNA to extract from this lot at all,' he said, shaking his head curiously.

Prudence watched as he climbed into his little Morris Minor and tried not to worry too much about the scampi distracting him as he took to the road. Then, still rueing how much of the morning had already slipped by, she jumped into the camper van and hit the road back to St Marianne's.

She was cruising around Devil's Corner, following the headland where the camper had broken down almost two weeks before, when the school came into view. Even at this distance she knew that the banquet was due to begin – for she could see the patchwork of colours in the car park that told her the guests had started to arrive. Already, they would be congregating in the lavishly deco-rated dining hall, no doubt being received warmly by Mrs Carruthers and the one or two staff she'd summoned to help her in Poppy's unfortunate absence. Perhaps some guests had already asked after an appearance by the fabled Mrs Bulstrode.

There was no more she could do for Poppy now, no more she could do at all until Suki received the call from

Detective Hall. Prudence had a job to do – and, no matter what the circumstances, she intended to do it right.

She left the camper van on the other side of the earthworks, where the police cordon had been taken down but work had not yet resumed on the new gymnastics facility, and hurried by foot to reach the school's front doors. Another family was arriving as Prudence reached the reception hall, and Prudence waved to them cheerily when she saw the looks of recognition spread across their faces. Then she ploughed directly through the front doors, crossed her fingers that all was going well in the domestic science classroom, and marched breezily to the dining hall instead.

Inside, twenty guests had already assembled – less than half those who were expected, but it still lent the hall an atmosphere of anticipation. Glasses of sparkling wine had already been poured – Miss Down seemed to have taken on the role of maître-d', which Poppy had been expected to fulfil – and Prudence was happy to take one from a silver tray as she spritzed through. The look on Mrs Carruthers's face, when she saw her, was filled with fury – but that fury had to be quickly mollified, for another set of parents waltzed up to her and swept her into a conversation of her own. 'It's all under control,' Prudence mouthed to her as she passed. 'I'm not going anywhere now.'

'See that you don't,' Mrs Carruthers's scolding eyes seemed to be saying. 'This is your time, Prudence. This is your show!'

The time wasn't quite right for Prudence to rally the parents and make a speech about the journey their daughters had come on this summer, so she was just saying some hellos, telling everyone how excited she was to have returned to St Marianne's and to be hosting this meal, when she saw a familiar face hoving into view. Prudence had quite forgotten about the governor Bernie Hogg since that first night at the Bluff, but he didn't seem to have forgotten her. 'Now, now, Mrs Bulstrode,' said the porcine man as he approached, his finger wagging like the caricature of an admonitory teacher, 'you never did take me up on my invitation. I should have liked to have wined and dined you this summer, Mrs Bulstrode. You and I might have had an estimable time. Some illuminating chats. Some—'

'I'm afraid these girls' education comes before a good time, Mr Hogg,' said Prudence, and turned on her heel to march back towards the doors. 'Ladies and gentlemen,' she declared, before she slipped through, 'I must attend to the kitchens – but I shall be back in but a short half hour to tell you all a little of the adventure our good St Marianne's girls have been going on . . . and in the most testing of times.'

There, thought Prudence as she left the dining hall behind, that ought to have struck the right note. She had to admit, even in spite of everything that had happened this trip, she still felt the flickering of joy at the idea of hosting an event here at St Marianne's – but the tragedy could not go unremarked upon; the death of one teacher and the imprisonment of another could not easily be whitewashed away.

She only prayed there was better news before the starters were served – if not the resolution of Adam Scott's murder, then at least the exoneration of Poppy Balloon. That, Prudence reflected, had to be the beginning.

She was crossing the reception hall, determined to march back into domestic science with all the confidence in the world – and hoping beyond hope that Suki had marshalled the girls as well as she might – when the front doors of St Marianne's opened up, and in stepped a woman who looked so close to her old friend Poppy that Prudence's heart near skipped a beat.

The woman's eyes met hers. She too had frozen in place, so suddenly that when her husband tried to enter the school behind her, he had to stagger to a stop, then inch his way around.

'M-Mrs Bulstrode?' said the woman. 'P-Prudence?'

Prudence had often experienced this moment: when you bumped into somebody you really ought to know, and had to pretend you knew exactly who they were until your memory caught up. In the busy, ever-changing world of TV, it was practically a daily challenge. Yet, within moments, the realisation hit her. 'You must be Hetty's mother,' said Prudence, putting her arms around the woman. 'I'm so glad I caught you. I can only imagine what you must be feeling.'

'I'm Helen,' the woman said, as Prudence stepped back. 'This here's Steve.' At her side, her husband gave a single nod – unable, it seemed, to summon any words. 'We got to talk to Mum last night. She said – she said you'd been able to visit.'

Prudence nodded.

'And she said . . . she said you were going to straighten it out, Mrs Bulstrode. She said you'd promised.'

Prudence glanced, instinctively, in the direction of domestic science. She'd made a lot of promises on this count. She only hoped her gamble was about to pay off. 'Helen, I'm waiting for a phone call. I believe there's a very good chance your mother is about to be exonerated, and a new line of enquiry almost certain to identify the real killer opened, by the time you cut into the haddock of Hetty's main course.'

'And Hetty,' Helen burst in, 'is she . . . is she cooking? When she called, we couldn't quite believe she was going to go through with it. She seemed so set on giving up.'

'She's doing divinely,' Prudence insisted, just hoping it was true. 'Helen, Steve, I think that, out of everyone here, you rather deserve a glass of something sparkling. Here, let me take you to the congregation.' She stopped before she ushered them through the dining-hall doors. 'Your mother's no more capable of murder than the haddock you'll be eating tonight, Helen. Have a little faith. You won't have to hold on to it for very much longer.'

'But it's everywhere, Mrs Bulstrode,' Hetty's father weighed in, drawing his trembling wife near. 'This "Crime Connoisseur" and how he unpicked the murder. They're interviewing him on *BBC Breakfast* tomorrow morning.'

Inwardly, Prudence bristled. 'They'll be interviewing him about his biggest slip-up since *Chefs Go Ape*,' she said. 'I *promise* you that.'

Prudence tried not to think about Benji Huntington-Lagan strutting his stuff across the daytime television sofas as she left the panicked couple to Mrs Carruthers and hurried to domestic science. She had to stop and steady herself before she marched through the doors – part of her had always known Suki wasn't quite ready for a challenge of this scale, and she feared what fresh hell she might find – but, the moment she stepped through the doors, the scents of simmering peas, curry sauces, fresh tangy ketchups and other vinegary delights amazed her. So too did the state of the kitchen – for, although the last two weeks had seen every corner of the kitchen covered in caramel, meringue, batter and all manner of other grisliness, the classroom was a pristine sight. Though every workstation bubbled with pots of peas, though every oven was warming and freshly made bowls of batter sat on every counter – though dozens of fish had been descaled, gutted and filleted in this very classroom – the whole place *sparkled*. The sharp scent of lemon undercut all the rest – and, indeed, Prudence could see a giant receptacle filled with fresh lemon segments, rinds and peels, no doubt masking the mass of discarded fish heads underneath.

Suki hardly looked up when Prudence came through the doors, for she was working diligently with Hetty in the corner, trying to get the best out of the fresh lime sorbet they were making for dessert. Only one or two of the girls even noticed Prudence's arrival, so consumed were they by mixing and adding spices to their batters. Prudence even noticed that not one of them was secretly sipping from the bottles of beer they had opened to make the batters unique. It was, she thought, a triumph of organisation and leadership – and little wonder, because there stood Miss Jubber, at the head of the classroom like a vision from fifty years in the past.

It seemed that simply being back in the domestic science block, no matter how radically it had changed, had given Miss Jubber fresh life as well – for, although she clung to the counter at the head of the classroom keenly, the wheelchair in which Ronnie Green had brought her had been left in the corner of the classroom. Her walking frame was beside her, but she seemed not to be relying on it at all; as if imbued with the youth of her days teaching here, all she needed was a chopping block and knife in her hands to keep her alive.

'Pru!' she cried out. This wasn't the first time Prudence had felt like a student this summer, but this was by far the most intensely she'd felt the emotion. Miss Jubber had summoned her to the front of the class, so off to the front of the class she went. 'These girls are in top shape, Pru, top shape! I can't say I sent many girls away from this classroom in quite the state of readiness these girls are in. And these recipes, Pru! Back in our day, it was boiled eggs and pork chops! If I left you girls knowing how to make a good Christmas cake, a couple of stocks, a decent roast dinner and a bread-and-butter pud, I was a happy woman. But these girls? These girls, Pru, will know so much more. Fine family meals they'll be cooking, each and every one.'

Prudence smiled. She was glad Suki hadn't heard that; Miss Jubber's prime directive might have been to make sure her girls could turn out good meals for their husbands and children, but time had rather moved on since then. 'Miss Jubber, if I can keep them away from takeaways and ready meals, I'll be more than happy.'

Miss Jubber was gazing at the classroom, a gummy

smile dominating her face. 'Do you know, Pru, I never thought to be back here. Never, not once, not since the day I left.' She turned to Prudence. 'You've provided an old lady with a moment to treasure. You've given me more than one of those in your day, but this one? This one's the best.'

Prudence looked across the classroom, to the corner where Hetty and Suki were working. 'If only it might have been in calmer circumstances, Miss Jubber.' At last, Suki caught her eye. 'Has he called?' Prudence whispered, though in her heart she knew it was too soon. Suki took the iPhone out of her pocket to check it but, in the end, just shrugged, then returned to the sorbet she and Hetty were stirring. 'It's been a long summer, Miss Jubber.'

'But a fine meal will make you feel better about that, Prudence.' Then Miss Jubber stopped, for she seemed to have had an idea. 'Do you know, Pru? I should be delighted if you'd take one last meal from *me*. I've shown you how to cook plenty, my dear, but I don't recall ever cooking a meal for you. Well, there are plenty of scraps lying around this kitchen. Plenty for a half-decent cook – even if she isn't in the best of nick – to make a meal out of. What do you say?'

The smile touched every corner of Prudence's lips. 'Miss Jubber, I don't think I'd like anything better.' Nothing, she thought, except perhaps a telephone call from Detective Hall, confirming every suspicion the skinhead protestors had about Elizabeth Duggan and her brooding husband Mac.

'Then I'll get to it,' Miss Jubber said. 'I may need a bit

of help with the chopping, but I've got plenty of kitchen hands here, Pru. I may even need some help with these ovens – I don't bend down so easily nowadays – but that's easily dealt with. Oh, and one final problem . . .'

Prudence stilled. *One final problem . . .*

'Yes, Miss Jubber?' Prudence finally whispered.

'Help me off with this wedding ring, would you dear? I don't like to get it too dirty. I hate the oily feeling of it – I always, always have . . .'

Miss Jubber had begun running her hands under the tap, then easing the wedding band off, but suddenly Prudence was reeling backwards. Suddenly, she was turning towards the door. 'Suki,' she called out, 'help Miss Jubber along, would you?' Then, without a hint of any further explanation, she bolted from the classroom, past the dining hall where the bubbly was still flowing, and directly out of the doors of St Marianne's.

She didn't stop until she got to the camper van.

She barely took a breath until she was sitting behind the steering wheel, the copy of *Sherlock Holmes* in her hands.

She opened it up, flicked through the contents.

There it was, written in black and white:

THE ADVENTURE OF THE EMPTY HOUSE.

THE FINAL PROBLEM.

Prudence let out an audible gasp. How on earth had she been so stupid? How had she possibly been so blind? Her mind spooled back to that lunchtime in the Bluff, the copy of Adam Scott's suicide letter with which she'd been presented. She'd said it out loud then, but barely thought of it since: *A child scatters capital letters in the middle of everything she writes, because she doesn't know any better. But Mr Scott ...*

Gripped by a fever even she did not fully understand, Prudence started to read.

Detective Hall was walking through the sands of Marazion Beach, wondering if he might stop in for a hot chocolate at the Chapel Rock Café (hot chocolate was his absolute favourite, even in summer), when the telephone started buzzing in his pocket. He fumbled the irritating thing three times before he got it to his ear, and only then realised that he hadn't yet accepted the call. Two fumbles later – and terrified the caller might give up on him before he even managed to answer (why did the world have to be so impatient nowadays?) – he brought it back to his ear and said 'Brian Hall speaking' in a lilting, sing-song voice.

'Brian, it's Bradley,' came the voice down the line. 'Listen, that test you wanted doing, I've got the results back in. Now, I can only say this to a ninety per cent probability, Brian, and that probably won't stand up in court – the samples are just too weak – but it'll give them cause to run something, if that's what you're after.'

Brian Hall stopped dead, his feet planted firmly in the golden sand, the breeze from the sea blowing sharp across his sun-burnished case.

'Give it to me, Bradley. Ninety per cent will be good enough for now. Enough to slow things down. Enough to convince that good Detective Rose to change course. There's a lot riding on this result.' He stopped. 'Well, go on. Let's have it.'

332

Moments later, the solitary dog walker passing by Brian Hall saw his eyes screw up in consternation, his jaw drop open, his head begin to tremble as he absorbed the news.

'Bradley,' he said, 'I've got to go.'

Then, scrambling back through the sand towards the place where his steadfast Morris Minor was waiting, Detective Brian Hall began scrolling through the contacts on his phone, desperate to make one more call . . .

Prudence was lost in the pages – devouring words written 130 years ago, yet feeling as if they were written for her alone – when she was startled from Holmes and Watson by knuckles hammering on the camper-van window.

When she looked up, certain it was Suki coming to summon her back to the kitchens, she saw the face of Ronnie Green glimmering back.

Quickly, she wound down the window.

'It can't be time yet, Ronnie. There's still time before service.' Half an hour, by the clock on the camper-van dashboard. That meant twenty minutes before she was due to stride in there and present the girls, telling the parents what fine young women they had raised. 'You can get some scraps from the kitchen, Ronnie. There'll be more than enough to go around. There'll even be a few beers from the batter going spare.'

'You've got me mistaken, Mrs Bulstrode. It isn't that at all.' He paused. 'Mrs Bulstrode, there's a problem. It's Mrs Carruthers. She needs to see you in the office, *right away*.'

Prudence was not in the mood to be admonished. If, by the end of the day, Mrs Carruthers had found the banquet wanting – and if, once she had eaten, she was of the belief that Prudence had been less than diligent in teaching the girls this summer – she would gladly return her fee for the course and prostrate herself in front of the governors, but until that moment she did not intend to be spoken down to.

'Mrs Bulstrode, please,' Ronnie implored. 'You should have seen the look on her face. She'll be serving up my liver with onions if I don't get you there quick.' He looked nervously back at the school building. 'And that bell's about to go for the banquet.'

Prudence's face was a storm preparing to break as she followed Ronnie back through the main doors of St Marianne's School for Girls, *Sherlock Holmes* still clenched tightly in one fist. The storm only intensified when, hurrying past domestic science, she saw Suki burst out of the doors, brandishing her iPhone and calling out, 'Grandma – Grandma, it's Detective Hall!' Ronnie's quick-march told her there was no time for stopping, so she cast Suki an exasperated glance and hurried on. At least Suki had the good sense to hurry after. Trailing them at ten yards behind, she followed them all the way to the door of Mrs Carruthers's office, then watched as Prudence was led quickly inside.

As soon as she stepped through the doors, Prudence knew what was wrong – for there stood Elizabeth Duggan, looking as haughty and imperious as Queen Elizabeth I about to fend off the Spanish Armada. At her side, his shoulders sunken, his head hanging low with the look of a schoolboy just told he was being sent to detention, stood Peter.

Prudence was appalled to see the dirt he'd already ground into those brand-new clothes.

She was appalled to see him here at all.

'By the look on your face, Mrs Bulstrode, I suspect you know why I've asked you here,' said Mrs Carruthers, shaking her head with the regret of a teacher who has just caught their favourite student smoking round the back of the bike sheds. 'Mrs Bulstrode, only twenty minutes separate us from this moment and the banquet to which these past two weeks were supposed to be diverted. Now, I am an understanding woman. I am, in my own way, a legend in these parts for my understanding.' *A legend for your modesty as well*, thought Prudence – though she decided it was better not to say anything. 'But you have taken this "helping the police with their enquiries" business a little too literally – and, I now understand, have descended into some criminality yourself. Mrs Bulstrode, do you deny it?'

Prudence gazed methodically around the little office, taking in each figure in turn.

'I'm sorry, Mrs Bulstrode,' Peter whimpered. 'I told 'em everything. Mac followed me to Carn Euny.'

'A DNA test?' Elizabeth Duggan intoned. 'Mrs Bulstrode, to orchestrate something of this magnitude takes a devilish and devious mind. Isn't it enough that you invaded my home on the flimsy pretext of a birthday luncheon? Isn't it enough that you prodded and pried into my personal affairs, when I am already living through my first husband's death, for the second time? I am minded to hand this matter over to the police – and I would do exactly that, Mrs Bulstrode,

335

if it wasn't that family loyalty demands I give this little *oik*,' and she slapped Peter around the back of the head, 'a second, third, fourth, seventeenth chance.'

'You seem to have spent this week tarnishing this school's reputation even further,' Mrs Carruthers went on. 'What am I to do with you, Prudence Bulstrode?'

Déjà-vu is a strange sensation, and it thundered into Prudence now. 'That isn't the first time I heard those words in this office, Mrs Carruthers. But I believe I was in the right then – it certainly *wasn't* me who clogged the girls' toilets up with cake batter – and I may yet be right now. In fact, I'm waiting on a telephone call that should prove the truth of this matter right now.'

'Your DNA test,' Elizabeth Duggan snapped, rolling her eyes heavenward, 'will show precisely nothing, except what I have told the world all along. Forty-eight years ago, when my first husband vanished off the face of this earth, I was carrying his child. That child grew up to be Peter's mother.'

Behind Prudence, the office door opened. In the corner of her eye, Prudence saw Suki appear. 'Grandma?' she ventured. Then, when her grandmother did not immediately reply, 'Grandma, she's *right*.'

Now, Prudence turned. Why was it, all of a sudden, that she felt like a schoolgirl caught in some playground scuffle, with all the eyes of the yard turning her way?

'Detective Hall received his report. He called us straight away. And Grandma . . . it came back positive. Peter and Mac Duggan just aren't matched. The lab was ninety per cent positive.'

336

Ninety per cent, thought Prudence. *Ninety per cent.* Was there doubt in that? Room for error? Ten per cent was not vanishingly small, and yet something deep inside told Prudence it was useless to hope.

Something told her it had been simpler than that all along.

She just hadn't wanted to see it.

She hadn't *dared.*

Elizabeth Duggan was already seething, 'I'm happy for them to repeat that test ad infinitum. I've never told a lie in my life,' but to Prudence it all seemed so far away. If Adam Scott really was Peter's grandfather, did it exonerate Elizabeth? It proved that Adam had given her a child – but did that necessarily prove she hadn't orchestrated his death?

Elizabeth was still talking, but suddenly Prudence felt the weight of the book in her hand. She turned her back on the office, fixed on Suki alone. 'I want you to take this,' she said, pressing *Sherlock Holmes* upon Suki, 'and hurry to the school library.'

'Grandma?' asked Suki, nonplussed.

'I want you in that new-fangled system of theirs, Suki. I want to know how far back the records go. Well, there's a chance, isn't there? Miss Down seems to be spending all her hours digitising every record that ever existed at this school. See if she's got a record of all the old library ledgers. I want to know if Adam Scott . . .'

'Enough talk of Adam Scott!' Mrs Carruthers exploded.

Perhaps she would have said more, but at that moment the school bell started resounding up and down the halls.

Prudence looked up. The hour was nigh. She could only hope the girls were ready.

'I want to know if Adam Scott ever took this book, or another one like it, out of the library. I want to know if he took it out dozens of times. Do you see?'

Suki didn't – not at first. But then her mind flashed back to another book, to the bonkbuster she'd spent the last week imbibing, and that tawdry story of Deb Elena and Andrew Simpson, the moment in the classroom when they might have given in to their passions and desires. *The Hound of the Baskervilles*, Suki remembered. That was what Andrew Simpson had been reading when Deb Elena tried to slide her hand up his thigh.

'Oh, and Suki,' added Prudence, 'whatever you do, don't let Miss Down know you're snooping about down there . . .'

There was so much that she didn't understand, but Suki knew her grandmother's sudden flashes of inspiration too well to give it much pause. Soon, she was hurrying off – and soon, so was Prudence. 'To the dining hall,' she announced, before she took that first step. Then she looked back. 'Mrs Duggan, I beg a half hour's grace from you. A half hour's grace and I might yet be able to set this thing straight. You might not have killed your husband, Elizabeth, but some-body here did. You might not have staged his suicide, but I have a sudden, strange feeling I know exactly who did . . . and that I should have known all along.'

The moment the bell started ringing, the domestic science classroom had sprung into action. Golden, crispy pieces of cod, haddock and plaice were being lifted from

338

the deep fat fryers. Little balls of tartare sauce were being positioned artfully on plates. Ramekins were filled with peas, with curry sauce, with ketchups and gravies, while thrice-cooked chips, crispy with beef dripping on the outside and fluffy as clouds in the middle, were being arranged into resplendent towers.

'Girls,' Miss Jubber thrilled upon seeing their plates, 'I don't believe I'm in a classroom at all. I believe I'm in a Michelin-starred restaurant, and you're all artists who've come here to cook!'

The door opened up, and in crashed Prudence. Every eye was suddenly upon her. 'Girls,' Prudence declared, 'your families have gathered. It's time for service.' Her eyes flashed around. How long would it take Suki to come back with some confirmation about that book? Did she *really* need it at all? Wasn't her instinct enough? Wasn't this the only explanation that made order from all the senseless pieces of this sorry story? The suicide note, in Adam's own hand. The tawdry story of *A Girl's Life*. The kissing in the library. The timing of that pregnancy announcement.

A-SALT AND BATTER-Y . . .

'Mrs Bulstrode,' Hetty called out from the corner. The plates she'd lined up looked divine: her crispy fried haddock topped in pink pickled onions, crispy fried pea shoots and balls of battered potato cake. 'What about my grandmother? You said my grandmother would be here.'

Prudence picked her way toward her. 'Not yet, Hetty. But . . . can you have hope just a little longer? I promise, my dear. I promise it's coming to an end.'

The bell rang again: two short, sharp blasts, the kind that summon the last stragglers to their seats in a theatre. The show was about to begin. The curtains were drawing back. 'Follow me, girls! This is your time to shine.'

Prudence marched to the door and held it open. First to pass through was Sophie, arms laden with baskets of cod croquettes and tempura pawns. Next came Hetty and her plates as colourful as rainbows. After that came seared tuna, curried lobster, sweet-pea fritters, fried scallops on röstis, pesto cod parcels, turmeric fish fingers, baked panko cod and a lemon butter sauce.

As the last girl ferried her tray of roast cod and orange raita through the door, Prudence looked back at Miss Jubber. The old dear was angling her walking frame, as if to disregard the wheelchair completely. 'Go, go, go!' Miss Jubber cried out. 'I'll get there Pru – but this is your moment too! If those girls are shining, then so are you . . .'

Prudence was torn. Her eyes flashed in both directions.

Then she hurried after the girls.

Through the dining-room doors, she could see that the families had gathered at the long dining tables, and that the girls were already being received with warm applause. Mrs Carruthers, Elizabeth Duggan and Ronnie Green had all joined the party. There they sat, at the head of the table, as the plates were spread round.

She opened the door, meaning to slip directly through, but the clatter of footsteps behind her made her turn. Here came Suki, careening around the corner with the volume of *Sherlock Holmes* still clutched in her fingers.

'Grandma,' she panted, 'you were right. Miss Down's been obsessive with the records. They go right back – right to the beginning. Mr Scott took out copies of all the Sherlock Holmes stories. Six volumes of them, if you can believe it, over and over.' She stopped. 'But Grandma, what does it mean?'

Prudence was frozen. By rights, she ought to be walking out there, singing the girls' praises, raising a glass and making a toast. There was Mrs Carruthers. There was Elizabeth Duggan. There, on the other side of them – tucked away, as she always was, as downcast and hidden in plain sight as she'd been back in Prudence's own schooldays – was Miss Verity Down . . .

'It means we know exactly who staged Adam Scott's suicide,' said Prudence. 'It means we should have known from the very start. It means we overlooked an old woman's desperate attempt to tell us what was going on, to reach us from the back of her diseased mind and set us on the right track. And it means . . .' she lifted her eyes, and Suki saw how sadly they were shining, ' . . . that we've very likely been dealing with two murders all along.'

For a beat, there was silence. The only sounds came through the dining-hall doors – where, in Prudence's absence, the girls had been invited to announce each of their dishes to the families waiting to eat.

Then Prudence heard the metallic click of a walking frame inching forward, and turned to see Miss Jubber emerging, at last, from the domestic science hallway.

'I'm afraid I've had to leave your dinner back there, Pru – we'll have to send someone to fetch it. Help me along, would you dear? I want to hear what these families are saying. I want to hear your speeches! Your grandmother's as good a teacher as she is a cook, Suki. She's as good a teacher as she was a student, and that's saying something.' Miss Jubber stopped. 'Help me through those doors. Prudence? Prudence, dear?'

Suki had only ever seen this deep a sadness on her grandmother's face once before – and that had been the afternoon of her grandfather's funeral, when Prudence returned to the kitchen garden to begin her life alone.

'I can't do that, Miss Jubber,' said Prudence, her voice filled with sorrow and regret. 'I won't be like Benji Huntington-Lagan. I won't do it in front of everyone. I won't draw the eye, make it about me – not when all those girls in there have worked so hard.'

Miss Jubber just furrowed her eyes. 'Prudence? I'm hankering after a few vinegary scraps, a little cod and tartare sauce. I'll bet it's the finest meal ever served in a school hall, dear. To take dinner at St Marianne's again – such a treat!'

'No, Miss Jubber. It's time we talked.'

'Oh, Prudence,' Miss Jubber said, with just a hint of the schoolteacher that she used to be. 'You're speaking in riddles, my dear.'

She inched forward.

This time, Prudence stepped into her way.

'I'm not the one talking in riddles,' she said, 'but there *is* a riddle at the heart of it. I suppose you knew it all along, Miss Jubber, and I ought to have done too. The thing is, nobody was looking for a riddle, so nobody found one. But there it's been, in plain sight for forty-eight years – Adam Scott reaching out to us from beyond the grave, telling us how it was done.' She paused. 'You must have thought the danger had passed, Miss Jubber. Along came Benji Huntington-Lagan to tie it all up and draw a line under the whole sorry affair. But it's been obvious from the beginning that he was wrong. That story he sold to the police, it never really accounted for the absolutes of the case: that Adam Scott was *seen* getting on to the boat that morning, that the suicide note he left behind was written in his own hand. I suppose Detective Rose may have stopped fudging it eventually herself, but for the time being she was won over. Well, she made the same mistake that Benji's been making his entire career. You see, Benji always mistook style for substance; he was interested in starriness above all other things; he didn't want to cook a lobster tail to perfection – he simply wanted to bake a cake and ice it well. Talent, yes, but cheap trickery as well.' Prudence paused. 'But you already know this, Miss Jubber. You know it because *you're* the one who met with Adam in that air-raid shelter. *You're* the one who clubbed him over the head and buried him there. *You're* the one who's been getting away with it for nearly fifty years.'

'Prudence, you're talking rot. Absolute rot!' Miss Jubber tried to inch her walking frame forward again – but, this time, Prudence placed a hand on it, bracing her in place. 'Suki, tell her. Your grandmother's under an enormous amount of stress. This trip has quite taken it out of her. These are wild, unfounded accusations. I'm an old woman. I'm tired. I need to sit down . . .'

For a moment, Suki looked genuinely perturbed.

'Two pieces of evidence that suggested the grandest of all conspiracies,' said Prudence in wonder. 'First, Adam was seen getting on to the boat. Next, he wrote a suicide note that even modern graphologists claim is definitely in his hand. I've spent all week wracking my brain, trying to work out how somebody might accomplish it. Benji Huntington-Lagan's tying himself in knots over at the Bluff, trying to plug the holes in his story, inventing lookalikes and local boys Poppy might have used. I myself looked at Mac Duggan and thought: in a certain light, with a certain gait, he might have passed for Adam, once upon a time. But we were all grasping at straws, bending the pieces in the hope they might fit. None of us was looking at it properly. None of us was *listening*. But I'm listening now, Miss Jubber, and there's only one possible way it all fits together. There's only one person who staged Adam's suicide.'

'You can't possibly think that I . . .'

'And that person was Adam himself.'

Now, Miss Jubber turned away. She heaved on the walking frame, turning it around one degree at a time. 'You're a rude girl, Prudence Cartwright, to speak to your old teacher like this. I came to this school to support you. I've been teaching your class for you, while you've been rushing around. I made you your dinner, for goodness sake! How *could* you speak to me like this? What makes you think I want to hear all this *nonsense*? It's been nearly fifty years!'

'Adam staged his own suicide, Miss Jubber, but you already know that – because he planned it all with you.'

'Rot!' Miss Jubber cried out, her voice breaking. 'Absolute rot!'

'I know it's true, Miss Jubber, because Adam told us himself.' And Prudence reached over to pluck the copy of *Sherlock Holmes* back out of Suki's hands. 'I wasn't the first to figure it out. That night I came to visit you, Mrs Arkwright already had a guest. She was sitting with Brian Hall, the detective who first worked the case – and, as we were leaving, she kept shouting it out. "Sherlock Holmes! Sherlock Holmes!" We thought, of course, that she was referring to Brian. Her mind was all addled, and she was mixing him up with the fictional detective. Well, her mind wasn't quite as addled as we thought. That was our mistake, assuming the worst of an old, frail woman. What she was actually doing was begging us to pay attention. Mr Scott's body had been dug up, the story was all over the news, the police were coming to investigate all over again – well, somehow, Mrs Arkwright joined the dots. She solved the riddle of the suicide note. She read between the lines and saw what it all really meant: that Adam Scott had faked his own death.

'You see,' Prudence went on, 'it was those capital letters that did it. I noticed them at the start, but they rather slipped my mind in all that followed.' And she closed her eyes as she tried to remember. *'"I solve this Final Problem and shall not see you again"*,' she said. *'"You will not live in an Empty House for very long."* Mr Scott was a very precise man. He loved a puzzle. Those sentences always had an air of the cryptic about them. Those capital letters could only have been deliberate. And deliberate they were.' Prudence opened up the book. *'"The Final*

Problem",' she read. '"The Adventure of the Empty House". Two of the later Holmes stories, so pertinent to everything we're discussing. Don't you see, Miss Jubber? In "The Final Problem", Sherlock Holmes dies. The last the reader sees of him, he's tumbling from the top of the Reichenbach Falls. For years, he's dead to the world. Then, by popular demand . . .'

'I saw this on the BBC,' said Suki suddenly. 'He isn't dead after all. He's staged it all to outwit Moriarty.'

'And in "The Adventure of the Empty House", he reveals the deception to Watson. Sherlock Holmes comes back to life.' Prudence paused. 'Who can say why Adam left those clues in his letter? I know it wasn't for you, Miss Jubber, because you knew what was going on from the start. Well, you *were* the one who was in love with him, weren't you? No, I like to think it was just Mr Scott's innate sense of playfulness. He made a puzzle of his suicide letter. He sailed out to sea, sat down to write his note, and couldn't help leaving one little riddle in the world. As far as I can tell, that riddle remained unsolved until Mrs Arkwright cracked it, forty-eight years later. I think Adam would have been happy with that. Forty-eight years, to crack his code. I imagine he felt rather satisfied as he left the boat – in, what, a rubber dinghy? – and made his way back to shore under cover of night.'

'Prudence, you're frightening me,' trembled Miss Jubber. 'You're as bad as that cad up at the Bluff. You're stitching things together badly. You're stitching *me up*.' Miss Jubber started wringing her hands together, seemingly unable to do anything else.

346

'I see you're covering your hand, Miss Jubber. Care to tell me why?'

'You're making me feel sick, Pru!'

The whole thing was making Prudence feel sick too. It was like a rot running through her memories, every good thing she'd treasured spoiling like unused vegetables.

'It's your instinct, Miss Jubber – your instinct telling you to cover that ring on your finger. You told me it was your mother's wedding ring, and of course I had no reason to doubt it. Only, you were lying in that, Miss Jubber.' Prudence closed her eyes. 'I didn't see it, even when it was staring me in the face, but it makes sense now. In the photographs in your album, back at the Cherry Garth, your mother's wearing a diamond ring. But the ring on your finger's just a simple silver band.' Prudence paused. 'When did Mr Scott give you that ring, Miss Jubber? A little while ago, Miss Down let me look through some of the old school photographs. I don't think you were wearing it in those. But then ... the trophy you presented me with, the Prize for Home Economics. Yes, I'm right, aren't I? The ring was on your finger in the picture they took – you and me, holding the trophy together.'

'It's ... it's just a ring!'

'No,' said Prudence, 'it's *his* ring. As close to a wedding ring as he could offer, given the fact that he was already married. A ring to signify the promise he was making, the life you would one day lead. You've been wearing it ever since, a symbol of how much you loved him – even though it was you, in the end, who took away his life.'

There was a long silence in the corridor. Only the hum

of voices through the dining-hall doors could be heard. Then, suddenly, the door opened up. In the corner of her vision, Prudence could see that Mrs Carruthers had arrived.

'We *are* waiting for you to give your speech, Prudence,' she said, firmly.

'Oh, she's already giving quite a speech here, Mrs Carruthers,' Miss Jubber sobbed, then leaned all her weight into the frame to pull it an inch further away from Prudence. 'Quite a long, rambling, *bitter, bitter* speech.'

Prudence's eyes flitted between them all. 'He gave you that ring because he loved you, Miss Jubber.'

Agatha Jubber froze. For the first time, the silence was so deep that not even the voices from the dining hall could be heard. Even Mrs Carruthers was still.

'I know he loved me!' Miss Jubber sobbed. 'He loved me right until . . . right until the end!'

Not even Mrs Carruthers had any words now. When Agatha Jubber looked back, her eyes were raw red marks in her old, dejected face.

'It was going to be so different, wasn't it, Miss Jubber? You, who'd already been stood up at the altar once in your life – and Adam, shanghaied into a marriage that would have stifled him the rest of his years. I think we knew, at a very early point, that he'd been having an affair with somebody in this school. Dot Ellen was the obvious candidate, but the way she wrote about it – in that thinly veiled memoir of hers – Adam rejected her because he was already in love. Poppy Balloon propositioned him, but he turned her down as well – Mr Scott

348

was too honourable to fall for a schoolgirl, no matter how close they were in age. Mr Scott's heart was already yours. It can't have been an easy affair. You, who lived with your parents – not like these other teachers, with their quarters on site – and Adam, going back to the wife he didn't love, and who didn't love him, every night. But there were places to meet, weren't there? The library, after hours. And those air-raid shelters, the very same ones we girls sometimes used if *we* wanted to sneak a boy into the grounds . . .

'I don't know when you fell in love, Miss Jubber, but I know it was real. Why else would you dream up a plan as audacious as this? A plan to rewrite the whole world? I think I'm right that it was Adam who dreamed it up. Only a man as in love with riddles and puzzles as Adam was, a man who knew the Sherlock Holmes stories inside out, might light on an idea like this. A suicide staged, just like Sherlock Holmes. One day, Adam would go down to the marina, make sure he was seen, and head out to sea. The next morning, he would be gone – and on the boat, only that tantalising suicide note left in his place.'

Miss Jubber stared at them all through ruddy, reddened eyes. At last, after a long, impenetrable silence, she began. 'It was only a game, when he started talking about it. Just a fantasy, I suppose – the two of us, dreaming of a way we could truly be together. But then . . . Barry Topps, and all that came after. Topps got the wrong end of the stick, of course. He thought Adam was debasing himself with our students. But it set things in motion. Topps had to be paid off, and Adam's father told him he had to put an end to his affair before it destroyed his marriage and brought the companies toppling down. Well, things got serious then. Adam knew he was being watched. And I suppose there came some kind of . . . desperation. We carried on for months. A stolen Christmas. The first kiss of spring. But we could see the end in sight – and Prudence,' she sobbed, 'we didn't want it to end.'

'So along comes Sherlock Holmes, and his "Final Problem". And it would have worked, Miss Jubber, wouldn't it? It would have worked, except that, when the newspapers reported on the memorial service to be held in Adam's honour, they reported on something else as well.'

Miss Jubber put her hand to her mouth.

'They reported on Elizabeth's pregnancy.'

Prudence dared to look back, through the dining-hall doors. In her absence, the meals had been served without a speech – and there sat Elizabeth, glaring at her through the glass in the doors, Bernie Hogg shovelling chips into his face at her side.

'The families had been banking on a baby for some years,' Prudence went on, picking up the story. 'If a baby came, the marriage would work. It's hard to keep two people together when they don't want it – but when they have common purpose? Yes, in those days, that might *just* work. A baby would have been heir to both companies. A baby would have sealed the union. And Adam Scott? Well, he was the sort of a man who might not honour his wedding vows, but was he the sort of man who'd walk out on a family? I think everybody knew not. I think you knew that as well.'

'I didn't know he slept with her still. I thought . . .'

'Tell us how it happened, Miss Jubber.'

'I can't, Prudence.'

'Tell us what happened after Adam Scott went out to sea.'

'I told you – I can't!'

Miss Jubber's scream billowed up, coursing past Prudence, Suki and Mrs Carruthers, catching – for the first time – the attention of the families in the dining hall. For a time, eyes darted their way. Then muted whispers filled the air. Moments later, the door was opening again – and Elizabeth Duggan entered the fray.

In terror, Miss Jubber wrenched her walking frame away. 'I won't,' she said. 'I can't!' But she had no power in her legs to run away, so Prudence followed her, at a steady pace, back along the hallway, back in the direction of the domestic science doors, urging the others to keep some distance behind.

'He was going to wait for me,' Miss Jubber said quietly, now that the others were out of earshot – now, especially, that Elizabeth Duggan could not see. 'There was a place I used to love as a girl, up in Colwyn Bay. We put a payment on a little cottage to rent – all of it under a false name, you see. And Adam was supposed to stay there, after he died at sea. By Christmas, I was going to hang up my hat at St Marianne's and join him. I'd tell my parents I was taking a job teaching at a girl's school in France – and off we'd go together. Who knew where? Who cared? We dreamed of the Highlands. We dreamed of the Costa del Sol. You know, the kind of places bank robbers used to go with their loot to live in the sun for the rest of their days. Anywhere, *anywhere*, where it could just be us. And then . . .'

'The baby,' said Prudence.

'It hit me in the heart, Prudence. It hit me in the heart.'

Prudence opened up the doors to the domestic science classroom, and in they both walked, back to the very place where their association first began. There, on the countertop, sat the meal Miss Jubber had lovingly prepared for her favourite student.

'So Adam came back from Colwyn Bay, didn't he? He came back to tell you he couldn't go through with the plan.'

'I don't know how he thought he was going to back out of it – not now, not now that he was dead. But I received a call one day, a call to the school office. They put it through, because he said he was one of the parents, but I knew it was him. It was another game we had, you see. And he said he had to see me, that we had to talk. A bit of me was thinking that he just couldn't bear to be without me until Christmas. He was lonely in Colwyn Bay, and he needed me. He needed to hold me and to . . . to ravish me! He couldn't stay away. Couldn't keep his hands off me. At least, that's what I told myself. A little piece of me thought it was the most romantic thing in the world.'

'So he came to the school.'

'Lord knows why he did it. But the air-raid shelter was our special place. It was where we could be *us*, you know? Until the very last moment, I was lying to myself, convincing myself he just couldn't be without me, not even for a few months. But that wasn't it.' Her voice cracked, and Miss Jubber had to pause before she went on. 'He hadn't come to love me. He'd come to tell me he was sorry. That he couldn't do it, not to abandon his child. He'd dreamed up some new story – he'd tell them he'd got washed up on the beach at Falmouth, and didn't know his own name, and keep up the ruse for long months until his memory started coming back. Then he could pick up where he left off. Back in his loveless life, I told him. Joyless, and loveless! But he didn't listen to a word I was saying. His mind was already made up.' Miss Jubber had started sobbing now, as if she was back in the air-raid shelter so many decades ago, reliving the words Adam had said. 'But what about me, Prudence? What about *me*? Off Adam was going, off to his new family life, and there I stood, a spinster again, my future taken for a second time.'

Prudence slumped against the counter, as if all the strength was leaching out of her as well. 'So you . . .'

'Don't say it, Prudence.' Miss Jubber stopped. The meal she'd made for Prudence still had some warmth. With trembling hands, she lifted it up, showing it to Prudence like some kind of offering. Only when Prudence showed no flicker of movement did she drop it back to the counter and say, 'I don't remember what happened. If you want the honest truth, there it is. We were fighting and I was screaming, and he took me by the shoulders and tried to tell me he'd always love me, even though he was leaving me now, and . . . and the next thing I knew, Prudence, he was lying in the earth at my feet, and the back of his head was sticky with blood, and . . . and there was a brick in my hand, and not a single breath in his body.'

'So you buried him there,' said Prudence sadly, 'and

nobody ever knew. Nobody even came looking – because, in their minds, he was already dead at sea. It was the perfect crime. And for forty-eight years it stayed hidden.' She breathed a disconsolate breath. 'I really thought it might have been Elizabeth. That's what all the protestors are espousing. Elizabeth and Mac Duggan killed Adam Scott because she'd fallen pregnant by him. But it never accounted for the suicide letter. It never accounted for Sherlock Holmes. Oh, Miss Jubber, *Sherlock Holmes*.' Prudence wiped away a tear. 'I don't want to be right about this, Miss Jubber. I'd give anything not to be right. I could understand a woman losing her mind when her lover turned his back on her. A dreadful accident, in the heat of the moment. But when poor old Mrs Arkwright shouted out "Sherlock Holmes" at Detective Hall that day, you heard it too, didn't you? You heard it – and, alone out of all of us, you understood what it meant.'

Miss Jubber plunged backwards, her hands losing their grip on her frame, and collapsed into her wheelchair. There she sat, her body wracked by sobs, as the classroom door opened up an inch – and Prudence saw Suki in the divide. With a subtle gesture, Prudence told her granddaughter to wait, then rushed to Miss Jubber's side. The old woman's breath was ragged, her eyes were closed – but this was only a fit of emotion, not the true undoing of her heart.

'Miss Jubber,' Prudence whispered, 'Adam's death wasn't planned. It happened in the terror of the moment. Oh, but Mrs Arkwright? Poor Mrs Arkwright? That's murder, Miss Jubber. Murder, plain and simple . . .'

354

'Gertie Arkwright used to pride herself on her tact. She knew about me and Adam, all right. I'm certain she did. But she kept it to herself.' Her breath became ragged; her head rolled from side to side. 'Why – couldn't – she – keep – *this* – to – herself?'

'I know you were scared, Miss Jubber. I know you were frightened the truth was going to come out. If anyone suspected Adam had set up his own suicide – well, that might lead them to some deeper discovery, and *that* might lead them to some deeper discovery yet. For forty-eight years, you'd kept your secret. You wanted to keep it until the end. But Mrs Arkwright, Miss Jubber. Poor Mrs Arkwright . . .'

'She wasn't long for this world anyway.' Miss Jubber sobbed. Then she looked up, with such a wild and feral snarl that Prudence staggered backwards. 'She should have kept her mouth shut. She'd forgotten her own mind. Why couldn't she forget this?'

Prudence still had hold of the library book. She set it down on the counter. 'You saw her with this, on her final night. You knew she'd asked to see me – and that put the fear of God into you. You knew what she was going to say . . .' Prudence paused. 'They found her face down on her pillow. That's what Daisy Lane said. And that's how she died, isn't it, Miss Jubber? Her face in her pillow, and your hands holding her there.'

'You can't tell them, Prudence.' Miss Jubber sobbed again. 'You can't tell a soul. It's all because of Adam Scott. None of this would have happened without Adam Scott. He gave me everything, but he ruined my . . .'

Miss Jubber's words frayed into formless nothings. She

wrung her hands together, ripped the ring Adam had given her off her finger, and cast it with vehemence across the room. When Prudence went to pick it up, she could see the faded inscription on the inside of the band: 'A Promise' was all that it said.

Suki was still at the door. As Miss Jubber continued to sob, Prudence went to her and said, 'You'd better call Detective Rose. If they listen to me this time, Poppy might still get here by the time dessert is served.'

'I already called her, Grandma,' said Suki, shaking. 'Is it true? Mrs Arkwright as well?'

Prudence looked back at the gibbering wreck of her favourite teacher. 'The past isn't always what we think of it,' she said sadly. 'We'll have to slow the dinner down, Suki. The girls will need to be back in here before long, prepping the desserts. Fetch Ronnie Green, and stay with him here. With a little luck, the police can come for Miss Jubber before the main course is over.'

'They're still waiting for you in there, Grandma. They're still expecting your speech.'

Prudence looked back. For a moment, she felt trapped between times: at once, the student who'd worked so diligently in this very classroom, and at the same time an aged cook who truly understood that the past had to be left behind. 'I'll be there in but a moment,' she said. Then, because in the middle of all the murder and devastation, it somehow seemed the only right thing to do, she said, 'The police are on their way Miss Jubber, but do you still drink Earl Grey? I remember, you used to get us girls to make you a pot of Earl Grey at the start of each lesson.'

Miss Jubber snorted back her tears and said, 'Yes please, Prudence. Three sugars, I think, at this time of life.'

The dining-hall doors opened up, and in walked a shell-shocked Prudence Bulstrode, to a rousing wave of applause.

It took all the willpower Prudence had to make it to the front of the hall and survey the crowd who'd assembled for the feast. She gazed out over the tables, the girls lined up in neat rows at the side, and felt suddenly as if she was in another space and time. There had been moments that had upended her before, moments that had changed what she thought of her life – the first moment she stepped in front of a television camera, the moment she held her babies in her arms, the time she'd come home alone without Nicholas and wondered at what life was without love – but only rarely did a moment come along that made you look back and recast your entire existence in a strange, different light.

She would have given anything for it to be somebody other than Miss Jubber.

In the celebrity world, there was an old adage: they said 'never meet your heroes', for when you met them, you realised they were but fallible people, brought down to earth. And as she looked out at the crowd now, she realised how true that old adage was. For fifty years, she'd thought of Miss Jubber as a shining star, the first one to guide her. Now, she realised that even stars could be tarnished. Even stars burned out.

'Ladies and gentlemen,' she said, and as she caught Hetty's eye she gave a soft wink, willing her to understand that, very soon, everything would be all right, 'I came here this summer with a singular mission in mind: to set your girls up for their own independent lives, with some age-old skills passed down through the generations. But the meals you've just eaten have come from your daughters alone – the products of their imaginations, and of their own hands. I might have shepherded them on their way, taught them a little of what I know across the last two weeks, but the truth is, your girls have taught me just as much as I've taught them. They've shown me that the world keeps turning. They've shown me that we who are old should have a little faith in the young. And they've shown me . . .' she thought, once last time, of Miss Jubber, and how the people you put on pedestals were not always as holy as you liked to think, ' . . . that we who are old are not *always* right. That things were not *always* better in the good old days, before KitchenAids and electric mixers and little iPhones in our hands.'

Even as the girls exchanged curious, stupefied looks at Mrs Bulstrode's final pronouncement, the applause began. She glanced towards the dining-hall doors, where a broken Mrs Carruthers was standing steadfast guard with Elizabeth Duggan, and saw movement through the glass – Detective Rose and some of her associates seemed to have entered the building and were, even now, picking their way toward the domestic science classroom – and it was only then that Prudence felt that the full weight of sadness would lift off her. She would, she supposed, carry it for a while longer – but perhaps there was room for a little hopefulness yet.

'Ladies and gentlemen,' she went on, raising a glass, 'in a few short moments your girls will be returning to our kitchens, then emerging in half an hour's time with the most delectable desserts in hand. Give them a round of applause, if you will – for the future of cookery is standing in front of you. As the sun sets on our own times in the kitchen, it rises anew!'

Chapter Twelve

The sun was beating down upon the ancient ruins.

Carn Euny looked resplendent at dawn. The first buttery light was making long shadows of the standing stones, and as Prudence and Suki left the camper van to pick their way into the scrubby field beyond the ancient village, those shadows seemed to lengthen and dance. Laden down with her hamper as she was, Prudence kept stopping – both to gather her breath and to admire the view. Coming back to Cornwall had filled her heart with so many rushes of emotion; leaving it again today was doing exactly the same.

The skinheads were gathered with their 'hogs' on the other side of the ruins – and there, in the midst of them, sat Peter, jawing with Pearl, each of them propped up against their motorcycles and drinking from cans of one of the foul, viscous energy drinks Suki had once tried to trick Prudence into tasting. As soon as they saw Prudence, they started waving. Then Peter leaped on to his hog, brought the engine to life, and cut a sharp arc around the field until he'd reached Prudence's side. 'I'll help you with that hamper, Mrs Bulstrode,' he declared, hoisting the wicker basket on to his lap. After that, he nearly tumbled off the motorcycle – but then, off he went, off to the furthest corner of the field, where the bonfire they'd built was already smouldering.

'They might have helped me with *these*,' said Suki, struggling with her half-dozen carrier bags filled with produce.

Prudence heard a second engine rumbling. 'I think your cavalry's just arrived,' she said, and inclined her head in the direction of the rising sun. There, up on the roadside where they'd parked the camper, a second camper van had just been parked – and out of it were pouring the girls from St Marianne's. First came Sophie – then, just behind her, came Hetty. At Hetty's side, sandwiched between two of the other girls, was none other than Poppy Balloon.

The girls came cantering past the ruins, snatching the bags from Suki and sweeping her along to the waiting skinheads, but Prudence decided to linger. Only when Hetty and Poppy, the last of the St Marianne's crew, reached her side did she start pottering forward again. She grasped Poppy's hand. Her old friend hadn't *quite* made it in time for dessert at yesterday's banquet, preferring the quiet of a night at home with only her family around her, something to help her find her feet after the discombobulations of the last days, and Prudence could see in her eyes how raggedly she'd slept. 'I'll have you feeling better, Poppy, you and all this lot,' said Prudence. 'Just give me an hour with that fire. Do you know, they asked for vegan chilli for breakfast – but I have something else in mind.'

Vegan chilli was not on the menu, but a great pot of scrambled tofu, rich with mushrooms, sun-dried tomatoes and olives, with a ratatouille on the side and fresh, sizzling flatbreads, was the order of the day. As the skinheads filled their bellies, and the St Marianne's girls overcame their nerves at talking to real live local boys, Prudence and Poppy reclined on one of the great boulders pockmarking the field. 'Do you know,' said Poppy at last, wiping the last of the ratatouille from her lips, 'I would have felt sorry for Miss Jubber if it wasn't for Mrs Arkwright. I never loved the old woman, she was a dragon in our time, but it seems a sorry way to leave the world, after so much struggle.' She paused. 'What will they do with Miss Jubber, do you think?'

Prudence shrugged. 'I suppose they'll avoid a trial, if Miss Jubber cooperates.'

'But a prison sentence, Pru? At her age?'

The question just lingered, for both knew the answer. Agatha Jubber, too often thwarted by life, would be thwarted in death as well. 'I wonder if it will be very different from the Cherry Garth for her,' said Prudence sadly. 'And you, Poppy? What does the future hold for you?'

Poppy had been debating the same thing all night. 'I've a few years left in me yet, Pru. And I should like to end my days at St Marianne's with a better taste in my mouth than I have right now.' She stopped suddenly and gasped, 'That's not a comment on your lovely breakfast, Pru! I only mean that . . . PVC don't give up that easily, do we?'

'We do not,' grinned Prudence, and raised her tin cup of tea in salute.

'Mrs Bulstrode!' Peter called out from the fire. 'Didn't you bring any dessert?'

'The cheek of the boy!' Poppy laughed. Then she had a sudden thought. 'Well, did you, Pru?'

'Open up the hamper, Peter,' Prudence called out. 'Share it around. Make sure everyone gets a piece.'

'Raspberry roulade!' laughed Poppy, when it came her turn. 'That's an indulgence for breakfast, Prudence, but I'll allow it just this once.' She marvelled at the light sponge-cake, the generous filling of whipped cream and raspberry preserve. 'To think, Pru, that something so simple set you on the road to the stars – while Benji Huntington-Lagan, and all his complicated, tricksy affairs, just can't quite get there . . .' She shook her head ruefully, trying not to let her bitterness at the man overcome this moment between two old friends. 'I'm sorry, Prudence. I should have told you about Mr Scott, all those years ago. I *really* should have told you last week, when his body was found. I had no idea they'd come looking for me. I had no idea Barry Topps even *knew*. Isn't it strange how the past just bubbles up? You never really leave it behind.'

Prudence took her hand. 'It just piles up behind you, when you get to our age,' she quietly said.

'And if Mrs Arkwright hadn't ordered up that Sherlock Holmes book, they'd have bundled up their case against me. Sent my file to the CPS – and maybe . . . maybe I'd be rotting in a cell somewhere, waiting for a trial. But there you were Pru, like you always used to be, using that head of yours, using those booksmarts . . .' She lifted herself up, for a sudden idea had presented itself. 'And look at you now, Prudence! Feeding all these raggedy boys and girls. It's like *another* book. Not Sherlock Holmes this time. No – *Peter Pan*! You're Wendy, and all of these are your Lost Boys . . .'

Prudence turned to her friend and grinned – but whatever she had been about to say next was suddenly cut off by the sound of another engine on the roadside above. All of a sudden, a cry went up among the Lost Boys. Peter's hand extended skyward – and, when Prudence craned around, she saw a police car with flashing lights sitting up on the roadside, the policeman who'd just emerged from the driver's seat remonstrating wildly, his arms flapping in the air.

In a moment, Peter had scampered over. 'I forgot to tell you, Mrs Bulstrode, the filth warned us off this place. They said we weren't meant to be wild camping so close to a site of special historical interest. I'm sorry, Mrs Bulstrode! You better get on the back of my hog. I'll get you out of here, you can count on it . . .'

Prudence shook her head sorrowfully. 'Peter,' she said, and took a little bite out of her raspberry roulade, 'should we *really* be calling the police constables, those from the very same service who just arrested your grandfather's killer, *the filth*?'

A dozen motorcycles had come to life. The skinheads were leaping aboard – and Prudence was surprised to see, now, that some of the St Marianne's girls had decided to forsake their camper and ride pillion instead.

'I don't fancy getting arrested again, Pru,' trembled Poppy.

Prudence stood. 'My old friend, you don't need to worry about that.'

The police constable was a stickler for the rules – and it seemed clear that this wasn't the first warning the skinheads had been given about building fires in this particular field – but he was also an admirer of a mystery resolved, and (he confided in Pru) he had never been wholly convinced by all the palaver surrounding Benji Huntington-Lagan, amateur detective extraordinaire. Even more crucially than this, he'd skipped breakfast this morning – and, while he was no lover of scrambled tofu and Mediterranean veg, preferring a hearty Cornish breakfast of smoked kippers and toast, he was happy to take a big chunk of raspberry roulade for his morning break. 'See that there are no more fires here, Mrs Bulstrode,' he told her as he climbed into the car – and Prudence's promise hung in the air as he drove off, jam and cream already smeared around his lips.

Soon, Prudence had said her goodbyes to Poppy and Hetty – who, together with Sophie, hadn't joined the motorcycle exodus – and she and Suki were guiding the camper van back along the glittering curve of the coast.

It felt different to be leaving. If there'd been a feeling of homecoming in the return to St Marianne's, there was a sense of finality about their journey today. Suki, who for once wasn't buried in her iPhone, had rarely seen her grandmother so filled with wistfulness. 'Is it Miss Jubber?' she asked at last. 'You loved her, in a way, didn't you, Grandma?'

'I think I did,' said Prudence, 'but the thing that's bothering me, the thing I can't really let go, is that somehow I still do. That's not to say I love what she is now, or what she did. But I can still remember being in that classroom, Suki. It's written into my story.'

'She wasn't a killer back then, Grandma. Maybe that's the difference.'

Prudence smiled, softly. 'Somewhere along the way, Suki dear, you became a very wise girl. Now, if I could only get you to remember that a crowded baking dish takes three times as long to bake, we might be getting somewhere.'

Now it was Suki's turn to smile too. 'I know something that will cheer you up, Grandma,' she said. They had just entered the cluster of seaside streets that made up St Austin, and she pointed through the camper-van window to a stand outside the newsagent on the little high street there. When Prudence slowed the camper down, she could very clearly make out the headline of the *Tregurnow Times*.

CRIME CONNOISSEUR COMES A-CROPPER!

HUNTINGTON-LAGAN'S THEORY GOES UP IN PINE-SCENTED SMOKE!

'GASTRONOMES DO NOT *ALWAYS* MAKE GREAT DETECTIVES,' SAY

LOCAL POLICE

'Dash out and get me one, would you, dear?' Prudence asked, then sat with her confusing cocktail of feelings until Suki scampered back.

There was one stop she wanted to make before they hit the road back into the east. Brian Hall was pottering in his front garden when they pulled up outside his house, pruning his roses while playing a game of chess against himself on the table by his front porch. It seemed that he, too, had taken a copy of the *Tregurnow Times*, because the centre spread – Benji Huntington-Lagan's face, and a detailed breakdown of how he'd led the police up a blind alley that almost let a killer get away with her crime – was open on the table, just beside his board.

'There he is, Sherlock Holmes himself,' grinned Prudence when she brought the camper van into the kerb.

Brian Hall hurried over. 'I have to say, Mrs Bulstrode, I've been reflecting on this whole sorry business – and I believe I rather let the team down. If I'd only realised the meaning of that letter forty-eight years ago, we might have all saved ourselves the hassle. Adam Scott might yet be alive. Gertie Arkwright even. And as for Agatha Jubber . . .'

Prudence shook her head. 'Case closed, Detective,' she said, simply. 'I'm sure Elizabeth Duggan will forgive all in the end.'

'Oh, I'm sure she will. She'll have to,' grinned Brian Hall. 'You see, the Duggans might have been innocent of murder – but there's plenty they've been guilty of along the way. Fishing out of British waters. Corporate espionage against that little fishing fleet in Prussia Cove. And don't get me started on all the insurance claims over the years!' He tutted and rolled his eyes. 'Yes, I'm sure Mrs Duggan may hold a grudge about our little DNA scheme, but she won't be doing anything about it, not with all the blind eyes turned in this county over the years.' He lowered his voice to a conspiratorial whisper. 'It's a seething pit of skulduggery in Cornwall, Mrs Bulstrode. A good man has to strive to keep his head up high. But me? I'll be content with my roses from now on.'

'Maybe this will help,' said Prudence, and passed him

a little package through the window. 'Just something sweet to celebrate a case finally closed.'

For Brian Hall, it was all the reward he needed.

On they drove, the azure sea spread out underneath them, the fishing flotilla of the Franks & Scotts already fanning out across the waters to bring in the morning catch. Soon they had reached Devil's Corner, and the very spot where Prudence's camper van had been stranded, playing host to Ronnie Green for several long nights. There, far below them, sat St Marianne's School for Girls. After a few more weeks of quiet, its halls would resound with the flurry of girls' footsteps once more. Up would go the gymnasium facility, forgotten would be the place where Adam Scott had lain alone for so many years, one year rolling so easily into the next. So did the seasons move on.

'Maybe you'll come back next summer,' said Suki.

'Oh, I don't think so,' said Prudence. 'Sometimes, Suki, it's right to say goodbye.'

There was only one more stop to make before Prudence and Suki left Cornwall behind. The sea was just as pure beyond the sands of Castallack Cove, and it would have been tempting to linger there, dipping their toes into the warm summer waters and eating mussels and cockles from the stand on the beach, but instead Prudence guided the camper up the long, switchback road that led to the headland above – and the place where the Bluff restaurant sat.

There was only one car in the car park. A familiar face, covered in orange whiskers, jumped out as soon as it recognised the camper van parking up alongside it.

Before Prudence had wound down the window, the face of David Hodge – the journalist who'd been here, slobbering over Benji's words, only two days before – was peering into hers.

'Mrs Bulstrode, I'm so glad it's you. I went down to the school earlier, hoping I could catch you – but Mrs Carruthers said you were gone. "And she can take all her drama with her," she said. I didn't think that was very generous, Mrs Bulstrode, given what you've done for them, and I told her so. I was going to put a call in to your agent, but I couldn't find them online and . . .'

'I don't have an agent any more,' said Prudence, climbing out of the camper and taking a small cardboard package with her. 'One doesn't need an agent when one is retired.'

'You can hardly call yourself retired, Mrs Bulstrode, not after the display we've seen this week. It's been a career change for you, Pru. You haven't hung up your hat, you've just changed it. And that's exactly what I wanted to talk to you about. My editor's keen to cover this story. We were covering it with Benji – but, hey, now that that's gone, it seems a shame to squander the research. A quick "find and replace" and it could be a story about you, Mrs Bulstrode. A big starry piece about how you not only debunked Benji's theory, but solved an age-old crime all on your own.'

Prudence stopped dead. 'I think I'm going to have to politely decline,' she said, simply.

Suki leaned her head out of the window. 'Grandma!' she booed. 'Why such a spoil sport?'

'Why such a spoil sport, indeed, Mrs Bulstrode? You

know, I'm not just a journo for the *Tregurnow Times*. I'm a proper writer. A Proper Writer – and that's with capital letters, Pru. I know how important capital letters were to this case! I think there's a book in this. A podcast. A TV serial. We'll get you back on TV in no time!'

Prudence heaved a weary sigh. Instead of answering, she turned her back, tottered over to the step of the Bluff, and left the cardboard package sitting there. Then, still ignoring the journalist's fevered conversation, she returned to the camper van.

'Mrs Bulstrode,' he cried out, 'here's my card. Call me! *Call me!*'

But the camper van had already pulled away.

'What was all that about, Grandma?' Suki began. 'That could have been something. You did a good thing here. People would want to read about it.'

'Then let them,' said Prudence. 'There'll be plenty written about old Miss Jubber and Adam Scott. But I'm not Benji Huntington-Lagan, dear. I don't need to be the face of it.' She grinned. 'I spent all my life being the face of cakes and crème pats. I travelled the world, telling stories about spices from Kashmir, from Persia, from East Asia. For my sins, I cooked for a troop of mountain goril-las with Benji back there. But I did all that because I loved the work, the sights and smells, the *food*, not because I loved the camera. Like I say, I'm not Benji Huntington-Lagan. But . . . poor Benji,' she sighed, 'he'll have a torrid time because of this. When you put yourself on a pedes-tal like he constantly does, it isn't easy when you fall. That's why I left a little present for him. Just a card to say no hard feelings, and a chunk of that raspberry roulade.

Well,' said Prudence, and looked sidelong at Suki with a devilish smile, 'I thought it might be just the thing to pep him up today, to give him a little bit of a boost.'

Suki was silent, but only for a moment. It seemed to her that the last thing Benji Huntington-Lagan would have wanted today was a note from the woman who'd exposed him as a fraud, and a piece of the very simple recipe that had made her such a star – when none of the cleverness and trickery of his own cookery had propelled him along quite the same path.

'Grandma,' she said, tactfully, as they followed the seafront road out of Castallack Cove, 'I'm not sure that's *quite* the nice gesture you think it is.'

The camper turned a corner, and suddenly the sunlight was everywhere, dazzling them as they drove. The way it landed on Prudence made her look almost angelic to Suki – but when her grandmother grinned, it was hardly an angelic smile that she wore. 'Suki,' she proclaimed, 'you *always* underestimate the older generation. My dear, dear girl, I know *exactly* what I'm doing.'

Acknowledgements

I can't believe Prudence and I have come so far, and yet here we are – a third adventure complete, a third mystery solved, a third killer brought to justice! I couldn't have done this without my beloved readers – thank you for taking Prudence and Suki so eagerly to your hearts. Along the way, I have had help from people too many to mention, but I am particularly grateful to my agent and old friend Heather Holden-Brown; to my editor Krystyna Green; to my copy-editor Howard Watson; to Amanda Keats, Beth Wright and the wonderful team at Constable/ Little, Brown who have worked so hard to bring Prudence to readers. I can't wait to see where this journey takes us next.